PRETTY BOY

PRETTY BOY

BY

SCHLEDIA PHILLIPS

THREE KEYS PUBLISHING

UNLOCKING WORLDS, HEARTS, AND MINDS

THREE KEYS PUBLISHING

www.threekeyspublishing.com

Schledia Phillips

www.schledia.wix.com/home

like her on Facebook at Schledia Benefield Phillips, author

or follow her on twitter @Schledia

or follow her blog at www.schlediaphillips.blogspot.com

Dedication

For my aunt Lynnie who fell in love with Ray.

Acknowledgments

I would like to thank my editor, Lynn Thompson, for her patience and dedication. Donna Huber, your editing services were invaluable. A special thanks to April May for her design idea, and to Linda Hill for the awesome design and artwork! Brian Smith, of Raven and the Blackbirds, thank you for your advice on music, musicians, musical instruments, and equipment. Now I'm looking for that gold record. Fred Molden, former player for the Minnesota Vikings, I know you are looking down on us all and smiling. Thank you for answering my questions about football. Trinity still cries for her Uncle Fred. Thank you to all my friends, family, and fans that have encouraged me in writing. I could not do it without you!

CONTENTS

CHAPTER 1

TOO PRETTY

Hearing the words *too pretty to be a boy* can be a terrible thing for a little man, and I heard it all the time. When I was just a toddler, friends of my mother would gloat and coo over me as if I was a baby doll. I distinctly remember it being embarrassing even at such a young age. I naturally gravitated to my mother's leg, wrapped my arms securely around it, and slipped bashfully behind her. People went on and on about my wavy, black hair and my deep-brown eyes, so I did my utmost to hide those features as I stowed myself away in the security of my mother's shadow. Mom would chuckle, stretch her arm around, tousle my hair (assuring me of my safety), and respond, "He *is* very handsome."

All too often my mother picked me up and held me tight as tears streamed down her face at the words, "He looks just like Blacky."

I noticed even then those words seemed to send a shock wave through my mom. She would gasp for breath as if she had just been punched in the gut with amazing force. The blow always brought the gasp, and forming within her crystal-blue eyes, a well of tears always followed the gasp. Ironically, as the sunlight glistened off the pools of water, radiance filled them. As the tears spilled over, she would run her hand through my hair, kiss my forehead and cheek, and respond,

"Yes, he does."

That usually led to an apology for mentioning Blacky. There weren't many variations of the apology; it was either, "I'm sorry, dear, I shouldn't have brought him up," or "I'm so sorry, Bonnye; I didn't mean to upset you."

My mother always graciously insisted, "It's okay; I talk about him every night while we look at pictures and watch our wedding video. I want to make sure Ray always knows his daddy."

My dad, Sean Winstrom (also known as Blacky), was a Marine. Unfortunately, he was sent to Saigon just two months before America pulled the last of her troops out of the Vietnam War.

Mom always told me my dad had a special job within the Marines. "He was so trusted by his fellow Marines that they would send him into a war zone to help gather wounded brothers together to get them home," she would explain. My dad was in the Recon division, so his job entailed going into dangerous situations and retrieving VIP's, and to a Marine a brother-in-arms was always a VIP.

Dad left out on February the 27, 1975; my mother was unaware of her pregnancy when he left. During that fateful trip to Saigon on April 21 of the same year, his helicopter went down. Mom found out she was pregnant the day before he died. I never had the privilege of knowing my father; I was still being formed inside my mother's womb, and my dad never had the chance to know of my existence.

Granny, my mom's mom, once told me about how ill my mother became when she learned of my father's death, and I nearly died on her as well. Granny watched in fear as Mom took to her bed and neither ate nor slept. Wrapping herself in my dad's Dress Blues uniform, she lay for weeks in a trance. After several weeks, Granny knelt next to Mom's bed, grabbed her hand, looked her in the eyes, and said, "Bonnye, I know you loved Sean dearly, and I know you are completely devastated right now that the man whom you planned to spend the rest of your life with is gone, but you have got to realize he lives on through that baby growing inside of you. You have to take care of yourself, or you're gonna lose his child."

Granny squeezed Momma's hand with one hand while gently caressing the top of her hand with the other. "I know you're depressed, but you need to realize God gave you a gift. He gave you a piece of Sean to keep forever. That piece of Sean is better than any picture or letter or even any home movie you might have. There is a baby growing inside of you that is a part of you and Sean and the love you two shared."

Granny's voice turned stern as she looked into the lifeless eyes of my mother and continued, "Now, I want you to get up, snap out of this, and realize how lucky you are to have that. I love you, dear, and I want to be able to hold my grandbaby in my arms and love him or her—whichever it's gonna be, and deep down inside I know you want to get out of this bed and live your life too. I know you want to be able to hold this baby in your arms and remember Sean as you see his eyes reflected through the child you two share, but if you wanna do that, you have to start eating, or the baby's not gonna make it, love."

At her last phrase, my mother's eyes broke free from their haze; she turned her head to face her mom and whispered, "Help me, Momma," as she tried to lift herself from the bed. Granny stretched her arms around Momma's waist to give her strength and support, and as Momma felt the warmth of Granny's arms firmly around her, she broke. She wept and moaned for the first time since my father's death. "I

3

want him back, Momma; I want him back. It's not fair; he was so young, and he'll never know he's a daddy. Why? Why did he have to die?" she wailed.

She had been in shock up until that point; she had been numb, but she finally faced the reality of it all. Slowly but surely she allowed the situation to sink in. Granny glowed with pride every time she relayed the story of how she saved my mother's and my life. According to Granny, from that point onward Mom began eating and sleeping and living again. Sorrow still draped over her, and you could see it echo through her eyes, but she would smile every time she felt her belly move, and then on November 24, 1975, I was born. Granny and Grandpa stayed right by my mother's side the entire time. Poppa and Maw Maw, my dad's parents, were there as well. I was welcomed into this world by a loving mother and four loving grandparents, and every one of them called me "Pretty Boy." My given name was Rayford Sean Winstrom after my dad.

My mother and I had a wonderful relationship. She was affectionate toward me; I'm sure it hurt to see my dad when she looked at me, but it never stopped her from smiling her beautiful smile and whispering how much she loved me. Before I was old enough to walk or talk, there were certain traditions she formed with me, traditions carried over from her relationship with my father. Every night she pulled out her album of ballroom dance music, placed it on the record player, picked me up into her arms, and danced away. By the time I was three, she was teaching me the actual steps to the fox trot, the rumba, and the waltz. She taught me the importance of properly escorting a lady to the dance floor and how to be a perfect gentleman.

Mom was a dancer. When she met my dad, he was stationed at Camp Lejeune in Jacksonville, North

4

Carolina. She was a native to the area; her parents owned the Dew Drop Inn, a nightclub, so she spent her weekends there dancing her heart away. Because of her status as the daughter of the owners, she was allowed to slip in, even at the young age of seventeen, and dance with all the handsome Marines who spent their evenings there. The regulars knew her age and feared her burly 6'4" father. They were quick to point out his stature to all the newcomers who were interested in dancing with her.

Mom shared the story of her and Dad's romance as she took me through the photo albums regularly. On the night of January 2, 1972, my mother watched as a newcomer to the Dew Drop made his way through the front entrance. His hair (black as a moonless night sky) was buzzed in the typical high and tight manner. From the corner of her eye, she eyed Chris, one of the regulars, point in the direction of her daddy while speaking to the tall, mysterious newcomer. She watched his head tilt, following the direction of the point, and then she saw him smile, stand to his feet, and head toward her daddy.

The gorgeous newcomer stretched his hand forth to shake the hand of the nightclub owner while introducing himself; then he turned and made his way toward Momma's table. When he reached her, he knelt down to see her eye-to-eye and said, "Hello, Miss Bonnye; my name is Sean, but they call me Blacky. Would you care to dance with me?"

Momma smiled. "Can you dance, Blacky?"

My dad grunted. "Not very well, ma'am, but I'm eager to learn, especially if you'd be willing to be the instructor."

Momma stretched forth her hand and allowed him to lead her to the dance floor. He knew nothing of dance; he stepped on her feet several times, but she could see his determination to learn. "So, are you always here

5

every weekend, or do you go to the drive-in theatre sometimes?" Blacky asked.

"I go to the theatre occasionally, but I never go on a date with a man who can't dance." She smiled. "So, if you're interested in taking me to see something on the big screen, you'll have to learn how to dance. I insist on being swept off my feet, Mr. Blacky."

My dad, smitten with her beauty, insisted he'd be there every weekend for lessons if she'd date him once he learned. Momma was a wonderful instructor. Within three months she had him twirling her around the dance floor. During the time they spent together gracefully gliding across the polished floor, they fell in love.

On November 2, 1972, my dad showed up at Momma's doorsteps with a bouquet of flowers in his hands. Surprised to see him standing on her porch on a Thursday, she questioned him with a smile. "What are ya doing here, Sean? Aren't you supposed to be on base?" she inquired.

He grabbed her hand and chuckled as he led her to the porch swing. "I have a four-day leave. I wanted to spend some extra time with you."

"And why is that?" she hesitantly asked. Momma knew Marines usually got an extended leave right before being shipped out somewhere. She knew she had to ask the question but dreaded the answer.

Momma vividly described how he placed the bouquet in her hands, knelt down on one knee, looked up into her eyes, and answered her fears, "Yes, Bonnye. I have to go away for a few months. I'm in the Recon division, and I have to go into North Vietnam to retrieve some important people, but before I go, I wanna know you'll be here waiting for me when I get back. I wanna know I'm the only man you'll ever dance with ever again. I wanna spend the rest of my life dancing with you. I wanna have babies with you and grow old with you. I love you, Bonnye. Will you be my wife?"

"His words ran together from nervousness," Momma would say, smiling each time she relived the moment and told me the story.

Tears streamed down my mother's cheeks as she responded with a smile and a yes. After his weekend of spending time with my mom, the Marines shipped him out. He returned in April, and they were married May 5, 1973. While on his mission, she kept her word and never danced with another man, and even after his death she stayed true to her word until after my birth. In her own way, as she danced with me, she was transported back in time to the memories of dancing with my father.

When I was four, my mother met a Marine by the name of Andy Donovan. Mom had brought me to see my grandparents at the Dew Drop. Sitting me on the bar, she chatted with Granny about my grandpa. He had fallen ill, and my mom was concerned. While I played with Granny's necklace, a man approached my mom from the side. Placing his drink down on the bar, he pulled out a stool, smiled at her, and asked for her name. She graciously smiled and answered, "My name is Bonnye. I don't mean to be rude, but this is my mother; we're talking about an important, private matter."

"I'm sorry, ma'am," he whispered as he gestured a sincere apology with the tilt of his head and hat, stood to his feet, and made his way back to his small, round table.

When Momma finished her discussion with Granny, we got up to leave. Hugs and kisses were given as usual. Momma reached down to hold my hand as we made our way to the exit sign glowing above the front door. She stretched her hand out to push open the door, but before she could wrap her hand around the bar, a strong, masculine hand grasped it and shoved it open. She cut her sparkling blue eyes around to see who the hand belonged to and gasped as she looked into the deep-green eyes of the Marine who had asked her name. "Oh, you startled me."

"I'm sorry, Mrs. Bonnye. I didn't mean to scare you. I just wanted to open the door for you; that's all."

"I appreciate it, Mr.—"

"Andy."

A perplexed look crossed my momma's face. "How is it exactly that you knew to call me Mrs.?"

He glanced down at her left hand and chuckled, "You're wearing a wedding band, ma'am, and you have a small child which typically implies marriage."

"Then why are you hitting on me if you believe me to be married, sir?" She placed her hand on her hip.

He hung his head in shame and defeat. "I suppose I should admit the truth. I saw you in here a couple of weeks ago. I asked around. I was told that you're widowed."

Momma sighed.

"I'm sorry to have said it so bluntly. I just didn't want you to take me as the kind of man who would make moves on a married woman...knowingly that is." He shuffled his feet around and squirmed.

Momma regained control of her composure. "It's quite all right, Mr. Andy. It's been a long time now since I lost my husband."

"Please, just call me Andy."

"Okay," Momma answered. A shy smile stretched across her face.

"Can I walk you to your car?" he asked.

"I suppose."

I looked up at my mother and watched as flattery washed over her face with each compliment he gave as we made our way across the parking lot. As soon as we

8

made it to the car, he opened the door so I could crawl in the back seat. As he went to place his hand on the driver's side door handle, he paused. "Mrs. Bonnye, would you allow me to take you out to dinner?"

Momma inhaled a deep breath. "I suppose if you want me to refer to you as simply Andy, then you should call me Bonnye," she said, lifting her head to peer into his eyes. "I do appreciate your offer, but I'm really not ready to leave Ray with anyone, Andy."

"That's okay. I have a little boy of my own. Victor. He's eight. I'm sure he'd get along great with Ray. We can all go out together."

Slightly biting her bottom lip, Mom pondered the idea. Her mind told her it would be nice to have someone to talk to of the opposite sex, but her heart made her feel as if she was betraying my dad; nevertheless, logically she knew he had been gone for over four years. With a sigh, she answered, "Yeah, that'd be nice."

Andy took us to the local McDonald's for burgers and fries on our first date with him and Victor; the next date was to the small seafood restaurant across town. Eventually, Mom and Andy went on a date with just the two of them. Granny offered to watch me and Victor since Andy's family lived in Mississippi. His wife had left them when Victor was only two-and-a-half years old. Andy didn't speak of her often, and when he did, I could see a strange emotion brewing behind his green eyes.

Eight months down the road my grandpa passed away. Andy stayed by my momma's side the entire time. She turned to him for strength and comfort. His presence during such a difficult time assured my mother he could be trusted to take care of her, so when he asked her to marry and move back to his home state with him, she said yes.

9

On July 14, 1981, my mom married Andy in a small ceremony on the beach in Biloxi, Mississippi. All of Andy's family lived in Biloxi. He chose not to re-enlist in the Marines. He took a job in Pascagoula at Ingalls Shipbuilding, and we made our home in the small city of Moss Point. My mother shined on her wedding day—one of the only times I had seen her smile other than when she danced with me. Granny made the trip down to give her daughter away, and once again, I found myself retreating and hiding behind my mom as Andy's family, one right after the other, approached my mother to give their congratulations. Upon spotting me they were sure to comment on how I was too pretty to be a boy! It was nice to see a gleam in my mother's eyes as they sparkled with tears of joy rather than the pain of hearing the words, "He looks just like Blacky." She still tousled my hair and assured me of her protection while responding with a smile, "He is a handsome young man."

School was another year away, and I had a new home and no friends outside of my new stepbrother. As soon as we settled in, he began picking on me, jeering at me and calling me *too pretty*. He always waited until Mom wasn't around to take his stabs. Andy caught him a few times and fussed. At the time, I thought hearing those words was the worst insult I could ever imagine. I also thought Andy's rebuke of Victor meant he would be a hero to me; I was wrong on both accounts.

CHAPTER 2

JUST RAY

Taking advantage of every opportunity he had, Victor tortured me with the words *too pretty*. Stuck in the house with my tormentor, I hid in my bedroom (my sanctuary) when my mom wasn't home. Fortunately, we didn't have to share a room. Glad to have a safe haven away from the harassments of my new stepbrother, it never bothered me that my room was the smallest in the house. Victor never physically hurt me, but he taunted me relentlessly. Somewhere in the darkness of Victor's mind, he perceived Mom and Andy's marriage license as a permission slip to tease me. We had gotten along fairly well until that beautiful day on the beach, but as soon as the ceremony ended, my suffering began.

Victor filled the remainder of my summer with jabs and pokes. Occasionally Andy would catch him harassing me and get on to him, but for the most part I had to endure his cruelty. One particular day, Mom had made a trip to the local grocery store. I decided to go out back and play, so I slipped on my play clothes and an old pair of tennis shoes and marched myself into the living room where Andy lounged watching television.

"Andy...um...Dad," I stuttered.

"Yeah," Andy hollered at me without even turning to look at me.

"Is it okay if I go out back to play?"

"Yeah, sure." He waved me off with his eyes glued to the television. He obviously didn't want his attention drawn away from the news.

I gladly skipped off toward the back door. I walked around the fenced in yard picking up sticks until I found the perfect one. I shoved my hand into my pocket and pulled out a wad of shoe strings. I plopped down by a skinny popcorn tree growing by the back fence. When in bloom, popcorn-looking buds covered the tree, hence the name. I tied the shoelaces together and attached them to a long, curved stick. Once finished, I had created a perfect bow and arrow. I ran through the yard hiding behind tree trunks and the shed while aiming at my prey—pretend monsters!

Standing silently behind the popcorn tree, I heard the sound of rustling leaves. My imagination ran away with the possibilities of a huge swamp monster making his way out of the nearby river or a giant tire-man coming my way to squeeze me to death. I had nightmares about that ever since I watched the commercial for the Michelin tires with the Michelin Man.

I inhaled a deep breath of air and held it; I stiffened my body against the tree trunk, desperately trying not to move an inch. Whatever crunched amongst the leaves, I didn't want it to find me. I could feel its presence inching its way toward me. I silently prayed, *Please, God, don't let the monster get me.* Then the rustling of the leaves abruptly ended. I heard shushing and heavy breathing. I froze in fear.

Suddenly from the other side of the tree, I heard a shrieking cry. I dug my fingers into the tree trunk as I clenched my fists. "Boo!" Victor and his new friend Mike jumped at me from behind, startling me.

"Aaahhh!" I screamed.

"Ha ha ha ha ha ha ha ha ha." He hit the ground laughing.

My face flushed blood red. "That's not funny, Victor. You two scared me."

He rolled around on the ground a little longer. Fed up, I kicked my foot into the ground causing dirt and leaves to fly into his face. With that, he jumped up. "Oh, you want your butt kicked now, don't you? I'm a lot bigger than you, you little punk."

I stood huffing and watched as he picked up my bow, yanked it apart, and shoved me face forward against the tree. "Hold him here, Mike," he spit. Mike held my arms against the tree trunk and pressed his weight against me, securing me against the tree. Victor used the shoelaces from my homemade bow and tied my hands together on the other side of the tree; then they left me there. Victor would occasionally return and taunt me calling me a wimp.

On his fourth return, he snidely jeered, "Oh, you're just too pretty to be a boy. That must be why you can't get free, you sissy." Then I heard larger footsteps from behind him. I looked up to see a hero coming to rescue me; I watched as my stepdad came to free me from the evil villainous monster named Victor.

"Victor!" Andy screamed. "Untie him immediately, young man; then you go straight to your room. Do you understand me?"

"Yes, sir," Victor stammered as he quickly untied the knots he had made in my shoestrings. As soon as he freed me, he took off to his room.

Andy came and knelt down in front of me. "I'll take care of him," he assured me. He pulled a cloth handkerchief from his pocket and wiped the dirt and tears from my face. "Hey, buddy, you think we can keep this incident a secret between us men?" he asked waving his hand between our proximities. "Your mom, she'd be really angry if she knew what happened, and I don't want to upset her. You understand?"

With a timid nod I shook my head *yes*. Andy stretched his hand down to grab mine and led me to the bathroom. "Go wash up, buddy. I'm gonna go have a little talk with Victor. Your mom should be home any moment now."

As I washed my hands and face with soap and warm water, I heard Victor's bedroom door shut. I couldn't tell what was being said behind the closed door, but I felt vindicated somehow. I felt certain Victor would never harass me again; certainly he had gone too far this time, and Andy let him have it good. I had only been back in my room for a few minutes when I heard the front door open and Mom holler for help with the groceries. I darted out to meet her, gave her a hug, and took off out the front door to retrieve a brown paper bag of groceries from the trunk of her car, never saying a word about the incident.

For some reason I sensed a bond had formed between Andy and me through our secret. Mom was never the wiser, and Victor did indeed leave me alone for a while. He played nice with me after that. Andy whispered to me the next day that he'd given Victor a good attitude adjustment, and he wouldn't be messing with me anymore. Of course, that would not last forever.

In early September Mom drove me down to Small World, a kindergarten in Escatawpa near her place of employment. She had put in an application at an insurance agency in the small town next door to us. I was all too happy to have a place to go during the day where I could meet other boys. I was a little on the bashful side, so I didn't make too many friends right off the bat, but I wrestled around on the playground with a boy named Tramane, the only black boy in my class, which seemed odd. Back home where Granny lived, I'd seen many people of darker skin walking around, and I saw them all the time at the grocery store in my new hometown.

Granny had a black lady, Mrs. Annie, who would

14

come clean her house twice a week; she had a little girl about my age named Sabrina. She was one of my playmates, so I thought nothing of it when I boldly approached him and stuck out my hand for a shake. "Hey, I'm Ray. What's your name?"

He gave me a strange look and responded, "Tramane." I noticed he didn't extend his hand out to meet mine.

"Do you wanna be friends?" I asked with a huge grin.

His eyes pierced through me with wariness. "You *want* to be my friend?" he quizzed.

"Sure, why not?" I shrugged my shoulders.

I scanned the room and noticed all the other children staring at us with shock boldly scribbled across their faces. Then I realized most of the children had shied away from him; I pivoted my head back and forth from him to them, but for the life of me, I couldn't figure out why they thought my speaking to him was so weird and seemingly forbidden. They saw an untouchable boy, someone different from themselves, but I had not been brought up to see color; I simply saw a possible playmate.

As I scrutinized my peers, I caught a glimpse of Tramane skimming through the stares and even glowers in some cases. He brought his head back around to look me in the eyes and assess my disposition; I supposed he searched for malice in my eyes, and when he found only a smile, he grabbed my hand and responded, "Yeah, we can be friends."

Tramane and I spent all of recess playing on the playground. While others gave us funny looks and veered away from him, I saw a friend who was really good at swinging me around on the old tire-swing hanging from the big oak out back. Tray (I shortened his name) was fun, and he was my friend. We sat next to each other when we colored and did finger painting as

15

well as during lunch.

When my birthday rolled around, I learned a lesson in life. My relationship with Andy changed dramatically that day; up until that point, he had spent a lot of quality time with me and treated me as if I were his own; he always referred to me as his buddy when he introduced me to others. He would even say, "This is my youngest boy Ray," with a gleam in his eyes and a smile on his face, but my birthday changed it all, and from that moment forward, I was just Ray.

I asked Mom if I could invite Tray to my birthday party; after all, he was my best friend. She agreed to his coming and gave me an invitation to give to him. I folded it once and stuck it in my back pants pocket. Excitement flooded me when I saw Tray walking toward our table. I jumped out of my chair and quickly pulled the crinkled invitation from the narrow pouch and handed it to him. A huge grin spread across my face, which grew even more as I watched joy wash over him as he eyed the colorful balloons on the front of the invitation. He knew they signified a party invite.

"So, do you think your mom will bring you to my birthday party?" I pressed.

"I live with my grandma, but yeah, I hope so."

"You don't live with your mom?" I crinkled my forehead in confusion.

"No, my mom left me with my grandma when I was a baby," he answered in a factual way.

"My brother Victor, his mom left him too. Now he has my mom. We used to see my grandma all the time, but we don't live by her anymore."

The teacher stepped to the center of the room and called everyone to order, interrupting our conversation. Tray took his invitation home that afternoon to his grandma and came back the next day excited over her approval. Eagerness permeated the following three days while I awaited my big day. The day of my party Mom kept telling me to get the ants out of my pants. I didn't have any ants in my pants and couldn't figure out for the life of me why she thought I did. I had not even been outside all morning.

Close to noon, Mom went to the refrigerator and pulled out the hotdog fixings when she realized we were out of mayonnaise. "Andy," Mom hollered. "We don't have any mayo, Dear. Can you run down to Wayne Lee's and pick up a jar real quick? People are expected to start arriving any minute now."

"You'll have to put the hotdogs back in the fridge, Bonnye. I'll start 'em when I get back," he yelled back as he snatched his keys off the entrance table and headed out the door.

Leaning over the back of the couch staring out the window, I anxiously awaited Tray's arrival. His grandma parked in the drive soon after Andy drove off. When I saw him get out of the car, I darted to the front door to let them in. Outside of two of Andy's nieces and one nephew close to my age, Tray would be the only playmate I had at my party. Adults weren't fun to play with, and I expected my party to be filled with them.

Mom made it to the door right behind me. She greeted Tray's grandma. "Hi, Mrs.—"

"Brown. Mrs. Aretha Brown," she whispered with a quivering voice as she extended her hand in a friendly gesture, testing the waters.

Mom grabbed Mrs. Brown's hand with firm approval of their invitation into our home. Mrs. Brown smiled.

"My name is Bonnye; I'm Ray's mom. Mrs. Aretha, would you like to come in for a cup of coffee while the boys go out back to play?"

"Yes 'am. That'd be nice."

Mom stepped to the side and welcomed them in

our home. "Ray, you and Tray go play out back," she insisted as she led Mrs. Aretha to the living room couch. I eyed wariness in Mom's eyes, so rather than obeying her, we crouched outside the sliding glass door and listened in. Tray's grandma sat quietly while Mom went to pour them each a cup of coffee. She brought both cups into the living room on a tray with sugar and creamer available. Both ladies sat and visited while awaiting the rest of the guests.

"Wait right here, Tray," I whispered as I slipped back inside undetected and eavesdropped from the kitchen.

Mom took a sip of coffee and inhaled a deep breath. "Mrs. Aretha, I have to be honest with you. My...my husband and I...well, we haven't been married for too long, and...um...How can I say this? We've never been in a situation for me to see his views on certain issues. Honestly, I've never even thought to ask how he feels about them until now. What I'm tryin' to say, Mrs. Aretha, is—"

Mom sucked in a sharp breath and slowly released it; her hands quivered with nervousness, so Mrs. Brown finished her thoughts for her. "What your tryin' to say is *you* don't have a problem with me bein' here, but you ain't so sure how your new husband will take it." Mrs. Brown scanned the room, stretching her neck to see down the hallway. "Is he home?"

"No ma'am, he went to the store for me, but he'll be back shortly. I really hope there's not a problem. I just didn't realize Tray was a colored boy. Ray never mentioned it."

"Your boy's a good boy. You know, he's the one who asked my grandson to be his friend. These kids...mmm...mmm...isn't it amazing how they don't see color unless they're taught to."

"Yes, ma'am, it is."

"You know, Tramane said he couldn't believe it
18

when Ray asked if they could be friends. He said every other boy in the class looked at them both like they was aliens or something. I think our world would be a better place if we had a few more kids like your boy there."

Mom grinned. "I think so myself. He's so much like his father." Sadness flushed over Mom's face, and she shook her head slightly as if to shake off a distant memory.

"Where's his father?" Mrs. Brown asked.

"He died in Vietnam. His helicopter went down on the way out. They were trying to bring the last of our men home." At the mention of my dad, I poked my head around the corner and spied on my mom. A hesitant smile crossed her face, and a rush of water made its way toward the dam created by her lids. She worked hard to keep them back, but they pooled together, inching their way over the perimeter created by the thin wall of skin; then one small tear drop made its way over the dam and trickled slowly down her face. As she stretched her hand to dry the tear that had escaped, she whispered, "He didn't even know I was pregnant." Taking a deep breath, she continued, "Ray looks so much like his dad that it's almost like he's still here with me in some ways. I probably sound silly, don't I?"

"Not at all, dear. Not at all." Mrs. Aretha placed her hand on Mom's shoulder and whispered so softly that her words were inaudible.

A strange silence filled the room, not a weird silence but rather quietness seemingly carried in on the wings of peace. Mom's shoulders relaxed, tranquil as if a weight had been lifted. The worry she had endured up until that point had been a raging storm. Startled, she jolted at the sound of the front doorknob turning

"Honey, I picked up the mayonnaise and a paper." Fury brewed behind my stepdad's green eyes when he stepped into the living room and laid his eyes upon their visitor.

"Hey, honey. This is Mrs. Brown; she's Tray's grandmother. You know, the little boy Ray talks about all the time from school?"

"Bonnye, I need to speak to you for a moment, please." He forced a pleasant tone through gritted teeth.

Mom gave Mrs. Brown a wary look and proceeded toward her husband. I tiptoed through the kitchen, inched to the door leading to the hall open, and eyed Andy. He stood in the hallway fuming underneath his calm appearance; as Mom approached him, his face contorted in an angry glower. He forcefully grabbed her arm and dragged her along with him back to their bedroom. As soon as the door shut, I poked my head through the door and heard the clicking of the lock. Despite their being behind a closed, locked door, Mrs. Aretha and I could hear his words clearly.

"What is that woman doing in my home, Bonnye?" he demanded an answer.

"She's Tray's grandmother. I didn't know they were colored folks, but honestly, Andy, I didn't know you would have this kind of response either," she spouted out in defense of herself.

"Oh, so you thought I might be a nigger lover?" he yelled.

"I'm sorry. It won't happen again. Just please allow me to be the one to ask them to leave."

Andy sighed, "Huh...okay, go on. Get 'em outa here."

At the sound of the bedroom doorknob turning, I yanked my head back through the door and left it cracked—keeping my eyes on their bedroom door through the small opening. Mom stepped into the hall, straightened her wrinkled blouse, and ran her fingers through her disarrayed hair. Blotting her face with tissue, her chest fell as she heaved a shuddery breath

Mrs. Aretha met Mom at the front door with an extended hand and a smile. A weak smile inched across

20

my Mom's face. She grasped her hands together firmly to refrain from taking Mrs. Brown's friendly gesture.

Dropping her hand, Mrs. Aretha said, "Ms. Bonnye, thanks for inviting me and Tray over for Ray's party, but we have somewhere else we need to be. I just wanted to stop by and let the boys see each other a minute or two."

Mom's face paled, and her eyes grew huge. "I'm sorry you have to leave, Mrs. Brown," she responded softly.

Mrs. Brown peered over Bonnye's shoulder. Seeing the coast was clear, she drew in closer and whispered, "Please, it's Aretha to you, Ms. Don't worry. We'll leave before we cause you any more trouble."

A tear escaped, and Mom quickly dried it. "I'm so sorry, Aretha," she whispered.

"It's okay, honey. Ignorance is still everywhere, and we women must put up with it more so than men."

"Thank you for understanding. I'll go out back and get Tray. Meet you at your car?" She raised her brows.

At those words, I darted off. Mom stepped out the back door and called Tray to her. She briskly walked him out to his grandmother with me following close on her heels.

"Tramane, we have a few places to go, sugar. I'm sorry you can't stay for the party," his grandmother explained.

"I don't wanna leave, Grandma," he cried.

Mom knelt down eye level with him. "I'm sorry you can't stay, Tray, but it was very nice to meet you." She slowly stood to her feet and watched as Tray's face drew into a pout.

"Come, on, sugar. Get on up in the car. We have t' get goin'," Aretha declared.

I waved bye to Tray, slumped my shoulders, and headed back in the house. My mom entered behind me to find Andy laying into me about not playing with

21

niggers. "We're respectable white people; we don't play with niggers, boy. You'll get a bad name for it. Do you understand me? I better not hear that boy's name again," he demanded.

I stood speechless with tears streaming down my face at the loss of my only friend. I didn't understand what was so wrong with being friends with Tray, but I feared the fury lingering underneath Andy's deep-green eyes. My mother tried to step in to defend me, but he met her with a stern glare and an order to let him be the father figure I desperately needed.

Andy's feelings for me changed. I had embarrassed him. As he so fervently put it, the entire neighborhood had seen a black family in our home, so I had brought shame upon him. All the warm feelings flowing from Andy toward me were turned off immediately. He no longer *had* affection for me. He placed a seal over his empathies, allowing none of it to drip or leak past. I was no longer his youngest boy or his buddy. I was...just Ray.

CHAPTER 3

BOY NEXT DOOR

A rift formed in my mother and Andy's relationship. It didn't take long for both Victor and me to see it. Mom slept on the couch for several weeks. Andy spoke harshly to her when he did bother to speak, and when he decided I existed and spoke to me, he spoke even harsher. Victor deciphered his dad's coldness toward me as permission for his torturous ways to return, so to test the waters and see if he would receive disciplinary action or rebuttals, he began with his jabs once again. In the beginning words formed his jabs—simple name calling, but eventually, when Andy delivered no punishment for them, he added in shoves, pushes, pokes, and a few smacks.

Victor had become the ultimate bully whom I could never get away from except in the retreat of my bedroom, so I spent a lot of time tucked in my small refuge, pulling out my army men and mounting war after war within the covers of my bed. I made mountains out of pillows, and with my hands I molded trenches into my bedspread. "Bang, bang, bang..." the imaginary guns fired away aiming at men on the other side of my bed. "*Boom!*" thundered the make-believe bomb as green men flew through the air, but no matter the shots or the roar of the explosions, the war continued on. My little green army men never gave up, and they surely never cried.

During those first few weeks, Mom tried to

intervene when she heard Andy's cutting remarks toward me or saw him shun me as I passed. I witnessed several arguments on my account, which made Andy begrudge me all the more. Every time she spoke in my defense, his resentment ran deeper like a seemingly bottomless well of heavy, cold water. The further down one goes within the well, the colder the water becomes. Likewise, my mother's words of defense sent me, rather than a bucket, plunging into the cold blackness of his emotions. They weighed heavily on me, constantly aware of his disapproval and stony indifference toward me.

After three weeks of mom sleeping on the couch, Andy awoke on a Sunday morning and elected to make an attempt at smoothing things over. I suppose he got tired of sleeping alone and decided she wasn't going to budge on her stance. He stumbled into my room and nudged me awake. "Ray, come help me with breakfast," he whispered.

I edged along behind him into the kitchen. I yawned and stretched before slouching into the chair. Andy started the coffee pot, began boiling water for grits, and scrambled a few eggs. "Stick the bread in the toaster for me."

I dropped a couple of slices of bread into the toaster and moseyed over to the refrigerator to get the butter. As each pair of toast popped to the surface, I slathered them with a thick layer of yellow heaven. Well, that's how my mom referred to butter anyhow. Andy grabbed the tray off the bar, slid a few slices of my toast on a plate, and made his way to the living room. Tiptoeing, I slid quietly across the floor, staying far enough behind so as not to have my presence felt. I ducked behind the kitchen door and watched as he set the tray on the coffee table and proceeded to wake my mom.

"Bonnye, Bonnye," he whispered as he shook her awake by her shoulder.

Mom fidgeted and moaned. "Um..." She turned facing the back of the couch.

"Bonnye, wake up, honey. We need to talk."

Mom broke free from the world of dreams and came back to the real world. She wiggled her way back over, facing Andy. Stretching, she intertwined her hands and extended them. She peeled open her eyes and looked at her husband. With outspread arms, Andy gently helped her sit up. Eyeing breakfast on the coffee table, she narrowed her eyes.

"Bonnye, I think we just had our first real fight, and we need to talk some things through so we can get past this. No one ever said marriage was always peachy. Couples do argue and fight. We're not gonna always see everything eye to eye."

Everything rolled off his tongue quickly. So quickly, in fact, Mom stopped him. "Andy, give me a minute, please. Can I have a cup of coffee before we start in on this?"

Reluctance tinged his reply, "Um...yeah...of course, honey."

Mom slowly stood to her feet, made her way to the hall bathroom, rinsed her mouth with Scope, then came back to join Andy on the couch. I stayed my ground, keeping an eagle eye in case my mom needed me to rescue her. I remained leery of my stepdad at that point. I witnessed the bruise on my mother's arm from the way he grabbed her on my birthday. It had faded over three weeks, but I seared the memory of it in my mind forever. I made sure to listen in on every word that transpired.

Mom took a sip of her coffee and allowed the warmth of it to run through her body. Inhaling deeply, she closed her eyes and breathed in the aroma of freshly brewed Columbian Supreme before taking another sip and allowing the warm, black coffee to trickle its way down her throat; then she braced herself, squaring her shoulders, for the inevitable—a conversation!

"Bonnye, I'm sorry...I'm very sorry I grabbed you so hard and that I blew up the way I did, but I'd like it if you'd give me a chance to explain why. Can you do that?"

Mom sighed, "Huh...I suppose I'll give you a chance to enlighten me on why you responded so harshly."

Andy looked up at her. "Do you believe blacks and whites should marry?"

Mom squinted. "No, I was brought up that we are supposed to marry our own race, but I was also brought up that we should always be kind to others no matter what color their skin happens to be."

"Well, think about it, Bonnye. If we allow Ray to have black friends and think that it's okay for him to be friends with them, then who's to say he won't start thinkin' it's okay for him to date one when he gets older?"

Mom gave in to his rationalization and agreed. "You're right. I can see how it could possibly lead to that, but I don't think it justifies your hurting me and almost slapping me, or the way you've been treating Ray either," she insisted.

"I'm so sorry about that. I have a temper, but I'm working on it. I promise; I won't ever hurt you again, and I'll be sure not to speak harshly to Ray." Andy leaned forward and placed his hands on his knees. "There's one more thing that needs to be taken care of. He needs to understand he can't be friends with that boy, and I know you don't want to teach him to be mean to anyone, so I was thinkin' maybe he could be transferred to another kindergarten."

"Okay," my mom reluctantly agreed. "I'll ask around and try to find one."

26

I eavesdropped on their conversation, so I heard every word that had been spoken. I surely didn't fathom what my being friends with Tray had to do with me marrying anybody. I didn't understand the logic adults seemed to have. I jumped up and darted off to my room. Slamming my door behind me, I pulled out my bag of green army men from under my bed and set up another war scene. Once I completed the site, I picked up two of the men and stared at them for a lingering moment; then I set them in their positions and picked up two more, contemplating what I knew to be true of them—they were all green. Army men weren't actually green, but they all wore green camouflage, and for some reason the makers of these little plastic men chose to make them green all over. I stored that fact away in the back of my mind as I pondered on why they might do such a thing.

With Christmas less than a week away, school let out for vacation. Since I had no desire to be bullied, I locked myself in my room daily. Growing tired of my bedroom day in and day out, I decided to venture out to the backyard on a particularly cold Saturday. The cold spells on the Gulf Coast were nothing like the cold spells back home where Granny still lived. On the coast, you could wear shorts one day and a massive coat the next.

I slipped into an old pair of jeans, pulled a sweatshirt over my head, situated a beanie over my wavy locks of hair, and creaked open my door. Sticking my head through the small opening in order to spy out the situation, I peered down the hallway to see if I could see Victor anywhere. I listened closely and heard the television going. My ears picked up the sounds of Saturday morning cartoons, clueing me in on Victor's whereabouts. I slipped through the small crack in the door, turned the knob in my hand, silently shut the door, and tiptoed down the hall to the back door. When I finally made it outside unseen, I lay against the back wall and took a deep breath. I had become one of my green army men fighting a war within the walls of my own home. My older step-brother morphed into my enemy, a much stronger opponent.

Suddenly I heard a rumbling coming from the empty house next door. Fright washed over me, and I shivered. My breathing grew rapid and shallow. I stayed glued to the back wall of the house. "Okay, you're a Marine like your dad; you can do this," I told myself. Inhaling one deep breath, I dashed across the yard to the privacy fence. Once there, I released the oxygen held tightly in my lungs through heavy panting; then I used the horizontal slates of wood as a ladder and inched my way to peer over the top.

I saw a man get out of a big black car and walk around to the passenger side where he opened the door for a blindfolded woman. With his help, she stepped out of the car and exclaimed, "Jason, what is it?" She smiled. "You're not really gonna keep me in the dark about this, are you?"

"Yes, I am, Dorothy." He smiled back as he led her toward the house. Once they were no longer hidden behind the car, I could clearly see she had a huge belly poking out in front of her.

I watched as he unveiled her eyes, revealing a beautiful blonde-haired, blue-eyed woman beneath the bandana. She threw her hands over her mouth and squealed as she cried. "Jason, you didn't?"

"Yes, I did. Merry Christmas, sweetheart. It's a four bedroom, so now, Mason will have a big bedroom." Patting her belly, he added, "Our little princess, Renee, will have a nice nursery, and I'll have a study. The master bedroom is huge; I can't wait for you to see it all. Come on," he said as he led her through the front door. My spying ended when the door shut behind them.

The next day I stalked to the living room's side window at the sound of a loud roar. Pulling back the drapes, I peered out as an enormous truck parked at the house next door and four Andre the Giant-looking men stepped out and began unloading beds, couches, tables, boxes, and a shiny, black piano. I spied the same tall, dark-haired man who had been there the previous day. He sauntered through the front door and disappeared from my sight, swallowed by the house. I wondered, *Maybe Mason's a boy I can play with?* But I never saw a little boy or the woman who had been with him, so with a sigh, I dropped the curtain from my hand and let it fall back into place.

Day after day, I searched for signs of a playmate, sometimes peering through the window while other times spying through the cracks in the fence. No blonde-haired woman appeared, and no little boy named Mason did either. I had begun to give up hope of finding someone with whom I could wrestle or play kick ball. (Victor would hurt me intentionally. I just wanted to goof off and have fun.)

On Christmas Eve Granny came into town. She had flown in, so I made the trip with Mom to the airport in Mobile to pick her up. I squirmed all the way there.

"Ray, stop wiggling around," my mother fussed.

"But I can't wait to see her, Momma. I miss her. I haven't seen her in a kazillion years."

Mom chuckled. "A kazillion years, huh? It's only been six months, sweetheart."

"Why can't Poppa and Maw Maw come too?" I inquired after my dad's parents.

"Poppa works in an office in one of those really tall buildings in downtown Houston, and his boss told him he had to work on Christmas this year, sweetie," my mom explained.

Disappointment washed over me, but as soon as I eyed Granny searching for her luggage, it fizzled away.

Granny rushed straight for me when she saw me at the baggage claims section of the airport. She whizzed right past my mom and picked me up in her arms. I left the airport that day with a red face. My face, however, wasn't red from embarrassment; Granny's lipstick covered it with huge red kiss marks. Granny treated Andy with just as much love as she had the day she gave her daughter to him, so it was obvious Mom had not let her in on the altercation that had taken place.

Andy worked diligently to get back in my mom's good graces. When we walked in the front door, he made it seem as if our home was straight off the television set of, "Leave it to Beaver," "Father Knows Best," or "My Three Sons." All anyone had to do was simply pick any one of those shows where the kids got into a bit of trouble every now and then but the parents always had the perfect answer, helping their children to make a wise decision. In their world, their homes ran rather efficiently, and life was grand. He made it seem as if he was as perfect as the fathers in those shows and our home ran as smoothly as theirs did, when in reality my home had become more like "Planet of the Apes." Of course, in my thoughts and mind, Andy and Victor filled the roles of the cruel, vicious apes who wanted nothing more than to destroy the dignity of the only remaining humans.

Tousling my hair as I passed, Andy uttered, "Hey there, buddy. Enjoy the ride to the airport? You get to see any planes flying overhead for a landing?"

"Yes, sir," I mumbled.

Ever since his talk with Mom, Andy made a few attempts at winning me over, but I hadn't forgotten what had transpired, and, of course, he hadn't apologized to me for the way he had been speaking to me. He simply wanted to be nice to me and expected me to dismiss it all, but I had no such plans because I could still see something lingering behind his green eyes. I wasn't sure what it was, but something I didn't trust dwelled beneath them. I had seen it surface at the mention of Victor's mother on occasion, and it rose to the surface on my birthday.

"Hey, honey," he said as he kissed my mom on the cheek. Wrapping his arms around Granny, he laughed. "So good to see you again. How was the flight?"

"Oh, it was fine, dear, but I sure could use a cup of that coffee I smell brewin' in there." Granny chuckled. Draping her arm securely around my shoulder, she made her way to the couch.

Andy brought Granny a cup of steaming hot coffee. They lounged around the glass and brass coffee table chattering away while I snuggled up next to her, falling asleep there with my head in her lap. I woke up some time later with Granny's hand gently caressing the side of my face.

I quickly sat up, thinking Christmas morning had arrived. "Did Santa come? Did Santa come? Oh no, I wasn't in my bed. Did he skip our house?" I cried.

Laughing, Granny replied, "No, sweetheart. Santa comes tonight. You just took a little nap, that's all." She chuckled again and added, "You've only been asleep for thirty minutes, darlin'. It's almost supper time. Why don't you go wash up?" she insisted, patting my arm.

"Yes, ma'am," I uttered as I pounced to the floor and dashed down the hall. "Woo!" I exhaled a sigh of relief as I made my way to the bathroom. I felt intense relief I had not missed Santa. For a six-year-old Santa skipping your house because you weren't in bed made for a pretty serious situation. Before Granny informed me I had only taken a nap and had not missed him, my mind had already mulled over possible ways to get him to turn around.

That night we all sat around the table and enjoyed

31

a huge turkey with dressing, squash casserole, green bean casserole, candied yams, and rolls. Andy's mom and dad came over and had dinner with us. My mom was a super cook, so good, in fact, I ate all the squash casserole she put on my plate, and that's saying a lot, I might add. After supper Granny tucked me in my bed and kissed me goodnight. A smile crossed my face as I closed my eyes and drifted off to dreamland.

When I awoke on Christmas morning, I bolted to the living room. Hitting my knees, I scurried through the packages searching for my name. I ripped through gift after gift labeled from Santa; then I came across a bright red present from Granny. I pulled the green ribbon loose and ripped the paper from the box to find a used tobacco pipe. Furrowing my brow in confusion, I held it high and exclaimed, "Granny, Momma told me to never, never, never, never, *never* smoke a pipe. She said it's what killed Grandpa!"

Granny knelt down next to me. "I know, sweetie. It's not for you to smoke. It was your Grandpa's; it's just an heirloom—something for you to remember him by." Taking the pipe from my hands, she grasped it and breathed in its aroma. "See, dear, it smells like your grandpa. This way, you'll always have something to remind you of his fragrance."

I stretched my hand to take the pipe back and took a big whiff. "Hmm..." Seeing a vision of myself sitting in my grandpa's lap while he smoked his pipe and watched the television, I sighed. "It does smell like Grandpa." I smiled at Granny; then Mom came strolling in the room with her hands on the handlebars of a red and black Huffy bike sporting a humongous yellow bow. "A bike, a bike, a bike!" I squealed. Like a flash of lightning, I darted to my mother's side and grasped the bike. "Can I please go out front to give it a ride, Momma?"

"Oh, I don't know. Let me get a cup of coffee in, and I'll take you outside. I don't want you on the road by yourself, Ray," Mom insisted.

"Please, Momma," I begged. Watching her stand firm on her decision with her arms folded tightly across her chest, I gave in with a huff. "Oh, all right, but can you drink it fast?"

Once Mom finished her cup, she and Granny took me outside to teach me how to ride my bike. Momma placed one hand on the handlebar and the other on the back of my seat. She briskly walked along with me as I peddled away. When she felt I had it down, she let go. I made it about 100 yards before crashing to the ground. "That's all right, sweetheart. Just get back up and try it again," Granny encouraged.

I got back up over and over again. My sixth time on the bike, I heard a rumbling noise coming down the street. It sounded like the same noise that echoed from the big black car I had been searching for ever since I had seen the dark-haired man and the blonde lady with a big belly. I put the brakes on and planted my feet firmly on the ground. Craning my head I spied the car, following it closely with my eyes as they pulled in the driveway next to ours. The dark haired man I knew to be Jason stepped out and slammed his door. Marching around to the passenger side, he opened the door and extended his hand. From inside the car, a dainty hand stretched to meet his. Out stepped the lady holding a bundle of blankets in her other arm. Removing her hand from the man's, she wrapped her free arm lovingly around the blankets. Glancing down at them, she sighed.

She glided toward the front door, eyeing the blankets she snuggled. The man remained by the car with the door still held open. "Come on, Mason. Let's go get a look at your new bedroom!" he exclaimed. A thrill of excitement washed over me as a boy with dark-blond hair climbed out of the back seat. I couldn't tell from where I stood, but I was certain he had to be close to my

33

age. A grin stretched across my face as I pondered that idea of a new friend. My mind swiftly scanned through the scenarios of all my alone time out back where Victor had free reign to torture and harass me because there were no witnesses.

There may have been a small amount of selfish motive involved in my excitement, seeing as I enjoyed the idea of having a friend right next door who could be a scapegoat of sorts. It wasn't that I would have put any of Victor's harassments off on anyone else, but rather I would use him as a guard. I hoped Victor would find someone else to unleash his frustrations upon if I had a friend over playing with me, a type of witness. At that thought, I gazed at the boy next door and smiled.

CHAPTER FOUR

PEE WEE

I passed most of my time in the backyard playing, outside of hiding in my room; unfortunately, Victor spent his time out back as well. Usually Mom insisted we play in the portion of the yard secured by a privacy fence, but she made an exception that day because of her and Granny's presence. Elation washed over me, along with a sense of relief, when I spied the boy about my age standing in the yard next to mine.

The boy next door craned his head in my direction, threw his hand out in a wave, and exclaimed, "Merry Christmas!"

A smile slid across my face and the same boldness I felt when I met Tray surged through my blood. I shoved the kickstand down on my bike with a thrust and went to meet him. The boy's dad continued to the door to let his wife and new baby in while his son made his way to my drive.

"Hey, I'm Mason," he said.

"Hey, I'm Ray; I live next door."

"So, you're moving in on Christmas day, huh?"

"Yep, my baby sister was born three days ago, so Dad said today was the perfect day to move in," he answered with a slight shrug of the shoulders.

"How old are you?" I began my onslaught of questioning, my bashfulness seeming to fade from the exhilaration of a possible new friend.

"Seven. How old are you?"

"I'm six. Are you in the first grade?"

"Yep, I go to West Elementary."

"You already go there? But you're just now movin' in?"

"Yeah, I know. We used to live a few streets over. This house is bigger. Momma wanted a bigger house because of my new sister, so Dad got her this house for Christmas."

My questions were brought to a halt when his dad poked his head out the front door and hollered, "Mason, come in and see what Santa brought. You can play with your new friend later today, okay."

Mason smiled. "I gotta go see what I got for Christmas. Meet you back out here for some football after Christmas dinner?"

"Sure thing."

After dinner I asked Mom and Granny if I could be excused. "Mom, Granny, can I go outside and play now?"

"Sure, honey," Mom responded but quickly added, "Go out back, okay. That way I don't have to worry 'bout you getting' run over by a car."

"But, Mom, Mason asked me to meet him after lunch out front to play football," I whined.

Andy quickly interjected. "Listen to your mother, boy."

I cut my eyes at him and rolled them, dismissing what he had said. "Please, Momma, he's my new friend."

It didn't take long for Mom to realize the significance of the situation. She waved Andy off and answered, "Okay, I'll walk you over to knock on the door. You can invite him to come play in our backyard."

Granny leaned over, placed her lips to my ear, and whispered, "I know she's overprotective, sweetie, but you're all she has left of your daddy. She can't bear the thought of losing you too." My head dropped, and my shoulders slumped.

Mom began clearing the table and instructed me to assist her. I helped her gather the dirty dishes and take them to the sink to rinse them as she placed them in the dishwasher. Once we finished loading it, she filled it with detergent and pushed the start button; then she walked me over to Mason's house and knocked on the front door.

Knock, knock, knock, echoed the solid oak door. "Mooooommmmm," I whined through gritted teeth. "There's a doorbell right there." I corrected her, pointing at it.

"Oh, it's okay, honey. Door-to-door salesmen and kids selling donuts are usually the ones who ring doorbells. Friends and neighbors just knock," she said, explaining her reasoning. I wondered if she just hadn't noticed the doorbell or if what she said was the truth.

The beautiful blonde-haired lady opened the door and greeted us with a smile. Mom returned the smile while reaching for the lady's hand. "Hi, my name is Bonnye, and this is my son Ray; we live next door."

"Very nice to meet you. I'm Dorothy. Why don't you two come in?" she asked.

"Oh, all right," Mom uttered as she stepped over the threshold into the foyer. "Ray met your boy earlier and wanted to see if he could come over and play out back with him."

"Yeah, Mason mentioned meeting a boy around his age. Have a seat." She pointed to the elegant couch in what was obviously a formal living room. "I'll go upstairs and get him. Would you like a cup of coffee?"

"Oh, yes, I'd love a cup," Mom trilled. I could see excitement bubbling in her eyes.

Is coffee really that good? I thought to myself. "Can I have a cup too?" I interjected.

Mom swiftly turned her head to look at me. "Ray, it's rude to ask for something in someone's home. You always wait 'til they offer," she scolded me in a gentle manner. "Besides that, coffee is not for kids, honey."

Coffee's not for kids? Exactly what are they keeping from us? I wondered. *Whatever it is, it must be good.*

Mom drank her cup of coffee and chatted with Ms. Dorothy while Mason and I played with some of his new toys in his new room. His house was awesome and enormous. We finished setting up his electric train set and watched as the train went round and round; of course, we set up a few obstacles along the way to see if the engine had what it takes to power through, and we were sure to applaud one another when our blockade caused derailment.

After Mom and Ms. Dorothy shared their life history over fresh-brewed coffee, Mason and I were allowed to go out back and play in the yard. I took my Huffy, he grabbed his new BMX bike, and off we went. We both had been given bikes for Christmas, so football was forgotten.

Over the next six months we wore a path around the perimeter of the yard with our bikes. We spent almost every day with one another. We entered many worlds together as we became army men fighting in a war, the bionic man and his bionic friend (we both wanted to be bionic, so we made up a story of his best friend being in an accident and becoming bionic as well), and Luke Skywalker and Han Solo saving the universe from Darth Vader. Every time Victor stepped outside we imagined him as Vader and pulled out our imaginary light sabers. We even pretended to be our favorite super heroes from *The Justice League.* Mason took on the role of Batman, and I played the part of Superman.

Andy worked on winning me over for a little while, and I managed to forgive what I had seen him do to my mom. While I still did not understand his issues with Tray, I forgave him for that as well. Of course, I had been taken out of Small World and placed in a kindergarten called The Pumpkin Patch. I made a couple of friends there, and Andy was pleased with my choices, but after a few months, he went back to calling me *just Ray*. He didn't ignore me, but my presence seemed to be an irritant to him. The casual "good morning" and "how was your day?" filled our superficial existence.

When summer hit, Andy scheduled camping trips every weekend for him and Victor. He explained to Mom that he felt Victor needed some extra attention from him. Since Mom and Andy had married, Victor had been "acting out" as Andy called it, so he thought weekend trips out amongst nature with just the two of them might help. Mom didn't mind so much because it gave her and me time together too, so every weekend over the summer, Mom pulled out her old ballroom dance albums and taught me to dance while she remembered my dad. Amidst the instructions of forward, slide to the side, one, two, three, she would tell me about him.

Summer came to an end all too quickly. It had been one of the best summers ever. I had a new best friend who lived right next door, so we played almost every day, which meant Victor didn't have an opportunity to torment and harass me. On the weekends he left with Andy (which did seem to help his attitude), and I had my mom all to myself—the perfect summer, but as I had been told, all good things must come to an end. I found that statement to be true. Life went back to normal. Andy stayed home on the weekends which meant so did Victor, and school was set to start.

The first day of school went off without a hitch. I woke up bright and early, put on my favorite Flash Gordon t-shirt and my best pair of jeans, brushed my teeth and hair, and ate a healthy breakfast before catching the bus with Victor. Victor sat in the back of the bus with the older children, which happened to be fortunate for me. It eliminated his opportunities to badger me.

I sat up front with Mason. His mom liked to drive him to school, but he asked if he could ride the bus with me, so she allowed him to do so for a while. That day when we got back on the bus to head home, Mason handed me a piece of paper. Across the top in bold letters were the words *Pee Wee Football.*

"They're having registration for the pee wee football teams this weekend. Do you think your mom and stepdad will let you play?" he asked.

"I don't know...maybe."

"I sure hope so. You think it would help if I went with you to ask? We could beg. That's what I do when I want my way," he said, informing me of his tactics of getting what he wanted.

"I don't know, Mason. I don't want to make my stepdad mad. Mom says we have to walk on eggshells around him sometimes. He gets pretty angry." I explained the tension that sometimes arose in my home.

"Oh, ok." He gave in. "You're gonna ask though, aren't you?"

"Yeah, I'll ask."

"Great!"

The bus pulled up in front of our homes, and we both stepped off. Mom wasn't home from work yet, leaving me stuck in the house with Victor for thirty minutes. Her boss let her off early every day in order to get home and fix supper, but in order to do that, she had to give up her hour lunch. Exhausted, she heaved a heavy sigh as she ambled through the door and plopped on the couch. Not wanting to bother her, I decided to wait until after supper to ask her about football.

As soon as I finished my dinner, I placed my fork

on the bare plate, cleared my throat, and asked, "Mom, Mason said they're having sign-ups for pee wee football this weekend. Do you think I could play?"

"Oh, I didn't realize you were even interested in football, dear."

"Well, I've never played before, but his dad played in high school, so he could help us out."

"You really wanna play?" She raised her brow in question.

"Um, yeah."

"How much does it cost?" She pressed a little further.

"Cost? Um, I don't know. He didn't say anything about that."

"Tell you what, I'll call Dorothy after we clear the table and wash up the dishes, okay?"

"Yes, ma'am," I responded as I hopped to my feet and grabbed dishes to take to the sink. Mom knew how to get me moving when it came to cleaning. All she had to do was hold something like that over my head, and I was up and running.

She made her phone call and okayed my playing pee wee football alongside Mason. She made arrangements with Ms. Dorothy to take turns taking us to practice, and Mr. Jason, Mason's dad, agreed to get us outside and work with us as well. We all gathered down at the community center early that Saturday morning to register. Mason's dad took us outside every day after school to do exercises and practice throwing and catching the ball. I didn't do well at either of those, but I held my own. Two weeks after registration we had our first practice. The head coach swindled Mr. Jason into being an assistant coach because of his experience playing football, so neither Mom nor Ms. Dorothy had to take us to practice.

Pee wee football, slightly different from junior high or high school football, didn't require tryouts for the team. With those, boys had to work hard to make the team. Of course, there were those picked to be back up; they sat on the bench and waited for someone to get injured or sick, and if no one did, they didn't play. With pee wee football, however, one played each position at least once, the point being to learn the game. Competitiveness thrust itself on the bigger boys.

During the first few weeks we spent a lot of time exercising and training rather than playing the game. The head coach, Coach Robby, noticed my speed immediately and suggested me as the perfect candidate for running the ball. My height and thin frame allowed me to whisk right past the stockier built boys, yet I lacked strength, so he set up scenario after scenario of the bigger boys blocking others to keep them away from me. The only problem I had was hanging onto the ball, (well, catching it to begin with). I kept fumbling the ball and not just when catching it mid-air if I happened to be lucky enough to catch it. I even dropped it several times long after I had caught it. I could be running with it securely in place, and suddenly it disappeared; it just slipped right out of my grasp without my realizing it.

It didn't take long for everyone on our team to realize I wasn't the athletic type. Coach allowed me to play some during each game, but I sat out more than any other boy on the team, and when I did get on the field, the guys yelled at me for fumbling the ball. Although he was the best player on the field, Mason was the only one who didn't rag me about being horrible at the game. He loved playing; he had fun, and he made up for my weaknesses on the field. I may have dropped the ball, but he made sure he caught it on the next go round and made a touchdown.

Mom and Andy came to every game, and Andy hung his head in shame every time I fumbled or missed the ball all together. The drive home after the game was usually spent listening to a lecture on how to catch the ball and how not to drop it or how a boy's manhood is centered on his athletic abilities. He insisted I had to find my sport. Mom took his talks as his showing an interest in me bettering myself and finding at which sport I excelled; I took them as the simple reprimands I saw them to be. Andy pointed out to me time and again Victor's athleticism. He played football, soccer, and baseball—the reason Andy stayed too busy to help me practice! He spent his time taking Victor to his practices and games. It didn't bother me because it meant less time that Victor was home.

The season ended the weekend before my birthday, and by the end of it, I was ready for it to be over. While glad I had attempted playing the sport, I knew it wasn't for me. I wasn't quite sure what would be for me, but I knew beyond a shadow of a doubt I would *never* play for a professional football team in the NFL. Mason, on the other hand, already showed signs of being a natural at the game, and from that point forward, his dad groomed him just for that.

At closing ceremonies we each received a small trophy. Mom beamed with pride as she watched me walk to the front to retrieve the small plastic football player set upon a pedestal, and I smiled because I had fun playing. I wasn't good at it for sure, but I had fun doing it nonetheless.

As we left, Mason handed his trophy to his dad and ran toward me. "Hey, dude, I thought of this cool handshake that can be ours," he exclaimed.

"Really? Show me."

"Okay, our hands come together like this; then we hit the back of our hands together like this. We slide our hand over our ear through our hair like this; then we grasp one another's hand and ram each other's shoulder. Waddaya think?"

"Cool, let's do it again so we can get it down pat."

We stood there practicing our new handshake until we had it smoothed out and timed perfectly. Mom and Ms. Dorothy laughed. "I sure am glad we moved next door to y'all. I think there's the potential for life-long friendship here." Ms. Dorothy giggled.

"I think you're right." Mom laughed back as she stretched out her arms to take Mason's baby sister, Renee. Like one big, happy family, we all walked to the parking lot.

The following weekend I fell asleep looking through my mom's old photo album filled with pictures of my dad. A starburst of light pierced my eyelids. Squinting, I pried open my eyes. Blurry green blades shot up around my face. I rubbed my eyes and brought stalks of high grass into view. Tall trees swayed overhead, and all sorts of plant life surrounded me. Green consumed everything. I wasn't in my yard. I wasn't certain where I was. My breath caught in my throat when I realized I was lost. The hair on the nape of my neck stood on ends and a cold chill trickled down my spine. Mom had pounded in my brain over and over again not to stray away from her because there were bad people out there who kidnap little kids, so I immediately scanned the area looking for my mom.

As comprehension of my aloneness in a jungle sank in, I panicked. In desperation I rustled through the wilderness enclosing me. Pushing leaves and limbs to the side, I scampered through the thick, heavy jungle and screamed for my mom. Sweat beads popped up across my forehead. Then I heard a voice calling my name; I had heard it before somewhere, but I wasn't sure where. "Ray, I'm right over here," the deep voice echoed. A bright light shone through the canopy created by the tall trees. Narrowing my eyes, I peered at my dad, drenched from head to toe, stepping out of a river. His crushed helicopter lay in a mangled heap on the riverbed. I stretched my hand out as I walked toward him, but the closer I got, the brighter the light glowed until it hurt my eyes. I squeezed them tight to shut out the light. When I peeled them open, I squinted as the rays of sunlight shot through my window blinds, hitting me right smack in the face, and looked up into the eyes of both my grandparents.

"Dad," I whispered as I sat up.

"No, baby, it's Maw Maw and Poppa," my grandmother responded. "We came to see you for your birthday."

I jumped to my feet and threw my arms around my Maw Maw's legs; then I climbed into my Poppa's arms. "This is the best birthday present *ever!*"

CHAPTER 5

MUSIC MAN

Maw Maw and Poppa Winstrom, as I called them, both sighed a big "awww" at my proclamation. Poppa inherited his mother's Italian traits, but of course, at that point his hair was mostly a handsome silvery gray, but the pitch-black peppered throughout reminded me of the pictures from his youth. My dad looked just like him, and I looked just like my dad. I'm not certain what it is, but there's something significant in being able to see where you came from. I knew I came from my mom, but I looked like my dad and his dad, so I had a special relationship with my paternal grandparents, despite the fact I only saw them once or twice a year.

One would think because of my mother's marriage and our moving closer to Texas that I would have more opportunity to see my dad's parents, but it had been a year and a half since I had seen them, so I unleashed a mighty waterfall of words, telling them of all my adventures on the Gulf Coast.

"Maw Maw, Poppa, you have to see my bike!" I squealed. Sliding down the side of my grandfather, I hit the floor running, and straight to the toy box I went. "Here's the Simon I got for Christmas. Look what it does," I squealed. Lights glowed as different sounds were made by the electronic game. Hoping to impress my grandparents, I followed its sequence for as long as I could; then I jumped to the next new toy showing off all the things I had gotten and mastered since I had last

46

seen them. I could complete the Rubik's Cube in record time—without removing any of the stickers, I might add. My grandparents sat patiently on the bed watching me go through my red, wooden toy box. At one point I gazed back at them and spied a silvery sheen glistening in both their eyes. Simultaneously they smiled, but no matter how hard they tried to look enthusiastic, sadness reflected from the thin layer of tears.

As a tear escaped my grandmother and trickled down her cheek, I bolted to her side. "Maw Maw, don't be sad. It doesn't hurt him to stretch his arms like that. He's Stretch Armstrong; you're supposed to stretch his arms out."

"Oh, darlin', I'm not sad, and I'm definitely not concerned for your doll."

I lowered my brow. "It's not a doll, Maw Maw; it's an action figure."

"Oh...action figure...sorry for the mistake, darlin'. Maw Maw isn't sad at all. These are happy tears. Did your momma tell you your poppa made that toy box for your dad when he was a little boy? You just looked so much like him pullin' all those toys out. I just felt such happiness that I cried."

"Yep, momma told me it was my dad's and Poppa made it for him when he was a little boy like me." Turning my head to peer into my grandfather's eyes, I asked, "And you felt such happiness that you cried too, Poppa?"

Poppa sat straight and tall. "I'm not—" Cutting her eyes at Poppa, Maw Maw interrupted his train of thought and corrected him with her glare. Clearing his throat, he continued, "Yes, Ray, it was the overwhelming happiness I felt that caused my eyes to water, but I didn't actually shed a tear, you know." He winked.

"So, are y'all comin' to my birthday party?"

"We most definitely are," Poppa said.

47

Satisfied with his answer, I went back to showing off my toys; then I grabbed an old pair of jeans and a t-shirt out of the drawer and headed to the bathroom to change. When I came back out, I grasped Poppa's hand with one hand and Maw Maw's hand with the other and led them out back to the bench. "You two sit here so I can show you all the neat tricks I can do on my bike."

They both sat and watched while I raced around the yard on my Huffy. I demonstrated for them every skill I had mastered on my bike. Eventually my flare of energy, probably due to a sudden burst of adrenaline at the sight of my grandparents, waned, and I wore out, so I put my bike back under the lean-to and led Maw Maw and Poppa straight to the kitchen.

"I'm starvin'. How 'bout you?" I asked.

"Well, sweet pea, we ate at the La Font, but I'd love a cup of coffee," Maw Maw answered. Poppa sat at the table while Maw Maw made a pot of coffee, and I fixed me a bowl of cereal. After turning the coffee pot on, she stepped to the table, and I noticed Poppa stand to his feet and pull her chair out for her to sit. When he did so, she gazed at him and smiled. I had never seen Andy do that for Mom, so I tucked it away in the back of my mind.

I sat with my bowl of Cookie Crisp and took a big bite before asking, "Maw Maw, Poppa?"

"Hmmm?" Poppa questioned.

"Maw Maw just made coffee, so that means Mom's still asleep. How did y'all get in the house?"

"Your stepdad let us in and went back to bed," Poppa answered.

"Oh, I was wondering if maybe y'all were bionic or something." I shrugged my shoulders.

With a giggle Maw Maw raised her brow. "Bionic, huh? That's interesting. I wish I was bionic; then maybe my bones wouldn't hurt quite so bad."

About that time I heard a small creak in the floor.

My grandfather stared past me and asked, "So, what time is the party?"

Simultaneously my mother and I answered, "One o'clock."

Hearing my mother's voice, I turned my head. "Hey, Mom. Maw Maw and Poppa are here."

"I see that. Have you been keepin' them company?" she asked.

"He sure has," my grandmother interjected. "He's already shown us all his new toys and demonstrated his expertise on a bicycle for us, dear. So, how have you been?" Maw Maw questioned as she stood to her feet to hug my mom.

"I've been pretty good. How 'bout you two?"

"Well, you know, life in Houston doesn't stop. We stay pretty busy."

We all sat around the table for an hour or more chatting and catching up. Mom filled them in on all the news of her life, where she worked, how she liked living on the Gulf Coast, and what she missed about home. None of them brought up my dad during that conversation, but my grandparents asked about her happiness with her new husband. She assured them of her contentment and that all was well on the home front. Before I knew it, time for me to get a bath and get ready for my party crept up.

When one o'clock rolled around, the house filled with visitors. Mason and his family came over, and I had a couple of friends from school that made it. Other than that, adult family members and a few step cousins packed our home. Andy grilled hamburgers and hotdogs for everyone. Mom bought a Transformers cake. It was the best! After indulging in cake and ice cream, I opened all my presents. I got a Connect Four game, a Clue board game, and a Fantastic Four board game from various friends and family members. Mom and Andy bought me a 9.6 powered Jet Hopper Turbo; I had seen one in the store and had been begging for it. Mason gave me a Transformers action figure of Optimus Prime.

The party surpassed my expectations; I had gotten everything I had seen on television I had been wanting, but the best present I received came from my grandparents. They saved their present, a gigantic gift, until last. I ripped the paper covered with colorful balloons to find a big box. Mom went to retrieve the scissors from the kitchen to cut through all the packing tape that sealed the blank box. Usually a gift bought from a store had a stamp of some sort on the box, but I stared at a blank box, so I knew right away their gift would not be like the others I had received that day. What I didn't realize at the time was that it would be a present which would change my life forever.

Mom came back with the scissors and carefully cut through all the tape; then I slowly opened the box to find an old acoustic guitar that had been polished and restrung. Carefully picking up the small acoustic guitar, I glanced at my grandparents. "A guitar?"

A bright smile crossed Maw Maw's face. "It was your father's. We bought it for him on his seventh birthday. Tony...your Poppa...came across it in the attic about a month ago while he was storing some old dishes for me. We thought it'd be perfect to give you on your seventh birthday!"

I tried to hold the guitar in the proper fashion but failed miserably. My grandfather strode over to my side to show me how to hold it. He pulled a strap from the case and attached it, being sure to demonstrate to me how to affix it properly. "I polished it up and bought new strings for ya. Here...hold it like this...and put this hand here like this...and take this hand and place it here," he explained the proper technique for holding a guitar.

I peered into his eyes and asked, "Can you play, Poppa?"

"Yes, sir, I can. I taught your dad. He was pretty good, you know?"

"Will you teach me?"

"Tell ya what. I'll show you a few things about it while I'm here. I bought you some books to go along with it." He picked up two books from inside the case. "It teaches about the frets and shows you how to play all the chords, and once you've gotten a grip on all that, you can move on to pickin'."

"Cool." I smiled.

I glanced around the room and saw two things simultaneously; a saddened smile crossed my mother's face, and Andy's green eyes flared. Mom shook free of the down-hearted mien and grabbed all of my new toys and games; she briskly transferred them to my room. "Ray, why don't you and your friends go in your room and play with your new stuff, okay?" she requested as she disappeared behind my bedroom door. "You can go spend the night with Maw Maw and Poppa at the hotel. Poppa can show you all of that stuff there."

"Yes, ma'am." Signaling to Mason, Joel, and Bobby, I uttered, "Let's go to my room and see what all this Jet Hopper can do." They all followed me to my room, and we played with my new stuff while the adults visited in the living room.

That day was awesome. I enjoyed playing with my friends, and I had a great time with my grandparents that night. Poppa kept his promise to show me a thing or two on the guitar, and he also gave me a few pieces of sheet music my dad had written as a teenager. He had found them folded up in the case. Despite living in Houston, one of the largest cities in the United States, my dad was a country boy. The songs he had written were soft country ballads, and I wanted to learn to play them all.

I grasped the sounds quickly and was able to tune my small guitar with a little practice. Poppa said I had an ear for it, and I was naturally gifted. From that moment onward if I wasn't playing with Mason, I spent all of my free time shut up in my room practicing, determined to learn my dad's songs.

The following summer Mason and I learned new tricks on our bikes and spent countless hours in our make-believe world of superheroes. Andy decided to make a ritual of his weekend camping trips with Victor, so I had the summer weekends with my mom again, and of course, we danced. Mom claimed I was by far her best student.

"You're even better than your father," she proclaimed on a warm Saturday night in June as she picked up a glass of wine and sat on the couch to indulge. I had never seen my mother drink wine except for the day she married Andy, and I found it odd for her to do so in my presence. Still too young to absorb the realization that something was going on deep in her heart, I gazed at her with innocent curiosity while she sipped away on the deep-red wine.

Plopping down next to her, I wrapped my arms around her. "Really? Am I...am I better than Andy?" I hesitantly asked.

Startled, she choked on the wine as she swallowed. "Uh, uh," she coughed. Clearing her throat, she glanced my way. "Honestly, Ray...I wouldn't know. I...I've never danced with Andy."

Perplexed, I wrinkled my forehead and stuttered, "Y...you haven't?"

"No, I haven't."

"Why?" I searched for understanding. She had always spoken of her love of dancing and what she believed about dancing and soul mates.

She contemplated my question for a brief moment. "I'm not really sure. I suppose it's because of your dad. I gave that part of my heart to him, and I can't ever imagine dancing with anyone else—besides you, of course."

Once the new school year began, football season kicked in. While I enjoyed playing, I knew from the previous year I sucked at the game, so I declined signing up for it when Mason brought me the flyer. I spent my afternoons in my room practicing my guitar; Victor stayed at football and soccer practice every afternoon, and Mason consumed his afternoons throwing the ball around with his dad or at his practices. I rode with him and his family every Saturday to watch the games, and we spent time out and about on our bikes on Sunday afternoons.

Before I knew it, another birthday and Christmas had passed. All of my grandparents made it to Christmas that year, so I had a particularly amazing Christmas. Poppa continually encouraged me with playing the guitar. They all seemed so proud of me, so I decided to give them a special surprise Christmas gift. I had been working extremely hard on learning one of the songs my dad had written, so on Christmas morning while everyone sat around the tree opening gifts, I went and pulled out my acoustic guitar. Despite my bashfulness, I announced I had a song to play for everyone. They all sat quietly and listened as I played the melody of a song my dad titled "Hold My Hand."

While playing for my family, a strange thing happened. It felt as if the strings of the guitar were merely extensions of my fingertips, and with every vibration the strings made, I absorbed the sound into my own body. I wasn't just hearing the music, I could literally feel it. As the last note rang, everyone in the room stood to their feet and applauded—even Victor, which surprised me so much that I couldn't stop staring at him with what can only be described as a dumbfounded look. It was a shining moment for me, the moment I realized my destiny. In that instant I determined I would spend the rest of my life making music because I was meant to be a music man. It almost felt like my mother's description of dance; the guitar and I were in a dance together, flowing. The sound waves singing through the guitar streamed through me, and I sensed the song it sang.

I made a conscious decision to spend every spare moment I had preparing for the dream implanted in my soul, so for the next couple of years, I did just that. I didn't lock myself away in my room as if some sort of prisoner bound to his love of music, but I devoted as much time as possible there, shut away from the rest of the world and the reality of my life, not that my life was horrible or even bad, but I knew all too well I would never measure up in Andy's eyes. Andy's mentality of how a boy should be if he expected to grow into a man was simple, barbaric even. Boys were supposed to be rough; they were supposed to wrestle and fight with other boys, and they most assuredly played sports. I excelled in school, so I was a pretty smart kid, and I had learned of ancient civilizations where *real men* were defined by the attributes Andy believed in, but I also read of the destruction to those places where the men knew only of blood, guts, and war.

Oh, Andy stood and clapped with the rest of them on that Christmas morning, but he constantly complained to my mother that I stayed shut up in my room like a hermit and had cut them out of my life—which I hadn't in my opinion. I still did all of my chores, and I still spent quality time with my mom, but Andy ragged me about anything and everything, insignificant stuff he felt I should be doing. He barked orders, repeatedly on my case about doing other things besides playing the "stupid" guitar, as he put it, but I knew the guitar was my life; it was a part of who I was, who I was destined to be.

A silent voice inside my head convinced me he was jealous of the fact I took after my father. I looked like a mirror image of him, and I developed a gift I obviously inherited from him. Even though I never knew him personally, he was a hero to me, someone I looked up to and strived to be like. I wanted to believe wherever he was, he was proud of me. Despite the fact he died without knowing of my existence, I clung to the belief he was informed of my mother's pregnancy the moment he was taken into the clouds of heaven, and he was given the task of being my personal guardian angel, so he was always watching over me.

No matter how carefully my father protected me from the heavens, there was one thing he couldn't do; he couldn't be a dad to me. I wanted and needed a dad. There was a time when I believed Andy would fill that role in my life, but after being disappointed in me on several occasions, he gave up trying to meet that need in my life. The inadequacies he felt I exhibited escalated as I grew older. My mother tried to encourage our relationship by suggesting I go on outings with him and help him in the yard or even throw a ball around with him, which only created a great monster inside of me. I resented being pushed into a relationship with a man who would never love me as a son because in his eyes I was a failure at those things at which he felt all boys should excel.

CHAPTER 6

BLOOD ON BLOOD

The summer before my fourth-grade year, my grandparents called and asked if I could spend the month of July with them in Houston. Although hesitant about allowing me to go so far away without her, my mom agreed to let me spend some quality and quantity time with my grandparents. Excited about visiting the big city, I dashed out the door and hurried to Mason's as soon as my mother exited my room.

I banged on the door and waited. Pressing my hands against the wooden door, I stretched on my tiptoes and peered through the peephole, searching for any sign of acknowledgment. I beat my closed fist as hard as I could on the door once more. A soft creak resounded through the door, so I laid my ear against it. Footsteps echoed closer before stopping. Mason's groggy voice demanded, "Ray, come back when the rest of the world is alive and movin'."

"What?" I squealed, as if holding a sacred secret. I shuddered and stepped back when the doorknob squeaked. "I'm goin' to Houston!" I blurted out as Mason tugged open the front door.

He rubbed his heavy eyes. "What? I'm sleepy, dude. Come back later." He yawned.

"Oh, did I wake you?"

"Yep." He yawned.

"Well, how'd ya know it was me knockin'?"

"Who else would be knocking on my door at seven

o'clock on a Saturday morning?" Mason peeled his eyes open slightly and stretched his arms above his head. "Where did you say you were going?"

"Houston." I beamed.

"You're not movin', are ya?" he moaned. His face dropped into a worried pout at the thought lingering in his mind of losing his best friend.

"Of course not!" I exclaimed. "I'm going next week to spend the whole month of July with my Maw Maw and Poppa, my dad's parents. I'm comin' back."

"Good," he sighed. Patting me on the back, he whispered, "Come on," as he led me to the den. Laughing, we sat for a few hours and watched several of our favorite cartoons.

The next afternoon, we both went out for our routine bike ride around the neighborhood; then Mason detoured off our typical route and led us to a deep ditch. He stopped and threw his hand up signaling for me to follow suit. Nervously scanning the area, he waved for me to come on; then he dashed down into the ditch, coming up on the other side on a patch of land full of high grass with multiple paths cut through it, the motorcycle field; the older boys in the area who had motorcycles would ride through the paths that had been worn down over time. He peddled faster and faster, keeping his eyes forward and his body hunched over the handlebars.

"What are you doin'? Where are we goin'?"

"Sssh," he shushed me. He made a sharp left onto one of the paths. "I wanna show ya what I found the other day," he explained once we were safely on the trail.

"Hey, you do realize Victor and his friends come out here? I'm not really in the mood to get beat up by my stepbrother."

"I know. I was spyin' on 'em the other day, watchin' the path they take, and I noticed there was one trail they never went down, so I marked it. As long as they are nowhere in sight when we get on it, we're fine. It's really cool. I can't wait to show ya what I found at the end of it," he rambled.

The pampas grass, intertwined with gangling trees, stood much taller than either of us, and the three feet wide trail coiled through a massive field. It wound in this direction and that direction before leading us out to a small opening with what had to be the biggest oak tree I'd ever seen in my life. Nailed up the side were wooden boards meant to create a ladder; the tree had grown around the ladder, but it was still usable. We jumped off our bikes and threw them to the ground without a second thought. Dashing to the tree, we both began to climb. Once up within the huge limbs, we could see a small piece of plywood had been fastened in place to construct what had obviously once been a tree house.

"Cool!" I exclaimed.

"I know. It's the best. I couldn't believe what I found. This will be our secret hideout." He smiled.

"Yeah, it's amazing, dude. We'll have to be sure no one sees us cross the ditch 'cause if Victor and his friends find this place, they'll be sure to take it over."

We sat for an hour on the platform just talking about silly stuff little boys talk about, but we both spoke of our hopes and dreams as well. Mason already felt sure he wanted to play professional football, and destiny carved my name in a guitar. The sun was still high in the sky as usual for that time of year, but Mason looked down at one of his many Swatch Watches trailing up his left arm and reminded me of the time.

We both climbed down our newly found tree house, but before we headed for our bikes, he grabbed me by the arm and stopped me. "Hey, wanna be blood brothers?" he grinned.

"Blood brothers?" I crinkled my brow in question. "Exactly what is that?" I hesitantly asked.

"It's a friendship ritual I heard my dad talking about with his friend Tim. They've been friends since they were little boys. It must've been somethin' they did when they were young like us, and they're still best friends because of it."

"So, if you and I do this ritual, we'll be best friends forever?"

"Yep, that's how it works, or so I hear." He chuckled.

"So, exactly what do we have to do to become blood brothers? I don't have to drink blood, do I?" I cringed.

"Dude, you're hilarious. It's not a vampire ritual. Apparently, all we have to do is prick our fingers under a full moon. Then we put 'em together and tell each other how we're gonna be friends forever. It's supposed to seal the friendship or somethin' like that. I just thought it sounded cool, and since there's a full moon tonight, I thought we could do it tonight in my backyard before you go off for a month to Houston," he rattled on and on.

Shrugging my shoulders, I uttered, "Yeah, sure. Sounds pretty cool. What time we gonna meet?"

"Can you sneak out around 10 p.m.?" he asked.

"I'll do my best."

We both got on our bikes and headed home. When we got to the end of the trail, we were sure to look both ways and listen carefully for the sound of roaring motorbikes. When we were both sure the coast was clear, we darted across the field and back through the ditch. We were both pumped full of adrenaline when we hit the pavement on the other side, so we made it back to the house faster than we had made it to our secret hideout.

I kept an eager eye on my wrist watch waiting for the long hand to hit nine, reminding me to meet Mason in fifteen minutes. The second it struck the nine I crawled out of my bed, pajamas still on, slipped on a pair of flip flops, and poked my head out of my bedroom door to spy out the activity in the house. It was Sunday night, and Mom and Andy both had to be at work early the next morning, so I knew they would at least be in bed, if not sleeping already.

I listened for the sound of snores. Silence filled the hall signaling the coast was clear. I edged my way down the hallway towards the back door, leaning rigidly against the wall the entire way. As I came upon Victor's room, rock music pervaded the atmosphere at a decibel that wouldn't arouse our parents. Uncertain if he had fallen asleep listening, I peeped through the door to find him propped against his headboard flipping through the pages of a comic book. I inhaled a deep breath, got down on all fours, and crawled as quietly as possible past his door. Once safely on the other side, I stood to my feet with my back firmly against the wall and exhaled, relieving my expanded lungs; then I made my way to the back door.

It took me all of seven minutes from the time I watched my clock strike 9:45 until I made it to my backyard. I made the trip from my backyard to Mason's with ease. By removing the lower nails, Mason and I had loosened two of the boards in the privacy fence that separated our yards. All I had to do was listen for Mason's owl call, letting me know all was clear, and swing the boards to the side while slipping through to his yard.

We both stood under the full moon and gazed upon it; then taking deep breaths, we looked back down at our hands while he reached in his pocket for his pocket knife. I stretched my hand toward him, entrusting him with it. I squinted slightly as he made a small incision

60

across my index finger. The cut hurt, but the real pain was knowing I wouldn't be able to play my guitar until my finger healed. It would be much too painful to do so because the nerve endings in the fingertips were so sensitive. The skin had already thickened on the ends of my fingers from the few years I had been playing, so Mason had to put more pressure behind my cut than he did his own. The extra pressure caused the knife to go down deep.

Mason sliced himself, and we placed our fingers together. Mason smiled the same crooked smile he often did; then he looked me square in the face and declared, "Ray, you're the best friend I've ever had and ever will have. Now we're more than friends; we're blood brothers, and nothing and no one will ever come between us...okay, now you have to say the same thing."

"Um," I cleared my throat. "Okay, Mason, you're the best friend I've ever had and ever will have. Now we're more than friends; we're blood brothers, and nothing and no one will ever come between us. Did I get it right?" I questioned with a furrowed brow.

"Yep."

"Okay, cool. What now?" I inquired.

"Nothin'. That's it. Now we'll be best friends forever, at least that's what I heard my dad sayin' to Tim. I mean, they're still best friends."

"All right. So, I can go home now? My finger really hurts." We both simultaneously glanced down at our hands. Blood oozed down my hand and arm. Apparently the cut on my fingertip was deep enough that the bleeding wouldn't stop.

Freaking out, Mason used his knife to cut a piece of his pajamas off. "Oh, shoot, man! Why didn't you say somethin'," he exclaimed while he frantically tied the small piece of cloth around my finger.

"I guess I didn't realize how deep you were cuttin'."

I winced.

"I'm so sorry. Boy, did I mess this up," he ranted.

"You didn't mess anything up. We completed the ritual, and that's all that matters. I'll be fine," I insisted.

"You may need stitches, Ray, and that *will* mess this up because nobody's supposed to know about the ritual. It's supposed to be a secret thing."

"Nobody has to know. I'll go home and wash it out and wrap it up. I'll be fine. We have gauze and tape at the house."

"You can't wrap it by yourself. Look, you go in your house, get the stuff, and I'll meet you in your yard. I'll wrap it for ya, okay?"

"Okay."

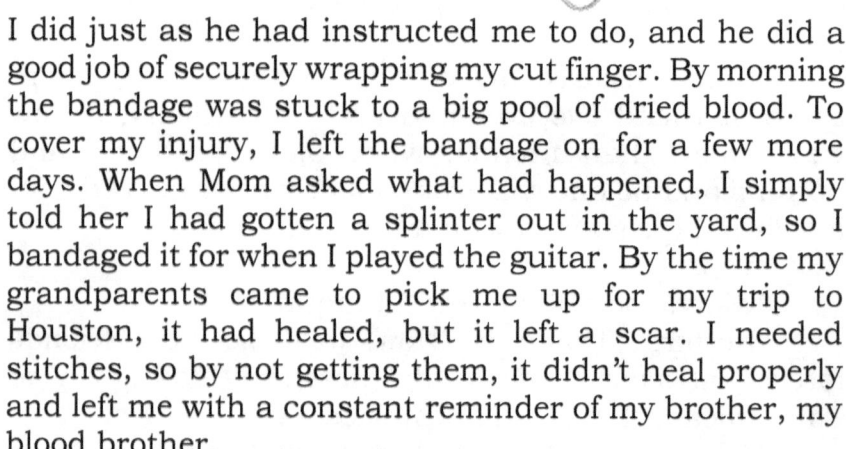

I did just as he had instructed me to do, and he did a good job of securely wrapping my cut finger. By morning the bandage was stuck to a big pool of dried blood. To cover my injury, I left the bandage on for a few more days. When Mom asked what had happened, I simply told her I had gotten a splinter out in the yard, so I bandaged it for when I played the guitar. By the time my grandparents came to pick me up for my trip to Houston, it had healed, but it left a scar. I needed stitches, so by not getting them, it didn't heal properly and left me with a constant reminder of my brother, my blood brother.

Houston was massive. I had never seen anything like it in my life. The drive in on the massive interstate system with lanes everywhere and overpasses with cars zooming overhead and exits that raced toward another interstate or highway system was thrilling for a nine year old. I imagined we would slow down when we approached our exit off I-10, but instead we shot right onto I-45 north and headed to Cypress, the area my grandparents lived in. They lived in a nice subdivision in the rapidly developing area which sat snuggly in the northwest corner of the Houston vicinity.

During that month my grandparents took me to the Galleria in downtown Houston. I went ice skating for the first time in my life. Poppa took me into work with him a couple of times; he took me into the tallest building in Houston and made me peer out the window down at the tiny people walking the streets, and he took me shopping in the underground mall. I enjoyed every moment I had with my grandparents, and they adored me. I even slept in my dad's old bedroom while I was there. Maw Maw said she had planned to turn it into a guest room when Dad joined the Marines, but she never got around to it, and after he died, she couldn't bring herself to change it.

My last week there, I sat picking strands of grass in the backyard. Music echoed. I craned my head toward the source; it sounded as if it had come from the house next door, so I crept over to see where it came from. It sounded so near and so real I felt certain it wasn't coming from a blaring radio, album, or cassette, and it sounded nothing like the music I had been teaching myself to play. This music was heavy and loud. I liked it. I had heard a few similar songs while at Mason's house, but we rarely listened to music together—we were always busy goofing off outside on our bikes. In my home my mom and stepdad listened to country music and Elvis except for Victor; he listened to hard rock. Unfortunately, he never allowed me in his room to listen along with him, and he had a pair of head phones he used on most occasions, so I rarely listened to rock myself. I followed my mom's example and that of my father's.

When I realized it reverberated from the garage, I slipped in closer and paid close attention to the humming of the guitar strings. Right about the time the song ended, I tripped over a decorative rock in my grandparents' yard and tumbled into an Althorn bush nestled against the neighbor's garage. "Shoot!" I screamed as I threw my hands in front of me to barricade my face from the spiny, flowered bush.

"Oomph," someone grunted from the other side of the wall. I gulped at the loud popping of an amplifier being turned off.

I wrestled my way free from the entanglement in the prickly bush. Just as I stood to my feet, a voice asked, "What are you doing?"

I looked down at my hands and plucked a few bloody thorns from my palms and stuttered, "I...I was just listenin', that's all...Scouts honor." My eyes grew huge as I caught a glimpse of blood streaming down his right hand. Glancing from his hand to his eyes, I gasped, "You're bleedin'."

"Yeah, your little scuffle out here with the bush startled me; I cut myself on the bridge."

"Seriously? Sorry 'bout that. You're awesome, man. I'd love to be able to play like that."

"Do you play?"

"Yep, but I have an acoustic guitar, and I can't play the kind of music you were playin' either." Awareness that he had no idea who I was hit me, so I introduced myself. "By the way, I'm Ray." I stuck my hand out to shake his without a second thought.

He stretched his right hand out to shake mine and uttered, "Paul."

I took in his appearance and analyzed the trend. "Are you in a rock band?"

He laughed. "No, not yet, but I'm gonna be."

"What song were you playin' just then?"

"*Hot For Teacher* by Van Halen. It's off their *1984* album. So where did you come from anyway? I know you don't live there. They're an older couple. I've never seen any children there at all."

"Oh, I live in Mississippi. They're my grandparents.

I just came to spend some time with them. They usually come to see us."

"I didn't even realize they had any children, much less grandkids."

"Um...yeah...well, my dad died before I was born, and he was their only child."

"Sorry, dude...hey, you wanna listen to a few more songs?"

I furrowed my brow. "You're gonna play with a cut hand?"

"Dude, pain is part of the game. I'll bandage it real quick."

I was shocked he invited me into his garage to hear him play. He was at least Victor's age, probably older, but I wasn't for sure, so it threw me off guard that he didn't mind my presence. Victor usually treated me as if an infectious disease consumed me, slamming doors on me and the like, especially when his friends were present. I jumped at the chance to sit and listen to his playing. I watched every move his hands made across the neck of the guitar as he played several riffs which captivated my attention and had me watching the way he manipulated the strings of the guitar. His fingers were like liquid lightning—smooth yet quick. His skills fascinated me.

After strumming away on a few of his personal favorites, he asked, "So you wanna learn to play an easy rock song?"

My jaw dropped. "Um, yeah," I spit out after a delayed moment.

"Here," he pulled the strap over his head and handed me his guitar. I couldn't believe it. I stared in awe as I held it in my hands. It was the most beautiful guitar I had ever seen. I wrapped the strap around me and gripped the neck. "You know any power chords?" he inquired.

"No," I stared in awe at the slick, red Stratocaster.

"All right, then. I'll show ya the ones needed to play the main riff of *Rock You Like a Hurricane* by the Scorpions."

"Scorpions. What a cool name."

"You never heard of 'em?" He raised his brows and widened his eyes.

"Nope." I hung my head from embarrassment.

"Okay, so you start off playing the E power chord on the seventh fret of the A string," he explained. He walked me through each step in slow detail. It didn't take too long to get it down pat. "You're pretty good for a...how old are you, kid?"

"Nine and a half."

"Well, you're pretty good for a nine and a half year old." He chuckled.

"Thanks."

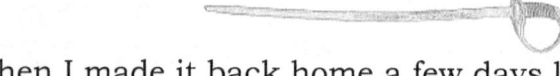

When I made it back home a few days later, I sat in my room trying desperately to get the short riff to sound good on my acoustic guitar. I must have been doing a fairly good job because Victor recognized the tune and poked his head in my door.

"Hey, Ray, are you playin' *Rock You Like a Hurricane*?" He narrowed his eyes in disbelief.

"Yep. I met a guy about your age in Houston. He taught me how to play it; it sounds a lot better on an electric guitar. Sure do wish I had one."

"That's awesome. Might be a cool thing to have you as a stepbrother after all." He stood in the doorway. "Mind if I hang out and listen?"

"No, not at all." I shook my head.

"I may have to introduce you to Kevin; he has an electric guitar. He's tryin' to get a band together. He's cool. You'd like him."

I wanted to let my jaw drop, but I didn't want Victor to see my shock, so I tried to remain cool, calm, and collective. I inhaled deeply. "Sounds cool," I uttered with a degree of nonchalance, but in my mind I felt a trickle of acceptance drip down into the deep, bubbling well of rejection that had been instilled in me through his constant harassments and his many torturous ways. Victor finally thought of me as cool. I was no longer just his nerdy, pesky stepbrother. He was a total jock, and I had always felt his eyes looking down upon me as a weak, sissy-like boy because I wasn't athletic (in much the same way that Andy looked at me, which always made me feel I didn't belong). My home was not mine; I simply resided there unwelcome, but now maybe, just maybe, I could fit in within my own home and feel that I belonged.

CHAPTER 7

WILD SIDE

The following weekend Victor introduced me to his friend Kevin. He allowed me to fool around with his electric guitar while watching in amazement as I learned several popular riffs. I spent the next several months learning a few things from him. During that time I noticed a difference in my relationship with Victor. A change had taken place, a diminutive change, but a change nonetheless. Kevin didn't need to convince me an acoustic was not quite the same, so as my birthday approached I petitioned my mom and Andy for an electric guitar. Andy opposed the idea because of my age, the noise, and the expense. He made it clear that ten years old was just too young for it. My mom was more stunned I didn't find my dad's acoustic guitar to be enough. I tried to persuade her it had nothing to do with that but that I wanted my musical talents to grow and expand. It was a hard one for her to swallow at the time, so she supported Andy in my not getting one right away.

By early spring I witnessed a complete metamorphosis in my relationship with Victor. We became friends. One night in April, I went to his room to show him my newest creation on the guitar and caught him sneaking out his bedroom window.

"Dangit," he grumbled. "You're not gonna go

squeal on me now, are ya? Just when I finally like you."

Those words of assurance confirmed I had not been imagining the bond I had felt forming between us. They were all I needed to let him slip away into the dark night. "No way," I insisted. "Where ya goin'?" I pried.

"Just down the road to Tommy's house. I'd invite you, but Tommy doesn't know you. He'd get mad at me."

"That's okay. You comin' back tonight?"

"Yep. I'll be back in a couple of hours."

"See ya in the morning then."

"See ya," he whispered before disappearing into the back yard. I tiptoed toward his window to watch his escape route. I found it funny he had apparently found mine and Mason's secret passage between our two yards, and yet he had never said a word to me about it or ratted me out.

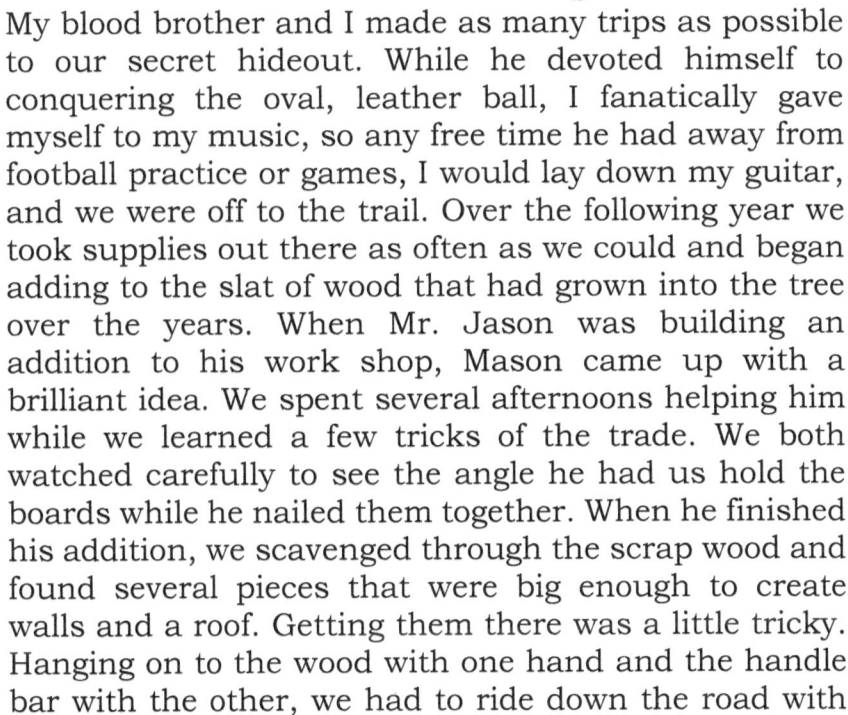

My blood brother and I made as many trips as possible to our secret hideout. While he devoted himself to conquering the oval, leather ball, I fanatically gave myself to my music, so any free time he had away from football practice or games, I would lay down my guitar, and we were off to the trail. Over the following year we took supplies out there as often as we could and began adding to the slat of wood that had grown into the tree over the years. When Mr. Jason was building an addition to his work shop, Mason came up with a brilliant idea. We spent several afternoons helping him while we learned a few tricks of the trade. We both watched carefully to see the angle he had us hold the boards while he nailed them together. When he finished his addition, we scavenged through the scrap wood and found several pieces that were big enough to create walls and a roof. Getting them there was a little tricky. Hanging on to the wood with one hand and the handle bar with the other, we had to ride down the road with the sheets of plywood between us. After a couple of trips, we both got the hang of it.

By the time we got the last slat of wood there, the sun started to fade, so we set a date to go back out with a hammer and nails to build our fortress. It took us several trips to our home away from home to finish putting up the walls. Fortunately for us, two pieces of plywood had big chunks taken out of them, so we used them as our windows. There was no hole big enough to be used as a door, so we decided to leave an open space between two pieces to serve as the entrance. We overlapped a couple of pieces of tin to create a roof. Pride swelled in our hearts as we stared at the tree house we built, but we knew it was not quite complete.

"It's so bare. There's nothing to sit on or anything. We need furniture," Mason insisted as we both sat admiring our hard work.

"We should both go through our rooms and see what we can bring out here," I said.

"We'll have to be sneaky, or else our parents will figure out what we're doing." Mason pointed out.

"Yep, there's no rush. We'll just find stuff our parents are throwing away and bring it out."

A light bulb went off in Mason's mind. "Hey, my little sister hasn't slept in her baby bed in years. I think my dad put it in the shed. We could use the mattress as a couch."

"You sure your mom wouldn't mind?"

"I'm sure of it. I heard her telling my dad she was thinkin' of selling it because they're not gonna have any more kids."

"Hmmm...if you say so."

A couple of days later, we slipped out to the shed and rummaged through trying to find the baby bed, but what we found was even better. Oh, we found the mattress, but we also came across some old, rusty camping gear Mr. Jason had thrown into the big can he used for storing things to be taken to the dump. There was a pot, a pan, a coffee pot, and a kerosene lamp. In the back corner of the shed, we discovered an old wooden chair with two removable cushions. They were old and dingy, but we didn't care. In a couple of trips, we had our new treasures in our tree house.

A couple of months later, my mom decided to redecorate the living room, which included new drapes, so when she threw the old ones out, I sneaked out back and dug them out of the garbage can. One panel was plenty to make a makeshift door, and the other could be used over the two holes we considered to be our windows. After examining the two panels, I shoved them in a duffel bag, threw the duffel bag over my handlebars, and took off to the tree house.

Signaling for Mason to follow, I honked my bike's horn as I darted from my driveway. Peddling with all my might, we made it to the tree house in record time. We both climbed the ingrown ladder. I pulled out the drape panels, stuck my hand in my pocket to retrieve four push pins, and pinned one of them over the opening we referred to as the door; then I found a pair of scissors nestled at the bottom of the duffel and began cutting the remaining panel in half, constructing two curtains to cover the windows. I dug in my pocket for more pins and secured them in place over the two holes.

By mid-October of '85, we had made a makeshift tree house. It wasn't the fanciest in the world, but it was ours.

Sitting in our home away from home, Mason peered out the opening into the blue sky as if something weighed heavy on his mind. "What's up, dude?" I asked.

"I was just thinkin'. You know what we need to do? We need to see what this looks like at night."

"What? You mean, you want us to come all the way out here when it's dark outside?"

"Yeah. You're not chicken are you?" He teased.

71

"No," I spit back.

"Besides, we have a lantern for light. We can build a small fire on the ground to cook some food, and we can drink coffee."

"I don't kn—"

"Wouldn't it be cool," he interjected. "We could plan to come out here on Halloween night, bring our sleeping bags, and tell ghost stories."

"Are you serious?" I gasped.

"Yep, serious as a heart attack."

I narrowed my eyes and glared at him. He looked completely serious and solemn. "Yeah, I'd say that's pretty serious. Where'd you get that from?"

"My dad says it all the time." He chuckled.

I looked at him like the silly boy he was. "Mason, you're as crazy as a bed bug." I laughed. "I heard that one from Poppa Winstrom." I gave my head a slight nod and grinned. "Man, you're a nut. How would we get away with doing something like that anyway. Our parents don't even know of the existence of this place. They're not gonna agree to us spending the night out here for sure."

Mason started his descent down the ladder and plopped to the earth beneath him. "Well, we can lie." He shrugged his shoulders once his feet were firmly planted on the ground.

I began my climb behind him. "Lie as in...I'm spending the night with you, you're spending the night with me kind of thing? You have to know that'll never work. Your mom and my mom are really good friends," I insisted as I glanced back over my shoulder at him.

"I'll come up with something. I promise," he assured me; then he shook his head and asked, "So, how crazy are bed bugs anyway?"

Hitting the ground with a thud, I let out a roar of laughter. I grabbed the handlebar on my bike. "They're pretty crazy," I answered as I thrust the kickstand back and climbed on.

Halloween was only a couple of weeks off, and Mason couldn't seem to come up with anything. Mason plopped on my bed as I grabbed my guitar and strummed a song I had written myself. Victor poked his head in my door and smiled. "Killer song, Ray. We've really gotta convince Dad and your mom to get ya an electric guitar." He shut the door, and as he crossed the hall to his room, I heard him grumble, "A waste of talent on that acoustic. I could get him in good with some serious players if he had an electric."

"That's it." My eyes beamed with life and hope.

"What's it?" Mason looked confused.

"I know how we can convince our parents to let us go camping on Halloween night!" I exclaimed.

"What's your idea?"

"Victor." I grinned.

"Victor? You've got to be kiddin' me. How could he help us, and why would he?" he argued.

"Victor and I have gotten pretty close over the last year or so. He's impressed with my guitar playing, so he likes me now. I know some of his secrets, and I found out he knows our secret passage between our yards, and he didn't even squeal on me. He doesn't even know I know that he knows," I explained as excitement bubbled away, causing me to jump to my feet and pace the floor.

"Still tryin' to follow this crazy plan." Mason's face contorted with bewilderment.

"I'll ask him if he can convince our parents to let him take us camping at one of his friend's house. We can all leave the house together and go our separate ways. We'd just meet back up the next morning at a certain time and come home."

"And you really think he'll do this for us?" A hint of

sarcasm filled his voice.

I rolled my eyes. "Uh...well...it's worth a shot. Do you have a better idea?" I threw back.

"No, I don't, but we've got to lay some ground rules. One, if he demands to know where we're gonna be, we're out. Got it?" he required an immediate answer to his stipulation.

"Yeah, I got it."

"And, two, we have to have his word he won't rat us out."

"That one, I'm sure we'll get. Like I said, I know some of his secrets, and he knows I know them. He'll be cool. I promise," I insisted.

"Okay, let's go ask him."

We both went to the door and tiptoed our way down and across the hall to Victor's room. I inhaled a deep breath and lightly tapped on the door. "Victor, it's me," I whispered through the door. "I need to ask ya somethin'."

Paper rustled just before a loud thud echoed from the floor. Heavy footsteps pounded across the wood-slated floor, inching closer to the door. My face paled gray as the doorknob turned. "Wuz up, dude?" he asked as he swung open the door. "Oh, hey, Mason. What you two need?" he asked. Using his feet to bounce his soccer ball in the air, he snatched it with his hands and flopped down on his bed.

"Wow! Dude, that was awesome. You're really good at sports, aren't you?" Mason praised him.

"Yep, I am, and I hear you're not so bad yourself. It takes adrenaline and aggression and anger. The three As." He passed on his jock knowledge.

"I'll remember that." Mason grinned.

"So, you two planning to tell me what's up?" he pressed.

I nervously scuffled my feet and signaled for Mason to shut the door. I knew Victor and I had bonded over

74

the previous year, but for some reason all the feelings and emotions that had been bottled up over his constant harassment of me prior to that time began to surface, and when that happened, fear gripped me right smack in the gut. It felt as if my stomach had become a coagulated mass and someone had taken a gigantic wrench, shoved it through, and clamped it around the dense lump of muscle and nerves. Every nerve ending in my body seemed to find its way to my stomach, and as the wrench tightened, they shot up my spine and wrapped around my chest, constricting my lungs and causing my heart to race. My only response was shallow, rapid breaths.

Finally the intellectual side of my brain caught up with the survival side and reminded me to take a deep breath and ignore the irrational fear that had taken over my body, so I did as my brain instructed. Through my nose, so no one else would see, I filled my lungs completely full. My speeding heart slowed down.

Everything seemed to be moving in slow motion. Every thought that passed through my mind seemed to be lengthy, but in reality, it had only been a fleeting moment since I signaled for Mason to shut the door. The light thud of the door behind me brought me back to reality.

"Yeah, we need a favor," I whispered.

"What kind of favor?" he inquired.

Mason interjected, "Well, first things first, we need to know that this stays between us three, and we need to know you're not gonna ask where we'll be."

Victor's eyes grew huge with intrigue. "I'm listening...That's as good as my word, by the way."

I cleared my throat. "Uh um, okay, we have a secret hideout, and we want to camp out there on Halloween night, but we know our parents won't let us do that, so we kind of need a cover story. I was thinkin' if they thought we were camping with you at one of your friend's house, they may let us go."

Astonished, Victor sat straight up in his bed. "I can't believe I'm hearing this. Are you two trying to cross over to the wild side?" He laughed.

Mason smiled a half smile. "That sounds fun."

"It is fun, dude, but you've gotta be able to hang if you're gonna cross over. So, what am I gonna get out of this?" He looked me in the eyes.

I gulped. "Well, I was thinking it'd give you a chance to hang with your friends while your dad and my mom think you're babysitting us, in a sense," I said, tugging on my shirt collar. "It would probably give you some brownie points with my mom. We would all be able to stay out all night, and you won't have to worry about my mom or your dad calling to check on us because you can't take phones camping."

"And tell me, Mr. Genius, what if your mom wants the number to my friend's mom so she can call and make sure it's okay that we stay over?" He raised his brow with the challenge.

"Hmmm...that wouldn't work, would it? Do you think they'd trust you with us if it wasn't at a friend's house?" I questioned, racking my brain for the solution.

Victor peered at his soccer ball. "Got it!" he exclaimed. "Okay, Tommy's parents own an empty lot a few blocks over. We can get permission to camp there from him. I'll get Dad to help me set up the tent and everything. He'll know where we are. I'll assure him it's a coming-of-age thing for you two. I'm sure I can get Dad on my side. He'll see the importance of it and explain it to both of your moms. I'll take my motor bike, and you two bring your bicycles. We'll convince him we'll take down the tent on our own and ride our bikes back the next morning. After he leaves, he can assure all parents of our location, and we will be free to take off to wherever we want." A pleased smirk crossed his face at his plan. "Yep, I'll help you two out with this."

Everything went as planned. Tommy's parents agreed to let us use their empty lot for a night of camping, Mason's parents agreed to allow him to go camping with Victor and me, and my mom entrusted me into Victor's hands. That one took a little more convincing than the rest, but I assured her Victor and I were cool. Of course, then I had to explain to her that *cool* meant we were getting along just fine, and she had no need to worry that he would be secretly torturing me while we camped away from home. Andy chunked our bikes in the back of his truck and drove us down to the lot. Victor led the way on his motor bike. We all worked together to set up the tent and stashed our bikes on the back side of it. We wanted Andy to see that they were hidden from sight in case he decided to drive by and check on us. We were fairly certain they wouldn't actually look in on us, but we set up a battery-operated lamp inside the tent and stuffed pillows under extra blankets to make it appear as if there were three sleeping shadows.

Once we completed our cover, we went our separate ways. We had no idea of where Victor went that night, and he never inquired of our location. We had clear instructions to meet back at the tent at six a.m., so we could be sure not to get caught. Victor patted us both on the back and sent us on our way. Mason and I spent the night in our tree house telling ghost stories. We both ended up getting so scared that neither of us slept a wink. Adrenaline pulsed through our veins every time we heard the rustling of tree limbs as the wind picked up and blew across the surrounding trees, and every time we heard the crackling of leaves, we imagined the worst. We just knew Jason was going to jump out with a machete, or Freddie would cut through the walls of our hide out with his razor sharp claw.

I looked down at the face of my watch and knew

the time had come to head back to the tent. It would take us at least twenty minutes to get there. Exhaustion consumed me. I was certain my feet would not be able to peddle as quickly as they normally could. We climbed out of our fortress; the place had served us as a safe haven from the racket of the night. It had protected us from the ghouls that roam the earth on October the 31. The sun had yet to rise as we crawled on our bikes and headed back to the tent.

We made it there five minutes ahead of schedule, set our bikes in the back, and crawled under the covers with the pillows that formed our make-believe bodies. My eyes grew heavy as I lay waiting on Victor. As I gave way to the weight of my lids, I heard a soft rumbling of a motor and drifted off to sleep with the lingering thought, *we had crossed over to the Wild Side.*

CHAPTER 8

I LOVE ROCK N ROLL

I petitioned for an electric guitar again on my eleventh and twelfth birthday to no avail. Victor even joined in with me, assuring his dad I had the potential to eventually make money off it. He failed miserably at convincing Andy, and I couldn't seem to get across to my mom that I wanted to play rock and roll. I determined within myself I would have an electric guitar by the time I made it to the seventh grade.

As the summer of '87 came to an end, I prepared to enter Magnolia Junior High without the guitar I had been longing for. Needless to say, that put me in a grim mood as I started the year. Victor knew my frustration and took pity on me. The Saturday before school was to begin, he asked me if I wanted to sneak out with him and go to Kevin's to jam. Feeling the festering anger, I quickly agreed, so that night as soon as Mom and Andy went to bed, I silently shut my bedroom door and stealthily made my way to Victor's room. His room had a window that opened into the back yard, so that was our best bet on getting out of the house. I had sneaked out through the back door to meet Mason in his yard, but this was not quite the same.

That evening as we slipped through the opened window, I thought of my adventure with Victor on Halloween night nearly two years prior. I had assumed, by crossing over to the *Wild Side* that night, we had tasted of rebellion and had become wayward boys, but I was destined to find out as I crossed the threshold of Kevin's door, we had only crossed the street on that momentous Halloween night.

What I had viewed as waywardness was simply the beginning of a lesson on the various roads of the world. There are scores of young boys and girls who cross the road of innocence, allowing their feet to barely venture onto the soil of mischievousness. It's quite simple to slip back across at that point and regain a proper perspective, leaving the mind untainted. My choice to deceive mine and Mason's parents guided me across the smooth pavement to the bumpy, troublesome path on the other side. I could have easily crossed back over to reclaim my childlike naivety, but I soon discovered my choice to crawl through the window and follow Victor to Kevin's took me farther down the street of corruptness my feet landed upon on that Halloween night, and the path I chose to take would be a hard one to follow; unfortunately, as I passed through the doorway into the backside of Kevin's garage, I discovered crossing back over to youthful innocence could not be done.

Silence filled the last half of our walk to Kevin's, but instructions pervaded the first half.

"Look, Kevin thinks you're a cool little dude and everything because you play so well, but in order to really hang with him, you've gotta be willing to test some things out, okay?" he questioned in a commanding way.

I stretched my neck and glanced up at him (Victor was six feet tall, and I had just hit five foot one.) "What kind a things do I have to test?" My eyes glimmered with innocence.

"You can't turn down a beer, Ray. That's a sure way to kill your social life with these guys," he coached me.

I crinkled my nose at the thought of the smell. I had smelled it on Andy's breath on many occasions, and there was a time or two I was certain I had caught a hint

80

of it on Victor's; now I was sure of it. "Does it taste as bad as it smells?"

Chuckling, Victor peered down at me, "Yep." Seeing the look of fright which seemed to cross my face at that thought, he patted me on the back and added, "Don't worry. You'll acquire a taste for it before long."

"Victor?" My voice quivered slightly.

"Yeah?"

"Am I gonna have to test anything else?"

He tousled my hair. "Don't worry, buddy. You're only twelve. I won't let 'em push anything else on ya. I gotcha covered," he assured me.

A sense of relief washed over me, and we walked the rest of the way side by side in silence. As soon as our feet grazed the cold concrete of Kevin's converted garage, Victor shoved his hand in a cooler and passed a Miller Lite my way. I thought it through and figured getting past the presumably horrible taste, from the smell that is, would be easier if I faced it like I would a swim in the icy-cold waters of Cedar Creek where I had been several times with Mason's family. To slowly step into the creek would be unbearable and excruciatingly painful, so in order to alleviate the lingering stings brought on by the freezing water, it is best to grab a hold of the old rope, swing out over the water, and plunge in all at once. Convinced diving into it was the best way to get past it, like a good little stepbrother, I popped the top and took a big gulp. I closed my eyes and cringed as the liquid passed over my tongue. I opened them to see everyone staring at me.

I finished off the beer and asked for another. I figured it would make Victor proud, and I enjoyed having a brotherly relationship with him. It felt good. That night Kevin took me under his wing and introduced me to the sounds of Joe Satriani.

Signaling for me to follow him to where he kept his albums and cassettes, Kevin gave a nod. "You like David

81

Lee Roth?"

"Yeah, man."

"A while back I read an interview with his lead guitar player Steve Vai. He went on and on about his teacher Joe Satriani, so when I saw this cassette at the Record Bar a couple of weeks ago, I snatched it up." He showed me a red cassette with a white alien dude surfing on a white board. "It's called *Surfing with the Alien*. It's wicked, man. You've gotta hear this man play. He's my new idol."

He shoved the cassette into his stereo system and pressed the play button. Closing his eyes, he stood in a type of reverence and awe. After his moment of silence, he contorted his face in a strained expression, wrapped his left hand around his invisible guitar, and began playing along as he entered his imaginary rock band world. I listened, appreciating the complexity of Joe Satriani's playing.

As the song came to an end, Kevin snapped out of his illusion. "Isn't he a god?"

"Yeah, he's amazing. I hope to be that good one day."

"Still haven't been able to talk your mom into getting you an electric?"

"Nope, I'm not givin' up though. I love rock and roll too much to give up. So, this guy taught Steve Vai how to play?"

"Yep, sure did."

I shook my head. "Wow!"

The night ended, and we made it back home and through Victor's window without getting caught. A thrill of adrenaline rushed through my body and mind that night. Getting away with something like that left a sense of excitement and guilt all at the same time. It wasn't just the sneaking out part that contributed to those emotions; the three beers I had at the young age of twelve and a half aided those sentiments. I was not yet a teenager, and I slipped with ease into a party scene.

Within a few days I graced the halls of Magnolia Junior High. In preparation for attending school with the "big kids," I had started to let my hair grow out a bit over the summer, so it looked a little shabby on my first day; it was layered throughout, hanging over my ears and extending midway down my neck. My hair was pitch black and wavy. Allowing wavy hair to grow out can be a difficult process, and my hair was in that phase of awkwardness.

Both Mason and I had been so excited about that day because it symbolized our growing up, yet at the same time we were slightly apprehensive because we would be at the bottom of the totem pole. Mason was sure to fit in; he had already made a name for himself amongst the athletes of the school. They were looking forward to his moving up and joining the football team. He was good at what he did, so he was quickly accepted, even by the superior ninth graders. Our first day went rather smoothly. As soon as we stepped off the bus, we found our way to a group of boys we both knew from the elementary school. We both felt a sense of comfort in being surrounded by our old friends. There were a lot of other kids from other elementary schools that came there as well, so the school was much larger than what we were used to, and that made it a little intimidating.

We were both upset to find out we only shared one class, English. We didn't see each other during school hours except for the bus ride to and from school, waiting for the initial bell, English class, and lunch. We were both glad we at least had the same lunch. It was the only time to hangout anyway. Within the first week of school, the football coach approached and recruited Mason for the team. That opened up a tremendous door of social opportunity for him, and because I was his best friend, it left a small crack in the door for me. It wasn't a wide-open door overflowing with friendliness and admiration like Mason received, but because of him most of the jocks at school tolerated me. I was quiet at school; I didn't cut up in class, and I didn't drool over the cheerleaders, making references to their body shapes like several of Mason's new friends did, so most of them viewed me as more of a tag along.

The night of the first football game of the season, Mason met Pamela, and a small wedge was shoved between us. The football players, along with the cool kids in school, gathered together in the parking lot after every home game. Games were on Thursday nights, so parents were usually insistent everyone be home at a decent hour. Because of that factor there was only thirty minutes for most, forty-five for some, to spend hanging out in the parking lot, and that is where he met the beautiful, blonde, popular seventh grader who quickly decided all of Mason's spare time should be spent with her, and anyone who dared to ask him to take a bike ride was a mortal enemy. She did not like me. While in their presence, she made her disdain of me apparent with every sigh and each roll of her eyes. Whether Mason and I were getting off the bus and she walked up to grab his hand and pull him away or if I happened to walk over while they were holding hands outside the cafeteria, her pungent disregard curled under her nostrils causing her nose to turn upward.

Before I knew it, Christmas had arrived, and it brought with it a complexity of emotions. I was beyond ecstatic when I ripped the paper off the biggest gift under the tree for me. It was the best present I could have ever imagined—a red Stratocaster! I glanced under the tree at the only remaining gift and knew it had to be an amplifier for my guitar. I wasn't sure if I had finally worn my mom and Andy down on the electric guitar issue or if they began to feel sorry for me because of the time I had been spending alone since Pamela had come into Mason's life. I wanted to retreat to my room to begin jamming, but Mom informed me and Victor they had one more surprise for us both.

We both sat back down on the couch and watched her pace the floor, ringing her hands. Andy sat in the recliner across from us with a huge grin on his face. Finally, she stopped dead in her tracks and blurted, "I'm pregnant!"

Neither of us moved an inch. We were both in a state of shock. "Well, boys, whatdaya think?" Andy pried.

Shaking his head, Victor stammered, "Um...what did you just say?"

With a crinkled forehead revealing her worried expression, Mom answered, "You two are going to be big brothers. Your dad and I are going to have a baby."

I cleared the lump in my throat and uttered, "Wow...um...yeah...that's great...I guess, so when will it be here?"

"It?" My mom furrowed her brow. "The *baby*," she corrected me, "will be here in August."

"Sorry. I didn't mean it was an *it*...I'm shutting up now," I pathetically tried apologizing. A light bulb went off. "Mom, where is the baby going to sleep?"

"Well, dear, that's one of the things we needed to speak to you two about. The baby will need a room, and since Victor's room is bigger than yours, Andy and I thought you two could maybe share a room, and we'd make your room into a nursery."

At that Victor blew up and stomped off; the house literally shook from the slamming of his door. A wide range of emotions bombarded me. I felt a little shafted by losing my room, my privacy, but Victor lost his as well. It bothered me that Victor was upset at my having

85

to be in the room with him because I thought we were close. I wasn't sure how to describe the intense feeling I felt over no longer being my mother's only child after thirteen years. *How could she do this? What about my dad? Does she love Andy more than she loved my dad? Will she love this baby more than she loves me? Didn't I do enough by sharing her with Andy and Victor? Now I have to share her with someone else, someone she might actually care about more.* The flood of words kept flowing through my mind, so I stood to my feet and excused myself. I knew of only one way to stop my mind from racing—music.

I grabbed my new guitar and amplifier, "Mom, Andy, if you don't mind, I'm gonna go try out my new guitar. I need to think." I gently shut my bedroom door, set my amp down, plugged my guitar in, and began playing *I Love Rock and Roll* by Joan Jett.

As the year forged ahead, numerous things began to change in my life. I helped Victor to rearrange his room to accommodate my presence. His room was a good bit bigger than mine, so it wasn't too difficult to fit two beds and two dressers in it. While making the transition, Victor assured me he wasn't upset about having to share his room with me, so that eased my mind to a certain degree. Sharing a room meant sharing a life. Victor and I spent even more time together, but I noticed I wasn't invited when he was with his jock friends; I was only involved in his life when he went to Kevin's to party. I was sure to take my Stratocaster as we slipped through the window at night. The more I hung with Kevin and his friends, the more I became like them. I jammed with them; I drank with them, and I began to dress like them. The longer my hair got, the more my appearance changed, and the more my appearance changed, the more I withdrew into myself. It was stingingly obvious I was not athletic; that combined with my curly, long hair gave two particular jocks, George and Kenneth, an open invitation to begin harassing me. It began as taunts in the hallway as I passed. *Hey there, pretty boy,* they would chuckle as I passed. I ignored them for the most part, but they didn't let up.

Along with spring came a fresh coat of pink paint in what was once my bedroom. I walked in the room to check it out and overheard a disturbing bit of information. Mom was telling Andy that Dorothy told her that she could have Renee's old baby bed that was out in Jason's shed.

"Oh, shoot," I whispered. "I've gotta tell Mason."

I took off in a flash and ran next door. Banging on the door, I was greeted by Pamela. "What do you want?" she snapped.

"I need to speak to Mason, Pamela. It's important," I insisted.

To no surprise she rolled her eyes and stepped out of the way, allowing me to come through the door. She glided to his side and clung to his arm. "Hey, dude, wuz up?" He grinned.

"I need to speak to you in private." I held my hand up, facing my palm and my scarred finger towards him.

He picked up on the significance of my signal and excused us. "Pamela, we'll be right back." He darted upstairs and into his room. Shutting the door behind him, he asked, "What's going on, man?"

"I just overheard my mom say your mom told her she could have the baby bed. We've got to get the mattress back out in the shed before she sends your dad out there to get it."

"Oh, no, we'll have to sneak out and do it tonight. Do you think you can get Victor to help us?"

"But then he'll know about the tree house." I stepped back.

"It's time for us to grow up anyway. Some other kids in the neighborhood can have it."

I was taken aback by his nonchalance at losing a piece of our childhood, a piece of our friendship. I knew he was right. It was time to grow up, but it stung nonetheless. We persuaded Victor to help us retrieve our things that night after dark. The task was not easy, but we succeeded in gathering our things together, most importantly the mattress for the baby bed, and stored it back within the wooden walls of the shed in Mason's back yard.

I began to drift away from Mason during school hours. I was still present, but I wandered toward the back of the group he hung with while he walked in front with Pamela at his side. It was a natural progression due to his jock friends who were popular and wealthy and his girlfriend who loathed my presence.

As I began to change and evolve into my own person, I realized something bothered me; it seemed junior high had a social structure that differed from the elementary. In elementary school one could be friends with whomever he pleased, but for some odd reason, junior high had cliques and groups that followed unwritten and unspoken rules of not crossing invisible lines and walls that separated us all. The walls may have been invisible, but they were clearly seen as one walked the halls and painfully felt when one walked face first into one of them, just as I did.

My collision with the invisible wall didn't take place on my first day in junior high; it happened near the end of my first year. By that time I was so captivated by the rock scene that I dressed like they did in some of their videos—obviously not like they did in all of them because I wouldn't have been allowed to wear zebra-printed spandex pants to school. My hair had grown past my shoulders, but because of the curliness, it barely hit them. That morning I had gone to school sporting an old tattered pair of jeans, black boots, my white 7800° Fahrenheit t-shirt, and a sleeveless, faded blue-jean jacket. I was walking next to Mason as we stepped off the bus when he came to an abrupt halt and turned to me.

Scuffling his feet, he shoved his hands in his pockets, stared at the gravel, and stuttered, "Hey, man...look...the guys from the team...well, they...they don't want you hanging with us in the mornings anymore."

It felt as if he had punched me in the gut. He was choosing his football buddies over me. "What?...Why?"

"They just said you're not our type. They don't like the whole heavy-metal scene. They said people like you are dope heads...Look man, this is my team we're talkin' about. I can't isolate myself from 'em. You understand?"

"No, I don't, dude. Is that what *you* think of me?" I grimaced.

"Nah, man. You know I don't think that, but you've gotta admit, you've really changed over the past six months."

"And you don't wanna hang with me anymore, is that it?"

"Look, Ray—"

I interrupted, "Look at what Mason?"

"You don't understand. They keep messin' with me asking *Where's my pretty boy,*" he said, mocking their tone.

My face fell as those words stabbed me. "I thought we were blood brothers, man."

Mason sighed. "We were. I mean, we are. That hasn't changed. You're my best friend, Ray, but I have to play football with these guys, and...in order for us to function as a team, I have to play the game the way they wanna play it. They're the majority, and in their game, they don't want you around...They don't control what I do at home, Ray. We can still hang together, just not at

89

school."

I glanced at the ground and mumbled, "Whatever," and walked off.

I had smashed face first into the dividing wall between the jocks and the rockers and found out prejudice did not confine itself to blacks and whites as I had thought. I distinctly remembered that dividing wall being set up in my life at a young age. I didn't understand that wall, and I most definitely did not understand the new one I had just experienced. I thought back and remembered the lesson of my green army men, and as I did, anger grew inside of me. In my mind I questioned why the rest of the world did not see each other the way those little green army men were meant to see one another—camouflaged. To them it didn't matter what color their skin was under the green paint, and it didn't matter what their clothes looked like; all that mattered was they were brothers.

CHAPTER 9

THE JUNGLE

I stormed off the bus and shoved my way past Mason. Slamming the door behind me, I threw myself on my bed with a huff. Victor flung the door open, marched in right behind me, and demanded, "Who messed with you?" I folded my arms under my pillow without responding. "I've never seen you like this, man. What's goin' on, little brother?"

I rolled over on my back, slipped my hands behind my head and sighed, "Huh...why don't you take me with you when you hang out with your soccer and football buddies?"

"Oh, that's what this is about? Mason's friends finally got to him, huh?"

"What's that supposed to mean anyway? Finally got to him." I rolled my eyes.

"Okay, sit up. It's time for a cold, hard lesson in teenage life," he commanded.

I propped my pillow against the headboard, sat up, and leaned against it. "I'm up," I snarled through a curled upper lip.

Propping his arms on his thighs, he leaned forward. "Look, dude, jocks are like jungle animals. Not all of 'em, but most of 'em pride themselves on being tough guys. They measure their manhood on how physically strong they are, and since you're not athletic, they probably consider you a wimp. The truth is, I'm the same way. I'm one of the top athletes in my class, and

91

that brings a certain amount of pressure. On top of the pressure from Dad, there's pressure from the other guys to be cool and superior; unfortunately, to some of them, being superior means making others feel inferior. That's why I don't hang with Kevin at school. The other guys on the team, they'd rag me big time if I did, but that hasn't stopped me from being friends with him. He's the first friend I made when we moved here, and he understands how things are. You just have to understand what Mason might be going through by being friends with you," he explained.

I groaned, "He did say they were givin' 'm a hard time."

"Look, just be his friend and try to understand the pressure he's under from them. I promise it gets better. He might not speak to you at school for a while, but by the time you get in high school, most of that will have died down, and you two will be able to speak at school without anyone givin' him too hard of a time. He may not buddy up with you in the hallway, but you'll be able to be civil to one another."

He leaned over toward my bed and tapped me on the shoulder. "Your friendship will survive, as long as you want it to, that is. You just have to be willin' to change."

"Thanks, Victor, but I'm just not so sure I'm willing to be a part-time friend. I mean, if he approaches me, I'll think about it, I guess, but I'm not gonna go beggin' for a friendship. I'm glad we're more like brothers now. I guess you'll be starting your senior year off with a baby sister. Can you believe it? We're gonna have a little sister."

"Tell me 'bout it. I just hope your mom don't expect me to be changing' no diapers. No way, dude, I won't be goin' there." He laughed.

We both chuckled at that thought, and my bad day fizzled away with the laughter.

The following morning I awoke determined not to allow Mason's betrayal to phase me, but I wasn't as prepared as I thought for the shunning that took place. Standing at the edge of our driveway waiting on the bus, I tilted my head and shifted my eyes toward Mason's yard. "Hey, man," I called out, but Mason stood rigid with his arms folded across his chest, never glancing my way. The loud roar of an engine signaled the approaching bus. Mason darted across the street. Climbing on ahead of me, he ignored my presence. I was invisible to him and that stung.

George and Kenneth met Mason as he stepped off the bus. As I turned the corner to exit, I eyed them huddled together, whispering. As I sauntered past them, Mason's foot shot out in front of me. I tumbled forward and smashed into the back of a dark-haired girl holding a thick stack of books. Her books toppled to the pavement along with us both.

"I'm sorry," I whispered as I brushed my hands on my pants and stretched my hand out to help her to her feet. Mason, George, and Kenneth all cackled behind me.

The girl glanced at my hand and turned away from me. She gathered her scattered books. "It's okay. I'm fine," she breathed.

"Oh, here, let me help you with that." I knelt next to her and grabbed several books.

Mason's shun stung me, but it was nothing in comparison to the humiliation I endured at his hand, or rather at his foot, all for the purpose of being accepted by his peers.

That summer my grandparents bought into a condominium in Gulf Shores. They figured I would enjoy spending a couple of weeks out of the summer with them there, a week around Christmas and a week in early spring. They were getting on up in age and wanted to spend as much time as possible with their teenage grandson. They were my only connection with my dad and I loved them, so I didn't have a problem spending a week or two of my summer with them. Besides, Gulf Shores had great beaches.

I enjoyed the quality time with Maw Maw and Poppa as well as several lone strolls through the hot, white sands of the beach. On my last day of vacation with them, I spent time sitting and watching the waves crash into the green water. As I peered out over the gulf, I pondered the conversation I had with Victor a few months prior and Mason's betrayal. I hadn't spoken to him since he tripped me for a laugh. Anger and rebellion rose up within me as I mused over these ridiculous rules society seemed to have written. *Civilization? Huh, how is enforcing social classes civilized?* From nowhere words began to rush through my mind, crashing over and over like the waves.

"Ignoring the Rules"

Walking the beach, I sit all alone.
I shouldn't just sit here; I should be gone.
The wind blows across and ruffles my shirt.
I wanna run down the pier and jump in feet first—
'Cause I wanna live my life
Ignoring the rules
Ignoring the signs.
'Cause I wanna dive into life
Ignoring the rules
Ignoring the signs.
'Cause I plan to live my own way.
To hell with your rules;
I don't care what you say.
I see all the lines as I walk the halls.
Run into one and you'll stumble and fall.

94

Invisible walls with flashing neon signs,
Telling me NO, controlling my mind.
But I wanna live my life
Ignoring the rules
Ignoring the Signs.
'Cause I wanna dive into life
Ignoring the rules
Ignoring the signs.
'Cause I plan to live my own way.
To hell with your walls
They can't keep me away.
'Cause I wanna live my life
Ignoring the rules
Ignoring the signs.
'Cause I wanna live my own way.
To hell with your rules;
I don't care what you say.

Ray Winstrom

I had created music of my own, but I had never felt lyrics rise up from within me before. The emotions stirring over the dividing wall shoved between me and my best friend emerged from the deep recesses of my soul, much like debris floating amongst the waters of the ocean that comes rolling to the shore with the crashing of the waves carrying it. The roaring of my anger and rebellion materialized through a song, and not only did I know the lyrics, but I could hear every note as I sang to myself. I didn't want to forget a single word, so I ran back to the condo, stormed through the door gasping for air, went straight to my room, grabbed a piece of paper, and scribbled away.

I returned home, and Victor and I spent the remainder of the summer hanging out with Kevin. On August 14, 1988, our little sister was born. Mom and Andy named her Lacey Kay. Before she arrived, I thought she would rob me of attention and love, so in a way I despised her, that is, until I took one single glance at her. I walked in the hospital room and watched as Mom held her so lovingly in her arms. She smiled and cooed at her little girl; then she stretched her arms toward me, handing me my baby sister.

"No way. I might break her." I backed off.

"You won't break her, Ray. Come." She patted the empty spot next to her on the bed. "Sit with me and hold your sister."

I knew she wouldn't take no for an answer, so I crept over to her side, slipped in next to her, and held out my hands. She placed her gently in my arms. I was awe struck at the tiny hands that reached up and grazed the side of her plump cheeks. "She's a little model already." Hearing my voice, she opened her eyes wide and peered at me through her hazy-blues. "Look at that. She knows I'm her brother." I felt an overwhelming sense of pride and protection all at the same time. Nothing would ever happen to this precious little girl, and I would make sure of it; unfortunately, I couldn't say that for myself or for Victor.

I was certain nothing in the world could bring me down as I began my new year in school. Mason stood awaiting the bus at the end of the driveway. He never faced my direction, and I never faced his. When we exited the bus, George and Kenneth both swiftly made their way to my side. "Hey there, pretty boy. How was your summer?" George taunted.

"Leave me alone," I grumbled, steadily walking toward the building.

Then I felt a massive blow to my shoulder. I stumbled back as I heard Kenneth proclaim, "George was speaking to you, pretty boy. Answer him."

Victor had been right; these guys were like jungle animals, and I determined right then and there not be their sissy, wimpy prey. Adrenaline coursed through my veins, creating an animalistic heightened sense of awareness that allowed me to perceive several things simultaneously. Straight ahead I witnessed George's beady eyes narrow as his face contorted into an angry grimace. Kenneth's face flushed red; his stance shifted, preventing my moving forward. Two gigantic, angry bullies stood before me looking for a fight, and I knew I would be fighting them both if I chose to lash back. I jerked my head to the side and eyed Mason just standing there with no obvious intent to intervene on my behalf. His palpable disregard of my presence combined with the fact he had once tripped me to give his buddies a laugh was bad enough, but the idea he planned to watch them beat me up and just stand there was devastating.

Coincidently just as I spotted Mason, I caught a glimpse of a tall, burly black boy pushing his way through the crowd. I was dead. I knew it, but for some reason I could not get my brain to shift into flight gear. I resolved to die fighting. *I don't even know him! Why does he wanna beat me up? Does he somehow know that my stepdad is a prejudiced jerk, and he's decided to take it out on me and join in on the fun?* The thoughts raced through my mind, but as he approached, a familiar glimmer shined through his eyes; I knew him.

I squeezed my eyes shut and shook my head. "Tray?" I whispered.

He shoved his way through the crowd encircling me like a pack of hyenas awaiting their portion of meat. Stepping between my attackers and me, he looked down at them both. "Leave him alone," he commanded.

"And what are you gonna do about it if we don't," George hissed, craning his neck to peer into the black eyes of the six-foot-one giant in front of him.

Cracking his knuckles, Tramane slowly stretched his neck and gave a nod to his friends who, unaware to

97

us all, had marched in behind him. "Me and my friends will have to rearrange your face, that's what."

George and Kenneth were both ninth graders, and they were both tall and stocky, although not quite the stature of the jolly green giant standing in front of me. With Tramane being the only one who stood in the way, they felt confident that together they could take him on, but when his friends entered the scene, they used their pea-sized brains, assessed the situation, and logically decided to back down. I think it may have been one of their more intelligent moments.

I heaved a heavy sigh and unraveled, slumping my shoulders and releasing my clenched fists. "Oh, my gosh. I just nearly died. Thank you, man. I don't know what I would've done if you hadn't shown up."

"You'd fought, and you'd lost; that's what." He chuckled and shook his head.

"How've you been? I haven't seen you since kindergarten. How's your grandma?"

"She's fine now. She was sick last year, so me and her, we had to go stay in New Orleans for her treatment. We just got back home a month ago," he explained.

"So, that's why I never saw ya around last year, huh? Well, I'm glad she's better, and I'm glad you saved my life back there." I grinned.

"So whatcha do to 'em?"

"Nothin', except exist. They're just jock bullies from the football team. They pick on me 'cause I'm not athletic like them. I had 'em both in P.E. last year, and I kept fumbling the dad-gum ball when we had to play, so they started messin' with me. Oh, yeah, and because I'm what they consider to be a dope smokin' head banger," I grumbled, rolling my eyes as I gave a loud huff.

"So, you like that loud stuff, huh?"

"Yep, sure do." My mind quickly pulled up a playback video of my last encounter with Tramane.

"Hey, Tray, I wantcha to know I'm sorry for what happened at my birthday party when we were little."

The bell rang to go to the gym to receive our schedules, so we started toward the building. "Man, don't worry 'bout that. My grandma made sure I knew you and your momma had nuttin to do with it."

"Yeah, my stepdad's a jerk."

"Dat's alright. We can be friends at school." He smiled and patted me on the back.

So, there I was. I had one friend who proclaimed he could only be my friend at home and another who couldn't be my friend at home. Life seemed too complicated to me. In my mind society had created a bunch of stupid rules, yet I knew I had to keep Tray's presence a secret, or Andy would flip again.

Victor and Kevin planned to take me to my first concert, Def Leppard, on September 9, but Hurricane Florence barreled upon us and canceled it out for the night. Fortunately her winds died down just before she moved over land, so she caused little to no damage on the Mississippi Gulf Coast, and the band shifted the concert to the following night. Gary, one of Kevin's friends, caught a ride with us to the Coliseum in Biloxi. Driving down Highway 90, he pulled out a bag of brown, dried-up grass-looking stuff, pulled out a small piece of paper, filled it with a small amount of the grass, rolled it up, and lit it. I crinkled my nose at the stench.

Gary took a big drag and held it in. "Wanna puff?" he asked as he handed it to me.

"Gary," Victor spoke in protest.

"What is it?" I furrowed my brow.

"It's a pinwheel. Pot...you know, dope."

I wrapped my fingers around it and looked up at the rear view mirror to see Victor glaring at me. "Don't do it, Ray."

"Why not? I get treated like a pot head at school anyway. If I'm gonna be accused of it, I might as well try it," I snarled. I brought it to my lips, inhaled, and glared back at him. I passed it back to Gary, and he passed it around to Kevin and Victor. It was passed back and forth until there was nothing left of it, and strangely I felt no change. *Well, what's the big deal about this stuff anyway? I don't feel any different. I think I'd rather have a beer,* I mused.

Gary glanced at me through droopy eyes. "So, do you go to the jungle often?" he asked.

"Um, what jungle?" I crinkled my forehead in confusion. I didn't know of any jungles in south Mississippi.

"Ha ha ha ha ha," he chortled. "The jungle; that's what we call Blade's garage."

"Who's Blade?"

"Blade, man, you haven't introduced him to your alter ego?" He leaned forward and smacked Kevin across the head.

"I'm Blade, Ray. It's kind of a nickname," he explained.

"Oh, I've never heard you called that before. Why do they call your garage the jungle?"

"Cause it's full of fun and games." He laughed.

I realized the fun and games he spoke of were alcohol and apparently drugs.

Victor parked the car in the parking lot of the Coliseum, and we all got out and walked to stand in the long line. He hung back and allowed Gary and Kevin to walk ahead of us. Trying to keep calm, he leaned in toward me and whispered in my ear, "I don't want you foolin' around with that stuff, Ray."

Flustered, I objected, "I didn't get anything out of it anyway. What's the big deal?"

"The big deal is you're my little brother, and you're not quite fourteen."

"But you do it," I argued.

"Yeah, I do it sometimes, among other things, but that's not the point. I'm seventeen years old, and you're only thirteen. Big difference, buddy."

"Well, why do you do it if you think it's bad?"

"Because I'm not as smart as you. Ray, you've got a lot goin' for ya. I share a room with ya; I've seen your grades. You're really smart—as much as you try to hide it. And I know, I know, it's not cool to be smart, but don't *stop* being smart 'cause you think it's not cool...just hide it if ya have to. Me? My athleticism and the stupid, funny things I do, along with going with the flow, which includes doin' a little drugs every now and then, is all I got. Be smarter than me, Ray. Don't get started 'cause then it'll be expected. They expect me to do certain things, and therefore, I do. Look, you didn't get anything out of it this time but next time you will, and it'll feel good, but when the high goes away, there's always a really bad feeling that creeps up on ya."

Victor slowed down to allow the others to get a little farther ahead and laid his hand on my back. "You remember that commercial about the brain bein' on drugs, and there's eggs frying in the fryin' pan?"

"Yeah."

"Well, it's true. It fries the brain cells, and you can't get 'em back once they're gone, buddy. I'm just lookin' out for ya; that's all."

Although I didn't agree with him at the time, I absorbed every word he said. I looked up to Victor. I thought he had a lot going for him. He was popular, nice looking, and fun to be around.

The year seemed to be moving in fast forward, and before I knew it spring lingered in the air, bringing its fresh, cool breezes interspersed with the sweet aromas of the blossoming flowers of the south. A gardenia bush grew right outside our bedroom, so every time we opened the window to allow the room to air out, the potent fragrance bombarded our habitat, saturating the air molecules with its puissant perfume. Lacey crawled around the house getting into everything. She was a doll, and everyone, including Victor, catered to her every whimper.

Along with the fragrance of spring came my grandparent's trip to Gulf Shores. I spent a week with them there and came home to an angry stepdad and an even angrier brother. When I opened the front door, I caught a glimpse of Andy huffing through the living room. His green eyes flared brighter than I had ever seen. Rage rose like heat in his body, singeing his face a deep crimson. He clenched his fists and seethed as he stormed into the hall. The backdoor rumbled as it crashed against the frame from its slam. My eyes grew huge. I tiptoed my way down the hall to mine and Victor's bedroom. I creaked open the door and slung my suitcase against the wall. Victor yanked one trophy after the other off the shelves and snapped them in half. "I hate him!" he screamed.

At the sound of the thud against the wall, Victor halted and glared at me. "Oh, it's you."

"E...verything," I hesitated, "o...kay?"

"No," he grumbled. "Look, I need to get outa here. Wanna come with me?"

"Sure, where to?"

"The jungle," he muttered.

CHAPTER 10

WIND OF CHANGE

Victor crawled behind the steering wheel of the car and revved the engine. "Come on," he hissed at me through a locked jaw. A thin layer of clear liquid glazed his eyes, depicting his level of anger.

"Coming," I yelled back as I slid my guitar and amp in the back seat. A gust of wind blew through my hair, leaving me with an eerie shiver. I plopped in the front seat and shut the door, cutting off all access of the strange breeze. I glanced at Victor through the corner of my eye but immediately noticed the red shimmer in his glare.

I thought it through and logically waited for us to turn off our road before I began my interrogation. "Ok, dude. You've gotta tell me what's up. Why in the world were you smashing your trophies? Angry doesn't even describe how you look right now."

He squinted his eyes and stared at the road. "Dad's on my back about college. I didn't get the soccer scholarship to Georgetown University he was hopin' I'd get. He wants me to study law there, but I'd have to get a scholarship 'cause he can't afford the tuition. Man, I hate this pressure." He slammed the palm of his hand on the steering wheel. "I just can't take it anymore!" he roared.

I deliberated what I should and should not say for a moment before interjecting, "I'm sorry you didn't get the scholarship. Whadaya gonna do? Do you have a contingency plan?"

"No," he shrieked. "Dad's been prepping me for this since before he met your mom. He'll want me to go into the military like he did probably, but I'm sick and tired of doing what everyone else wants me to do with my life. My football and soccer friends want me to be all tough, and some of 'em even want me to bully skinny little nerds around, and my dad's been planning my life out for me without ever asking me what I wanna do with *my life*." The decibel of his voice escalated. "It's my life. Can't they understand that? So what I'm good at sports. Does that mean I have to play them? Who ever said I wanted to? Huh? Yeah, I like sports, and I'm good at 'em." With each of the following, drawn-out words, he slammed his fist into the dash board, "but it's *my* life!" Victor's hand began to shake; he drew in a deep breath. Slowly exhaling, he mumbled, "I'm just sick of it all. I wanna do what I wanna do. I'm tired of having the way I'm supposed to act and everything I do being dictated to me."

He boiled over with anger and resentment. A deluge of blood rushed to his face and neck, turning them crimson. I glanced at him through my peripheral vision. I swear I saw waves of heat rolling off his skin. Tears of anger dripped slowly from his eyes. Seeing the fury on his face, I chose to turn my head in order to save his embarrassment and to remain silent as we headed for the jungle. Within a few minutes we pulled up at Kevin's garage. Victor grabbed the bottom of his shirt and wiped his face. We both eyed a car in the drive neither one of us had ever seen. I grabbed my amp and guitar. Using my foot to shut the car door, I headed for the back door. Along the way a strong wind burst across my body and knocked me back a few paces, almost as if it carried with it a warning to stay away, turn around, or leave. I didn't understand it, but in a spooky way, it seemed as if the wind had tried to prevent me from entering the car to begin with, and now it begged me not to step foot in the jungle.

I stood against the strange breeze, knowing I would not leave my brother's side. He needed me. When we crossed the threshold, Kevin introduced us to his cousin from Mobile, Alabama, and his friend. "Hey, guys, this is my cousin Ricky and his friend Todd. They're starting a band and want me in it as the lead singer."

A huge grin crossed my face, and I jumped in front of Victor to shake their hands. "Hey, I'm Ray," I said as I shook Ricky's hand. "Need a lead guitar player?" I chuckled and glanced at Victor with a sheen radiating in my eyes.

"Huh, naw, man. Todd here," he tapped Todd's shoulder, "plays lead, and I play bass. We have a friend, Jess, who plays the drums. He couldn't make it here tonight, but he's awesome. We just drove over to ask Blade here to join us."

My face dropped. I tried not to appear too disappointed, but it was a difficult emotion to hold back. The corners of my mouth crept back up when Kevin interjected. "I haven't heard ya play yet, Todd, but I have to tell you, this little dude," he whacked me on the back sending me forward, "is awesome. Y'all need to at least hear him play in case we ever need a fill-in or something."

"Well, let's hear it, dude." Ricky snickered, gesturing for me to take the stage.

I knelt down to open my guitar case, and I heard Todd whisper, "You're not really gonna seriously listen to this kid, are you? He's just a kid; he can't be a fill-in for me."

"Just hush, Todd. Of course I don't think he's gonna be good enough. I'm just gonna enjoy watchin' him try his heart out," Ricky mumbled back.

I did my best to let their murmurs roll off my back,

but it bothered me to be treated like a child. I wrapped my plain, black strap around my shoulder and contemplated what might impress them. Guns and Roses were all the rage, so I decided on one of their recent hits, *Sweet Child 'O Mine*. Ricky made eye contact with Todd to see what he thought. Todd's face turned sour as he tinged his critique with venom. "That's a fairly simple piece there, and you don't really fill it with the right pizzazz." He snorted, waving his hands and fingers in front of my face in a taunting way.

I took a deep breath and thought back to my days before my electric guitar. I wrapped my hand around the neck of my guitar and began to play *Andantino* by Carcassi. I looked up from my guitar and saw amazement twinkling in Ricky's eyes. Todd rolled his eyes and grunted. "Seriously? You're gonna try and impress me with that classical junk?"

"Junk?" I threw back. "Tell me if you can play this," I spit. I glanced at the placement of my right hand as I wrapped my left hand around the arm of the guitar. I inhaled a deep breath. I heard Todd give a disgruntled sigh. Then I let Caracassi's 25 Estudios loose.

When I looked up that time, I saw astonishment bulging out of Ricky's widened eyes. I had him hook, line, and sinker, but I clearly saw something different in Todd's eyes. I witnessed a battle brewing under the surface, and I knew he would never accept me.

"You are good!" Ricky exclaimed.

I hung my head. "Thanks," I whispered, but I couldn't resist lifting my head in pride at my accomplishment. I knew I had sparked jealousy in Todd, and I felt an odd sense of pleasure in that.

I heard Todd scoff as he stepped in front of me. "Huh, yeah, not so bad. You'll pass." His words dripped of rancor and sarcasm.

To ease the tension invading the room, Kevin stepped between us. He quickly glanced back at Victor,

106

who had been crouched over in a corner paying no attention to the guitar battle I had been in, and saw a red glare in his eyes. In that glance he saw something was terribly wrong. "Hey, let's have a beer."

He pulled a six-pack out of the small refrigerator and began passing them out. When he approached me, I turned it down. I was bent out of shape by Todd's attitude, and I didn't want to have a drink with someone like him. Still boiling from his confrontation with Andy over college, Victor snatched his from Kevin's hand; he sought to drown it all with a couple of drinks. I knew why we had ventured over there to begin with. Kevin was Victor's friend with whom he could chill and just be himself; coincidentally, Victor's idea of chilling usually involved a cold beer.

After they all had a few beers, Todd pulled out a bag of white powdery-looking stuff. I wasn't sure what it was, but apparently the rest of them knew and darted toward the small table and chairs set up in the corner. I stepped behind Victor, leaned over, and whispered in his ear. "What's that y'all are doin'?"

"It's coke. Something I don't want you to even consider trying, Ray."

"I really wish y'all would stop treating me like I'm a baby," I spouted.

Victor stood to his feet, grabbed me by the arm, and dragged me across the garage to the opposite corner. "Ray, I don't think you're a baby. It's just that this stuff is really dangerous and highly addictive. I've only done it once before, and I wouldn't be doing it right now if I didn't need to blow off some steam. You didn't even wanna beer. Why do you all of a sudden wanna try this?" Frustration flooded his face.

"I don't," I hissed and yanked my arm free. "I just hate being treated like I can't do stuff because I'm younger; that's all."

All at once Victor recognized, much like he

107

despised being told what to do, I didn't want to be told what I couldn't do. He understood where I was coming from, but he still didn't want me to participate, so he calmed himself with a deep breath. "All right, dude. I'm sorry. I'm not trying to treat you that way, I promise."

"Don't worry about it. I'm starting to get kind of used to it."

Victor laughed, tousled my hair, and went back to the table. He never wanted me to do anything except drink a beer or two. He turned out to be a protective big brother. I had smoked marijuana a couple of times since the Def Leppard concert we attended together, and he didn't like it one bit. He threatened to beat Gary up for introducing me to it. This time something told me to listen to his warning. A thought of my baby sister and how protective I felt over her invaded my mind. I shivered as cold chill crept up my spine, reminding me of the eerie breeze earlier that evening with its hint of warning. From the opposite corner I watched as Victor leaned over and snorted the white drug for the third time. Suddenly a sense of urgency rushed through my body as the memory of the warning lingered. I didn't understand it at the time, but I knew deep down in my gut something bad was about to happen.

As Victor raised his head; Kevin's eyes bulged. Victor's hands trembled. He arched back in the chair. His body jerked with amazing force, sending the chair and his body crashing to the cold concrete floor. His eyes rolled back in his head as his body flailed.

"What's goin' on?" I screamed.

Kevin and Ricky reached under Victor's body and picked him up. Kevin stuck his hand in Victor's pocket and hollered, "Crank the car, Ray," as he threw me Victor's keys.

I darted out the back door, ran around the building to the street, jumped in the car, and cranked it. Kevin put Victor in the passenger seat and commanded, "Get in back; I'm drivin'."

I climbed over the seat into the back. "What's goin' on, Kevin? Tell me!" I screamed. Tears trickled down my face as panic set in. I couldn't breathe. I didn't understand what was happening to Victor, and Kevin wasn't answering my question.

Finally he hissed, "I don't know for sure, Ray. I think he just overdosed."

"What? Oh my gosh! Is he gonna be okay?" I cried.

Victor grabbed his head and shrieked; then he slumped forward. Kevin stretched his right arm out and lifted Victor's upper body, pressing him to the back of the seat. The car swerved all over the road. "Dammit," he grumbled. "Hold him," he snapped, yanking his arm back and straightening the car on the road. Victor's body slumped forward as soon as Kevin released him. From the back seat I wrapped my arms around his body and pulled him back. His head flung backwards over the seat; he stared at me through open, lifeless eyes.

"No! No! No!" I screamed. "Victor!"

Kevin sped up and made it to the hospital in record time. "We were gathered together with some guys we didn't know at the Point. They offered him the drug. Neither of us did it," he instructed me. "Do you hear me, Ray?"

"Yeah, I hear ya."

"Where were we?"

"At the Point."

"With who?"

"Some guys we didn't know, and they had the drugs," I answered robotically.

He pulled in the drive-through in front of the emergency room doors, jumped out, and hollered, "Park the car while I carry him in."

A security guard saw him struggling to get Victor out of the car and ran over to help carry him in. I parked the car in the first available spot and ran into the waiting room demanding to be taken back with my brother. "Where is he? I wanna know what's going on," I cried.

The triage nurse grabbed my shoulder. "Calm down, son. We need to ask you two some questions. We need to know what happened, so we can know how to treat him."

"Okay, okay. Ask," I insisted.

They pulled us both to the side and began asking, "What was your brother doing?"

In a rehearsed manner I answered, "We were down at the Point; some guys came up and offered us drugs. Victor walked over to where they were parked and snorted some; then he started shaking uncontrollably. We got him in the car to bring him here. On the way here he grabbed his head and screamed; then he slumped over. That's it... Is my brother dead? Please, tell me. Is he dead?"

The nurse peered into mine and Kevin's eyes. Guilt washed over me, and I was certain she could see it staring back at her. Finally she whispered, "I'm sorry. I don't know the answer to your question, but if you'll go sit in the waiting room, I'll check. Before you sit down, I need the name and number of your mom and dad."

"Victor's dad is Andy Donovan. Our number is 555-7030."

"He's your brother?" she questioned.

"Yeah, he's my stepbrother."

"Okay, dear, I'll be back in a few minutes." She disappeared through the double doors.

I eyed the large clock hanging in the waiting room and watched the minute hand move slowly. Thirty minutes had passed when I saw the same nurse briefly return to the triage desk, glance my way, speak softly to another nurse, and slip away out of sight. I stood up and dashed toward the tall, red-haired nurse behind the desk. "My brother? Did she say anything about my brother?"

"Who, dear?" she questioned.

Exasperated, I answered, "The nurse you were just talkin' to; that's who. She was supposed to find out about my brother. His name is Victor Donovan. Will you please check on him?" I begged. As the last syllable rolled over my tongue, I felt the same spooky breeze blow across my back. I did a one-eighty to see the double doors open. Mom and Andy rushed through them. I saw the devastation dripping from their damp, reddened faces. Tears streamed down my face. I knew in my gut what the nurse had refused to tell me—he was gone.

My mother sped to my side. "Are you okay? They didn't have you identify him, did they?"

"No, mom. We brought him in. I told them who he was and gave them the number to the house. They called you? Is he okay?" I asked, hoping my instinct was horribly wrong.

Andy pushed my mom to the side and grabbed my arm. "Were you doing anything? I wanna know right now," he demanded, shaking me.

"No," I yanked my arm free.

Mom cried, "Andy, stop. Leave him alone. Can't you imagine how devastated he is?"

Andy looked up at the nurse and commanded her in his military tone, "Test him right now."

"Andy!" Mom shrilled. Kevin stood and inched his way toward the exit sign and ducked out without being seen by Andy or my mom.

"I'm not playing around, Bonnye. I want him tested. Victor is dead because of what they were doing, and I'm not gonna let him get away with participating in it without consequence."

My heart sank as I realized my worst fear. Victor was dead. The wind warned me with its frigid breeze and the eerie shiver it sent through my bones.

Everything in my life from that point forward would be different; everything would change.

I felt my head as it began to swirl; then I felt myself slump to the floor, wailing. "Aaaaahhhhhh..."

Warm arms wrapped gently around me. No words were spoken, but I could hear delicate sobs coming from my mom.

The nurse walked around the desk and helped me to my feet. She glanced at my mother and asked if she wanted to go through with the blood work. Mom peered at Andy and perceived the seriousness glaring at her through his deep-green eyes. She turned to the nurse and whispered, "Yeah, I think he'll be okay. Just give him a minute."

The nurse took me through the double doors into the emergency department and into an empty room. She pointed to the bed and requested I sit. At first I sat on the edge of the bed, but as soon as she exited the room, I crawled into a ball on the bed and wept. I jerked up when I heard the door creak open. A tall, slender black man shoved a cart through the door. He introduced himself as a lab worker and drew some of my blood. His wary eyes pierced through mine, searching for guilt. Guilt resided there, but not the guilt he hunted. I was guilty of not listening to the sound of wind and the warning it carried with it.

Andy was satisfied when the emergency room doctor reported my tests all came back negative, and we were allowed to go home. Mom and Andy spent the next day at the funeral home making arrangements, and I spent the day in my bed. I just kept lying there staring at Victor's side of the room and his smashed trophies. Eventually I fell asleep, but sleep didn't release me from the torment of seeing his lifeless eyes staring at me. I kept hearing his warnings of the dangers of drugs and how he felt pressured to do them to be cool.

I awoke to a slight knock on the door. "Come in," I

rasped. It seemed my voice had gotten lost in dream world.

Mom poked her head in the room. "Honey, please come eat breakfast. We have a lot going on today, and you'll need your strength."

I sat up. "Breakfast?"

"Yes, dear, you slept through supper last night. You've been asleep for sixteen hours. It's seven a.m."

"Okay. Give me a minute." I stumbled out of bed, slipped into the hall bathroom to brush my teeth, and tiptoed quietly past Lacey's room. I glanced through the small opening in her door to see her sleeping soundly in her baby bed. She was all I had left. I had my mom, but Andy needed my mom now more than ever.

That evening we arrived at the funeral home promptly at 5:45 p.m. Andy was keen on punctuality, and we were to be there by six. He always insisted we be fifteen minutes early for all appointments, and the fact that this appointment was for his son's wake didn't change his philosophy.

That evening and the next day were both horrible. People poured in in droves. All of Victor's friends and classmates, all of Andy's friends and co-workers, Andy's family, as well as ours, filled the small room overflowing with greenery and wreaths of colorful flowers. Mason and his family came. With his girlfriend at his side, he shook my hand and said he was sorry for my loss, but that was it.

After the funeral everyone came back to the house, carrying trays of food. I slipped off to my room to escape the crowd. A small package sat on the edge of my bed. Slinging my suit jacket over the back of the lone chair in our room, I wondered aloud, "What's that?"

I looked to Victor's empty bed and thought I heard him respond, "I think it may be a peace offering." Chills ran up my back. It felt so real, like I could see and hear him speaking from another world.

113

I sat on the edge of my bed, picked up the gift, and gazed at it. "A peace offering," I heard a voice cry out from the opposite side of my half-opened door.

Spooked, I threw the box down and looked for the owner of the voice. The door creaked as Mason swung it open wide. "Hey, dude."

"Hey, man."

"Can I come in?"

"Sure."

Mason shut the door behind him and sat next to me on the bed. "Ray, I'm really sorry...about everything...not just about Victor. I've been a major jerk, and I hope you can forgive me."

"It's okay, dude. Honestly, Victor kind of explained everything to me. He felt the pressure you feel too, so he understood. He asked me to understand where you were coming from, but I didn't want to. I guess I should do what he asked with him being dead and all." I picked the box back up. "Peace offering, huh?"

"Yep."

I opened the box and pulled out a cool guitar strap. It was black, covered with red flames. "Wicked, man. Where'd ya find this?"

"Oh, I have my connections." He laughed and bumped his shoulder into mine.

I stretched my hand and grasped his, "Blood brothers?"

"Blood brothers," he replied as he tightened his grip and grinned.

"So, who's the pretty girl you had with you?" I pried.

"Oh, that's my girlfriend, Samantha. We've been goin' out for a couple of months now. She's a ninth grader, so she spends her time on the first hall. That's probably why you haven't seen her around."

"That or the fact I've been avoiding you," I chuckled. "Well, she's really pretty. How'd ya meet her?"

"She's a cheerleader. You know me; I like those cheerleaders." He laughed.

"Yeah, you're pretty typical when it comes to that kind of thing. So, you really like her, huh?"

"Yeah, dude. I think I might actually love her. I'm not really sure; I've not ever been with a girl until her if you know what I mean."

My mouth dropped, and I interjected, "Been with? Y'all've been together been together?"
My eyes grew huge.

"Yeah, it kind of happened the other night."

"Wow, okay. Um...don't really know what to say to that. Please don't give me any details."

"I won't." He shoved me again.

"I'm glad you found love and all." I chuckled.

"Me too." he stared at the wall.

We sat together in silence, and I reminisced over the last year. So many things had taken place during that time. Tramane had saved my life and become a sort of body guard for me at school. We picked up right where we left off in kindergarten although our friendship stayed within the confines of the school yard. Because of his stature the football coach recruited him to be on the team, so my taunting ceased. However, a strong gust of wind blew through my life and brought with it change, both good and bad. Victor was gone forever, and despite his past harassments, he and I had grown close. I learned many things from him. In the midst of the devastation brought through the wind of change, a bond, which had been broken, was forged once again. While mine and Mason's relationship had been altered through the events that transpired, our friendship was rekindled, and peace was made. Change blustered through my life like a category-three hurricane, breaking and destroying our lives, but change can be good, and lives can be rebuilt.

CHAPTER 11

GRADUATION CELEBRATION

My life had been changed all right, not only my life but my nightly dreams as well. They were invaded by a recurring nightmare. In each dream I stood far away watching as Victor laughed a distorted, muffled chortle with his friends; then he convulsed uncontrollably. All of a sudden I was alone, but I wasn't sure where because darkness enveloped me. There was no light present at all. A cold hand grasped my shoulder from behind. As I pivoted to gaze upon that which grabbed me, I came face to face with the lifeless eyes of Victor.

I would wake up in cold sweats. What I had seen that night would not loosen its grip on me. I lived under the nightmare's torment for months until I wrote a song about my experience.

"Lifeless Eyes"

You invade my dreams
So real it almost seems.
As I look into your eyes,
I can hear your cries.
There's nothing I can do;
There's nothing I can say
When your lifeless eyes
Glare at me that way.
I'm captured by
The gaze they hold.

They draw me in;
Your death is cold.

Your lifeless eyes send chills right through me;
Your lifeless eyes won't let me be.
Your lifeless eyes are all around me;
Your lifeless eyes straight through me see.

I awake from my dreams
So real they always seem;
I wear my own disguise
So I can hide from your eyes.

There's nothing I can do;
There's nothing I can say
When your lifeless eyes
Glare at me that way.
I'm captured by
The gaze they hold;
They draw me in
Your death is cold.

Your lifeless eyes send chills right through me;
Your lifeless eyes won't let me be.
Your lifeless eyes are all around me;
Your lifeless eyes straight through me see.

Yeah, your lifeless eyes send chills right through me;
Even in my dreams guilt follows me.
Would your lifeless eyes, please set me free.

Ray Winstrom

Despite the guilt I felt for not stopping Victor from doing something so dangerous, I determined not to go down a similar path and allow my life to end in like manner. I held Victor's wise words in my heart and set my mind on my music and my education. Over the following three years, I honed in on my skills in metal music as well as classical, and I dove into my school books. Victor complained athleticism was all he had; he didn't have the brains to get a scholarship. He relied completely upon his ability to pass a ball down a long field amongst his teammates and drive it past the goalie. He *was* good at it, but apparently it wasn't enough to get him into the college of Andy's choice. That, coupled with his inability to stand up to peer pressure, led him to make a wrong decision he could never change, fix, or make amends for, so the day after his death, while I lay in my bed staring at his empty one, I resolved in my heart to take the intelligence he always spoke of my having and begin diligently applying it.

As a result of my endeavor, I rose to the top ten percent of my class. I wasn't the brightest kid in town—that was a girl I had heard of but never met. After some investigation I discovered her name. Rumors floated throughout the school, suggesting Aralyn Liddell was destined to be valedictorian come graduation time, but with graduation still far enough in the future, I had a fighting chance, and I loved a challenge.

I kept my grades a secret from my friends except for Tramane. With Tray it was different. He felt a sense of pride in his friend's grades. In exchange for his constant protection from the bullies who desired to rip me to shreds simply because I lacked athletic abilities and because they held a certain level of disdain against guys with long hair, I tutored him in those classes which were more difficult for him. He wasn't dumb by any means, but he wanted to be able to get into a good college. His grandparents had always taken care of him, and he knew it would make them proud to see him better himself. They had grown up during the time of segregation, and during those days, a college education for a black boy or girl was a rarity.

Tramane knew his family's history and how hard it had been for blacks since they were freed from slavery. Their freedom did not give them rights. As a people they fought hard to gain rights. His grandfather worked hard to earn the position of Paint Supervisor; nevertheless, without a college education he knew he had attained the highest level available to him. It had taken him years to work himself up to that position, and he didn't want his grandson to have the same struggles in life, so he and his wife drilled getting an education into Tramane from his earliest days. Knowing they wouldn't be able to afford much in the way of college, they encouraged Tramane to focus on his academics as well as his athleticism. Tramane shared his family's story with me, and I was all too happy to partake in the betterment of his life.

Once I passed my driver's test, Andy handed me the keys to Victor's old car. He balled the keys in his fist, inhaled a sharp breath, and extended his arm toward me. With a sigh he diverted his eyes to the ground and managed to loosen his grip and drop them in my hand. He mumbled something about being careful to take care of the car as he ambled to the kitchen. He had a hard time relinquishing anything belonging to Victor. My room, which I shared with him, remained the same. All of Victor's clothes still hung in the closet next to mine, and his side of the room was dusted and placed back in the exact position it had been on that horrible day, so it surprised me when Andy passed the car on to me. I had not expected it. Having a car made it much simpler to tutor Tramane. I was able to meet him at the library after school and often on Saturdays without Andy being aware.

Six months after Victor's death, Kevin approached me. "Hey, man. How ya been?" he asked with a hand shake.

"Um...all right, I suppose," I mumbled, slightly shrugging to my shoulders.

"Look, your brother, man, he really believed in you, you know, and I thought...maybe, just maybe, we could start a band together...in his honor and all." He cringed slightly before interjecting, "I think it would make him proud to know you're in a band with his buddy."

I stared into space for a fleeting moment. "I'll think about it."

"I was thinkin' we could call the band Silver Blade after the nickname Victor gave me."

Kevin had become a huge Joe Satriani fan, and the album *Surfing with the Alien* was his favorite, and since the album was named after the Silver Surfer in the *Fantastic Four* comics, Victor had started calling Kevin, who already had the nickname Blade, Silver Blade.

Kevin had backed away from drugs and alcohol after Victor's death; I had completely shunned it all. The idea his life had dramatically changed as a result of Victor's untimely demise and the fact he desired to honor Victor in such a way drew me to strongly consider the proposal. "Give me a day or two to think it through, okay?"

"Sure thing. Just give me a holler when you make your decision, all right, man?"

"I will," I assured him as I smacked my hand against his mid-air.

In reality I didn't need a day or two. I made my decision within hours of his request. We spent the better part of my ninth-grade year meeting with his friend, Nick Wright; he played the bass guitar, but we still lacked a drummer we felt had the right stuff. My first day in high school, I met Ron Hickson in jazz band. He was a year older than me. He was goofing off on the drums as I walked through the double doors of the band hall, and he was good. We recruited him within a week and began regularly scheduled practices. While I divided many hours between studying for myself and tutoring Tramane, I spent the remainder of my time practicing with the band, Silver Blade.

Mason and my friendship went through a major overhaul. We both still retained a portion of the blood bond we established as merely children, and I still bore the scar on my fingertip, a constant reminder to me of the oath we made under the full moon that night—the promise we would always be best friends and nothing and no one would ever come between us. Every time I glanced at the small, white scar, I faced the painful reality that no magic existed within the ritual. The mark always ushered my mind back to the day Mason told me we could no longer hang out at school because something had already come between us. His desire to be popular severed our status as best friends. I hoped there was at least a little magic in the bond of blood brothers.

In April of '92, Mason approached me to offer Silver Blade their first gig. It was on that day the *someone* portion of our oath would be introduced, and our friendship and the mystic ritual of which we partook would once again be put to the test. I thought Pamela had been the someone to test our oath. I was mistaken.

Leaning uncomfortably against my headboard with books strewn all over my bed, I held my three-inch thick history book in my hands as I studied for a test. *Knock, knock, knock.* I jumped at the sound of firm banging on my bedroom door.

Thinking it was Andy, I responded, "Sir?"

The door slightly creaked opened and in popped Mason's head. "Hey, dude..." His jaw dropped, and he slung the door open wide and lumbered across the room, approaching the end of my bed with a knitted brow. "Oh, my! Do you have a major test in every class tomorrow or what?" he scoffed as he tossed a few of my books to the floor, making room to sit.

Flushing red, I closed my book and quickly interjected my excuse, "Um...yeah...I have a huge history test tomorrow, and...well...the band will be practicing tomorrow afternoon, so I figured I better go ahead and study for the tests in my other classes too."

"Your mom and stepdad stay on ya 'bout grades? I know my parents do. Boy, if they only knew I do all right compared to some of the guys I know. I mean, I'm no A student, but I make B's and C's except for P.E.; I always have an A in there," he rambled on.

"Yeah, I understand, dude. Parents can be kind a harsh sometimes when it comes to grades." Promptly changing the subject, I quizzed him, "So, what's up, dude?"

"Oh, I actually came over to see if Silver Blade was ready to set up a gig."

I sprang forward to an upright position. "Yeah, we are. You know of something?"

"Well, you remember my cousin Brent?" he started.

"Yep, is he gonna have a party or something?" I interrupted.

"Yes and no. Slow down and let me get it all out, okay?"

I inhaled a deep breath of excitement and conceded. "Okay."

"Well, you know graduation is just a little more than a month away, and there's this girl I know, Laila, who likes Justin. She's been crushin' on him for a couple of weeks. She's actually dating Keith, but she was tellin' me she was seriously thinkin' of breaking up with him."

I raised my brow in confusion as I sat patiently listening to the story he spilled. I had yet to see what this had to do with him or Silver Blade.

"Anyway, Laila is graduating, and she has a sister; she's in your grade. Well, you know how I've dated a lot of girls since Samantha?"

I nodded my head in acknowledgement. "Yeah."

"Well, I think I've been going out with the wrong kind of girls all this time. I've always dated girls like Samantha and Cassie and Linda." His list went on. "You know, the knock-out gorgeous girls who come from money, and they're popular. It just seems to me the chase is too easy. Those girls, except for Samantha, all want to go out with me 'cause I'm the quarterback, and they all think I'm hot. All I have to do is ask, and they'll sleep with me. I think I need someone different, a challenge."

"And your challenge is this girl?" I questioned, narrowing my eyes at him.

"Yeah, Laila's little sister. Given, she's nowhere near as beautiful as her sister, but she's pretty; she doesn't act like she's pretty though. I've seen her around, carrying a big heap of books. She's like really smart from what I hear."

My interest swelled. I wanted to know who this girl was. "What's...her name?" I hesitantly asked.

"Aralyn Liddell. I think a girl like her might be just what I need." He smiled a crooked smile.

Hmmm...no way...he can't like the girl I'm in competition with! She's too smart for him. Trying to hide the shocked expression perched on my face, I shook my head. "I'm confused, dude. What does this girl have to do with a gig you want Silver Blade to play?"

"Oh...um...well, my cousin Brent offered to loan me his house to set up a graduation celebration, a party right after graduation for seniors only. Of course, I'll be there because I'm giving the party, and I'll prearrange with Laila to have her sister there. Y'all can play there that night. I figured it'd give y'all some experience playin' before a crowd."

123

"Ok, I'll talk to Kevin about it. I'm sure he'll be excited. So...this girl is just a challenge for you—a game?" I pried.

"I wouldn't call it a game, but it'll definitely be a challenge. From what I hear, she's never had a boyfriend, so she obviously doesn't just throw herself on guys. I think it'd be nice to date a girl with some substance."

"Hmmm...okay. I've heard of her, but I've never met her. I hear she's very quiet. I think she hangs around with Andrea Maples and her group of friends. They're all pretty smart from what I hear...You sure you want substance?" I threw in my last pitch of effort in discouraging the relationship.

"Yep, I'm sure," he assured me, and I settled in my mind that unbeknownst to this young girl, she was a challenge on two accounts.

Kevin was enthused at the opportunity, and before we realized it, time had passed us at the speed of light it seemed. We were a cover band, so we mostly played songs by famous recording artists. I had a couple of friends graduating that night, so I sat, impatiently I might add, waiting to watch them cross the field at the Moss Point High School stadium. I had watched so many games take place on that field, but I had never had the thrill of being out there amongst the excitement of it all. Somewhere in the back of my mind, those thoughts made me feel a bit inferior in comparison to other guys, especially to my childhood friend Mason.

I fidgeted in my seat and watched as Tom held his head high to receive his diploma. I knew Tom rather well; he was good friends with my stepbrother Victor before he started fooling around with drugs. I twisted my wrist toward me to read the face of my watch. *8:15, I've gotta get; Doug'll never know that I had to slip outa here,* I thought to myself.

Standing to my feet, I made my way down the

creaky, old bleachers. I tried my best to keep the noise to a minimum. I knew better than to come watch a few friends graduate; I had my first gig, and I needed to be out in the boonies of Helena setting up the equipment. That responsibility seemed to have fallen on me. Blade, the leader of the band, made his plan clear. His responsibility was to move amongst the crowd and mingle with the guests before we started. Ron and Nick were both good at what they did, but they were slackers when it came to duties; I stayed frustrated with those two. They strolled in fifteen minutes late to every practice, while I showed up early to make sure the sound system was ready to go.

I pulled out my keys and climbed into my red '88 Chevrolet Sprint Turbo and headed toward Helena. It wasn't long after I passed the small airport on Saracennia Road that I slowed down to make a right-hand turn. I had a small piece of paper in my hand with the map Mason had given me scribbled across it. I had been to his cousin Brent's house with him when we were kids, but it had been a long time ago, so I needed a map to make it back out. Mason drew a map and ran-off copies to pass out to all the seniors at the school. He purposely restricted the party to seniors to keep the numbers down, with the exceptions being himself, band members, and Aralyn.

Nestled in the middle of a couple of hundred acres, a humongous two-story home stood. It seemed as if everyone in Mason's family had money. I turned down the long drive, eyed the small sign pointing to the four-wheeler worn path Mason told me to search for, and drove toward the glistening blue lights covering the shed. I pulled around back to park my car, got out of the car, opened the hatchback, and began unloading equipment. I had not been able to get out there earlier to set up, so I had a good bit left to do in preparation. Mason had given me a key to the shed to let myself in, so I unlocked the door and began working.

I didn't mind doing the work myself. It gave me time alone to think. I could write great songs in my mind while I dilly dallied with setting up the equipment—as long as I was alone, that is. The creative side of me seemed to need seclusion.

Before long seniors (as well as Ron and Nick) began to trickle in the side door, so I turned the stereo system on to give them background music until time for us to play and went about hooking up our sound system. Interestingly enough, my friends decided to join me in completing the hook up when there was just a few wires left to connect and a couple of knobs left to turn. Just as I finished and stood from my crouched position, a spark of red caught my eye, drawing my attention. I shifted my eyes and craned my neck to gaze at the beautiful girl wearing the strapless, crimson top.

CHAPTER 12

CLOSE ENCOUNTERS

The flash of red may have been what caught my attention to begin with, but the gorgeous girl wrapped in the leather skirt and shimmering top piqued my interest. She stood behind three other girls whom I didn't know. Her pale complexion, vastly differing from my own, hinted of her frailty. Not that she looked sick, but rather she had been preserved by a protective covering which had wrapped itself around her, shielding her from the harmfulness of the sun's rays. Her brunette hair fell halfway down her back in long curls. Despite the heavy layers of make-up, natural beauty shined from beneath its covering. Her hands trembled, revealing her hesitance, as she grasped a wine cooler. She ambled across the room by herself, holding the bottle and looking around like a lost puppy.

Her bright-blue eyes scanned her surroundings. It seemed as if she was intent on finding a particular object the way she peered through the room. An alluring force tugged on my chest, pulling at me and persuading me to leave the small platform and draw near to her. Even though I had never had a girlfriend, there were some pretty girls I had been attracted to, but I had never experienced magnetism until that moment. It forcefully drew me to her. I had never understood the power a beautiful girl could hold over a guy before that moment. Something in me wanted to approach her and help her find whatever she was searching for.

I mustered up the courage to walk toward her and to ask her if she needed help finding someone or something. I inhaled a shuddery breath. My heart pounded wildly against the cavity of my chest. *Mason is going to have to give me his secret! How does he do this over and over again?* I wondered. Slowly exhaling, I lifted my foot to take the first step in her direction.

Without warning the sound of the microphone clanking restrained my step. I heaved a sigh as Kevin yelled, "Happy graduation, everybody! Most of you know me, and for those who don't, I'm Blade Parker. This is my band, Silver Blade, and we're gonna play a few songs for you tonight. On drums we have Ron Hickson. Give him a hand!" he yelled as everyone began hooting and hollering. *No way,* I winced at my lost opportunity as Ron played his short drum solo; then Blade jumped over to Nick, "On the bass guitar we have Nick Wright. Give him a hand," he encouraged the crowd. *Okay, quick, think. Play something that might impress her. When we take a break, make your move then,* I emboldened myself. The crowd cheered, and Blade grabbed the microphone again and faced me. "And last but most definitely not least, on lead guitar we have Ray Winstrom." I played a complex piece with the intent of making a good impression on the mystery girl.

Jealousy churned within me as I watched Johnny Weatherton approach her. *Wait, no...he seems to have been shot down; he's walking away from her...Oh, man, he was just getting her another drink. I hate that guy. Who does he think he is? Him and his goofy, skateboarding self, thinking he's all that,* I complained to myself. I played along with the band as we rocked on, but I kept an eagle eye on Johnny and the gorgeous brunette being sucked in by him. He took the empty bottle from her hand and chunked it into a nearby garbage can, showing off no doubt. They were obviously having an interesting conversation because she smiled. Her smile entranced me, tugging on my thoughts, but I found myself begging for it to go away. A smile suggested a possible attraction; I prayed she wouldn't be interested in Johnny in the least.

Blade cut his eyes back at the rest of us, signaling the song up next. *Stupid slow song. He's gonna ask her to dance,* I grumbled inside. Blade interrupted my train of thought, "We're gonna slow it down for a minute. Here's a favorite from Cutting Crew, *I Just Died in Your Arms Tonight.*" Blade stepped to the side, laid his fingers on the keyboard he recently purchased, and began the song.

I watched as she sought a place to set her drink and followed him to the dance floor. She looked nervous and uncomfortable dancing with him. He certainly couldn't dance, that's for sure. *Strike one. Ha, Johnny Weatherton, we'll see about that. I can dance. I'll sweep her off her feet and right out of your arms, buddy.* I narrowed my eyes and shot darts at him. *Oh, no!* I cringed. Distraught over seeing his hand on her waist, I scanned through the rest of the room and caught a glimpse of Mason talking to the black-haired girl she had walked in with; he seemed to be upset with her. *I wonder if that's Aralyn. I hope he isn't already messin' things up with her.* I searched the room for Justin; Mason planned to set Aralyn's sister up with him in exchange for the set up between them. From the corner of my eye, I noticed my mystery girl squirming. She peered at her friend and Mason with a scowl of frustration glaring through her eyes. *Oh, wait a minute, my lady in red must be her sister Laila. She looks steamin' mad. I guess Mason didn't keep his end of the deal. Boy was he right. She is beautiful! I'm gonna have to talk to him about introducing me to her and shunning Justin. He sure is missing out; where is he anyway?*

Blade gave us the signal to switch gears. He began

on the keyboard with *Jump* by Van Halen. I watched as the girl I presumed to be Laila recoiled from Johnny and stormed toward Mason and her sister. There seemed to be a bit of a tiff going on between the two girls; then as we began playing *You Give Love a Bad Name*, Justin marched into view. He gave Mason a swift pat on the shoulder, grabbed the black-haired girl's hand, and led her to the dance floor. An ache shot through my finger as my scar pulsed in pain, skidding down the string under intense pressure as my grip tightened. My challenge, his challenge, my interest, and his were all one and the same—Aralyn. She was the *someone* portion of our ritual, and I feared she was more powerful than the oath we had made. For more than a month, she had merely been an irritant reminding me I couldn't compete with her if she were to be my friend's girlfriend; he was determined she would be his girlfriend, and considering his status and looks, he usually got his way when it came to his desires. As I watched them exit the shed together, my battled ensued, *Compete with her secretly over grades and scholarships, compete with Mason to win her love, or keep my blood oath and walk away from it all?*

They were gone for an awfully long time, much too long to have just visited the restroom. When they returned, the night had dwindled down. We shut down around midnight and mingled with the crowd for the remainder of the night. We had all decided to wait until morning to come back out and retrieve our amps, microphones, and other equipment. From across the room, I witnessed the close proximity between Mason and Aralyn. I resigned myself to the fact I had lost the battle before it even began.

I stepped outside to get a breath of fresh air. In truth I needed time alone to think, so I walked through the yard, weaving through the cars, and contemplated the intense emotions surging through me earlier. They had completely thrown me off guard, and if she dated my friend, I wasn't sure I would be able to be around them when they were together.

Just as I convinced myself I needed to keep a distance, Mason, Aralyn, and her three girlfriends came out into the parking area. Mason securely held Aralyn's hand in his own. They both smiled. A light giggle slipped through Aralyn's lips. One of the girls shrieked, "What the? How are we gonna get outa here? Guys, we're blocked in."

Aralyn dropped Mason's hand. "Are you sure, Rhonda?" She sought out their car and saw clearly that three vehicles had trapped them in. "Laila, we have to call Mom and Dad by 12:30. We'll be in a *lot* of trouble if we're even a minute late," she insisted.

Laila flew into hysterics, "Oh, my gosh, those idiots. You don't pull behind someone when there's a tree in front of 'em. I'm supposed to be responsible for my little sister. I'll be grounded for life. I can't be grounded for life; I haven't even been on a date with Justin yet. We've got to *move* these cars!" she screamed frantically.

Feeling sorry for the girls and inwardly wanting to help Aralyn out, I approached Mason. "I'll get the cars outa here, man." Turning my gaze toward the four young ladies, I asked, "Do any of you have a pen and a small piece of paper in your purse?"

Laila snapped, "Whadaya gonna do? Leave 'em a note?"

I couldn't help but laugh. "Ha, no. I was actually planning to take down the license plate numbers and announce for them to move their vehicles before they're towed."

She stepped back and sucked in a large gulp of air. Releasing it slowly, she gained control over her fit of rage. "Oh...yeah...that'd work. Sorry," she added with a hint of smugness in her tone as she turned up her nose at me.

The girl who still remained unknown to me scrambled through her purse and retrieved a pen and tore off a small piece of paper from the envelope of a graduation card that had been given to her that night and handed them to me. I smiled. "Thanks." I made a conscious effort not to look in Aralyn's direction and refused to make eye contact with Mason. I took a quick inventory of the cars and saw instantly no two were alike, so I decided to go with color, make, and model. *Most of those people in there are too drunk to remember a license plate number anyway,* I told myself. Straightaway I went to scribbling down the information and excused myself. "I'll have 'em out of your way in just a moment," I promised.

"You sure you don't mind?" The unknown girl pouted in a flirty way.

"I'll take care of it, no problem."

I headed back to the shed, grabbed the microphone, and announced, "Would the owners of a blue Ford Escort, a black Pontiac Trans Am, and a white Ford Ranger please move your vehicles *now*, or they will be towed." I watched as all three owners stood to their feet and made their way out to their automobiles. It felt good to do something to help Aralyn out, but I had to keep reminding myself not to think that way. *You can never compete with Mason, Ray. Don't even think about it.* I repeatedly reminded myself.

The following Thursday Mason knocked on my bedroom door. "Hey, man, you goin' to Gulf Shores this summer?" he asked as he walked through and sat on the edge of Victor's bed.

"Look, dude. Can you sit in the chair?" I pointed to the only chair in my room. "No offense but Andy gets upset about Victor's stuff being messed with."

He straightened the covers on the bed and strolled over to the chair. "Still? Man, he's taking it pretty rough. Do you think he'll ever get over it?"

I strummed my guitar. "I'm beginning to wonder myself. I mean, it's still hard for me, and he was only my stepbrother." I sat my guitar down in its stand. "I'm planning to go, but I may not be able to spend a whole week. Kevin has gotten three calls since Friday night. We've got several gigs set up already. By the way, we'll be playing at a party in Gulfport next Saturday. It's some big birthday bash for a girl named Brook. You're invited as my guest. Her fiancé said we could each invite a friend."

"Gigs already, huh?"

"Yep, a couple of seniors knew some people looking for a band to play some parties. So, why do you ask about Gulf Shores?"

"Just wonderin'. I was kind of hoping you'd have a few performances out of it. I got a job with Mr. Lee doing construction, so I won't be around during the daylight hours at all. Nights are all I've got; my usual summer vacation is blown, that's for sure. I's just wonderin' if yours was too." He chuckled.

"I'm supposed to leave the day after the Gulfport party to head over. When do you start with Mr. Lee?"

"Bright and early Monday morning, and I've gotta date with Aralyn Saturday night," He grinned.

"Oh, really." *Why does he have to fill me in on this?* I cringed inwardly. "What are y'all gonna do?"

"Well, it's a double date with her and her sister. Me and Justin are gonna take 'em to Mobile for dinner and a movie; that's all."

"So, she liked you, huh?"

He smiled a crooked smile. "Of course, who wouldn't?" He chuckled.

"Oh, yeah, right. I guess I forgot. You're irresistible." I rolled my eyes.

133

"Apparently not," he scoffed.

"Whadaya talkin' about?" I asked, unsure if I wanted the answer to the question that immediately rolled off my tongue.

"Well, let's just put it this way: she'll definitely live up to the challenge I was looking for." He raised his brow.

My blood began boiling, and I could feel the heat rolling off my skin as it rose to the surface. I wanted to lunge for his throat and demand to know what he had done to her, but I knew I had no right to do so. She didn't even know I existed. "Mason, what did you do?"

"Well, I tried, of course. No one's ever turned me down before, but she did. She had the will power to turn me down even though she'd had a few drinks."

Without thinking, I narrowed my eyes and glared at him. "So, that's really what this is about? She's really just a challenge to you. You don't see her for anything more than that?" *Okay, let's see how he answers this. Maybe I could warn her of his intentions if he's only looking to score.*

"No, no, no, dude. I like her. I really do. Like I said, she's got substance. What do you care anyway?" He shifted in the chair and folded his arms across his chest.

"I care because I think she has more than substance, Mason. She has a heart, and let's face it, you're known for breaking them."

"Why do you care if I break her heart? Do you like her or something?" he jeered.

Stunned, I spouted, "No...I could just tell she had an innocence about her; that's all. She's obviously not like the other girls you've dated. Those girls wanted to go out with you to be the popular girl of the week or month, however long it lasted, but she came across to me as a serious kind of person, you know...I just think you should be careful."

134

"I plan to, man. I wasn't joking around when I said I thought I needed a different kind of girl. I think she'll be good for me. She's really nice, you know."

"Well, I'm glad you see that. Just be careful, man."

"Okay, dude, enough of the lecture. You sound like my mom."

Mason left and went on his date a few days later, and during that time, Kevin got several other shows set up for us. Our summer nights would be spent jamming, and that was sure to keep my time and mind occupied. I could easily flush out all thoughts of the girl in the crimson top.

The following Saturday I pulled up at the fancy house a few blocks away from the beach in Gulfport. Arriving before the rest of the crew, I knocked on the door. A young woman, apparently the guest of honor, answered the door. It was obvious she had been preparing herself for the spectacular event; it was her twenty-first birthday bash. She greeted me, showed me to the great room where the function would be held, and excused herself. I unloaded the equipment in my small car and began setting up.

As expected, the rest of the gang showed up just in time to finish up with the easy stuff. I had just completed my task when I saw Mason enter the large room. From across the way, he shuffled across the floor, heading toward me. Aralyn sauntered behind him, holding his hand and glancing around at the elaborate home. *Ah, man. Maybe if I pretend to be busy, he'll go on past,* I contemplated, so I knelt down in front of my amplifier, pretending to be hooking the wires up; unfortunately that didn't discourage him from bringing her over to introduce us.

"Hey, man," Mason called.

I reluctantly turned my head to face my inner

battle with a forced look of interest, but as soon as I saw her standing there wearing a Queensryche t-shirt and faded jeans, I couldn't help but smile. Girls Mason usually dated didn't dress that way, but her style boosted my interest. "Whuz up, man?" I asked as I unconsciously swung my arm through the air, colliding with his, in our old childhood handshake. *What are you thinkin', you idiot?* I argued with myself, secretly thankful Mason participated in our old tradition. I could just imagine how silly she thought we looked. I didn't know why, but I couldn't seem to think straight with her around me. It was as if my brain turned to mush.

"Ray, this is Aralyn," he introduced me.

Yeah, I pined. "Yeah, right. You were at the graduation celebration, weren't you?" I squinted as if I had to strain to pull her face up in my memory banks.

"Yeah, I was," she answered. *Ah, her voice is so sweet and delicate sounding. I could listen to her talk all day. She probably doesn't even remember my kind gesture that night.*

I knew I had to busy myself because I couldn't stop looking at her, so I faked a need for the restroom before we started playing. I made my way back to the room just before Blade introduced us. We played a couple of songs, and I noticed an attractive teenage girl watching every move I made. Her auburn hair glistened under a starburst of light. Her brilliant green eyes locked with mine as she danced closer to the make-shift stage. Her black top draped over one shoulder and sparkled under the blinking strobe light. She was discernibly interested in me.

During our first break Mason slipped away from Aralyn and approached me. "Hey, dude. I see you've got yourself a fan over there." He laughed and smacked me on the shoulder.

"Yeah, looks that way."

"You should ask her out, and we can double. She's

hot. Man, look at her legs in that miniskirt."

I cut my eyes to him and folded my lips over my teeth. "So, you planning on stayin' with Aralyn for more than two weeks?" I asked in a smug way.

He chuckled. "Ha, yeah, man. You know, I think I could really fall for her. She's amazing. I mean, did you ever expect to see *her* wearin' a t-shirt like that? She blows my mind, and she's so smart too."

"Yeah, I didn't imagine a girl dressed down like that was your type, buddy." I couldn't help but put a tiny stab in there. "So I'm guessing the date last weekend went well?"

"Yep, sure did. It's nice having someone interested in me, not just my looks or the position I play in football, you know? And, by the way, meat head, I'm friends with *you*, aren't I?"

"Yeah, I guess you are." I laughed. "I'm happy for you, dude. Just treat her right, and I'm sure she'll do the same."

"I plan on it. Well, I better get back over there before I get into a fight with that guy who just walked up to talk to her." He smiled. "Later man."

"Later."

Just as Blade called us back up front, the young lady approached me, "Hi!" she trilled, sticking her hand out for a shake. "My name is Loraine. What's yours?"

"Ray. Nice to meet you, Loraine. Look, I certainly don't want to offend you, but I kind of have to get back up front. We're fixin' to get started back."

"Oh, okay. I totally understand. So maybe we can chat during your next break?" she asked with a hopeful gaze. Her heavily layered hair dangled over her bare shoulder.

"Yeah, I'd like that." I stared into her shimmering, pale green eyes. Anyone who cared to give her a single glance could easily see her attractiveness. She seemed to be really into me, so I figured I might as well go for it, considering I would never be able to win Aralyn's heart—she belonged to my blood brother.

In a matter of just seven songs, we were excusing ourselves for yet another break. I set my guitar in its stand and turned to see Loraine just a few feet away from me.

"Hey there again," I uttered.

"Hey." She smiled. Stretching her hand toward me, she asked, "Can I, can I touch your hair, please? It looks so..."

I had never had a girl ask to play with my hair, so I stood slightly shocked for a brief moment. "Yeah, sure. I suppose."

She ran her hand down the length of my hair and intertwined her fingers through my natural waves. "So, Ray, how long have you been playing?" she asked, taking an interest in my talent, as well as my hair.

The feeling of her fingers mixed up in my hair sent a tingling sensation down my neck, so I nervously stuttered, "Oh, s...since I w...as about se...ven." I shrugged.

"Wow, You're like really good, you know," she commented as she pulled her hand free.

Blushing, I looked to the floor. I had never received so much attention from a girl before. "Thanks," I mumbled softly. "So do you go to school over here? You look too young to be out already." I sought more information about her.

"No, actually, Brook is my cousin, so she invited me, but I live in Hurley. It's a small town above..."

I interjected, "Yeah, I know where Hurley is. I live in Moss Point."

"Really? Hmmm...I'm going to be a senior this year. How 'bout yourself?" she quizzed.

"Junior."

"Well, I don't mind that you're a year younger than me." She placed her hand on my chest and smiled. "So when and where will you be playing again?"

I glanced at her hand as she traced her fingers over my heart and answered, "We'll be playing at a house in Mobile weekend after next."

"So you don't have anything going on next weekend?" She batted her eyes at me.

"Oh, um...no...I mean, I'll be in Gulf Shores throughout the week with my grandparents, but I should get home Friday night. Would you possibly be interested in going to dinner Saturday evening?"

A bright smile gleamed and flittered across her face. "I'd love it!" she exclaimed. "Here's my number." She pulled a pen from her purse, grabbed my right hand, and scribbled her number on the back of it.

"Okay, I've gotta get back up there, but I'll call you Saturday morning to make sure we're still on and get directions." My confidence wavered, so my statement came across as more of a question.

"I'll be waiting." She leaned in and kissed me on the cheek. That was a close encounter I could enjoy.

CHAPTER 13

SUMMER NIGHTS

My summer nights were set to be spent living it up in diverse ways. I planned to spend as many days as I could in Gulf Shores—summer evenings on the sandy shores are always fun. We already scheduled multiple nights jamming out, and now there was the possibility of spending evenings with a beautiful girl. Life was good.

My mom knew I joined a band, but she wasn't too keen on my staying out late on the weekends. She worried I would end up like Victor. I tried explaining to her I had no desire to do those sorts of things, but she wouldn't give in on an 11:30 curfew. In order to be able to play our shows, I had to deceive her and Andy, so I arranged to spend the night with Kevin on those weekends. With Kevin being four years older than I, Mom did not like the idea, but ironically I found a friend in my stepfather.

Because Kevin was Victor's childhood friend, Andy encouraged our friendship. It kept Kevin coming around the house, which made Andy feel better somehow. Andy convinced my mom I should be allowed to spend as much time as possible with him, persuading her that being around Kevin probably helped me to deal with Victor's death. In a way I think he understood on a level my mom didn't because it did help. For some reason Kevin's presence linked me to Victor. Andy recognized and felt the same link every time Kevin passed over the threshold of our home. Each time Kevin stretched his hand out for a shake, Andy yanked him into a tight hug and told him he loved him. Tears always inundated Andy's eyes.

Victor's death had changed Andy in many ways, but he remained unmoved on the issue of race. Fortunately my grandparents did not view friendships amongst diverse ethnic groups in the same manner as my stepdad. Early in the week when I had spoken to them, I asked if I could bring one of my friends along, so when I pulled out of the drive to head to Gulf Shores, I made a pit stop across the river in Escatawpa to pick up my friend Tramane.

My grandparents treated Tramane the way he deserved to be treated—as an equal. They enjoyed conversation with him almost as much as they did with me. Realizing I had grown up, they extended me freedom to stroll along the beaches for the majority of the day as well as the evenings, requiring we only spend a small portion of our day with them. That portion usually consisted of the three meals we ate daily.

Every night multiple people held parties on the beach, so there were plenty of opportunities to entertain the crowds with a few songs as we all gathered around the small fire that served as the center piece, drawing everyone to its entrancing flames. Unlike winter beach parties, this fire didn't serve the purpose of warming our chilled bones. The warm temperatures of June did that well enough without assistance. This bonfire served one purpose and one purpose only, to roast hotdogs and marshmallows meant to fill the bellies of those who swarmed around to watch the blue and yellow flames wrap around the object at the end of the stick. Where there was food, there were always people laughing and telling stories.

On our last night there we sat in the sand, with our bare feet within reach of the water as the waves rolled in, and gazed at the stars hanging over the surging Gulf of Mexico. Ripples of serenity rode the swelling waters to the shore. In this place no controversy could exist. "I may have a date Saturday night," I finally blurted out.

"Seriously, bro.? With who, might I ask?" Tramane questioned with a look of skepticism in his single, raised brow.

"Her name is Loraine. I met her at the gig last weekend in Gulfport."

"Yeah, right." He chuckled.

"Whadaya mean, yeah, right? You don't think I can get a date—with a pretty girl, I might add?" A grin broke out on my face.

"No, I think you can get a date; I just can't see you drivin' to Gulfport to pick her up. That's a long-distance relationship."

"She doesn't live in Gulfport. She lives in Hurley." I shook my head. "Besides Gulfport wouldn't be long distance if she did live there. Granted, the phone calls would be, but an hour is not that long of a drive."

"Oh, so you gonna date one of those hick girls?" He fell over on his side, laughing uncontrollably.

"Okay, Tray. She's not a country hick. She's actually quite beautiful." I splayed my fingers, dug them into the sand, and spattered his back.

Sitting back up, he brushed the moist sand from his back. "Okay, okay! Sorry, I just couldn't pass that one up, but seriously, so you okay with this Aralyn chick and Mason now?"

"Yeah, I guess I have to be. He's my friend, and he really seems to like her. Who knows, I may go out with Loraine and never give Aralyn another thought."

"I hope so 'cause girls coming between friends ain't right," he insisted.

My eyes popped open bright and early Saturday morning. I craned my neck and spied my composition notebook lying on my nightstand. Loraine's phone number stood out in bold black marker, scribbled across the front. I had transferred it there from my hand when I returned home from Kevin's the morning after meeting her. I rolled over and stared at the notebook for what seemed like an hour. My stomach twisted in a horrendous mass; calling a girl made me a nervous wreck, so I figured it was better to go ahead and face the giant known as fear right off the bat. I nestled my upper body in the pillows against my headboard, grabbed the notebook and phone, inhaled a sharp breath, and dialed.

"Hello," her voice croaked.

"May I speak to Loraine?"

"Ray?" Her voice perked up.

"Yeah, you still interested in grabbing dinner together?"

"Absolutely. I told you I had no intentions of backing out on our date."

I picked her up at five p.m. sharp at her home burrowed in the woods behind the middle school she had attended. I pulled out on Highway 614 and headed to Mobile. She filled the car with conversation that required little input from me. I was thankful for her bubbly personality, but I found the twirling of her fingers in my hair to be a distraction while driving. Soon after the highway morphed into Airport Boulevard, I pulled into the parking lot of a small Italian restaurant.

As soon as I opened the car door to let her out, she grabbed my hand, not letting go until absolutely necessary. It turned out to be necessary when the waiter seated us, and I had to have my hand back in order to sit in the booth across from her.

Her eyes glistened. "You don't want to sit over here by me?" She patted the spot next to her; an entrancing smile flitted across her delicate face in a flirty way. "There's plenty of room, you know." She pouted.

Pulling my thoughts together before speaking, I hesitated before giving my response. "Oh, I can...I just figured I'd be able to see you better from here." I didn't want to offend her in any way, shape, or form, but she came on a little strong, and I wasn't quite sure if I'd be able to actually eat my food with her grabbling all over me, so I thought about my response before blurting it out and figured a compliment would suffice. I sat impatiently on the edge of my seat waiting for her retort.

Finally her smile spread even farther across her face as she interpreted the meaning of my response to be my desire to gaze upon her beauty. "So, you want to be able to look at me? Does that mean you think I'm pretty?" She winked.

"Yes, I think you're very pretty." I smiled in return and quickly eyed the menu, engrossing myself in the scrumptious options in a scrutinizing manner. "I think I'll have the veal with gnocchi and carbonara sauce."

"What is a gnocchi? I've never heard of it, much less had it."

"Oh, they're delicious. It's a potato pasta. My grandpa makes 'em from scratch. That's where I get the Italian in me from. Try 'em. You'll love 'em, I promise." I assured her.

"Okay, I will." She sat up straight and tall, pleased with herself for trying something new and intriguing.

The waiter brought our meals, and we both dove in, enjoying every bite.

"This is so good, Ray. Wow, I'm glad you suggested it. So, did your grandpa teach you how to make 'em by chance?"

"He promised to pass the tradition on to me next summer when I drive out to Houston for a visit." I smiled down at my plate. It was difficult to look her continuously in the eyes. I was afraid she might find me out—that I had never been on a date before, that is.

"Oh, he lives in Texas? Do you go every year?"

"No, they bought into a condo in Gulf Shores a few years back, so they drive over here a few times a year, and I go spend a week with them there. That's where I was this past week...with my grandparents in Gulf Shores."

"But they're not coming next summer?"

"No, my grandmother had already scheduled the week for the condo, but she got a phone call from her baby sister; she's going to be in Houston that week for a business trip. She wanted to spend some time with her, so Grandma told me I could use the week at the condo and bring a friend or two if I promised to drive out to Houston for a week to spend with them."

"That's so neat. I've never been out of Mississippi, with the exception of driving to Mobile. I wanna see the world. I hate being cooped up in a small town. I know I'm from a small town, but I'm not really a small-town kind of girl. I spend a lot of time with my cousin Brook. You know, the girl having the birthday party?" She shook her head searching for my acknowledgment.

"Yeah, I remember. She's your cousin, huh?"

"Yep, I'm over that way a lot. That's where I wanna live, on the beach watching the waves roll in from the front porch of my gigantic house." Her eyes grew huge.

"I don't know. I kind of like the peacefulness of small towns. Don't get me wrong, city lights do attract, but I think when it comes to settling down, I'd rather be out in the woods somewhere."

Apparently my proclamation had taken her off guard as she took a sip of her Coca-Cola, and she choked out, "Uh, uh." She set her glass down on the table. "Hmm...well, I hope you're not looking to settle down any time soon."

"No, of course not. I have things I wanna do with my life before I settle down."

"Good." She grinned.

She appeared to be enjoying herself, and she seemed interested in me, but my own insecurities rang heavily on my mind. *This is nice. She keeps smiling, so surely she's interested in another date, but what if she's just a really nice girl, and she doesn't want to hurt my feelings, so she's only pretending to be into our conversation. I could just let this be a perfect date that ends perfectly without the worry of her turning me down by taking her home, giving her a kiss on the cheek, and never asking her out again,* I mused over the temptation to leave no room for future rejection. In the end a strange sensation shot through me and defeated my lack of confidence. I had never felt it before, but I was certain it had something to do with her beauty.

I stirred in my seat and tried uselessly to suppress my fascination. "So, the band is playing at a Fourth of July bash in Mobile next Saturday. Would you maybe like to come with me? I know you wouldn't know anyone, but I'd be able to talk to you during our breaks. If you'd rather not, I'd understand." I quickly threw in the last bit of information in fear she might say "no."

"Yeah, I'd love to. I don't care if I don't know anybody as long as you promise to spend time with me while you're on your breaks!" she squealed in excitement.

"Okay, great. I'll have to pick you up early though because I'll have to set up. Is three o'clock too early?"

"Nope, not at all."

Oddly we were *both* quiet during the drive back to her house. The silence flooding the vehicle had me on edge, so I reached for the radio knob and turned it to 97.5. They always played the top forty, and being unsure of her choice in music, I calculated it to be a safe bet. I turned onto her long drive, shifted into park, flipped off the headlights, and turned the ignition off.

My right hand fidgeted with the keys as I gripped the steering wheel with my left. Staring at the floorboard, I tilted my head in her direction. "Stay right there."

I dropped my hand from the wheel and opened the door. I sucked in a deep breath of confidence as I ambled to her door. The car door opened with a loud creak. She grasped my outstretched hand and pulled herself to my side. With interlocked hands we strolled to her front door. Squeezing her hand, I shifted to face her. "I had a great time tonight," I whispered.

She craned her head and gazed into my eyes. "Me too." She smiled.

Inhaling a sharp breath, I leaned in to kiss her gently on the cheek, but just as my lips grazed the side of her face, she turned into them with an intense kiss, my first kiss, and it was amazing. I drove home that night in a daze.

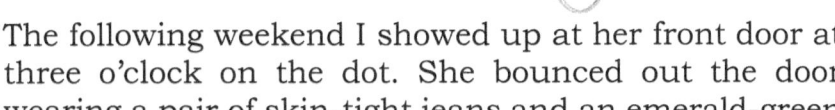

The following weekend I showed up at her front door at three o'clock on the dot. She bounced out the door wearing a pair of skin-tight jeans and an emerald-green sequin top.

"Okay, you've gotta come in and meet my dad," she insisted as she grabbed my hand and snapped the gum she chewed.

My face washed ashen with fear. I had never met a girl's dad before. Thoughts rushed through my mind faster than Flash Gordon. *Oh, no! How can I get outta this? What if he threatens to kill me if I ever hurt his daughter? What if he's a monstrous biker dude? What if he's not and he decides that he doesn't like me because of my long hair and he figures he'll save himself the trouble of doing it later, so he kills me now? Okay, if I walk through this door and see any form of weaponry,*

I'm outta here.

I took a deep breath and stepped over the threshold into the unknown. It felt as if I passed through to the twilight zone—a land where the next step you take could lead you on a frightening journey. Sweat popped up across my forehead as we rounded the corner and turned into the kitchen. I yanked my hand from hers and dropped it by my side. She recognized it immediately and smiled.

Her dad sat at a small desk shoved in the corner of the dining area. A large computer sat in front of him, and he was glued to the screen. "Daddy," she called.

"Just one second, dear," he begged as he finished up his task before turning to meet me. His glasses had slipped down his nose, so as he glanced up to look me in the eyes, he shoved them back to the bridge.

"Well, hello there. Ray, is it?"

I stepped forward, offered my hand, and responded, "Yes, sir; it's Ray. Nice to meet you, sir."

He cut his eyes toward his daughter. "Well, Loraine, I think I might like this one. He has manners. Not your usual pick."

"Daddy!" she cried, turning her mouth down in a pout.

"Oh, all right. She said you're playing in a band tonight and you'd have to tear down before bringing her home. What time do you expect to have my daughter home?"

"Yes, sir, I am, but I've already talked to the guys; they're gonna tear down without me tonight. We're scheduled to play 'til 11:30, so she should be home no later than 12:30."

"Sounds good. All right, you two behave, and you," he pointed to me, "drive carefully. Mobile is full of crazy drivers."

"Yes, sir, I will."

As soon as we pulled out of her drive, Loraine

turned to me. "Ray, when we get to the end of the main road, take a right, and will you pull into the Jiffy Burger, please? I'm starving'."

"Yeah, sure. Not a problem." She obviously wasn't one of those girls who were afraid to eat in front of a guy.

We pulled up to the window of the small burger joint and ordered her a burger, fries, and a Coke. She occupied the empty space in the car with chatter all the way to the house in Mobile. She filled me in on how she didn't have a great track record when it came to dating and how she usually picked bum guys. Which in turn, she explained, is why her dad responded in the manner he did toward my politeness.

Once at the venue, Loraine pounced to the ground and scuttled around to the trunk to meet me. She grasped a microphone stand and pulled it from the back of the car. "I got this," I insisted. Pointing to the courtyard, I added, "There's a bunk of folding chairs over there. Go. Sit. Relax. I can handle all this."

"I'm no weakling." She winked. "Besides, I wanna help."

I gave in with a sigh and made certain she carried only light weight items. The day started off without a hitch. Because of her assistance I finished setting up a little early, so we had a few moments to walk around the area and talk. Excitement bubbled from her as we strolled, hand in hand, around the grounds—being in her presence made me feel good. Her enthusiasm seemed to be rubbing off on me. I found myself laughing and joking around. It felt amazing.

Time slipped by, and I had to leave her amongst a group of older guys searching for a girl to spend the night with. I didn't like that feeling; it stirred something within me. Fueled by jealousy, my confidence rose. In front of everyone, I pulled her into my arms, brushed her hair away from her face, and pressed my lips hard against hers in a passionate kiss.

I kept a watchful eye on her while we played. When I stepped off the stage for our first break, she approached me with two beers in her hands. Handing one of them to me, she giggled. "I'm having an amazing time here. These people are really nice. They didn't even ask me how old I was when I asked for the beers."

I graciously accepted her offering, but inside I battled. I had not taken a single drink since Victor's death. Kevin had already resorted to drinking and even fooling around with a few drugs, but I had kept a firm hold on my resolve not to do any of it, but that night I gave in. There was something about her bubbly presence I didn't want to upset. After a couple of beers during breaks, I loosened up and relaxed a little around her. I found myself laughing throughout the night. I honestly enjoyed being with her.

When the night rolled to an end, as I told the guys thanks and bye, I noticed her pull something out of her purse and walk around to the other side of the car in a secretive way. Curious, I followed along behind her fearful of what it might be. Knowing some of my friends fooled around with drugs was upsetting enough, but the idea she may have a habit such as that was more than I could handle.

Just as I approached, she spit something from her mouth. "Whaddaya doing? What was that?" I asked, my tone clearly vexed.

"Hmmm?" She spun around to face me sporting a bright smile and boldly displaying a small bottle of scope. "Just making myself minty fresh."

"Whew, scared me there for a minute. I didn't know whatcha were up to."

"Well, I figured you wouldn't want to take me home to my dad with beer breath." She smiled.

I chuckled, "Ha, you're right." I squinted. "Especially considering that you, my dear, are the one who got it for yourself and tempted me with the same. I would hate to have to tell your daddy that you were a bad influence on me." I grinned.

Her mouth dropped open. "You wouldn't!"

"Hmmm..." I raised my brows playfully and folded my arms across my chest.

She dropped the bottle back inside her purse, threw it in the car, and stepped toward me, definitely crossing the boundary of personal space. She stretched her neck to peer directly into my eyes, wrapped her arms around my neck, drew her face within inches of my own, and whispered, "I could just tell him that you are a bad influence on me. Whatcha think about that?"

Without giving me an opportunity to answer, she gently pressed her lips against mine. I inhaled the sweetness of the aroma rolling off her soft skin. It intermingled with her minty breath. Swirling around her, the two fragrances combined. To relish the moment, I closed my eyes and breathed it all in again, but this time the two scents merged with another appealing, flowery smell lingering around her hair. The mixture of them all danced around my head causing an overwhelming sensation and desire.

Not wanting to be *that guy*, the one who takes advantage of a girl to fulfill his own fleshly cravings, I pulled myself away. "Maybe you could tell him I'm a good influence on you."

She dropped her arms and slumped her shoulders. "Yeah, you are actually. You're the nicest guy I've ever been on a date with."

"That's nice to know. So, you ready to head back to your place?"

"Not really, but I suppose if I'm ever to go out with you again, you'll have to get me home on time." She laughed.

When I pulled in her drive, I shut the car off and strode to her door, opening it for her. Walking her to the front door, I asked, "So, next weekend I don't have to

151

play anywhere. Would you be interested in another date?"

"Would love it. Where to?"

"Oh, I was thinking something magic." I grinned.

She smiled, leaned in, and kissed me. "Goodnight, Ray."

"Goodnight."

CHAPTER 14

MAGIC

Not wanting to seem too eager, I waited until Monday to call Loraine.

"Hello," her father said.

"Good afternoon, Mr. Hartford, may I speak to Loraine?" My voice shook slightly.

"Hold on just a moment, Ray, and I'll see if she's in her room." The phone clanked as he set the receiver down on something hard.

A few moments later I heard a muffled shrill in the back ground arguing with a deeper voice. When she answered the phone, her voice rang like a sweet melody. "Hello."

If I hadn't just heard the harshness in her tone only moments before, I would have sworn by the gentleness of her timbre she was an angel floating amongst the clouds. "Hey, what's up?"

"Oh, nothing, just arguing with my dad; that's all."

"What are y'all arguing about?"

"Oh, he was messing with me about your call."

"Hmm...Why? Does he not like me or something? I thought he did."

"No, he likes you just fine. He was just picking on me; that's all. I don't really wanna talk about it, okay?" she insisted.

"Okay," I quickly complied.

"So, what are you up to?" She swiftly changed the

subject.

"Well, I was just thinking maybe we could do a double date this weekend. The magic I had in mind is a lot more fun with another couple involved."

She sat silently for a moment, and when she responded, reluctance lingered in her voice. "Oh, yeah, I suppose. Who did you have in mind?"

"Well, I thought about asking my friend Tray. He likes this girl at school named Raquel. I figured it'd be easier for him to ask her out if it was a double date, so I thought I'd help him out."

"Oh, sure. Anything to help a friend out with a girl."

Our conversation continued for another thirty minutes with her chatter filling my silence. She went on about her boring Sunday, briefly mentioning she had waited inside for my call which never came. She seemed a little miffed with me about that because she had apparently missed out on an enjoyable horse ride with her mom. I apologized and explained I didn't want to seem too overbearing. She accepted my apology and insisted I call early the next morning because she planned to spend her afternoon shopping. I called Tramane and told him my plans for the weekend and suggested he invite Raquel to join us.

Early Saturday morning I called Loraine and told her to be sure and dress casually. When I pulled up in her drive, she came charging out wearing a pair of shorts and a halter top. She had her auburn hair pulled in a ponytail. She bounced in the car. "So, where ya takin' me?" she giggled.

"Um...shouldn't I have come to your door?" I hesitated.

"Nope, Daddy's not home," she insisted.

"What about your mom? I haven't met her yet."

"You wanna meet my mom?"

"Of course. You don't want me to?" I lowered my brow wondering if she was ashamed of me or something.

"Oh, no, I don't mind, but you'll have to drive through there." She pointed to a gate in the back. "She's in the barn with the horses."

"Ah, the horses. I didn't realize you had horses when you said you missed out on a horse ride."

"Yep. Well, actually they're Mom's. She loves 'em more than she does me, I think."

"Will she feel we've bothered her?" I questioned.

"Oh, no, she'll be pleased. No other guy has ever asked to meet her. Go ahead, drive on back."

I backed up and pulled onto the small, worn-out path through the side of her yard that led to the old, tattered barn; it needed a lot of work. I drove past the gate and pulled in front of the faded red building. When the roar of the engine cut off, a tiny woman stepped out from the shadows of the stables with her hand raised above her brow, blocking the evening sunlight. Loraine inherited her beauty from her mother. She bore the same flaming hair and sparkling eyes, but her mother's natural skin revealed hundreds of freckles. I had never noticed freckles on Loraine. I wondered if she had them hidden beneath her make-up.

I stepped out of the car to meet the woman wearing an old pair of jeans, boots, and a button-up plaid shirt. She brushed her hand across her dirt-smudged face and flattened the stray hairs blowing in the light breeze against her head. She grinned and propped her hand on her hip. "Well, hello there, Ray. I've heard lots about you. It's nice to meet you."

"Nice to meet you too, ma'am."

She stuck her hand out to shake mine. "Lynnie."

"Ms. Lynnie," I acknowledged as I took her hand in mine for a firm shake.

"So, where ya takin' my girl?"

I glanced back at Loraine, still seated in the car. "She doesn't know yet, but I was planning to take her to Biloxi to Magic Golf across the highway from the beach. I figured we could play a round of goofy golf and maybe race each other in the go-carts."

"Sounds like you two will have a great time. What time can I expect her home?"

"What time do you want her home?"

"Let's say midnight. How's that sound to you?"

"She'll be here; I give you my word," I insisted.

"Drive careful, Ray, and it was real nice meetin' ya."

"You too, Ms. Lynnie."

I walked back to the car, climbed in, cranked her up, and drove out to the main road. "Your mom seems nice. You look like her."

"Yeah, I know. I hate it."

"Tsk." I shook my head. "What? Are you crazy? You're beautiful, Loraine."

"Only because I cover my freckles with Clinique continuous coverage," she mumbled.

"I don't know what that is, but I don't think you need to cover anything."

She smiled. "You're too sweet, Ray. So, you don't mind freckles? Even a lot of them?"

"Nope, not at all. Your mom obviously wasn't wearing any clinake cover stuff, whatever you called it, and she's pretty."

"I'm not like my mom in that respect for sure. She's a pure country girl. She never wears make-up, and she lives to tend to her animals, especially her horses. I don't think I've ever seen her in anything but jeans."

A few moments of silence passed; then she reverted back to her original question. "So, you still haven't answered my question. Where are you taking me?"

Well, we're going to Tramane's house in Escatawpa; then we're going to Raquel's house in Moss Point; then we're going to some place magic." I grinned.

I relished in her response to my teasing as she threw her arms around me, causing me to swerve, and begged, "Please, please, please, please tell me."

"Nope, I'm thinking of making you keep your eyes closed for the entire drive." I laughed.

"It's not funny, Ray." She jutted her bottom lip out in a pout and folded her arms across her chest with a huff as she slouched back in her seat. "I'm used to getting my way."

"Not today you're not," I assured her.

"Okay, I give in." She dropped her arms and kicked her feet up on the dash. She arched her neck to glance at me. "I thought you said your friend's name was Tray?"

"Tray is short for Tramane."

We pulled in Tramane's drive. I knew Ms. Aretha wouldn't allow me to drive off without giving her a hug, so I climbed out of the car, walked around to Loraine's side, and opened the door. "Come on, I want you to meet Ms. Aretha."

Her expression was slightly apprehensive. "Oh, okay." She held her hand out for me to take. Holding her hand, I escorted her to the front door.

Ms. Aretha came to the door looking rather poorly. "Well, hello there my precious Ray," she greeted me.

"Hey, Ms. Aretha. How are you feeling?"

"Not so well today, son. Doc say it ain't looking so good." She glanced to my right. "Well, my, my, my, what have we here? Who's this beautiful little lady you's got with ya?" She reached out and pulled Loraine into a tight hug.

"Ms. Aretha, this is Loraine," I introduced her.

"So, you his new girl I been hearin' 'bout?" She chuckled.

157

Loraine's face lit up, and she glanced my way. "I hope so."

"Well, any friend o' Ray's is a friend o' mine. You two come on in. Tramane'll be ready in jus a minute. He back there tryin' to get all lookin' good for Raquel. You shoulda seen him the minute she said she'd go. He's jumpin' round this house like a mad man." She laughed.

"So, are you gonna have to go back to New Orleans for treatment, Ms. Aretha?" I pried out of concern for her wellbeing.

"It's lookin' thata way, son. I ain't told Tramane though. He's gonna be upset to leave again." She shook her head.

"He cares more about you than where he's livin', Ms. Aretha."

"I know, I know." Heavy footsteps came burling down the hallway. "Well, speak of the devil. Look at how handsome my boy looks. Y'all have yourselves a good time tonight."

"We will," Tramane spoke up, a bright smile spread across his face.

"I'll have him home around eleven. I have to have her home by midnight, and she lives in Hurley, so I wanna make sure we're not late."

"All right." She kissed us both on the cheek and gave Loraine another hug before sending us on our way.

We picked Raquel up, drove down to Pascagoula, hit Highway 90, and headed west toward Biloxi. I drove slowly once we hit the beach, and we admired the red, orange, and yellow hues of the sunset across the water, a beautifully painted picture that brought inspiration for a new song.

"Sunset Boulevard"

Beaches so white, water so blue
And here I am sittin' next to you.

158

We drive down the street
Watchin' the crowds hit the beach;
They all gather around
Because when the sun goes down,

It's Sunset Boulevard
Where the party never ends.
Sunset Boulevard
Where the night life begins
On Sunset Boulevard
I hear it calling my name
Sunset Boulevard
Where life is one big game
On Sunset Boulevard.
As the sky turns orange and red,
It's time to rise up out of bed,
Grab my guitar in my hand,
And gather up the band.
Give a girl a call
And ask if she'll watch the sun fall

On Sunset Boulevard
Where the party never ends.
Sunset Boulevard
Where the night life begins
On Sunset Boulevard.
I hear it calling my name
Sunset Boulevard
Where life is one big game
On Sunset Boulevard, Sunset Boulevard.

Beaches so white, water so blue
And here I am sittin' next to you
On Sunset Boulevard, Sunset Boulevard
Sunset Boulevard.

Ray Winstrom

I turned into the parking lot of Cucos on the beach in Biloxi, and we all piled out of my small car. Our waiter led us to a corner booth. The evening was spent laughing and joking around, getting to know one another better. I glanced across the table just as Raquel blushed and smiled up at Tray. Happiness swelled in me for him. She seemed to enjoy his company, and I was pleased to see Loraine didn't seem to have a problem with their skin color. I had been slightly concerned about that because I knew there weren't many Blacks in the Hurley area, as well as the fact that her face clearly expressed trepidation when I mentioned his name being Tramane. My concern turned out to be unwarranted as I watched the two girls lean across the table to one another, giggling. I wasn't sure what they were laughing about, but I was fairly certain it had to do with Tramane and me.

We finished dinner and drove down the street to Magic Golf.

"Goofy Golf?" Loraine asked with a grin.

I smiled, "Yep, goofy golf."

"Now I know why you said it would be more fun with another couple. I have to admit, I was kinda worried maybe you just didn't want to be alone with me again."

She took me off guard with that proclamation, and I sat there with my hand on the keys still in the ignition. Tramane grunted, "We're gonna go check out the prices, okay, dude." He excused himself and Raquel.

"Yeah, sure," I answered. They slide out of the back seat and walked hand in hand to the small building.

Finally turning to face her, I whispered, "I'm really sorry if I made you think that. I had no idea you would take it that way. I just thought I'd surprise you with a fun night out, other than a party I was playing at."

"Don't worry about it, Ray. I'm a little neurotic sometimes. I haven't had the best of luck with guys, you know. I was like in love with this guy William. I called him Willie. I really thought we were in love, and after giving him eight months of my life, he decided to call it off. He just dropped me like a hot potato. Said he wasn't *into me* anymore. I haven't ever really gotten over that." She paused briefly and looked to the floor board. "Ray, I'm sorry. I probably shouldn't be sayin' all of this right now, but I felt I needed to be honest with you. Willie was instantly *into* another girl, and it left me a little insecure and crazy jealous, so you should know, I'm probably not gonna like any females you're friends with, and I'm probably gonna think things like what I thought about you not wanting to be alone with me. I know you haven't even asked me to be your girlfriend or anything, so I'm being a little crazy about all this, but I really like you. You're the sweetest guy I've ever met." She blew out a heavy breath filled with the worry she'd been carrying.

"Wow, that was a lot of information, Loraine. Thanks, I mean, for the sweetest guy part. I'm sorry you went through that. I really am." I stopped to process the overwhelming thoughts invading my mind. I liked her, and I knew I hadn't asked her specifically to be my girlfriend. I had never been on a date until two weekends prior, so I wasn't sure what was considered to be the proper amount of time dating a girl before you asked her to be yours and have her promise not to date anyone else and give your promise to do the same. "Loraine, I really like you a lot, but we only met three weeks ago, so I wasn't really sure if it would be too soon to ask you to be my girlfriend or not. I'm kinda new at all this," I explained.

"Whaddya mean new at this? You've had other girlfriends, haven't you?"

"No, I haven't. Does that bother you?" Feeling an odd sense of shame, I hung my head.

"No, that doesn't bother me at all. I just wouldn't have known it from your kiss, is all. I figured you, being so good looking and being in a rock band, would have had lots of girlfriends."

I tried to hide the embarrassing blush I felt coming on by turning away. I peered out the front windshield looking toward the open water. When I felt composed enough to face her again, I turned back around. "So, are you interested in being my girlfriend?" I held my breath.

"Are you asking?" She gazed directly into my eyes as if searching for something.

"Yes, I am." I stared back into hers.

"Then, yes. I'm interested." She grabbed my hand.

I smiled. "We better get out there. They're gonna think we've abandoned them for the night."

We got out and joined Tramane and Raquel. The girls wrapped their arms together and skipped off to the first hole. I couldn't hear what they were saying, but I could clearly hear their giggles echoing through the warm night air.

Tramane stopped me. "So, you think she likes me? She's so hot. Did you see the way she slipped her hand in mine when we got outta the car?"

I laughed. "Yeah, man, I did, and I think that's pretty strong affirmation she likes you, dude."

"Thanks for invitin' us. I'd probably never gotten up the nerve to ask her out on a single date."

"I know what ya mean. If Loraine hadn't made the first move, I'd never asked her out. I'd thought she was too pretty to ever be interested in me."

"Yeah, she is." He shoved me and cracked a laugh.

"All right, I hear ya." I chuckled back as I caught my balance. A slight shove from the jolly green giant could send a guy flying.

The end of the night came all too quickly. Before I knew it, we had dropped both Raquel and Tramane off at their homes and were heading up to Hurley on the dark, unlit highway. Loraine scooted over as far as she could, reached up to the steering wheel, grabbed my hand, and intertwined it with hers. We pulled in her drive, and I parked the car. She leaned in and kissed me. "Thank you for a magical night," she whispered.

CHAPTER 15

RUNAWAY

We played gigs over the following two weekends. Loraine insisted she didn't mind tagging along. Mason and Aralyn showed up to both events but stayed in amongst his group of jock friends. I only briefly spoke to them and introduced them both to Loraine.

Before I knew it, summer break sneaked to an end. I hated to see it slip by and fade into a distant memory. I had had great, magical summer nights, but all good things must come to an end, or so I had heard. Like a runaway my summer vacation packed her bags in secret, preparing to steal away unexpectedly.

The first weekend of August brought with it reminders of school being just around the corner. My mother, anxious to meet Loraine, arranged a day on the town for us all. She insisted the following Saturday had to be spent at the Singing River Mall shopping for school clothes, and she promised we'd top it off with a chili-cheese burger from Edd's in Pascagoula. We both conceded to her planned-out day: her way to get to know Loraine.

We spent several hours searching through the racks in the stores. Loraine found several shirts for me that she liked and a few pair of jeans she insisted would look good on me. I hung in as long as I possibly could while, store after store, they riffled through stacks and racks of clothing. I moseyed over to a bench in the footwear department and plopped myself down. Shopping with women was not exactly my idea of a fun day. Me? I'd walk in, pick out a few items I liked, check out, and leave; unfortunately, I learned an undesirable truth about females that day; that's *not* the way they shopped—they chitter-chattered while they rummaged through piles of clothes. Occasionally they'd get so caught up in conversation that they'd stop shopping all together while they widened their eyes and dropped their mouths open in amazement over something the other had said.

"We're done. Ready for Edds?" Mom asked.

Finally, I thought. I wasn't positive if they were satisfied in their choices and felt their task was complete, or if it was the fact lunch had long passed, and they were famished. I suspected it was the latter. As for me, the succulent scent of pizza baking at Giovanni's prompted the churning of hunger pangs. The mouth-watering lusciousness of those chili-cheese burgers was losing its hold on me.

Mom's words were like the sweet sounds of heavenly music in my ears. "Yes, I'm starvin'."

Driving into Pascagoula, we caught the draw bridge just as it began its journey up, so traffic was congested as we entered the city famous for its crazy church-going squirrel. Spotting the huge ice cream cone above the small white building, my stomach growled. Mom pulled up on the side of the drive-in and sent me and Loraine to the window with her order. As we stood in line, Loraine grabbed one of the poles supporting the metal awning and twirled around it.

The employee hollered, "Next." So I stepped up to put in my order.

"One double chili-cheese burger, two regular chili-cheese burgers, three small fries, and three chocolate shakes."

Without writing a word I had said down, the lady
165

dressed in white calculated my tab (without a calculator) and put in my order. We all devoured our chili-cheese burgers and finished them off with the delicious chocolate shakes. Big cities may have had hundreds of fast-food chains, but Pascagoula had Edd's. People drove from all the surrounding towns to the little white building to stand out front waiting for the opportunity to put in an order for their famous chili-cheese burgers. It was a treat for all.

Mom released us to enjoy the evening alone, so we drove up and down Market Street with the rest of teen-age society, pulling in at various shops to meet up with friends and find out what party might be going on. Nights on Market Street were never dull. It was full of partying and an occasional fight over a pretty girl. There were no parties to be found that night, but that was fine with me. I spent plenty of time at them playing my guitar. I enjoyed an occasional night out just to hang with some of the acquaintances I had made over the years. Of course, we were sure to see a couple of those acquaintances attempt to enter the likes of Thunder's Tavern, only to be kicked to the curb for being underage. There was an occasional teenager who had a friend in a bouncer; they were the ones who made their way past the entrance into the darkness of the popular adult hangout.

The band had a gig set up the following weekend. Blade had met a guy named Wyn at the Biloxi party we had just played, and he was having an end-of-the-summer blow out, as he called it. Bound for his senior year in college, he desired to party it up before having to buckle down for the year. As usual I picked up Loraine and headed for his Biloxi home. We pulled up at the large two-story home, and Loraine was gracious enough to help me with the lighter-weight equipment she could handle.

We set up, and the party began. Loraine sulked at her boredom while I played. She huddled in a corner and crossed her arms over her chest. I eyed her as she slipped off with a huff and ambled to the kitchen area. She bounced back in the room with a beer in her hand and a smile on her face. We were just about to take a breather when I spied Mason and Aralyn squeezing through the horde of people gathered in the den where we were set up. He tugged her along behind him, weaving through the crowd of bodies; an air about her suggested sadness much more than usual. Granted, I had only been around her a few times, so I didn't know her well enough to assess whether or not she was happy or sad, but she usually smiled several times throughout the night, even though I always sensed a sadness lurking beneath the surface of her smiles; however, on that particular night, an unmistakable aura engulfed her. She looked as if she had been let down big, and for some odd reason my heart ached for her.

Our last song for that set ended; I placed my guitar in its stand and made my way toward Loraine, but before I could get there, a girl I knew to be Jennifer bebopped her way right in front of me, threw her arms around me, and kissed me. Shocked, I gently pushed her away. "Whoa there, Jennifer, I have a girlfriend, and she's right over—" I peered across the room to point in Loraine's direction and saw her shoving her way through the mob of people. She rammed into Mason, jostling him back into Aralyn, causing her wine cooler to slip from her hand and shatter on the floor.

Mason twisted around in protective mode to see if she was all right. "You okay? Sorry 'bout that. Ray's little girlfriend should be out on the football field. She's a strong little thing." He chuckled.

"Looks to me she's a mad little thing," Aralyn responded.

Loraine ran away, and I immediately chased after her. As I passed Mason, he threw his arm out to catch me. "What in the world did you do to her?" he asked.

Catching my balance, I spit, "Nothing, man. Some girl just jumped in front of me and kissed me. I pushed her away, but I guess Loraine must've took off before seeing that part."

"Go catch your little runaway," Mason encouraged. "I'm sure it'll be okay. She should know by now you're the guy who would never do something like that to anyone."

"I hope so." My forehead crinkled in worry.

Aralyn stretched out her hand, laid it on my arm, and whispered, "I'm positive she'll believe you."

A strange sensation took place in my body at that moment, and I was all too eager to run off and leave her presence. Whatever attraction I had felt for her that first night had left some sort of residual effect to her touch. I had been fine seeing her at a few parties throughout the summer, but when she touched me, something happened, and that was something I resolved to fight to the end. She was my friend's girlfriend, and I had a girlfriend whom I cared about and was determined not to lose.

I searched all throughout the yard to no avail, and before I knew it, Blade's voice echoed my name over the microphone. I had no choice but to give up my search and begin anew during our next break. I reluctantly went back inside to the party, grabbed my guitar, and gave Blade a stern look. He simply shrugged his shoulders. From the mass of people, Mason questioned me with his eyes to see if all was well. I shook my head *no*.

My eyes skimmed over the crowd, searching for Loraine. As I scanned the room, my eyes fell upon Aralyn. She guzzled her drink. I nodded my head with a sigh, dropped my eyes to my guitar, and played the solo of our very own song. Each time I searched for Loraine, my eyes were drawn to Aralyn's face, and I watched as she downed one after the other. I had never seen her consume so much. As a matter of fact, I had only seen her drink one or two wine coolers, but she went through them rather quickly, and gloominess draped around her like a dark shroud. I didn't understand why I could see these things about her, and I was seriously wishing that intuition would go away.

The songs moved in slow motion as I impatiently waited for our break to arrive, anxious to finish my search and resolve the issue. As we started the last song of the set, Aralyn stumbled into Mason and looked up at him. She looked as if she was going to be sick. Mason slipped his arm under hers and supported her weight as they left the room.

As soon as the words *All right* slipped through Blade's lips, I shoved my guitar into its stand and charged through the mass of people. A few of them tried to stop me and engage in conversation, but my sights were set on the staircase by the front door. I had explored every blade of grass outside but had forgotten to check out the second story of the house.

I skirted around Jennifer and stopped at Wyn. "Hey, Wyn, do you know if anyone is upstairs or not?"

"Yeah, dude, but there's a few empty rooms, I'm sure. Go on up. I don't mind."

Running all the way to the top, I took a deep breath and looked down the hall at all of the closed doors. I would have to knock on them to see if they were occupied or not. I could only hope she would answer if she sat behind one of them. I knocked on the first door and was greeted with a harsh holler. I leaned in close to the next door. "Loraine, you in there," I whispered.

Then I heard a familiar voice, "I don't want to remember my first time as being drunk at a party. I want it to be with the person I'm going to spend the rest

169

of my life with." Aralyn's speech was slightly slurred. She was obviously drunk and still able to say *no*.

"But, Aralyn, I love you. It's not like it wouldn't be special." Mason did his best to convince her.

"I love you too, but *no*," her voice rang loud and clear. Pride welled up inside of me. Despite being drunk and being in love, she had a strong resolve.

Not wanting to invade their privacy, I swiftly pulled away from the door and moved on to the next one. I dropped my head and sighed in defeat as I approached the last room on the opposite side of the hall. I hammered my fist on the door.

"Please go away," she sniffled.

"Loraine, it's Ray. Can I come in?"

"No, you kissed that girl."

"Loraine, I didn't kiss her, I swear. Please let me in so I can explain," I begged.

I heard her scuffle through the room and place her hand on the doorknob. "Please, Loraine."

There was a slight turn of the knob, and then she stood before me with tear-filled eyes. "I know what I saw, Ray."

"Yeah, you saw a kiss, but what you saw was her kissing me. I know of her through Blade, but seriously, Loraine, I didn't even realize she was there until her arms were around me and she was kissing me. I didn't kiss her back, and I pushed her away, but I guess you took off before you could see that," I explained.

She glanced at the floor. "Seriously you didn't kiss her back? And you pushed her away?"

"I swear to you I did. I would never do something like that to you."

"It just shocked me so much when I saw it; I was gone before I even realized what I was doing."

"Shocked you? Huh, I've *never* had anything like that happen in my life until a little while ago, and I went to tell her I had a girlfriend and saw you leaving. I

170

searched all over outside for you until Blade called me back up."

"Yeah, I heard him call for you. I just figured you were off making out with her. She's so much prettier than me."

"Are you crazy? No, she's not, and I swear I was looking for you. I couldn't wait to finish that last set so I could find you."

"Really?"

I leaned in toward her with a kiss and whispered, "Really."

She wrapped her arms firmly around me and kissed me back. "I hate to have to break away from this, but I'm fixin' to have to get back down stairs."

She let me loose and replied, "I know. Do I have time to go to the bathroom and freshen up before we go down?"

"Yeah, I'm sure there's a bathroom up here somewhere, but it's not on the other side of the hall for sure. I've already knocked on all those doors trying to find you." I smiled.

We left the seclusion of the bedroom and found the bathroom directly across from the staircase. After Loraine freshened up and rejoined me, we sauntered downstairs hand in hand. As we passed Jennifer, Loraine cut eyes at her like nothing I had ever seen before. It looked as if a tigress lay hidden beneath her tiny frame, and she prepared to pounce on her and rip out her jugular! Darting at lightning speed behind Wyn, Jennifer nimbly removed herself from view and accessibility. She secured her arm in his, and he welcomed her.

While we played the next set, I eyed Mason pace across the room and join Wyn's group. Jennifer, the flirtatious girl who planned to leave with someone that night, stood in between Wyn and Mason, her right arm secured around Wyn's. My mouth dropped at her cunning and sly ways when I caught a glimpse of her running her left hand up and down Mason's arm without Wyn's knowledge. Mason tilted his head, glanced down at her, smiled a half smile, and began talking to her. With a clenched jaw, I narrowed my eyes and searched the room for Aralyn.

When our set ended, I shoved my guitar in its stand with a clank. Blade, his eyes ablaze, shot past me and joined the small group huddled on the other side of the room. CJ nudged Wyn and Mason. He pulled out a small bag of cocaine as they hemmed in closer around the small lamp stand nestled in the corner; he separated a few lines for them on the glass top. Disgusted Blade would participate, bile rose in my throat and my face contorted in an angry glower. Victor was his friend, and he watched him die. How could he? I grabbed Loraine's hand, pulling her behind me as I angrily strode away from them, and secured us a seat on the other side of the room. I plopped down with a huff.

She sat down on my lap and asked, "What's wrong, Ray?"

"Nothing." I lied.

"Don't lie to me, Ray Winstrom. What's wrong?"

"Blade and Mason are over there snortin' coke. I don't like it at all." I sighed.

"You've never done it?"

"No," I answered swiftly. I jerked my head to look her in the eyes. "Have you?"

Her head dropped in shame. "Yeah, with Willie. He liked to party a lot."

Overwhelming disappointment in her washed over me, pushing the bile that had risen into my mouth. I swallowed hard against the saliva filling my mouth. Deep inside I knew I couldn't hold something from her past against her. I had participated in my share of things as well, and I would have done it that night all those years ago had Victor allowed me. I wanted to fit in with them, so I understood the pressure she might have felt with her boyfriend being the one she wanted to fit in with.

After a few moments of silence, she finally blurted out, "You're not like gonna break up with me over that, are you?"

I gazed in her worried eyes. "No," I assured her. "I'm just a little shocked is all. I guess I never thought of you doing anything like that. You seem so innocent."

"I'm far from innocent, Ray. You're just a gentleman is all, but I'm glad. I feel safe with you." She smiled and caressed the side of my face before leaning in and kissing me gently.

A loud roar of laughter broke out from amongst the coke-snorting circle. I heard Mason's laugh echo above all the others. My eyes shot in his direction just as he craned his head to check out Jennifer's perfectly shaped body; then from the corner of my eye, I saw Aralyn enter the den and freeze in place. Her mouth dropped open, and her eyes widened. Outside of those movements, her body remained as still as a statue. She was obviously trying to process what she was seeing. From her angle it wasn't possible to see Mason and Jennifer flirting back and forth. All she had seen was he had just inhaled something. Blade looked up and saw her standing in disbelief at what her eyes were taking in. He elbowed Mason. Mason turned his gaze upon her, and she took off—another runaway.

Without a second thought he jolted to life and went after her. Jennifer just simply turned her attention back to Wyn. I heard Mason hollering her name in search of her.

"Tonight's full of runaways, isn't it?" Loraine laughed. "Maybe you should go fill him in on the upstairs tip," she suggested.

Not wanting to admit to her I already knew they

173

had been upstairs once, I complied. "All right, I'll go tell him to look upstairs before he gives up."

"I'll be right here waiting for you when you get back," she promised with a smile.

When I stepped outside, Mason visibly shook. Fidgeting, he paced toward me. "I can't find her, man. I think I may have really screwed this up."

"I knew you fooled around with some light stuff, but I didn't know you messed around with the hard stuff. You probably should've filled her in on that."

He ran his hand through his hair in frustration. "I didn't want her to know. I thought she was passed out upstairs. She's so pure. I mean, my goodness, she'll drink a few wine coolers and that's it. Tonight was like freaky. I've never seen her drink so many. Something was botherin' her or somethin'"

"So, what was going on with Jennifer over there?"

He yanked his head toward me and confessed, "I...I was frustrated. I've been seeing Aralyn for a couple of months now, and she's so smart and good and well, she's innocent. I really like that about her, but it gets frustrating at times. I took her upstairs to lie down because she got sick feeling. Jennifer made it clear she would've slept with me. I'm horrible, ain't I? I don't deserve a girl like Aralyn."

I didn't know what to say to that. In my heart I didn't believe he was good enough for someone like her, but he was my friend; I couldn't tell him that. "Look, you'll find her, and if you really do care about her, you'll get your act together and treat her the way she deserves to be treated. Answer this question for me. Are sex and drugs worth losing her over?"

"No, they're not."

"Then go find her. I'm sure she'll forgive you, man."

"Thanks."

With a pat on the back, I sent him on his way. It wasn't long before he found her balled up on the ground

174

behind his red firebird. When they returned to the party, I was finishing up my last set. With a smile on his face and his arm draped over her shoulder, he pulled her close to his side. We caught two of the runaways in our midst, but the summer vacation that had packed itself up (ready to steal away) handed over a goodbye letter dated for the nineteenth of August, the first day of school, and there was no catching that runaway.

CHAPTER 16

MIDNIGHT MADNESS

The nineteenth landed upon us all. Although summer vacation had slipped right through our fingers, she left us a staunch reminder of her presence—a heat wave, so we all reluctantly headed back to school while we daydreamed of summer days on the beaches watching the waves crash to the shore.

I pulled up to the school, parked my car, and looked to the empty seat next to me. While it would have been nice having Loraine go to my school and see her sitting there, it wasn't her absence that bothered me. It was that of Tramane's. His grandmother's doctor had sent her back to New Orleans for treatment just two days before school began, so I was without my best friend. Apparently Tramane's mother had finally settled down and lived on the outskirts of the city. She offered for them to permanently live with her while her mother went through her treatment. The doctors didn't seem to think she would pull through, but she determined never to give up. Despite her resolve to survive and beat cancer, she knew she had to plan for the worst because she had her grandson to take care of, so she agreed to live with her daughter and give Tramane a home and a chance to get to know the mother he never had growing up. They packed up and left quickly, with no plans to return. They put their house up for sale, and I agreed to keep up the yard until it sold.

I mingled with the crowd in the Atrium of the building and found my name written on a list giving me my homeroom teacher. The powers that be stuck me in building A with the likes of Mr. Broxson, the government and economics teacher. He was known for his military strictness, and I had been forewarned of his harassments of guys like me (the ones who didn't fit his profile of a good, decent, honorable guy). I was thankful I only had him for fifteen minutes at the beginning of the day.

He marched through the room handing out our schedules. I stretched my hand to grasp the paper and peered up at his narrowed eyes and set jaw. Gulping, I mumbled, "Thank you, sir."

When the bell rang, I stood to my feet, opened the door, and held it, allowing the three girls seated behind me to exit the room first; then I headed around the corner to room A29 for my first-period class with Mr. Stanley, the AP English and literature teacher. Pride in my accomplishment swelled inside of me, prompting the raising of my head and the jutting of my chin. My hard work had paid off and gotten me into the accelerated program in the school.

The room sat empty and silent, so I set my books down in the second row, second seat (I had a thing about 2s) and went to the water fountain. The back of Mason's head caught me unaware as I rounded the corner back into the room. *What's he doing in an AP class,* I thought to myself; then he shifted his weight, revealing his reason. With books in her arms, Aralyn stood before him, gazing into his eyes.

I inhaled a sharp breath and passed on the other side of him. He caught a glimpse of me from the corner of his eye and turned to me with a grin. "Hey, man, you have Mr. Stanley, huh," he stated with an ounce of shock ringing through his voice.

"Yeah," I replied. A sudden hesitance over the class

177

ran through my blood like a quick pulse of adrenaline.

"Wow, dude, I didn't know you were so smart." He laughed as he jokingly knocked me in the shoulder. I made a keen observation at that moment: jocks liked to overtly express their masculinity and show off to their girlfriends by shoving and smacking their friends around.

I laughed back. "Yeah, don't tell anybody, man."

Aralyn picked the desk right in front of the one I had secured for myself and set her books down. Mason grabbed her hand and uttered, "I'll meet you outside your class when it's over. I'll have to move pretty quickly."

"I'll keep up," she promised.

Mason turned to leave the room, laid his hand on my shoulder, and mumbled, "Don't let anybody mess with her."

I nodded in agreement. What else could I do? He was my friend, and he was asking me to watch out for his girlfriend. I sat down in the desk I had already claimed and kept silent. Part of me wanted to speak to her, but I decided it was best to simply keep my word and watch out for her, and that did not require speaking.

Shutting the door behind him, Mr. Stanley entered the room. "Once the door is shut, the door is shut," he commanded. "Unless you have an excuse in your hand, you will not be allowed to enter my classroom. This class is set up for those who mean business and plan to attend college. My expectations of you will exceed that of other classes. You will write more as well as read more than you ever have. I expect your full attention while I am speaking," he stated as he explained the rules and regulations of the classroom environment. He shuffled through some papers and began passing them out. "Pass these back, please. It is your reading list for the year. You will give book reports, both written and oral, write essays and critical analyses, as well as write a research paper," he instructed.

Teenagers squirmed all across the room. Looks of fear and dread revealed themselves in their furrowed brows and widened eyes. Worry lines crinkled across many faces. I couldn't see Aralyn's response, but I didn't imagine she bore any of the shocked and anxious looks exposed on the other faces in the class. My face showed worry and dread, but it wasn't the dread of the reading, the essays, or the reports or even the worry of the research paper; it was the dread of facing her every day and the worry that by accidentally touching me, she may cause the strange emotion to consume me. If that happened, I wondered if I would be able to keep the code of friendship and blood brothers as well as my word to Loraine that I would never do anything like that to her.

Aralyn looked down at her watch and began slowly gathering her things together. Relief washed over me when the bell rang minutes later, signaling the end of first period. She rushed to stand to her feet and tripped. Instinctively I threw my arm out to catch her. A bright smile crossed my face as I realized that no sensation took place when I caught her. *Maybe it was nothing*, I mused about the residue of infatuation left through the gentle touch at Wyn's party.

"You okay?" I asked.

Embarrassed, her face flushed red. "Yeah, thanks for catching me. That would've been humiliating if I'd smashed my face in the floor," she whispered.

I glanced down and eyed an untied shoestring, the source of her clumsiness. She had a large safety pin covered with multiple colored beads, a friendship pin, pinned to her tennis shoe; I hadn't seen anyone wear one since junior high.

"Your shoe's untied," I uttered.

"Oh, no wonder," she mumbled as she bent over to

179

tie it. Her hands carefully looped the laces back together. She stood back up, smiled, and grabbed her books.

Mason poked his head in the door. "You ready? I've gotta book it."

"I'm ready," she answered as she looked back toward me. "Thanks again."

"No problem."

I had Mrs. Nettles for trigonometry in building B during second period. Math was a breeze for me; it just came naturally. I strode back to building A for third period at the loud ringing of the bell. Mrs. Morrison, my tenth-grade English teacher had submitted my name for placement in a new class that required a teacher recommendation. I rounded the corner back into Mr. Stanley's class for poetry and creative writing. I sat in the same desk as I had during first period and waited for the bell to ring and the class to begin.

My eyelids barred my surrounds as I drifted off into music land and began playing a song out in my mind. I naturally picked up the two pencils sitting in the groove of my desk (I always kept two pencils out) and used them to add the percussion sounds to the song clearly playing out in my thoughts. The shrieking of metal over tile flooring jostled me, disrupting the flow of music. My eyes flew open wide, staring at the back side of a head full of long brunette spiral curls. Shifting in her seat, the girl twisted her body to face me. I dropped the pencils at the sight of Aralyn.

"Your teacher recommended you for this class?" she asked, her tone mingled with a hint of arrogance.

I had never heard her speak in such a manner. Her voice typically rang with humility. "Yeah, I know. I don't look like the intelligent type with the long hair and all, besides the fact I play lead guitar in a rock band." Trying to make her feel I wasn't insulted, I laughed.

"Sorry, didn't mean to sound that way," she

180

apologized. "It's funny how stereotyping rubs off on everybody." She laughed and her face flushed a bright pink. Another embarrassed giggle crossed her lips.

"It's all right. I get it all the time. So, you like to write?" I pressed on to a subject change.

"Yeah, poetry mostly. How 'bout you?" she asked.

"I write songs, some poetry as well," I responded just as Mr. Stanley shut the door.

Aralyn swiftly turned to face the front of the class, and I pulled out my notebook and opened to a blank page.

Football season kicked in high gear. The Moss Point Tigers ranked among the top in the state, so I proudly attended several home games with the exception of taking Loraine to her homecoming game for the Hornets and one other big rival game she was desperate to attend. Aralyn sat in the bleachers every Friday night cheering on Mason, the star of every game, with her new-found friend Sheena at her side.

Prying open my eyes, I woke up one morning to get dressed for school and dropped my feet to the floor. A cold sensation shot through my entire body. Goose bumps popped up all over my arms and legs from the nippy air. Fall had crept up unaware and abruptly changed the weather from sticky hot to a crispy chill. I breathed in the freshness of the air and could almost swear I smelled the popcorn popping, the butter drizzling over it, the caramel apples, and the cotton candy found at the Jackson County Fair. I ambled down the hall and into the backyard before dressing completely, closing my eyes and relishing in the cool breeze. Weather in south Mississippi seemed to have mixed emotions, so I wanted to take a moment to enjoy it. She was finicky and couldn't decide if she wanted to be hot or cold, so she fluctuated between the two until she finally settled on her heart's desire. The weather would change at the drop of a hat. I knew I could wake up the next day to smothering heat that sucked the oxygen right out of the air, so I allowed the wind to blow across my half-naked body while I absorbed the refreshing waft.

October the 23 was a home-game night and Midnight Madness at the fair, so Loraine and I made plans to spend the evening together. During the game Daniel Lamont and Justin Freeman approached me. Daniel swatted me across the shoulder. "Hey, man, wuz up?" He chuckled.

"Not too much. Just watchin' the Tigers shred these Greyhounds," I enthused. "What's up with you?"

"Oh, just seeing who alls goin' to Midnight Madness when we leave here. You and your girlfriend going?" he pried.

"Yeah, we're going."

Justin stood several feet back and glared down his nose at me. He nudged Daniel. Daniel discreetly glanced back at him, gave his head a nod, and whispered, "He's okay, dude. He's cool."

I pretended not to hear. Loraine tightened the grip she had on my hand, leaned over, and kissed me on the cheek. I smiled and acknowledged Justin's presence with a nod. "Hey there, Justin. How's life after high school?"

He huffed, "Fine."

"You going to college?" I asked.

"Yeah, I'm at State. I just came home for the weekend to see my parents, so I thought I'd catch up with Mason at the game and see if he's interested in a little partying at the fair."

"Oh, his girlfriend, Aralyn, is sittin' right down there." I pointed to where she sat.

"He's still datin' her?" he hissed. "I thought he'd gotten over his *good* spell by now. She's such a nerd.

Now her sister, she's hot!"

Without thinking twice, I narrowed my eyes and spit, "You're just jealous because her sister dumped you; that's what I hear anyway, and if you plan on partying with him tonight, you better not let *him* hear you say anything like that. He's protective of her."

Taken aback by my outburst, he threw out his hands, signaling peace. "Chill out, man. I was just messin' around. You can't deny it. Nobody thought he'd like being with just one girl, not after Samantha anyway."

Daniel jumped in the conversation. "It's true, Ray. We all thought he was out to seize and conquer, but..." He craned his head towards Justin. "He apparently wasn't. He really cares about her, so Ray's right, you shouldn't mess with him about it. He'll kick your ass, man."

Loraine stood up. "Okay, guys. I'm swimmin' in testosterone here. Just go down there you two and see what their plans are."

The two of them walked down the creaky bleachers. As soon as they were out of hearing range, Loraine gazed at me. "I hope you're that defensive of me," she murmured.

"I would be if I needed to," I quickly responded.

She smiled. "Good. I was getting a little jealous there."

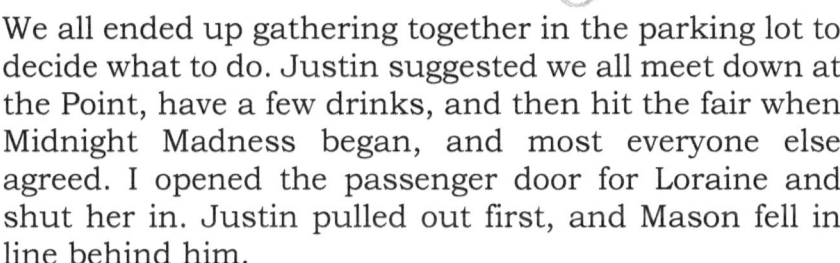

We all ended up gathering together in the parking lot to decide what to do. Justin suggested we all meet down at the Point, have a few drinks, and then hit the fair when Midnight Madness began, and most everyone else agreed. I opened the passenger door for Loraine and shut her in. Justin pulled out first, and Mason fell in line behind him.

Justin slammed on breaks at the Point, jumped

from the cab of his truck, and hollered, "Whoo, Mason! Let's get this party started." He opened the tailgate, pulled a cooler to the edge, grabbed a plastic cup, filled it to the brim, and handed it to me. I shook my head *no* and declined, "Nah, man. I don't want any."

He cocked his head to the side. A sinister grin crossed his face. "What's the matter, Ray? Not man enough to handle a real drink?" he taunted.

He threw the first punch, and it struck my ego, causing it to rise to the surface. "I can handle anything you can, Justin." I grabbed the cup from his hand and guzzled it down. "This is pretty good. Tastes like lemonade."

Loraine spoke up, "What is it, anyway?"

"Bullfrogs," Justin answered; then he looked at me. "I guess I was wrong about you, buddy." He laughed. "You're handling it just fine." He scoffed while filling another cup.

Loraine faced me. "Ray, let me have your keys."

"Why?" I asked. "I'm fine." I glanced at Justin. "You sure this has alcohol in it?"

He snickered. "I'm sure."

Loraine tugged on my shirt. "I know you're fine, but I'd feel better if I drove tonight. Please," she pouted.

I reached in my pocket and handed them over without an argument. Justin grabbed a McDonald's bag with lids and straws. "Here, we can drink 'em at the fair and nobody'll know." He chuckled.

Something in the air that night invaded my mind and senses, and I did some things that were not in my nature to do. Yeah, I had my days of drinking, and I even tried marijuana, but I had seen several of my acquaintances mess their lives up through drugs and alcohol. I knew three guys who had been expelled for having alcohol on school premises, and I knew of two guys who were presently serving time at the juvenile hall for drugs. On top of the death of Victor, all of these things kept me away from drugs all together; I would only occasionally drink a beer or two, but for some reason unbeknownst to me, I gave into the pressure that swelled around me at the Point.

Loraine climbed in the driver's seat and pulled out onto the road. We all walked around the fairgrounds with our cups of bullfrogs. I came out of the shell I usually stayed in, laughing and joking around. We had been at the fair for a while before I felt the effects of the drink begin to hit me. I turned to Loraine. "So, you gonna ride the Zipper with me?" I grinned.

"Um...I don't know if I wanna get on that thing."

I wrapped my arms around her. "I'll be right there next to you. I'll keep you safe."

She stood on her tiptoes and kissed me. "Umm...in that case, I suppose I will."

I turned to Mason. "Hey, man, we're gonna go ride the Zipper."

He grabbed Aralyn's hand. Facing her, he asked, "Hey, babe, you wanna go with them to ride the Zipper?"

"Oh, I guess. I've never been on it before. It looks kinda scary." Her eyes skimmed over the frightening sight before her.

The four of us stood in the long line awaiting our turn to ride the ride that flipped you and turned you in several ways all at once. We climbed in our little cage and shut the door; I immediately began rocking us back and forth. Loraine screamed the entire time as we zipped around. When we got off, she cried, "I'll never get on that thing again, Ray Winstrom. I won't be drinking anymore tonight. I think I might be sick."

Realizing her paleness, I straightened up. "Are you all right? Do you want me to take you home?"

"No, I'm okay but no more rides like that. I wanna ride the double Ferris wheel. Come on." She tugged at my arm.

"Okay, okay, I'm coming." We dashed off. Mason

and Aralyn tagged along behind us.

We climbed aboard and were taken to the top where the ride suddenly stopped and allowed more people on. We sat high up in the sky and looked out over the small city of Pascagoula. Loraine snuggled up next to me. "Ray..."

"Hmmm?" I mumbled with my arm over her shoulder.

"I love you," she whispered.

Taken off guard by her proclamation, I inhaled a deep breath and held it in. I knew she expected to hear it in return, and I knew I cared deeply for her, but I wasn't sure if it was love I felt. I had never been in love before, and I didn't want to just throw those words out there and then not be able to take them back. Therefore, I pulled her close to me, kissed her on the forehead, and sighed.

As we exited the ride, Daniel handed me the remainder of my drink. I realized as I slurped the last of it through the straw that I'd consumed more than I could handle. Loraine craned her neck and eyed me at the sound of my slurred speech and suggested I take her home. Dangling my keys in front of my face, she climbed in the driver's seat. Blackness swallowed us as she drove down long, winding roads to her home. Gravel churned under the weight of the wheels as the car turned into her drive. The house seemed empty, engulfed in darkness. She pulled the keys out of my ignition and faced me. "Come on."

I didn't argue with her. I simply nodded in compliance.

As we approached the door, she pulled out her keys to unlock the door and asked, "Hey, will you come in and check the house out for me? My parents aren't home, and I'm kind of leery of being here by myself at night."

"Yeah, sure. Where are your parents?"

"Mom had a horse show to attend this weekend, so Dad went with her. They won't be home until tomorrow night," she informed me.

I walked through the door, flipped the light switch, and paced through the house checking to see if anyone happened to be hiding behind doors, in closets, or under beds. Once I was certain all was clear, I joined her in the living room. "You're safe."

"Thanks," she whispered. I stumbled slightly as I headed for the front door. She reached out and caught me. "Ray, I don't think it's safe for you to drive home, and I'm really kinda scared of staying here by myself, so why don't you stay here with me?" she begged. "At least until I fall asleep," she quickly blurted out. I sat on the couch, and she joined me, wrapping her arms around me. She laid her head on my chest. "Ray..." she whispered.

"Yeah," I answered back as I ran my hands through her auburn hair.

She craned her neck, stretched her lips to mine, and kissed me gently. My heart rate increased. Before I knew it, the gentle caressing of our lips became fervent and heated. Her mouth grazed my cheek and found its way to my neck. Without saying a word, she let me know what she wanted, and I found myself suddenly consumed with desires I had never followed through on before. Nervousness took over my body, and I instinctively pulled away. I didn't want to take advantage of her vulnerability. She had already expressed a struggle with jealousy and proclaimed her feelings of love for me. I didn't want to hurt her. I knew she had been hurt in the past, and I didn't want to be *that guy*, the one who took advantage of a wounded girl seeking to be loved.

"Why don't you love me, Ray?" she pouted. Brokenness revealed itself through her eyes as water began to fill them, causing them to glisten.

"Loraine, I do...I just..."

She interrupted my train of thought and explanation as she pushed herself back into my arms, and I lost my resolve in the madness of midnight.

CHAPTER 17

LOST DREAMS

After that night things changed between Loraine and me. My feelings for her deepened, and I found it more difficult to control the temptation of physical desire when we were alone.

School was going well. I put plenty of hours into study. While most of my classes were an easy A for me, I had to dedicate many hours to my English and poetry classes. It wasn't that the classes were difficult, but both were time consuming. After breaking the ice with Aralyn by laughing off her insult when she stereotyped me, she began to turn in her seat to face me every day during both classes, and conversation naturally flowed. In the beginning she would ask me questions about Loraine and make comments about how pretty she was or ask me stuff about Mason from when we were little kids, like what kind of stuff did we do together (she was getting insider information). Eventually, however, the small interludes shifted gears, and the questions became about my writing.

She was a poet, so she couldn't help but be intrigued by the songs I wrote. The truth of the matter was I couldn't help but wonder what she wrote, so I informed her of the songs she had heard us play at various parties that I had written. Most of them were songs about rebellion and partying; that's what most teenagers wanted to hear, but I had just written one on a slightly slower scale that was more of a love ballad. I shared with her the lyrics.

"Pierced Heart"

I saw you on the dance floor;
You were looking mighty fine.
You captured my heart
When you looked straight into mine.
You pierced me in the heart
When you looked in my eyes.
You pierced me in the heart;
My love I can't disguise.
You pierced me in the heart;
I see you walking my way
You pierce me in the heart.
Baby, please don't leave; stay.
My desire I can't control;
Don't keep me in the dark.
Please tell me you'll stay with me,
And you'll give me your heart.
You pierced me in the heart
When you looked in my eyes.
You pierced me in the heart;
My love I can't disguise.
You pierced me in the heart;
I see you walking my way.
You pierced me in the heart;
Baby, please don't leave; stay.
I move towards you
As we sway across the floor;
I hold you in my arms,
But my heart longs for more.

Ray Winstrom

In return she shared several of her poems with me.

One in particular stuck out in my mind.

"The Wilderness"

I stand in a wilderness
At night all alone;
A frightened little girl searching for a home.

I stand in a wilderness
Searching through the green;
Silently standing by, longing to be seen

I stand in a wilderness
Shivering out of fear;
The rustling of the leaves warns me someone's near.

I stand in a wilderness
With nowhere to hide;
He breaks through the trees to stand by my side.

I stand in the wilderness
No longer do I fear;
He completed my life; I now see it all so clear.

~Plain Jane~

I knew, when I read that one, she had handed Mason her heart completely. I was happy for him but worried for her. Although I knew he cared for her, I also knew what he had almost done, and I knew if he ever did anything like that to her, it would shred her heart into pieces.

Two weeks before we were to be let out of school for Christmas holiday, Mr. Stanley instructed us to write a poem about one of our lost dreams. I stared blankly at the piece of paper on my desk and pondered the meaning of a dream. My dreams were in the process of coming true, so I couldn't say I had a lost one. To me a dream was a longing in your heart for something wonderful to take place in your life. My dream was to be a rock star, and I didn't consider that dream to be lost but rather on the horizon.

Without saying a word, Mr. Stanley exited the room. He often did that with our class because he could trust us to behave, and he knew he left us with an assignment that would keep us occupied. I squeezed my eyes shut and pinched the bridge of my nose. With a sigh I dropped my hand to my desk and peeled open my eyes. I glanced up from the blank page sitting as still as a stone on my desk. I tapped Aralyn on the shoulder and whispered, "Are you having a problem with this one?" I figured if we talked about the concept for a minute, it may spark an idea or two for each of us.

"Nah, uh," she answered. "Why? Are you?" she asked. Her voice rang with a hint of amazement.

"Yeah, what are you doing yours on?" I pried.

"My sweet sixteen," she whispered.

I squinted my eyes in confusion. "Your sweet sixteen is a lost dream?" *How can her sweet sixteen be a lost dream? She just turned sixteen, and she's obviously in love with Mason. Girls in this school would kill to be with him. She must be referring to being sixteen and never been kissed. Girls like that idea, don't they?* I questioned my own musings.

"Yeah, it's a long story. It was basically shoved to the side—not exactly a girl's dream." She tried to brush off the subject.

Brushed to the side? That's not right, I told myself. "Sweet Sixteen is a rite of passage for a girl. What happened?" I pressed. My interest was piqued.

"Well, my sister Laila, I'm sure you've seen her; she's gorgeous. She was voted Most Beautiful last year, well...my parents bought her a beautiful white formal dress for her sweet sixteen and threw this huge party for her at the Escatawpa Community Center. She was practically a princess for the day. All of her dreams came true that day, so I guess I had built myself up for the same, but apparently, my parents spent all of their money on buying my sister a new car for college and getting her set up in a dorm, so they couldn't afford to have a sweet sixteen party for me. I didn't get the beautiful white dress and the wreath of flowers in my hair." She stared across the room in a daze, almost as if picturing how the day was supposed to have unfolded. She pulled herself back to the real world and continued, "My sister is spoiled. Can you believe she was upset about having to wear that dress twice?" She huffed and shook her head. "I thought my parents were going to surprise me that day, so when I got home from the beach, I went to my room and put on a pretty dress, expecting to see my family gathered around the room, dressed all nice, but it was just my parents and Laurie and my sister. Laila laughed at me and asked me why I was so dressed up. I kinda lost it and screamed at her. My best friend moved away a few days later, and Mason, he didn't even know it was my birthday to begin with, but when I told him about how horrible my day had been, he promised to take me somewhere special the following weekend to celebrate," she said, laughing slightly at the last word. "But he forgot about it and took me that party you were playing at instead. No offense!"

I scanned through my mind searching for a party that suggested her being upset. "Which one?" I asked.

"The one at that guy Wyn's house."

That's why she was so gloomy that night. Mason didn't even realize he had broken his promise to her. He didn't know why she had been upset all night. Of course he knew what upset her later that night. "Whoa, he didn't?" I shook my head. "You deserve better than him." It slipped out before I even realized it had.

She quickly removed eye contact and hung her head. "You shouldn't say things like that," she mumbled.

"Well, it's true; he's said it himself."

"Really?"

"Yep, the night of that party at Wyn's, as a matter of fact. Mason fools around with some stuff." She yanked her head back up and looked at me with huge eyes of disbelief. "He told me you caught him that night. That's when he said it."

She pulled her eyes away from me again as if she felt some sort of shame. "Yeah, I don't like that kind of stuff. You don't mess with it, do you?"

At that moment part of me felt I could spill my guts to her about everything I had ever been through in the arena of drugs, but I held my tongue and generalized my answer. "No way. I like my brain cells. Don't get me wrong, I've dabbled with some stuff before, but I found out real quick that it's not for me. I plan on going to college and making something of myself. I don't want to waste my life and let it go down the drain. I've seen too many people get hooked and screw their lives up," I explained. I had divulged small bits of myself. "So, can I read your poem?" I asked.

Without saying a word, she handed the paper back to me.

"Sixteen Candles"

My lost dream
Would be my sweet sixteen.
Wearing a dress of white
On a starry Friday night.
In the background a lake
And a dazzling cake
Made with three layers of white,

194

Trimmed with rosebuds, pink and bright.
On my head a wreath rests
Made of white baby's breath.
Made a princess for the day
I watch as sixteen candles burn away.
Blowing them out, I make a wish
That Prince Charming would give me a kiss.

~Plain Jane~

I read the poem and looked at her with a smile. "It's good. A lake, huh?"

"Yeah, it's my dream. Actually my dream is to have an outside wedding in front of a lake, but sweet sixteen is close enough." She sighed.

The sound of heavy footsteps came burling down the hall. We both knew it was Mr. Stanley. She snatched her paper back and turned around in her desk. He burst through the door and stormed in the room. A loud thud echoed through the building as the door slammed shut. The entire class stiffened in fear at the sight of his crimson face. He stomped back to his desk, shoved a few things around, slammed a book or two down, and mumbled a few choice words under his breath. No one even wanted to know what had infuriated him. A fearful hush filled the remainder of the class.

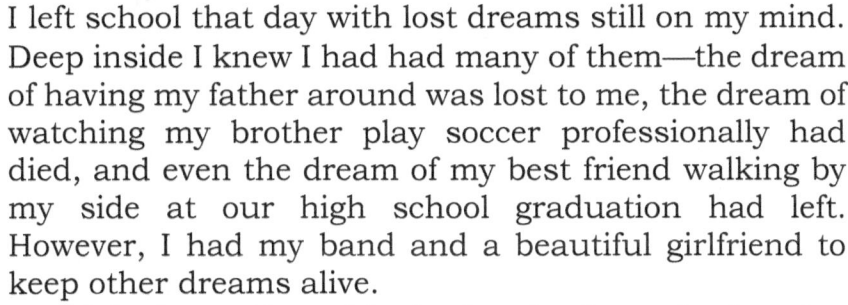

I left school that day with lost dreams still on my mind. Deep inside I knew I had had many of them—the dream of having my father around was lost to me, the dream of watching my brother play soccer professionally had died, and even the dream of my best friend walking by my side at our high school graduation had left. However, I had my band and a beautiful girlfriend to keep other dreams alive.

I had practice with the band after school and a

195

date with Loraine that night. Her parents were out of town for the second time since I had been seeing her. This time it was a business trip of her dad's to New York. They added a few extra days in and decided to make it a second honeymoon, so Loraine planned a candlelit dinner for the two of us at her home.

The sun dipped from sight early in the month of December, and the moon hid itself on that particular night, swallowing the countryside in blackness as dark as midnight despite the early hour of 8:00 p.m. My headlights flashed across a small low-riding, souped-up truck parked on the side of the house as I turned onto the drive. Gravel crackled under the tires as I inched my way closer to the mystery vehicle. I pulled up next to her dad's car, which he had left for her to drive while they were gone, and got out, easing the door shut. I narrowed my eyes at the unfamiliar truck; it didn't belong to any of her friends I had met over the past several months.

The pitch-black house struck me odd. Loraine was afraid of the dark. Curious, I strode around the side of the house in order to inspect the truck. My mind raced with thoughts. *This must be her friend Wynona's boyfriend's truck. Yeah, she mentioned they were going shopping this weekend in Mobile. I just assumed she meant in the morning...But wait a minute...both vehicles are here, so it can't be Wynona. They would have to take one of the vehicles shopping, and if they were back, the lights would be on. She wouldn't want Wynona here for our romantic dinner...It can't be a guy. Loraine wouldn't do that to me,* I assured myself. I stared at the truck. *Would she?*

I couldn't take it any longer. I had to know what was going on. I had to know why the lights were out, and I had to know who that truck belonged to, so I crept to the front door and marched right in. Eerie silent engulfed the house, so I twisted the knob and inched the door shut. The hinges creaked as the door found its

196

home. I turned the knob to the lamp by the door hoping to find her sleeping on the couch. Empty, the couch and living room were empty. I tiptoed to the kitchen and flipped the switch, peeking in to see if she might be in there by chance, and then I heard it. Laughter echoed through the house. I yanked my head around and glared toward her bedroom at the sound.

Shock pierced through my entire body in an instant. I wanted to believe I was having a horrible nightmare, so I reluctantly rounded the corner and headed for her room. A starburst of light glowed from the crack at the base of her bedroom door. The light reflected off the opposite wall drawing my attention to the horseshoe hanging next to the collage of pictures of her mother's prize horses. Coldness covered my chest and gripped my heart, twisting it, as the deep, male voice stabbed my mind. I instinctively yanked the horseshoe from the wall. *I'm gonna mess this guy up*, I told myself. As I crept up to the door, she giggled, and I cringed, not certain I wanted to see what I envisioned as taking place behind the door. I placed my hand on the knob, took a deep breath, and prayed before turning it, *Please let it be a family member she never mentioned.* Warning her, the door squeaked as it opened. Hearing the noise and catching a glimpse of my silhouette in the doorway, she yanked herself free from his kiss and jolted to life.

"Ray!" she hollered.

They were both fully clothed, but her face was riddled with guilt. My hands shook with adrenaline as I clutched the horseshoe. I fought the urge to beat him to a pulp and dropped the horseshoe just before charging through the house and slamming the front door as I left. Right behind me, she grabbed my arm before I made it off the porch. "Ray, stop...Please," she begged with broken sobs. I stopped in my tracks, but I couldn't face her. "Please look at me," she cried.

197

I twisted my body around in her direction but stared off in the distance. From the corner of my eye, I could see tears streaming down her face. It felt as if I were in a wrestling match and was being held in a head lock, and I was to the point where my ears were beginning to bleed and my eyes were seeing black spots. "Is that Willie?" I finally found my voice.

She looked down at her feet. "Yes."

"Did you sleep with him?"

"No, I swear I didn't, but...we are back together. I'm sorry, Ray."

I gasped, "Ah..." I had just been sucker punched in the gut with amazing force. I couldn't help it; at those words my eyes naturally gravitated to hers. Pain shot through them as I gazed at her.

She grabbed my hand, running her thumb repeatedly over it, and whispered, "I love you, Ray. I do, but...he's my first love...and...I didn't realize until today that I never really stopped loving him."

"I guess that's that. Goodbye, Loraine." I headed for my car.

"Ray," she called.

I stopped. "What?"

"This wasn't an easy choice. I can't help what my heart feels."

"Just stop twisting the knife, would you?"

"Please don't hate me."

I stood still for a fleeting moment. "I don't *hate* you, Loraine," I mumbled just before shutting my car door. I pulled out of her drive. I had thought out a list of lost dreams on my drive over, and now I had another I could add. I had lost Loraine.

CHAPTER 18

FROM A DISTANCE

*O*ver the following months I found it difficult to smile. I ran into Loraine and Willie once on Market Street. I glared at them from a distance. It had only been a month since she dumped me for him, and I wasn't prepared for the wave of rage that crashed into me at the sight of them together. I suppressed the anger boiling to the surface, screaming for me to approach him and pick a fight. I was better than that, and I knew it, but it didn't make the battle to stifle those emotions any easier.

Before long the senior class voted on and announced the theme of prom, and I cringed inside. I wasn't going. That was all there was to it. I wasn't enthused with the idea of being around happy couples, so I passed by the fliers being posted without a second glance, and I shrugged off any mention of it. It was only February, but the Prom committee planned it all well in advance.

The season changed. Life and its many colors arrived on the scene after a short, cold winter. Grass turned green again, and flowers bloomed in brilliants shades of orange, yellow, red, blue, and lavender. Amazingly I started to feel better. Along with winter, sadness left me. One Sunday morning in late March (before Mom and Andy had stirred to life), I woke up, threw some clothes on, and went to the kitchen. I grabbed a bowl and a box of cereal and sat at the table. I tilted my head at the loud thud of the morning paper smacking the front door as the delivery guy thrust it to the porch. Apparently the driver of the car overshot his aim. I opened the door and brought the paper in for Andy. He liked to read it while he drank his morning coffee. Deciding to scan through it for myself, I poured a glass of orange juice and plopped down at the table with it. As I flipped through, my eyes widened at a picture of Loraine and Willie in the local section, announcing their engagement. She would graduate in May and marry in August. I lump twisted in my chest and rose up my throat. I swallowed hard, pushing it and my pain back down before ripping the page out, crumpling it up, and throwing it in the trash.

The next day at school Daniel approached me. "Hey, dude, I met this girl who would be a perfect date for you to take to the prom." He grinned, trying to sell me on the idea.

"No, thanks. I'm not going to prom."

"Look, I'm gonna ask Sheena. You should come along. Ask Michelle to go. She's in my Biology II class. Apparently she saw me talking to you the other day, and she sat next to me in class and started asking a lot of questions about you. She wanted to know if you had a girlfriend. She even said she thought you were cute, man."

"Daniel, I appreciate it, but I'm not interested."

About that time Mason and Aralyn strolled up. Mason started in on our childhood secret handshake. I knew something was up. I appeased him and joined in. He smiled. "Hey, dude. Look, there's this girl Linda she's a real pretty cheerleader who asked me about you last week. She doesn't have a date yet for prom, and she wanted me to see if I would be able to talk you into taking her. Whaddya think, man?"

I sighed, "Ah, man. Don't do that to me. I don't wanna go to prom, okay."

"But she's nice, and we all want you there," he insisted.

"Look, I'm just not up for it," I said, dropping my head. The blustering bell for homeroom saved me from further conversation. "Well...gotta get to class," I mumbled as I darted for Building A.

First period had me crossing Mason's path again as I passed him and Aralyn standing outside the classroom.

Mason grabbed my arm and pulled me back. "Dude, seriously, this girl is real pretty, and she really needs a date."

Aralyn tugged on his arm. "Mason, don't push him. If he doesn't wanna go, he doesn't wanna go." She came to my rescue.

"Okay, okay," he grumbled as he leaned over and kissed her on the cheek.

Mason headed off, and she looked up at me before entering the room. The look in her eyes told me she understood on some level what I felt.

Mr. Stanley left the room while we worked on our research papers. Aralyn turned in her seat. "Sorry for Mason pestering you before school," she whispered.

"It's all right. They must've all read the paper," I huffed.

She bit her bottom lip in apprehension. "Yeah, he saw it. I'm really sorry, Ray."

"It's okay, Aralyn. I'm all right. I promise. It hurt when she broke up with me, and it took me a while to get over it all, and just when I thought I was finally able to be happy about it all, I saw that stupid announcement." I shook my head. "I'm over her; I really am. It just threw me for a loop is all."

She laid her hand on mine, and I was caught off

guard by my physical response. An electric flow rushed through my veins, and she whispered, "You're a good guy Ray. You're handsome and kind, and one day you'll find a sweet, beautiful girl who appreciates you for everything you are. She'll be totally captivated by you, and she'll love you with everything within her."

I couldn't say a word. I just looked through her eyes, and I could almost swear I saw straight through to her soul.

Two weeks before prom, Aralyn sat all bubbly in her desk. She was full of smiles, and I had to know why. I tapped her on the shoulder. "So, what are you so excited about?" I asked.

She turned to me. "I went shopping over the weekend with Sheena and bought my prom dress. It's *so* beautiful!"

"I hope my little sister is as excited as you are about that kind of stuff when it's her turn." I laughed.

"You have a little sister?" She smiled.

"Yep, Lacey. She's a pretty awesome little girl. She's all into dance; she wants to be a ballerina when she grows up." I chuckled. "So, did you find what you were looking for?"

"More than what I expected. It looks like a princess dress." Her mouth stretched in a beautiful smile, revealing her pearly-white teeth.

"Well, I hope you have fun." I settled back in my seat.

Her face dropped. "Ray, I understand why you don't want to come, and I know Mason and Daniel have been driving you crazy with trying to fix you up and all, but I wish you would come. It won't be the same without you there, and you have to admit, prom is one of those rite of passage things; life is not the same without it...Even if I wasn't dating Mason, I'd still go, and I think you'll regret it later on if you don't. That's all I'm gonna say about it. I promise I won't harass you anymore on the subject." The bell rang, and she turned back around in her seat, pulling her notebook out.

Later that day I walked to the office and bought a lone ticket for the prom. I didn't tell anyone I had changed my mind and given in to Aralyn's request. On prom night when I pulled in the parking lot, I eyed Daniel and Sheena walking across the sidewalk laughing. Climbing out of my car, I straightened my red cummerbund and dusted crumbs from the sleeve of the white tux. My little sister had given me a big hug before I left the house, and I had just seen the gift she had left me, oatmeal cookie crumbs.

I caught up to Daniel and Sheena just inside at the packed ticket table.

Daniel glanced around the room and eyed me. "Dude, you came. What made you change your mind?"

"Oh, just decided I would regret not going to my junior prom."

"Well, if you'd told me you'd decided to come, I coulda set you up with Michelle."

I shook my head. "That's okay. I wanted to come stag."

We finally made it to the table to turn in our tickets and entered the dance hall. Mason's football buddy Terrance and his girlfriend Jackie slipped in behind us. Terrance jokingly punched Daniel in the shoulder. "Yo, man, lookin' sharp there."

"Lookin' snazzy yourself." Daniel laughed.

Terrance threw his hand in the air and signaled across the room to Jackson, Ayesha, William, and Patricia. They joined us, and from a distance I spotted Mason and Aralyn. My senses jolted to life as I gazed at her. She was so beautiful. Her royal-blue dress captured and enhanced the beauty of her eyes, and her smile glistened with a sparkle like the morning sun when it first shines in through a window, breaking the hovering darkness. My ponderings on her beauty happened so quickly I didn't realize what was taking place until a few moments later, so as soon as I picked up on the inappropriateness of my thoughts, I reined them in and looked in the other direction.

Aralyn leaned in and whispered in Mason's ear. He nodded his head in agreement and then suggested, "Hey, guys, how about we go grab some punch."

All the guys, except me, headed over to the punch bowl on the other side of the room. I wasn't interested in punch at the time, so I hung back. Occupying myself so as not to look at her, my eyes skimmed over the decorations in the dance hall. A smile crept across my face when I caught a glimpse of her spinning awkwardly. Beauty encapsulated her, yet she remained clueless to it. Skittish, her eyes stayed glued to the floor as she held out her skirt and showed off her dress to Sheena.

My eyes fell upon Cassie, Prissy, Donna, and Linda—the congregation of cheerleaders—as they clumped together. Scowls covered their faces, making clear their disapproval of Sheena and Aralyn. They were all popular and wealthy; well, their parents were anyhow. They stood whispering amongst themselves, but Sheena and Aralyn seemed intent on not allowing the shunning to affect their evening.

Wearing a wig, Ralph Peterson, the class clown, bounced onto the dance floor during Whitney Houston's "I'm Every Woman" doing a silly dance. It was obvious he had preplanned the show for all. Everyone stood on the sidelines, watched, and laughed. He finished his hilarious portrayal when Chicago's "Look Away" came on. Aralyn turned to Mason. "Can we dance, please? I love this song," she begged.

Mason cringed. I felt a tap on my shoulder as he faced me. "Hey, man, will you dance with my girl?"

Shock ran through me, along with screams of *No, don't do this to me!* I had already suppressed attraction once that night. I glanced at Aralyn and looked into widened, embarrassed eyes. I mumbled to Mason, "Sure, man."

I walked toward her and held out my hand for hers. With a bow I asked, "Will you do me the honor, Ms. Aralyn, of joining me for a dance?" I figured if she had to feel the embarrassment of her love pawning her off on some long-haired guy, she should at least be treated as a princess during the dance.

Her face flushed pink as a smile flitted across her face. She looked down at the floor and answered, "It would be an honor, Mr. Winstrom."

She wrapped her arm in mine, and I pulled her in close as I spun us both onto the dance floor. She seemed to be enjoying herself, and she was actually a pretty good dancer. I wondered who had taught her and how she practiced because I knew Mason hated to dance. Without looking at me, she asked, "Have you taken dance or something?"

I smiled. "Nah, my mom, she loves to dance; she taught me. She's had me dancing with her ever since I was old enough to learn the moves." I chuckled.

"You have all kinds of hidden talents," she whispered.

I spun her around and brought her back to me, looked in her eyes, and mumbled, "As do you." Something deep within her eyes reached out and drew me in. I couldn't pull myself free from its magnetic force. I felt my heart revealing itself to her, and I didn't know how to shut it off. Part of me didn't want to shut it off as I saw her true beauty unfold through her eyes. Loveliness, intelligence, talents, and a sense of humor all wrapped themselves up into one humble young woman.

She gasped. Pulling herself away, she uttered, "Song's over." She practically ran across the convention center to Mason's side.

Ah, man. What's going on with me? What was that? Why could I see into her heart like that? She knows I'm attracted to her now, so I'll lose her as a friend. She's gonna be all freaked out around me now. I beat myself up over the incident.

Mason laughed with Terrance, William, and Jackson. Aralyn strode toward him. As she approached, he stretched his arm out and pulled her to his side. She stood quietly while he continued to joke around with his football buddies. I approached Daniel and started a conversation to get my mind refocused. "Hey, the weekend of June 11 I have full access to my grandparent's condo in Gulf Shores. Do ya wanna ride over with me?" I questioned.

"Are you kidding me? You don't even have to ask, dude. I'm so there." He threw his hand in the air to high-five me, and that started an on-going conversation that reeled in my stray thoughts.

"Yeah, they can't go this year, so they offered it to me as long as I promised to drive out to Houston to see 'em."

"Who else you planning to ask?" he pried.

"Oh, I'm not sure yet. It's a three bedroom, so there is room for one more guy."

Daniel slipped away from Sheena, hung his arm over my shoulder, and whispered, "If things are going pretty good between me and Sheena, can I bring her along?"

Daniel put me on the spot. "Well, I suppose you can bring her." I had hoped to take Loraine with me during that week, but, of course, that would never take place with her wedding just around the corner.

Daniel dropped his arm. "What about Mason. He'd

love a weekend in Gulf Shores. You should ask him," he insisted.

"Maybe. I haven't thought much about it 'til now. I better check with Kevin first since he is the lead singer of our band. He might get offended."

The D.J. played song after song; couples danced their hearts out as the night moved along. Before we all knew it, the principal stepped onto the platform, approached the D.J., and borrowed his microphone, signaling the time had arrived to announce the king and queen of the prom. Mumbling something I couldn't hear, Mason pulled away from Aralyn. I cut my eyes across the room, following his steps. He signaled to Sheena as he took long, quick strides toward her. She dropped Daniel's hand and met Mason halfway. She leaned her head toward his as he whispered to her. A smile broke out on her face, and she nodded yes before returning to Daniel's side.

"Good evening, juniors and seniors," announced Mrs. Moore. "It's time for us to announce the king and queen of the 1993 Once in a Lifetime Prom!" she said, her voice bubbling with excitement and anticipation.

She put on a good show for the school because everyone already knew who would get it. It was always the two most popular people.

"The queen of this year's prom is Cassie Bennett. Come to the front please." Mrs. Moore smiled.

Cassie threw her hands over her mouth as if surprised and shocked to be chosen. Tears streamed down her cheeks as she walked toward her fantasy.

"And the king of this year's prom is Mason Davis." She clapped.

Mason slipped his hand from Aralyn's. As he passed me, he leaned over and whispered, "Hey, will you dance with Aralyn and then cut in on me and Cassie?"

"Yeah, sure." I didn't have time to object.

"Thanks, man."

Mason marched to the front. Mrs. Moore placed the crown on his head, and he smiled. She retrieved the queen's crown from its pillow and placed it on her head before proclaiming, "Now the king and queen will share their traditional dance."

The D.J. played "Once in a Lifetime," the theme song for the prom, and Mason hesitantly grasped Cassie's hand and led her to the dance floor. I understood his leeriness because I knew Mason and Cassie, one of the many beautiful, popular girls he had dated briefly, shared a tense history. His label of being a heartbreaker stuck for good reasons. Cassie was still crazy about him. She flirted with him every chance she had. He usually appeased her neediness by flirting back, but he kept a careful distance between them in Aralyn's presence. Cassie hated Aralyn because she had only been someone for him to sleep with. Aralyn, on the other hand, was someone he cared about. I was quite positive Aralyn's naivety kept her in the dark as to why Cassie hated her so. Knowing her, she probably blamed it on a school social-class issue and merely attributed Cassie's constant snubs and evil glares to her status in the upper, popular class while she sat quietly in the lower, nerd class, when the truth of it all was simple jealousy.

I approached Aralyn and tapped her lightly on the shoulder. She glanced back to see who had drawn her attention. "I've been instructed to dance with you for a minute and then cut in on Mason and Cassie," I whispered.

She gasped, "Oh, All right." I could see her nervousness as she wrapped her arm around mine. I led her to the dance floor, spinning her out before bringing her back into my grasp. I moved us smoothly across the floor, making my way toward Mason. Cold awkwardness wrapped all around us, and I didn't want that to be the case. Aralyn was my friend, and I desired for that friendship to stay intact, so I decided to speak up and try to break the icy film of unease. "I'm sorry if I offended you earlier. You seemed anxious to get away from me."

She looked up at me and smiled. "You didn't do anything, Ray. I'm just not used to dancing with guys; that's all." She blew off the subject, trying to be ladylike.

That was the perfect opportunity to bring a little laughter into the situation and shatter the odd feeling. I narrowed my eyes in disbelief. "So, you're used to dancing with girls then?" I smiled.

She hung her head and laughed out loud. It worked. In a fraction of a second, the weird feeling between us disappeared. The ice melted just as I spun her to Mason's side. "May I cut in, Mason?"

Mason smiled at me and mouthed, *Thanks, dude.* He handed me Cassie's hand and took Arlayn's. Cassie glared up at me and grimaced. I was probably the last person she wanted to be seen dancing with. She liked preppy boys, and I was far from that. I ignored her disgruntled sighs and decided to show her what she was missing by shunning a guy like me, so I danced my heart out. I happened to glance over just as Mason placed his forehead next to Aralyn's and whispered, "Aralyn, I love you." My heart ached even though it had no right to hurt.

Try as I might, I couldn't pry my eyes away. I saw the glimmer in her eyes as they met his and she whispered back, "I love you too." I watched as he grabbed her hand and led her across the community center. My eyes followed them as they made their way to exit the building. I was once again faced with reining in my attraction to her when it suddenly punched me in the chest with overwhelming disappointment.

CHAPTER 19

HEARTACHE TONIGHT

Within a few weeks the end of school and another graduation were upon us. I perceived a big difference in Aralyn after the prom. She withdrew into herself even more so than normal. Concern she still held something against me for looking at her the way I did, ate at my gut, keeping it twisted into a mangled mass. Sitting in third-period poetry class, I caught a glimpse of her scribbling away. I wondered what she could be writing on the last day of school. No teacher required work to be turned in on that day. It simply filled a calendar slot.

Curiosity got the better of me, so I poked my head over her shoulder. "You're writing on the last day? Mr. Stanley said it could be a free one," I mumbled.

"Yeah, I know. It was something I needed to write. I'm not even gonna turn it in," she responded with a sadness lingering on her face.

I couldn't take it anymore. I had to know why she had been acting so odd at school. "Aralyn, can I ask you something?"

She turned her body in her desk to face me. "What's that?"

"Are you okay? You haven't been the same since the night of the prom." I couldn't look her in the eyes at that point, so I shifted them away from hers. I began wringing my hands. "You're not like upset Mason made you dance with me, are you?"

"No, Ray," she sighed.

My eyes were drawn back to hers. A brief smile flitted across my face as relief washed through my being; then it disappeared as I realized what I needed to do. A nervous lump formed in my throat. I cleared it and released a deep breath. "I feel like I need to apologize to you."

She squirmed a little in her seat. "For what?"

I looked down at my desk and answered, "Well, I know you caught me looking at you that night." It was hard to speak of the situation. I shifted in my desk under the weight of the awkwardness. "I was just taken off guard. I mean, you and I have gotten to be pretty good friends, and Mason asked me to dance with you—you are an amazing dancer, by the way. You looked so beautiful that night. The combination of it all just caught me off guard. I didn't mean to cross a line. You're not mad at me, are you?" I squirmed. It all flowed out as if it had been pent up behind a dam and was bursting forth.

"Of course, I'm not mad at you, Ray. I think we both felt a little awkward dancing together because we're such good friends. To tell you the truth, you're the best friend I have. Sheena is a good gal pal, but we don't really share our feelings, and I've never even shown one piece of my poetry to Mason. He's my boyfriend and I love him, but that's just a part of me I can't bring myself to expose to him. You're the only one I've shared that part of myself with, outside of Mr. Stanley," she chuckled, "and my best friend Laurie who I've only seen three times this entire year." She hung her head. "Truth be known, she's no longer my best friend. She was when she was here; I'm so sad that she's not anymore, but it was inevitable. On an intellectual level I knew it would happen."

I sat silently as she exposed her heart to me. I couldn't believe it. I knew she imparted pieces of herself

211

when she shared her poetry with me, but in that moment she verbally expressed to me I had a small piece of her heart, obviously not in an attraction way (of course, with Mason as her boyfriend, I didn't imagine she ever would be attracted to me. All the girls desired Mason.), but I did possess a special place in her life, an extremely special place. She just revealed my place as her best friend. Her proclamation overwhelmed me, and shock riddled me as I read the poem she passed back to me.

"River of Grief"

A river of grief came and snatched me away,
And all I could do was take a deep breath and pray.
As the rapids tossed me against the cold, hard stones,
They each let out their own cry, their own moan.
Each stone left its mark as it cried out to my heart,
"I was molded by you; in your life I play a part."
I was drowning in memories of all the hurts of the past
When upon a sandy shore I finally crashed.
The river had consumed me and left me for dead;
Then I woke up from a dream, crying in bed.
I determined that grief was a dangerous river,
And of my heart it could have only one tiny sliver.
I resolved in myself I could never swim back through;
If I attempted or tried, I would always be blue.
The river of grief may have snatched me away,
But I learned through it all how to live each day.

~Plain Jane~

My heart sank as I understood the grief she spoke of. I gazed at her as I handed it back to her, and I was certain my eyes gave away my heart.

The following afternoon I sat on the edge of my bed

writing a song about Loraine. It wasn't a beautiful love ballad; it was a song about the heartache I felt that horrible night and how I would never trust again. My bedroom door flung open. Mason invaded my room. "Hey, dude. That song is rockin'." He plopped himself on the bed beside me and lay back, throwing his hands behind his head.

I figured something was up, so I set my guitar in its stand and asked, "What's up, dude?"

"I'm going to State this weekend for football recruitment, and I'm a little worried about leaving Aralyn," he confided.

"Why? She's a big girl. I'm sure she can do without your presence for a couple of days," I threw back.

"No, man. She's a mess right now. When we got home from school yesterday, her dad was gone. He left, man, just up and abandoned his family without a word. I've never seen her like that before. I've always envisioned her as this perfect girl who happens to be pretty, smart, and together. I mean, she always has her head on good, you know? But she fell apart, and I didn't know what to do but stay by her side and hold her."

I inhaled a deep breath. Imagining him holding her in that kind of manner wasn't something I wanted to do, but I had no right to be jealous or anything for that matter. "Look, I'm sure you being there was all she needed, and you can't help that you have to go to Starkville next weekend. She'll understand. Just spend every waking hour with her until then...He just left them without any explanation?"

"Yeah, and her mom, she's a basket case right now. She won't even talk. I just wish there was something I could do to help get Aralyn's mind off it."

Just then it hit me. There was something I could offer. "Look, the weekend of the 11th, me and Daniel are going to Gulf Shores to stay in my grandparent's condo. Why don't you come along and bring her. A weekend out

213

on the beach might help her."

"Thanks, dude." He sat up and slapped me across the back. "I'll wait 'til I get back to tell her though. I think she needs time to be upset right now."

"Yeah, you're probably right."

On the Friday of our weekend away, I met Mason out front. He climbed in his red firebird while I climbed in my little car. We made a pit stop at Daniel's house, and then I followed Mason to Aralyn's, learning where she lived for the first time. Mason jumped out of his car, handed her his keys, and kissed her on the cheek. "Drive careful," he instructed.

She smiled at him. "Worried about me scratching your car?"

He shook his head. "No, worried about it scratching you."

As soon as Mason shut my car door, we drove down the street and stopped while Aralyn made a turn onto Sheena's road and picked her up. Once they were set, they pulled up behind us and followed us all the way to the condo. We got there around eleven a.m. and carried our luggage up both flights of stairs. As I unlocked the door, I announced, "I'll take the smallest of the three bedrooms. It's just me by myself, so it's the simplest way to solve the issue. You guys can flip over the other two."

Daniel pulled out a quarter and threw it in the air. Mason quickly claimed heads, but in the end, Daniel and Sheena won the bigger room. Sheena took off like a kid with candy to the bedroom to unpack her things. After unpacking and eating lunch, we made our way to the beach. The girls laid out their oversized beach towels and rubbed each other down with tanning accelerator, but we boys wanted to play, so we headed straight for the waves. For a fleeting moment I stood gazing at the two ladies lying on huge beach towels while one wave after the other crashed against my back. *She seems happy for now,* I thought. Realizing what I allowed, I turned and dove into the next wave.

When the sun started to set, it was time to pack up and allow our crinkled skin to return to normal, not to mention the fact we were starving, so we packed up our things and found a small burger shack. The girls stared at us in amazement (mouths agape) as we each scoffed down two double cheeseburgers and fries. They each left half a burger sitting on their plate while they picked at their fries, and of course, they insisted on feeding their leftovers to the birds in the parking lot.

The day had been great, and Aralyn seemed to be enjoying herself. I caught her laughing throughout the day. My heart swelled at each giggle that slipped through her lips. It felt good to know her mind had been freed of her current worries. Exhausted, we all had showers and headed to bed. We had a long day of fun in the sun ahead of us the following day, but we had no idea of how far from fun and how long it would turn out to be. We had no clue of the heartache that lingered.

"Aaahhhh!" a scream came just before a thud. I stopped playing my guitar on the spot, searching the large crowd for the cause of the noise. I glanced at Blade and heard him scream, "Aralyn! Aralyn!" My eyes narrowed as I stared at him. It was Blade all right, but Mason's voice echoed from his lips. I did a triple take and stepped back. Realizing reality invaded a dream, I spoke to myself, *Wake up, Ray, wake up. Something's wrong with Aralyn.* I shook myself awake; then I heard my name. "Ray! Ray! Where's the hospital?" I jumped from the bed and pounced on the floor.

As I threw on my clothes from the previous day, I heard glass shatter. "What's wrong with her, Mason?"

Sheena screeched.

"I don't know; she just collapsed. I need to get her to the hospital *now!*" Mason yelled.

Frantic, my hands shook as I buttoned my jeans. I shoved my wallet in my pocket, shuffled my feet into my flip flops, and grabbed my keys as I bolted through my door. "Go to my car; I'll drive you. I know how to get there," I bellowed.

Mason carried her down both flights of stairs and climbed in my car. Visibly shaken at the sight of her limp body lying in his arms, my hands trembled as I slipped the key in the ignition. Her face paled ashen. I didn't know what could have possibly been wrong with her. Panic stricken, I raced to the hospital, weaving in and out of traffic. Victor's lifeless eyes and slumped over body flickered before my eyes. My lungs clenched. I screeched to a stop in front of the emergency room entrance. Mason climbed out and carried her in through the double doors. I sped off to find the nearest parking spot. Slamming on breaks, I shifted into park, yanked the keys from the ignition, and ran to the building. Panting, I strode into the emergency room and scanned the room for Mason. They had been taken back, and because I was not a relative, the nurse would not give me any information on her wellbeing.

I found a pay phone and called the condominium. Sheena answered, "Hello?" Her voice rang with a question.

"Sheena, it's Ray. Mason and Aralyn are in the back, but the nurse won't tell me anything. Can you get a hold of her mom or sister?"

"I can. Please call me and let me know what's goin' on as soon as you find out," she begged.

"I will," I promised.

I paced the waiting room floor for fifteen minutes before harassing the nurse again for any information I might have been able to acquire. "Please, can you at least tell me if she's okay?" I pleaded.

"Look, all I can do is go back there and tell them you're out here wondering. The young man with her can fill you in, okay?" The nurse sighed.

"Okay. Thanks."

The nurse left the station and didn't return for a long time. I waited thirty minutes and called Sheena again. She had been unable to contact Aralyn's sister or mother, and I had no information for her. I had paced the floors for an hour and a half when the nurse returned. She signaled for me. "Sorry, I got your message to him a long time ago, but I've been too busy to get back out here to let you know anything," she explained. "The young man with her said to let you know she seems to be okay. He would come out here, but she is insisting he stay with her. They have tests to run."

"Thank you," I sighed. Relief washed over me. I called Sheena to give her the small bit of information I had retrieved. I found a coffee machine and a seat in the large room and decided to calmly wait.

After another hour passed, Mason came out looking exasperated. He plopped down in the seat next to me and began, "She..." He placed his head in his hands and wept. I had never seen him cry, so it scared me to death. I figured it had to be something serious for him to break in that manner. After only a moment, he gained control of himself and finished, "She was pregnant, Ray."

"Was?" I questioned with huge eyes.

"Was...she had a miscarriage; that's what's wrong with her. She was in so much pain, and she's so scared. She wouldn't let me leave her side, but when they came in to do the procedure, they drugged her up and took me out."

I placed my hand on his shoulder. "Man, I don't know what to say. I guess I'm in shock. I know you have

217

to be. Look, I'm here for ya, for both of ya, whatever you two need. If you just wanna talk, whatever, okay?"

"Thanks, man."

A nurse approached us and informed Mason that everything went well and he could go back and see her in another fifteen minutes. We glued our eyes to the overly large clock hanging above the nurses' station. The minute hand inched around in slow motion as we both fidgeted. Several hours later they released her, and we drove back to the condo in silence. Occasionally I would glance at them both through the rearview mirror as we drove back. Two people I cared about had just had their lives forever changed.

Daniel and Sheena both bombarded her with questions about what had been wrong with her as soon as we crossed the threshold. Protectiveness over her honor rose up within me at that moment, so I spoke up, "Doc said it's food poisoning. She'll be okay." Mason cut his eyes my direction before glancing back down at Aralyn.

Aralyn sighed and Sheena threw her arms around her. "I'm so glad that's all it ended up being. We've all been worried sick."

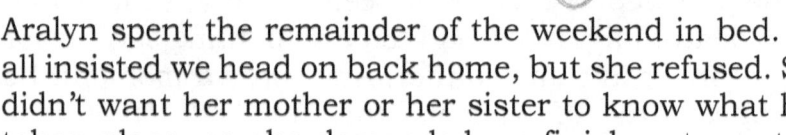

Aralyn spent the remainder of the weekend in bed. We all insisted we head on back home, but she refused. She didn't want her mother or her sister to know what had taken place, so she demanded we finish out our trip. Fortunately for her, Sheena had been unable to contact either of them.

I waited a week before I stepped next door to check on Mason and Aralyn. When I knocked on the front door, Mason's mom answered, "Hey, Ray, how are you?"

"I'm doing good, Mrs. Dorothy. How are you?"

"Can't complain. Mason's in his room. Go on up," she said, welcoming me in their home with a smile.

Approaching his room, I saw clearly that his door was wide open, so I poked my head in his room and mumbled, "Hey, man."

He stood in his closet going through boxes. He turned around. "Oh, hey, dude. What's up?"

"Just wanted to check on ya. How's Aralyn doin'?" I pried.

"I'm fine and so is she. It's kinda weird now, but I guess it'll just take time."

"Have ya heard anything about college?"

"Yep, I made the team. I leave on the fourth of August to start training. Classes don't start for another three weeks after that."

"Well, let me know if you need any help packing. I'm headed to Houston to see my grandparents. I just wanted to stop in and check on you both."

"Thanks, dude. I'll be sure to let ya know when I start actually packing. Be careful over there."

"All right, man. See ya later." I waved goodbye and left to hit the interstate heading west.

When I returned home a week later, I stepped next door and knocked on the door. The sound of heavy footsteps echoed, drawing closer. The door flung open.

"Hey, man, come on in," Mason said, holding the door open wide.

"How are you doing?"

"Okay."

"And Aralyn, how is she?" I asked with a raised brow.

Mason inhaled a sharp breath, glanced over his shoulder to his mom in the living room dusting, and nodded toward the backdoor. I followed him to his backyard. He shut the door behind us and paced across the yard wringing his hands. I eased down on the bench, waiting in anticipation. Finally he blurted out, "I broke up with her."

"What?" I howled.

He cut his eyes at me. "I couldn't face it. She was pregnant, Ray. I could've been a father. I'm not ready for that sort of thing. I was talkin' to Justin about it, and he pointed out to me how it would've ruined my life and how because of it, she'll probably wanna pressure me into marriage real soon."

"Mason, I can't believe you listened to Justin. He's a total prick. How could you do that to her?"

Anger boiled beneath the surface in both of us. He narrowed his eyes at me. "Why do you care so much anyway?"

"Because I'm not a jerk, that's why. Man, you convinced her to sleep with you, and then you wanna drop her because of something like that?"

"Don't you judge me, Ray. Don't act like you never slept with Loraine. Besides I waited a loooong time for Aralyn. That says something, doesn't it?"

"Whether I slept with Loraine or not is not the issue. I would've never done that to her. And yeah, the fact that you waited says you care, but this...it shows a different side of you. Man, you don't even deserve her. She's the best thing that ever happened to you, and you're gonna just throw it all away, sheesh. I think you've been tackled one too many times, buddy."

Mason took long strides, walking off the anger rising against me. I could see his nostrils flaring. "I don't know what else to do!" he screamed. "I'm freakin' out, okay. It was the hardest thing I've ever done. I'm not exactly proud of myself. You shoulda seen the way she cried. It was horrible..."

A picture of her anguish flashed through my mind. I inhaled a deep breath and shook it off. "Look, man, calm down. Let me ask you something. Do you love her?"

"Yeah, I do. I know I don't deserve her, but I do love

her."

"Then you need to really think about this. Do you want to lose her? Justin is not the best person to get advice from. He doesn't know her. He doesn't know how she'd respond to the situation. She's not like any of the girls he's ever dated. I don't think she'll pressure you to marry her any time soon. I imagine she wants to go off to college somewhere before she gets married."

"Yeah, you're right. She probably does. Man, why did I listen to him?" He shook his head and heaved a heavy breath.

"Because you've been through an emotional situation, and you weren't quite sure how to handle it, dude. You'll be okay," I assured him.

"You're right. I've got some thinkin' to do. Thanks, man." He hugged me.

As he hugged me, I cringed at what I had just done. Against my better judgment and against my own attraction, I convinced him of his stupidity in letting her go. I tossed and turned in bed that night, my own heart aching, as I contemplated what I had done and what I knew he would do.

CHAPTER 20

AFTER THE RAIN

Torrential rains began falling the next night. Strumming my guitar, I sat in my bed and stared out the window watching the sheets of rain hit the glass. It was a hard and heavy storm that particular night. The black night sky crackled with streaks of lightning. With every pop a bright flash lit the sky, and with every bright flash I eyed the rain pelting against the house. I closed my eyes, listened to the rhythm of the rain, and began playing and singing this song:

"Rain"

Rain is falling all around,
And it's drowning out the sound
Of the broken heart crying inside of me.
I crawl out of bed
Longing for you instead
Of the lonely sleep the night is sure to be.

I'm not looking for our love to fade away;
I don't want to say goodbye.
Please don't walk away.

Rain, come wash my pain away;
Rain, help this heart no longer ache.
Rain, tell her she must stay;

222

Rain, don't let my heart break.
Rain beats on the window pane;
As I listen to its sound, I go insane.
I close my eyes, and I see you;
Your love won't let me go.
Baby, I want you to know
That there's nothing my heart won't do.

Rain, come wash my pain away;
Rain, help this heart no longer ache.
Rain, tell her she must stay;
Rain, don't let my heart break.
Rain, tell her she must stay
'Cause without her my life won't be the same.

Ray Winstrom

A few days later Mason gave in to his own torment and asked Aralyn back. They both seemed happy, so I was happy for them. Of course, I couldn't deny a small part of my heart wondered if they truly belonged together. I had seen a side of Mason that upset me greatly, and I knew she deserved so much more than him, but ultimately he was a good guy and my friend. I knew he wasn't simply using her as so many had thought. There were several guys spreading rumors, saying he was just waiting to conquer. They assumed he hadn't already because Mason didn't go around bragging about the fact they had been together. That fact alone made me feel a little better about him. Most of his friends were the type of guys who bragged constantly about their triumphs with certain girls, and more times than not they falsely boasted of their conquests. It was those unfortunate girls who afterwards bore the label of being easy, yet all along the label was based upon a lie as so often they are.

The day Mason left for college I stepped over and

223

said my goodbyes with a promise to go see at least one of his games. Later that afternoon I heard a car rev, so I glanced out the living room window to see if someone had pulled up. I spied Mason's car pulling out of his drive. My eyes cut to his driveway, catching a glimpse of Aralyn standing there alone.

At least thirty minutes later I stepped outside to check the mail. As I ambled to the mailbox, I turned my head to the side and saw her still standing in his driveway with her eyes shut. She was in the same exact spot as earlier, so it concerned me. A gust of wind blew her hair across her face, yet she did not move. I moved to her side, laid my hand gently on her shoulder, and whispered, "Aralyn?"

With her eyes still closed, she answered, "Mason?"

"Nah, it's me, Ray. You okay?" I asked.

She opened her eyes and shook herself free from the daze she had been in. "Oh, Ray. Sorry. Yeah, I'm all right. I was just seeing Mason off is all. It's kinda hard, you know?"

Taken aback by the reality she didn't realize how long she had been standing there, I stuttered, "Um, Aralyn, that's why I came over. I heard his car leave thirty minutes ago. I looked out the window to see who it was and saw you standing out here. I just came out to check the mail; when I saw you still standing over here, I thought something must be wrong. You've been standing in that spot for thirty minutes. Are you sure you're all right?"

"Oh, wow, I didn't realize. I could've sworn I had only been standing here a few minutes."

"You sure you're okay? I raised my brow in uncertainty.

"Yeah, I'm sure," she answered, still dazed.

"Why don't you come in and drink a glass of tea or something?" I suggested.

"That's okay. I'll head on home."

"I insist." I grabbed her arm and pulled her toward my house. She gave in with a sigh and followed on my heels.

I fixed her and me a glass of tea, and we sat down at the bar. She fidgeted with her glass a little in between swallows. Silence filled the room for a brief moment. I didn't like the weirdness of it, so I decided to break the ice, "So, senior year starts in just a few weeks; you ready?"

"Yeah, I am. I've got a lot of studying to do in order to stay on top. I plan on graduating in the top three," she said with full assurance.

"Top three? You'll be valedictorian for sure, Aralyn." A bashful smile flitted across her face. "So, what Ivy League college are you planning to attend?" I pried.

"No Ivy League for me. I'm planning to go to the University of South Alabama. They have an excellent creative writing program there, and I want to major in English with a concentration in writing. I've researched a lot of colleges, and they have some great poetry classes." Her face beamed as she expressed her love for words and the English language.

"Wow, I expected you to go all out with college. You're so smart and all. Have you had your IQ tested?"

"My IQ? No, I've never felt it was necessary. I don't think intelligence is just about a person's IQ level. I mean, do you realize most serial killers have extremely high IQs? If all of a person's smarts are in their heads, then they are sorely lacking!" she exclaimed.

"Hmmm....I guess I didn't know that. That's kind of scary."

"It is. A brain that functions on that sort of level without a heart to guide it is an extremely dangerous thing...speaking of dangerous things...what are your plans after high school?"

"Well, I'm going to college for sure, but my dream is

225

to be able to make a life in the music industry. I wanna be able to sell my music as well as play it, but I think it's important to have a backup plan, so I'm gonna study drafting. There's several directions I can go with a degree in drafting, so I'll have a little room to play with so to speak."

"Hmmm...so you've really put some thought into your future, huh?"

"Of course. So, you planning on being on yearbook staff this year?"

"Ummm...they asked me to be the editor. I accepted. It'll be fun." She smiled. "I'm the girl who's behind the scenes making sure everything is written properly and not in any of the pictures." She gave her head a nod.

"Well, I know one layout you're sure to dominate—graduation. They'll have a picture of you giving your speech. You'll proudly stand in front of everyone and encourage your classmates to press on to higher education."

She bashfully smiled and looked down at her glass of tea.

We sat and divulged our expectations of the coming year as well as our desires for the future. Eventually she eyed the clock hanging on the wall and insisted she needed to get home, so I walked her out to her mom's car parked on the side of the road in front of Mason's house. Gentleman-like, I opened her door before saying good-bye.

School started a couple of weeks later, and I was certain it was going to be an amazing year. I had Aralyn in my calculus class, Daniel in my government class, and Sheena in my history class. I was surprised and disappointed Aralyn and I didn't share our English class. The three of us spent more time together during school hours, and they all showed up for my first gig of our senior year.

Aralyn sat right in front of me in calculus, so she turned around to talk to me for a few minutes every day before the class began. We always had pleasant conversations full of laughter, so I picked up on it immediately when she no longer turned around to chat. After two days of silence, I tapped on her shoulder to gain her attention, but she refused to face me and simply responded, saying she didn't feel well. When she didn't show up the following day, I assumed she had been telling the truth about not feeling well, and she was sick. When the third absence passed, I grew anxious and concerned, so I decided to call her when I got home from school. I was slightly apprehensive about making the phone call because of her being Mason's girlfriend and all. I didn't want to cross a line, but I shoved those thoughts aside and put my concern for her front and center.

The phone rang three full rings before I heard her voice desperately calling, "Hello."

"Aralyn?" I guessed.

"Mason?" she said, her voice full of questions mingled with excitement.

"No, it's Ray."

The excitement level in her voice dropped. "Oh, hi, Ray. I'm sorry, I haven't had much sleep. You sounded like Mason for a minute there. I guess I'm going a little delirious."

"I was just calling to check on you; you haven't been at school in three days. Are you all right?" I asked. She sounded horrible, and I couldn't shake the gut feeling I had that something was terribly wrong.

"Oh..., yeah, um, I'm a little sick is all. I haven't felt too good. I'll be okay. Don't worry about me. I appreciate your call," she answered, her voice cracking.

"Do you think you'll make it tomorrow?" I pressed.

"I'll try. I need to go; I think I hear something," she said before slamming down the receiver without saying good-bye to me.

I went to school the following day with the anticipation of seeing her there and the determination that if she did not show, I was going to see for myself just how sick she was. I couldn't shake the feeling there was more going on than a sickness, and I had to see for myself, so when she was a no-show, I left school and headed for her house.

No car sat parked in the driveway, so I assumed her mother had gone to work. I knocked lightly on the door and stood patiently. Hearing loud thuds, I braced myself. It sounded as if someone may have broken in, and the place was being ransacked. Then I heard her voice cry, "Ouch!" at the sound of another thud just before she flung open the door.

I stood staring at her for a fleeting moment, consumed with shock at her unsightliness. She slouched in front of me with non-matching wrinkled clothes. Her hair, matted as if it hadn't been brushed in days, stuck to the side of her sallow, sickly face. She grasped a wad of it and shoved it behind her ear. Black mascara smeared her raw cheeks. Her puffy, red eyes gave her hours of crying away.

"Ray?" she belched. I knew it; she was drunk.

"Aralyn, are you drunk?" I demanded an answer.

"Um, I think so," she hiccupped.

I pushed my way past her and began my interrogation. I was fuming mad. She wasn't sick at all. She was plastered, and I wanted to know why she was throwing her life away like that. "What's going on with you? Four days, Aralyn, you've missed four days of school in a row. Have you looked at yourself in a mirror? You look like walking death. I'm serious. Have you eaten at all because you look like you just returned from an audition for a part in Michael Jackson's "Thriller" video? This is not you; you've got dark circles under your eyes, and your face is sallow. You are a beautiful young woman with a bright future ahead of you. Why are you drunk in the middle of the day?" I plopped myself on the couch and waited for an answer. My tone had been harsh, but I couldn't help it. I had seen too many of my friends throw their lives away and watched Victor die. There was no way I was going to just sit by and watch her throw hers away without trying to wake her up to the reality of what she was doing. I cared too much not to.

She plunked herself next to me, laid her head on my shoulder, and cried, "It's been a week. I haven't heard from him in a week. I'm going crazy. I can't think straight. I can't even breathe; it feels like something is crushing my lungs and the harder I try to breathe, the tighter it squeezes."

A swell of guilt rose within me. If he intended to drop her, I bore part of the blame because I had convinced him he should be with her the last time he broke her heart. The idea the pain she endured was due to me was unbearable, and I didn't want to believe it could be true. I wanted to believe he was extremely busy and she had missed his calls. "Ah, man. I'm sorry, Aralyn. I didn't know. Have you called him?" I whispered, searching for hope. She seemed to be the old-fashioned type of girl who would not call a guy but wait patiently for him to call her.

"Yes, but his roommate always answers and says he's not in. I think he might be back with Samantha," she bawled.

"Samantha? She goes there?" I was confused. Oh, I knew exactly who Samantha was, but I couldn't understand why Aralyn would think he would be back with her, and I didn't realize she went to school there. I was quite confounded by the fact Aralyn would know where Samantha went to college.

"Yeah, he cheated on me with her back in June. It was only a week after my dad left. I can't believe he did that. I mean, I can see my not being enough, you know. I'm not pretty; I don't have the kind of figure guys are usually interested in, and I'm not popular at all. I can see why he would rather be with her, but I...I...I thought he loved me. How can you cheat on someone you love? I know he was drunk, and I understand temptation, but did he not even think of me at all? Why didn't he see a picture of my face and think about what I was going through at the time?" she squalled.

I had been disappointed in Mason when he broke up with her, but at that moment, what I felt far surpassed disappointment. He never confessed his infidelity to me. If he had, I would've never suggested he should be with her. I sighed and pulled Aralyn closer to me, and as I did, I felt a strange tingle in my finger that had been cut by Mason all those years ago. The numbness tingling through my fingertip diverted my attention for a brief moment as I pulled it toward me and stared at my hand for a fleeting second; then I gently laid that hand on the side of her face and whispered, "You'll be okay. I promise." She laid her head back down on my shoulder and cried. I sat silently while she let all of the pain flow out through her tears.

Determined she would be in school if I had to drag her out of bed, I showed up on her doorsteps every school morning after that day. I refused to stand by and watch her life waste away. She often dragged herself out of bed to go, but she seemed lost.

One Monday morning in September I pulled in her drive to see her standing on her front steps waiting for me. Excitement crept up inside me. I thought maybe after so many weeks of zombie-like life, she finally snapped out of it. She climbed in the car, slipped Mason's ring off her finger, and placed it in my hand. I gazed at her face. Her eyes were locked on my hand and the ring when she mumbled, "He...asked me to...give this to you."

When she finally pried her eyes away from the small object, she glanced at me, and I peered deep into her eyes. What I saw there frightened me; it almost reminded me of Victor's lifeless eyes I had written a song about a few years prior. I didn't know what I could say to help her. I knew I couldn't change anything. Her life was falling apart before my eyes, and I was helpless. The Fates she often referred to in her poetry were raining down one heart rending event after another. All I knew to do was to keep silent and let her know I would be there during and after the rain.

CHAPTER 21

HOW CAN I FALL?

Within a week I could tell she was slipping away from me. Every day when I picked her up for school, I sensed the faint stench of alcohol; it was obvious she was trying to hide it from me by covering her breath with mouth wash. She did a good job of refraining from eye contact, which made it more difficult for me to see through the outer surface and try to decipher what had taken place since our last talk. I knew she had been broken by the break-up, but I sensed there was more going on.

I picked her up every day; we drove silently to the school. With each passing day, she shut off to me more and more, so I wondered if I was wasting my time trying to help her through the difficulties she faced. The morning of October 28 I made up my mind to give up trying to get through the barricade she had built around herself. *She's never gonna let you through, Ray,* I told myself. *You're wasting your time. Just make sure she gets to school every day and that's it. Stop trying to pry into her life. Stop trying to save her. She's built a fortress around herself with good reason.* I gave myself a good firm lecture as I headed for my car. When I opened the door, I nicked my finger. The sting caught my attention. I glanced down at the small white scar and grimaced. *You know, I hate you right now. I wish you could see what you've done to her!* I ranted to myself as I stared at the reminder of my blood brother.

As I cranked the car, music flooded my mind from out of nowhere. The beautiful lullaby played through so clearly, and it brought an aura of peace to me at that particular moment. I couldn't hear the words to go with the music, but I got the impression they would come in time. I pulled up at Aralyn's house and knocked on the door as usual, and she came out taking her usual slow strides with the same solemn look perched on her face. Throughout the day the same lullaby played over and over in my mind, so I pulled out a blank piece of music composition paper and began writing out the notes I heard strumming in my imagination.

At the end of the day, I stood in the school parking lot and waited for thirty minutes, but Aralyn never showed. I assumed she had gotten a check-out or possibly another ride home. Occasionally if Daniel was taking Sheena home, he would offer her a ride as well. I drove home and set my mind to take my own advice. Advice is a tricky thing; some of it is full of wisdom and understanding while some is based purely upon emotion and not all emotions are good.

When I pulled in Aralyn's drive the next morning, determined to merely pick her up and no more, I was flabbergasted to see a small bashful smile break across her face when she opened the door. Simultaneously she opened two doors, one into her home and the other into her soul. "Hey, Ray. How are you this morning?" she asked.

I stood stunned for a fleeting moment. Stammering my way out of shock, I responded, "Um...I...I'm good." I furrowed my brow and questioned, "How are *you?*"

She grabbed her books off the small table inside the door and headed for the car. "I'm actually doin' good." She smiled back at me while I shut the door.

"Really?" I questioned.

"Yep!" she exclaimed.

233

"Well, you've got to tell me what brought all this on," I insisted.

I opened the car door for her; she climbed in. When I shut myself in, she explained, "Well, oh, yeah, sorry about yesterday afternoon. That's kinda what this is about. Mr. Stanley asked me to stay after to talk to me. He kinda jumped on my case about my grades and all. He questioned me a lot about what was going on in my life, and then he told me he was afraid I was going to mess up my opportunities. It all just kinda hit me, and I decided I had to get my act together. I still have time to get my grades up to a good, high GPA, so I'm bucklin' down."

Relief washed over me, and I smiled. "I'm glad to hear it. I've been worried about ya."

"I know you have, and, Ray, just so you know, all of your efforts have not gone unnoticed. I'm sorry you've had to be the one trying to pull me outa this murk I've been sloshing in, but I do appreciate every ounce of your time. You're the best friend I've ever had."

Best friend? Ouch, I guess that's me. What am I supposed to say to that? I've got to admit she's the best friend I've got, but I'm attracted to her as well. She's just so much more to me than that. I reined in my thoughts and responded in a safe manner. "Well, as your best friend I'm glad you seem better today. I was beginning to wonder if you were gonna waste your life away while I watched. It was pretty hard to see. You were startin' to remind me of Victor in many ways."

"Victor? Who's Victor?" She loosened her seat belt enough to face me.

"Oh, I guess I've never mentioned him to you, have I?"

"No, you haven't."

"Victor is...was my stepbrother. He died a few years ago," I choked out.

"Oh, gosh, Ray, I'm sorry. What happened?"

234

"We were over at Blade's house, and his cousin and a friend of his came over; they had cocaine with them. Victor was all mad at my stepdad because of the pressure he put on him about getting a scholarship to Georgetown University. When Victor didn't get the scholarship, he trashed all his trophies, and we took off to Blade's. He just wanted to blow off some steam, so he jumped at the chance to do a little coke and feel better. Of course, he pulled me to the side and insisted I was not to touch the stuff," I imitated Victor's voice as he lectured me that night. I even pointed my finger at Aralyn and shook it as I shared his words. I shook my head in disbelief. "I was so mad at him for that...He overdosed; he died on the way to the hospital...I had my arms around him when it happened. When I looked into his eyes and there was no life there, it freaked me out really bad." I told my story.

"So...how is it...I've reminded you of him?" she questioned in a cautioned manner.

I glanced at her while we sat at a red light and answered, "The eyes. I saw no life through his eyes, and you've had the same kinda look, like there was no life left in you." She gazed back into my eyes, and I saw something there. I saw hope lingering beneath the surface. It wasn't the hope she would fall for me like I was apparently falling for her, but it was the hope that the winter of her life had passed and spring was on the rise. Life began to flourish inside of her.

"Oh...you're pretty perceptive. I've kinda felt dead inside. I hate to admit that. I haven't talked to anybody else about what's been goin' on." She hung her head. "Ray?"

"Yeah," I answered.

"Do you think a person can mess up and do something really stupid and still be a good person?"

"Everybody makes mistakes, Aralyn. Mistakes don't make a person bad. So, tell me, do you think I'm a good person?" I questioned in return.

"Yeah, I do. You're the best."

"Well, trust me. I've messed up plenty. I told you I've fooled around with stuff, but I made up my mind not to go down that kind of path." As the words flowed out of my mouth, I realized I had left the street of unscrupulousness (with lessons learned in hand) which I had strolled down after crossing over to the wild side as a young boy, yet I was unable to regain the youthful innocence I once held. "Aralyn, innocence is something that can't be regained once lost; that's a wretched thing to see happen in a person's life. From a distance I've watched it happen to you, and quite honestly it's been hard. It's almost as if innocence is embodied in those rose-colored glasses adults speak of. When you have them on and look through them, the world is beautiful and flawless, but once you take them off, you see all the bad that's out there and realize you've been protected by those glasses. The next time you put 'em on, they don't work the same. You still see the bad, but I think they still paint a beautiful picture of the world. They just no longer hold the power of innocence in them, and they can no longer protect the wearer from the bad stuff that's out there."

"Hmmm...nice analogy. I think it's time for me to put those glasses back on. I know I can't get my innocence back, but I wanna see the good in the world again."

I pulled into the school parking lot and made my way around the car to open the door for her while she gathered her things. We walked into the building heading for her first class. I eyed several girls giving Aralyn strange looks and whispering amongst themselves; then I heard a couple of girls snicker as we passed. *What is goin' on with these girls?* I thought to myself. Anger brewed inside me when Dusty, Marcus, and Caleb strutted past. They all three looked her up and down. Dusty stopped and grinned. Caleb made eyes at her, but what Marcus did pushed me over the edge; he moaned in a sexual way. I wanted to jump on all three of them right then and there, but I knew I'd have to leave her side to do so. It was obvious something was going on; I needed to be there to protect her from whatever it was.

It didn't take too long walking the hallway and watching the snooty looks and hearing the jeers before we both had it made distinctively clear as to what was going through the dark minds of all the bystanders. Abigail strode right up to Aralyn and asked, "So, how'd you do it?"

I narrowed my eyes at her. A perplexed look crossed Aralyn's face. "Do what?" she asked. Bewilderment rang through her voice.

Abigail laughed, "Oh, come on, for a teacher he's hot. How'd you get him to sleep with you?"

What is she talking about? What teacher? My eyes scanned the hallway watching as all ears seemed to lean in for the answer.

Aralyn hesitated for a fraction of a second before screeching, "*What! What* are you talking about?"

Abigail rolled her eyes and shook her head. "Everybody's been talking about it since last night. The whole school already knows; don't act like little Miss Innocent. Mona saw it with her own eyes," she boldly proclaimed.

Almost as if frozen solid in place, Aralyn stood speechless. She began to hyperventilate, staggered back a few steps, closed her eyes, and covered her ears with her hands; then she gasped for air and screamed, "Stop!"

I stretched my hand out to steady her and let her know I wouldn't leave her side during the vicious assault, but she winced and jerked away from me. Right before my eyes I saw her knees buckle, and her body fall limp. I threw myself toward her and caught her before she could hit the floor. Lifting her to her feet, I draped her arm over my shoulder. "Come on, Aralyn. I'll take you home," I promised her.

My heart sank inside me; a variety of emotions overwhelmed my mind and heart. Anger boiled in my blood; fumes of revenge steamed to the surface and forcefully coursed through my veins. I *wanted* to inflict pain on those taunting her, but my compassion for her ran deeper. I knew I needed to get her away from the constant stares as well as the sexually provocative gestures guys were making. I held her weight as I led her to my car and headed for her home.

Outside of her rapid, short breaths, she sat frozen with her arms wrapped around her torso as if they held her together. A strange glare shot through her eyes. I peered deep into them as we sat silently at the red light on Dantzler Street, and what I saw within them was much worse than the lifeless eyes of Victor; I could see all the stitched up wounds she'd received throughout her life. The stitches worked themselves loose, and all the cruel teenagers at school pulled the threads out. I observed her wounds as they unraveled, and I watched her wrap her arm around her body in an attempt to prevent herself from falling completely apart. I glared into the eyes of cold, numb existence as all the blood ran from her veins and left her lifeless body to go through the motions.

I parked my car in her driveway and helped her to her house. In her trance-like state, I led her back to her bedroom and helped her to bed. She curled up in a ball on top of her covers, so I stepped into the living room to retrieve a throw. I laid it gently over her motionless body. She stared at me with empty eyes. I couldn't leave her in that condition, so I slid to the floor beside her bed and hummed. I didn't know what else I could do. I wanted to crawl up next to her, wrap my arms around her, and tell her she'd be okay, that I'd protect her. I wanted to tell her I'd do whatever I had to do to keep anything else from happening to her, but I knew I wasn't the one she wanted in that place. I knew I was hurting myself by being there for her because I was falling hard and was sure to get hurt, but no matter how logical self-preservation seemed to be, I couldn't for the life of me pull away from her.

Every ounce of life and vitality I had seen make its way to the surface of her heart earlier that morning had been slaughtered. The rose-colored glasses she slipped back on to watch and engage in the world through had been trampled upon, and I was helplessly watching her die a thousand times over with every painful breath she took. Up until that point in my life, it was the most difficult thing I had been through. Truthfully my pain wasn't all caused by her agony; there was heartache of my own. I struggled within myself over the fact I selfishly felt anguish within my own heart while I gazed at her. The knowledge I would *never* compare to Mason in her eyes tortured me. I was merely her best friend.

The lullaby that had brought me peace came to my mind, so I hummed it for her. As I hummed it, I heard a few of the words, but it was only the first line, *I see you from a distance*, I sang in my heart over and over again as I hummed for her. Her eyes began to grow heavy. They closed slowly and opened even slower. After a few times of drooping over her blue eyes, her lids gave way to the weight and stayed shut. I waited until I was certain she slept peacefully before I left.

I called to check on her several times over the weekend. Her mother informed me her daughter had been sick all weekend, and she wasn't sure if she'd make it to school on Monday or not. At that I knew she was clueless as to what was going on in her daughter's life. Nevertheless, I determined to show up Monday morning and make sure she made it to school, and that's exactly what I did.

On Monday morning I knocked lightly on her bedroom door. When I heard no reply, I creaked open the door. I didn't want to catch her off guard and dressing herself or anything, so I whispered, "Aralyn, Aralyn," as I pushed open the door. Still in her pajamas, she glanced up from under the covers and moaned. I stood straight and tall, folded my arms across my chest, and commanded, "Get up. I'm not leaving here until you do. You need to be in school."

She groaned and pulled the covers over her head. I strode across the room and knelt next to her. Pulling the covers back to reveal her face, I whispered gently, "Look, I know it's gonna be hard to be there, but if you *don't* show your face, it'll make you seem guilty, and hey, you've got me. I'll be right there, and if anybody says anything in front of me, you can pick 'em up off the floor after I put 'em there." I chuckled. I had always been good at making her laugh and lightening the pressure of different situations for her, yet that day I did not succeed. Despite my failure at bringing a slight giggle through her lips, I did manage to convince her to face her foes.

With a loud sigh and in a distinctively resistant manner, she gave in, pulled back the covers, and sat up. I stepped back toward the door. "I'll wait in the living room while you dress," I uttered.

"Okay. It'll only take me a minute," she assured me. "I'll try to hurry, so you won't be late for school, Ray," she hollered through the door.

"Take your time, Aralyn. I got here early to allow time for waking you up," I insisted.

Within five minutes she stepped out of her room wearing an old pair of jeans and a pull-over shirt. "Five more minutes is all I need," she hollered before walking into the bathroom to brush her teeth and fix her hair.

I heard the water shut off. She stepped into the

living room. Her hair had been pulled back into a simple pony tail, and her face bore little make-up. I imagined when she looked at herself in the mirror, she saw Plain Jane, the pen name she had given herself; nevertheless, that's not what I saw in the least. I saw a beautiful soul locked away in a cold, dark place. I had been allowed a peek into that place on several occasions, and I saw the beauty that flourished there despite the hurtful and even tragic events which caused her to encase herself away.

"Ready." She forced a small smile.

I opened the door and waited for her to exit. "I won't leave your side. I promise. I'll get to every class before you have the opportunity to step into the hallway," I assured her.

She looked up at me and smiled. "Thanks, Ray." Then she threw her arms around me and hugged me. At first shock rippled through me, so I just stood there, but as I breathed in the sweet scent rolling off her skin, an urge to hold her in my arms and pull her body close to mine consumed me. I longed to be more to her than a friend. My hands naturally gravitated toward her. I placed my right hand against her back and with my left I cradled her head as I returned her embrace. I closed my eyes and absorbed the moment. I was positive what she felt in the hug was not what I felt. She was merely hugging her best friend in thanks for being there for her, but I was holding a beautiful, young girl whom I had allowed into my heart.

Sure enough, heads turned when she stepped out of my car. Several people's jaws dropped from shock while others whispered amongst themselves with widened eyes. Of course, there were plenty of sinister glares given. Those were the ones who seemed to heartlessly desire to torture their victims.

As promised, I stayed close to her while I walked her to class. I spoke individually with each of my teachers, explaining my need to leave class early, and was given permission to meet her at the door of her class. It wasn't necessary to speak to my calculus teacher since we shared that class. Oddly enough, none of them required too much information. It slipped from one of them that she had heard the rumor and reported it. I stood outside Aralyn's fourth-period class with Ms. Robinson as teen-ager after teen-ager filed out heading to lunch. After Ms. Robinson exited, I poked my head in the door and saw an empty room. I headed to the cafeteria and glanced around trying to find her. I waited around for her to enter the cafeteria doors for a good ten minutes. When she didn't show up for lunch, I took off to the office to see if she had been checked out or something.

On my way to the attendance office, I passed a tall, slender black woman wearing a business suit being escorted to the front entrance by Mr. Wells. I overheard him mumble, "Thank you for your assistance, Ms. Dexter. Please let me know your findings on the situation."

From the corner of my eye, I saw Aralyn slip from the principal's office. I darted to her side. "Hey, I was worried. You okay?" I furrowed my brow. Her eyes were moist and red.

"I'll be okay. They just interrogated me; that's all. They're investigating this. Mr. Stanley could lose his job because of that stupid, idiotic girl. Uh, I'm really hatin' her right now, Ray."

Instinctively I wrapped my arm around her shoulder in protective mode. "I'm sorry today's been so hard. Are they sending you home?"

"No, I'm going back to class. Right now I'm just mad," she fumed. She never recoiled from me. With my arm around her, I walked her to our shared class.

242

Three days later during my time in the office as an aide to Mr. Wells, I spied an open letter from Mr. Stanley lying on the desk. When Mr. Wells left the room to attend a conference, I took advantage of the opportunity and made a photocopy of it for Aralyn. It was Mr. Stanley's resignation letter. Apparently Ms. Dexter determined her investigation to be inconclusive. Mr. Stanley would not be fired or charged with anything, but they would not say he was innocent either. That led Mr. Stanley to resign and leave. He stated in his letter that his presence would only cause Aralyn further harm.

That afternoon when we pulled in her drive, I handed it to her. She read it with tears streaming down her face. After that day Aralyn sank deeper into herself and withdrew even farther from the world. Everything about her existence seemed to be wasting away, and all I could do was watch her fall farther into the blackness that had consumed her.

CHAPTER 22

ROSE-COLORED GLASSES

Autumn left, and winter set in, and just as the weather turned cold, Aralyn did as well. She ceased talking to me about her feelings during our short drives to and from the school. I knew she drank even heavier than she had before. Her spiral downward didn't seem to have an end in sight. It drove me crazy watching her life go down the drain the way it was. I wanted to make her feel better, but I didn't know what I could do; then it came to me to give her a gift. Christmas was right around the corner, so it would be the perfect reason for doing so.

I approached my mom in the kitchen for advice. "Mom," I called.

Mom stood at the sink washing dishes. "Yeah, hon?"

"Can I talk to ya for a minute?"

She turned her head to peer at me and saw the serious expression perched on my face. She set her dish towel down and signaled for me to join her at the table. Andy wasn't home yet, and I was glad. "What's wrong, sweetheart?"

"After Dad died, is there any gift someone could've given you to make you feel better?"

"Oh, wow, I'm not really sure, Ray. Whenever you've lost somebody you love that much, nothing makes you feel better really. I don't think there's a gift anyone could've given me that would have taken away my pain—outside of you, of course. You're the gift your dad left me without even realizing it." He placed her hand upon mine and smiled. "What's goin' on?"

"Nothin' really. I just want to get something to make someone feel better, but I don't know what to get."

"Is this a girl?"

"I don't wanna say who it is. It's just somebody I know who's havin' a rough time right now."

"Well, I can't help you if I don't know whether the gift should be male or female."

"It's a girl, Mom," I sighed.

She smiled and set about her prying. "So, is this a girlfriend?"

"Huh, no, Mom. It's just a friend. She's just goin' through a lot. I don't want her to think I'm makin' moves on her with the gift. I just wanna do something nice; that's all."

"I don't know what to tell you, dear. I think any gift coming from a friend who cares helps when you're going through difficult times, but the best medicine is laughter."

Like a bolt of lightning, it hit me. "Thanks, Mom." I leaned over and kissed her on the forehead. "I know what to do." I raced up to my room and began writing a silly little song about the rose-colored glasses we had discussed, certain a good laugh would at least help.

"Rose-colored Glasses"

I was walking along the other day
When I saw you passing by;
I noticed you without rose-colored
Glasses to cover your eyes.
You looked so sad as you gazed at life
Without your glasses on;
Life without your glasses
245

Left you feelin' all alone.

These rose-colored glasses
I had them lying around.
These rose-colored glasses
Will do 'til yours are found.

I'll walk right on over to you
While you sit all alone.
I'll offer you my glasses.
I'll even let you wear them home.
I know that they don't work the same
Once they're taken off,
But if you'll just wear my glasses,
At the bad things you can scoff.

Ray Winstrom

I used my dad's acoustic and made a recording of my singing the silly little ditty; then I went shopping for a pair of rose-colored sunglasses. I wrapped the cassette tape with pink wrapping paper and used the glasses for a bow. If laughter was the best medicine as Mom informed me, I wanted to be the one giving her a good roll-on-the-floor chuckle. Embarrassing myself by singing a crazy little song was not important to me at the time.

When I pulled in her drive to bring her home on the last day of school before Christmas break, I shifted my car in park rather than reverse. "Are you going out of town over the holidays?" I asked in a nonchalant way.

"No, we'll be right here. How 'bout you? Any plans?"

"Nope. Oh, hey, I've got something for ya." I reached in the back seat.

Her eyes bulged. "Me? Wh—?"

"It's nothing, really, just a friendly gesture. I was

hopin' it'd make ya laugh is all."

Her eyes shifted to the floorboard as she chewed on her bottom lip. She inhaled a sharp breath and stretched her trembling hand out to receive the gift. Her eyes flittered and fell upon the sunglasses taped across the top. A smile stretched across her face. "My very own rose-colored glasses. Thank you, Ray. I need 'em."

A half smile inched across my face. "Merry Christmas, and just so you know, most of my music is serious. I just thought you needed a good laugh."

"Music?" she questioned. She tore the paper off the small gift and saw a homemade tape titled "Rose-colored Glasses."

"Just promise me you won't listen to it while I'm around, and no one else will ever hear it," I requested with raised brows.

She smiled and tilted her head to glance at me. "I promise. Thank you, Ray. Oh, um...I...I didn't expect anything. I don't have a gift for you." She hung her head.

"I didn't expect one," I assured her.

When I walked in the door of my home, the phone rang. Expecting Poppa to call, I briskly darted across the room to answer it. "Hello," my voice rang with excitement.

"Ray?" the voice giggled.

"Yeah."

"It's Aralyn. I just had to call. I needed that laugh. I love it. You're so sweet. I can always count on you to make me feel better," she said, her voice light and airy as if all the weight pressing her had been lifted.

"I'm glad you liked it. You better keep your word now. No one else is to hear that," I instructed with a laugh.

"So, maybe we'll run into one another over the

holidays. You have any gigs set up?"

"Believe it or not, we don't; but I'm sure we'll see each other," I threw in.

I wanted, *I needed* to figure out some reason to be able to see her, so I called Daniel when we got off the phone and talked him into having a small gathering with a bonfire at his house over the holidays. He took one look at the calendar and knew immediately what we all needed. "Hey, dude, New Year's Eve is on a Friday, just a little over a week away. Let me talk to my parents and see if it's okay to have a get-together before we go inviting people."

"Oh, yeah. Better get that straight first. Look, let's keep it small." I wanted to make sure I had plenty of time to spend with Aralyn, and because of our band's popularity, fans often kept us occupied in conversation.

"Trust me, dude, my parents won't go for a big party. Close friends only, I assure you of that."

By the next morning Daniel called to confirm his parents agreed to allow the "small" get-together. He called Sheena and asked her to tell Aralyn about it, but I had no way of knowing if she would show up or not without calling her, and I wasn't sure if I was ready to put myself out there like that. Being there for her was one thing, but admitting my interest to her was another story. I had convinced myself if I called to see if she would be showing up, she would surely pick up on my reasoning. Therefore, I waited rather impatiently, I might add, for December 31 to roll around. *I'll just be her friend who happens to be at the same party, so it'll be natural for me to talk to her all night long. If you talk to her all night long, she'll know you have feelings for her other than friendship, you big dummy, but I already spend a lot of time with her. Surely she won't suspect anything other than friendship,* I argued with myself as I paced my bedroom floor.

That night I spent extra time getting dressed.

248

Considering the thickness and waviness of my hair, I put extra conditioner in so it would be tamer than usual. I felt like a schoolboy with his first crush as I readied myself. I made sure I smelled good. I even bought a bottle of Obsession cologne, secretly praying the commercials were accurate and I would be irresistible to her. I slipped on my black Z Cavaricci pants Mom had gotten me for Christmas, pulled a black turtle neck over my wet head, and found a nice button-up shirt to wear over it. I made sure I looked sharp for the party.

I arrived late, so I wouldn't seem too eager. I pulled up to the curb and eyed Aralyn standing next to Sheena at the bonfire. From behind I could tell she wore black leggings and a dusty-blue sweater dress. An invisible force wrapped around my chest and squeezed it with amazing force. I spied Daniel, inhaled a deep, painful breath, and strode toward him.

As soon as he spotted me, he crowed, "There you are! Where you been? You're late, dude. I was expecting your help to get ready."

"Oh, sorry, man. I didn't realize."

Hearing my voice, Aralyn tilted her head to face me. The orange glow of the flames cast warmth on her face. She smiled, pointing to her rose-colored sunglasses. A loud chuckle slipped past my lips at the sight of her sporting sunglasses at night. Relief washed over me, loosening the tightness in my chest.

"Hey, Ray. You made it. I'm glad. I need someone to keep me company. Sheena and Daniel keep slipping off away from the fire where it's dark."

There were several chairs positioned around the fire. I found one and sat down. "Yeah, he's probably afraid his mom will look out the window and see him kissing Sheena if he's by the bonfire." I chuckled.

She grabbed a chair and pulled it close to mine. Things were going just as I had planned. Daniel's parents were home, so there was no alcohol. That led most teenagers to seek another place to hang, so we had a small group of people. It was nice to be around Aralyn and not smell liquor on her breath. She seemed to be doing well.

"So, can you see the good in the world again?" I asked.

"Yeah," she sighed. "The holidays have been nice. I've spent some time with my sister. Laurie even popped over for a few minutes on Christmas Day." Her eyes sparkled.

"That's really good. I'm happy for ya."

"How about you? How was your Christmas?"

"It was nice. Got to see my grandparents."

We spent the star-filled night standing around the bonfire laughing and joking around. With every giggle that escaped her lips, hope rose within me, hope she'd pull through and be okay. My mom had been right. There was something about laughter that had a magical healing effect. Unfortunately, I was unable to sustain Aralyn's happiness, and within a week her laughter ceased.

Toward the end of January, she showed up with her sister's friend Rhonda at a party I played. Alcohol was readily available that night; she took advantage of that and drowned her sorrows. After downing two drinks, she stumbled to the kitchen, returning with another. I watched from the makeshift platform as Cliff Taylor cut his eyes toward her, thrust his chest out, and strutted to her side. Her head lolled to the side as he traced his hand down her arm. Shoving his hand in his pocket, he pulled out two white pills. I knew Cliff, and I knew pain pills were his thing. He waved them in front of her, whispering something I could not hear. I narrowed my eyes as she grasped them without much deliberation. By the time we had a break, she could barely stand up straight, and Cliff made his moves. He ran his hands through her hair, leaned over, and pulled her lips to his. Jealousy and rage took over my being; I charged toward them. Aralyn placed her limp hands on his chest trying to push him away from her as she drunkenly muttered, "No."

I placed my hand on his arm and shoved him to the side. "She said *no*, Cliff." Consumed with anger, I grabbed her by the arm and dragged her out of the room. *What is she thinkin'? She should know better than to take pills like that. If I hadn't been here, he could've forced himself on her. Nobody else was paying any attention.*

As I led her outside into the cold night air, my anger subsided at her words. "My hero. My own personal Superman. You saved me," she slurred.

I wrapped my arms around her and sat her on the porch swing. "Come here. You need to sober up, Aralyn," I whispered as I sat next to her. I hummed my one-line lullaby as I rocked us back and forth. Before long I felt her head hit my shoulder. She passed out cold. I laid her back on the swing and stepped inside to inform Blade I'd be taking her home and most likely would not return that night. He understood the situation and excused me. I drove her home, put her in her bed, and left. She neither remembered my rescue nor calling me her Superman, and I never brought it up to her.

Silver Blade received a great opportunity; in February Kevin received a call from an intern at an agency saying the guy he worked for was interested in listening to us play. Kevin told them of the gig he had set up for the twenty-sixth of the month, and they agreed to show up. We spent every afternoon preparing for the event. Our lives were about to change, yet I had no idea how significantly mine would.

Despite my need to work on the band's songs, on the twenty-fifth I woke up with a flood of words rushing through my mind, the words to my lullaby. I pulled open the drawer of my nightstand, grabbed my notebook, and scribbled the words down before dressing. I picked Aralyn up as usual; she seemed to be in a particularly good mood. She told me she was determined to get her head on straight. I simply nodded in encouragement. When fifth period rolled around, she didn't show up for class. As soon as the bell rang to go to the last class of the day, I sought out Sheena throughout the halls.

Laying my hand on her shoulder to gain her attention, I called, "Sheena."

She faced me. "Oh, Ray, there you are. I was looking for you. Aralyn—"

I interrupted. "What about her? Is she okay? She wasn't in class."

"I took her home. She's pretty messed up. Somebody told her the school wasn't gonna let her graduate; then *Kristen and Carrie*," she snarled their names, "taunted her about it in the bathroom when they saw her crying. Somebody needs to teach those two girls a lesson. Anyway I wanted to let you know what was going on."

"Thanks, Sheena. I'll check on her after practice this afternoon."

School let out, and I headed to Kevin's garage for practice. The entire time we rehearsed our set, a battle raged in my mind. I wanted to go check on her right then, but I wrestled with letting Kevin down again. He already had to stop a gig halfway through because I couldn't follow through, and here we were about to play for a real live music agent. Logically, my brain concluded she'd still be there when practice ended, so I shoved aside the advice my heart screamed at me.

252

I wasted no time. As soon as practice ended, I raced out to my car and sped through the streets. When I went to pass my house, I eyed Mason's car sitting in his driveway with the trunk open. His front door swung open, and he exited toting a big box. I had not seen him since Aralyn had given me his ring to return to him, so it still sat in my glove box. I pulled in, opened the box, pulled out the ring, and went to say hi and bye. I thought about our blood oath and wanted things to remain peaceable between us, so I refrained from lashing out at him.

"Hey, dude. Aralyn said you needed this back. Sorry I've had it so long, but you haven't been in town that I've known of."

He took the ring from my hand. "Well, I was here for Christmas, but your car wasn't home that day, so I figured you weren't home, dude."

"I's probably at Kevin's or Daniel's. So, what you loading up?"

"Oh, some more of my stuff. I won't be comin' back here. Looks like I'm gettin' married."

"M..married?" I stammered.

"Yep."

"Who to? When did this come up?" I pried. *Oh, man, this is gonna kill Aralyn. I hope to God he didn't go over there and tell her,* I thought to myself.

"Samantha. You remember her, right?"

I cringed. "Yeah, I remember her."

"Well, I kinda ran into her at a party back in June when I went up for football recruitment." He shook his head. "I was really drunk, and I slept with her. She tracked me down after I got back up there and told me she was pregnant," he explained.

"And you're the father?" I questioned.

"Apparently so..."

"I wonder how come my mom hasn't said anything?"

"My mom feels I've shamed the family. She probably hasn't told her. We're gonna wait until the baby is born to get married."

"So, this is why I had to give you that ring?" I scoffed.

"Yeah, I didn't have the guts to tell her in the beginning, but I finally found the courage to face her and tell her."

I knit my brow and shook my head. "What? When?" I grasped the back of my neck with a trembling hand.

"Just a little bit ago. I went over there to tell her and say goodbye, but—"

"But what?" Fear gripped me right smack in the gut, twisting my stomach into a mangled mass.

"But I...I still love her, and I ended up sleeping with her. I don't even know how it happened. She said something about not being able to help who you fall in love with, and I kissed her. It happened before I told her why I had stopped by. She started screaming at me and threw me out when I told her. She's gotten a little feisty."

That was all it took for me to look down at the small white scar on the tip of my finger and determine she was definitely the someone portion of our oath, and the love I felt for her far outweighed the friendship I had with him. Without a second thought I balled my hand into a fist. "You're an idiot," I yelled as I drew back my hand and unexpectedly thrust my fist right smack in his face.

I jumped in my car and raced to her house. I needed to get to her as quickly as possible. At that point I didn't care if I got a ticket. I needed to see her; I needed to know if she was okay. I turned in her drive and eyed the empty carport. Her mom's car wasn't home, so I knew she was by herself. Throwing the gearshift into park, I jumped out and slammed the door. I sprinted to the door and charged right in. "Aralyn, Aralyn," I called as I made my way to her bedroom. I flung open the door to see her lifeless body sprawled on her bed, and on the floor in front of it an empty bottle of vodka and a medicine bottle lay. "Oh, my god," I hollered as I sped to her side and picked up the medicine bottle to see what she had taken. I shook the near-empty bottle of sleeping pills. My hand trembled as I flipped it over to see the date it had been filled. I needed to assess how many she had taken. It had been filled on the twenty-third, and it was the twenty-fifth. I knew she had to have taken almost the entire bottle. I twisted the cap and opened the bottle to try and count how many were left. My heart pounded ferociously in my chest. Adrenaline rushed through my veins. I had to save her. I just had to. I couldn't live without her. I dropped the bottle to the floor and begged, "Please, Aralyn. You have to live."

CHAPTER 23

SUPERMAN

Panic overwhelmed my body, crushing my lungs with its heavy weight. All the feelings I had for her rushed to the surface. They would be suppressed no longer. She lay dying right before my eyes. Hopelessness consumed my heart. I had to do something to save her. She had called me her Superman, and now I needed to be just that. My mind raced back to a childhood image of myself dressed as Superman while Mason pretended to be Batman. Irony filled our childhood choices. Mason had been much like Bruce Wayne in that he was a lady's man, unable to give himself to one person, but I was the one whose heart was devoted to one girl, and I would've done anything to save her life. Like Superman, had it been in my power to do so, I would've cheated the universe and broken every rule to keep her with me—including turning back time.

Instinct took over; I laid my head on her chest and searched for a heartbeat, desperate to find one; unfortunately, the sound I longed for could not be found. "No," I screamed. *How could she do this to me? How could she leave me like this?* I couldn't imagine my life without her. *Why, Aralyn? Why? Why did you have to love him so much? I was here; I would've done anything for you. I would've given my life in return for yours,* I struggled within myself. The thought of losing her caused my chest to constrict harder. It tightened around my heart causing it to beat frantically as if it was going to explode right out of my chest, almost as if my heart sought to pump for us both.

Seeking to spare her life, I thought back to my health class and tried to remember the exact location to place my hands. I laid my hands over her chest and said a small prayer hoping I was correct before I began compressions. I feared breaking a rib or puncturing a lung, but I knew if she was to come back to me, I had to try. I needed her blood to flow. I needed her life revived. "You can't die," I pled with her dying body. "I love you," I confessed. Anger arose from my aching chest. "Don't leave me," I commanded her. The angel of death was near. I felt his presence. Anger at him spewed from my soul. *You can't have her. I won't let you take her from me,* I wrestled with him as I pumped her chest. One, two, three, four. *I can't remember; is it four times or ten.* I struggled to do it correctly. *Just do it ten times,* I instructed myself. Five, six, seven, eight, nine, ten.

I pressed my lips to hers. I had imagined kissing them on several occasions; I had even dreamed of the first time I would touch my lips to hers. The idea of her lips touching mine had always been a sweet thought, but her lips felt nothing like I had imagined. Unlike my dreams her lips had turned cold. This was no dream; it was a bitter nightmare. With all my might I forced the air from my lungs into hers. After two full breaths being pushed into her lungs, I began to fall apart. My eyes flooded with tears, distorting my view of her, and I didn't want that to happen. I wanted to be able to see her clearly in case she flittered or moved. If her chest expanded in the slightest, I wanted to see it. If her eyes opened to peer into mine, I wanted to gaze into them.

My thoughts were being consumed by my emotions, and I was afraid of breaking down and losing my grip. I couldn't allow that to happen. I had to keep focused. I reined in my feelings and held back the tears with the barricade I created through my lids. I took a deep breath, caressed the side of her face, and begged, "Please don't leave me."

At that precise moment one single tear made its way past my barrier. It fell to her chest just as I placed my hands back over her heart to begin pumping it for her. I continued through the ritual of compressions and breaths until I heard a light gasp. I frantically searched for a heartbeat again, and that time I found a faint one. I knew I needed to get her to the hospital for professional help, so I cradled her in my arms and picked her up. As I carried her to my car, I whispered, "Stay with me."

I laid her limp body in the front seat and reclined it. I struggled because I didn't want to release her from my grip, but I had to be able to drive. I climbed behind the steering wheel, put my flashers on, and drove like lightning to the hospital. "I'm so sorry, Aralyn. I should've been there," I apologized for my absence in her greatest time of need. "Why didn't I get there earlier?" I fussed at myself as I slammed my swollen fist, the fist I punched Mason with, down on the dashboard.

I slammed on the breaks as I drove up to the emergency room entrance. I scrambled my way around the car, opened the passenger door, and lifted her into my arms once again. As soon as I walked through the double doors with her wilting body securely in my arms, the nurse jumped to her feet from behind the triage desk. She hollered for help, and a male nurse rushed out of a small room with a gurney. He slipped his arms under her dying body and took her from me. They disappeared through the swinging doors on the other side of the room, and my nightmare continued as I paced the floor awaiting the verdict of whether or not I had been able to save her.

They drilled me about what happened. I simply told them I knew she had been talked into trying a few

258

things and I had found her with an empty bottle of vodka and a near-empty bottle of sleeping pills. I had remembered the generic name typed across the bottle and gave them the specifics of it. "It's an overdose," the female nurse hollered back to the male nurse. "They'll have to pump her stomach," she informed me.

Every minute seemed like hours as I paced back and forth; then I remembered my car sat in front of the door blocking any ambulances from access. I approached the nurse and assured her I would be returning as soon as I parked my car. When I walked back in the waiting room, the nurse approached me. "Excuse me, but are you related to the young woman you brought in?"

My mind scanned through my options, *Should I tell her the truth? If I do, she'll not tell me anything about her. If I tell her she's my sister, then I'll have access to her.* "She's my sister," I responded.

"How can we contact your parents?" she inquired.

"We don't have a way to contact our dad." I pulled the answers quickly from my brain. "Mom is out of town, but she didn't leave a number to reach her. She's just gone for the weekend. She left me in charge. I'm eighteen; I guess she thought we'd be safe."

"And your name is?"

"Ray. Ray Liddell. My sister is Aralyn Liddell. Is she okay?"

"I'm not sure. I'll let you know as soon as I know something."

Finally the nurse relieved the aching in my chest. She called me to her and escorted me back to the room Aralyn lay in. "She flat-lined once on them, but they were able to get her back. You did CPR on her?" she asked.

"Yes, ma'am."

"Well, you saved your sister's life, young man. Good job," she said, encouraging me with a pat on the shoulder.

I walked into the cold room where Aralyn lay sleeping. After another hour they moved her to a private room on the first floor. I pulled a chair to the side of the bed, grabbed her hand in mine, and watched as she slept peacefully through the night. Eventually my eyes grew tired; I laid my forehead on the edge of the bed and dozed off.

The sun shot through the curtains and woke me only moments before the nurse came in to check her vitals. She still slept peacefully. I jumped up and scooted the chair back to its original position. "Don't mind me, young man. You slept right through my last visit. No need to pull away and get up," she assured me.

I stretched. "Nah, I need to be up. Do y'all have a coffee machine?"

"Sure do. There's a small room right around the corner with fresh coffee. Go fix you a cup, dear," she insisted.

I slipped out of the room, poured myself a cup of black coffee, came straight back to the room, and waited for her to awaken. It was nearly eight-thirty when she decided to peel open her eyes. I had just started humming my lullaby when she began to shuffle on the bed. I jerked my head to life when I heard the rustling of the covers; then I heard the sweetest croaky voice in the world call my name. "Ray?" she whispered.

The chair screeched across the floor as I jumped to my feet and leapt to her side. I grabbed her hand and whispered, "I'm right here."

"Where am I?" she glanced around the room, trying to decipher her surroundings.

"You're in the hospital," I answered.

"Oh, ummm…is my mom here?" she questioned, knitting her brows in bewilderment.

"No, I didn't know where she was or how to contact her."

260

"How long have I been here?" she questioned me further.

"Since last night," I replied.

Her brow furrowed in confusion. "How did I get here?"

Never letting go of her hand, I answered, "I brought you here."

"*You* brought me here? Why am I here?" she asked.

"They think you overdosed...accidentally. They had to pump your stomach. They said you flat-lined once. It really scared me."

She turned her head and glanced away from me. "They think I overdosed?"

"Yeah."

"What happened? How did you know I was in trouble? What made you go to my house?" Her questions ran together with impatience.

"Sheena told me she took you home. She told me what happened at school. The band was scheduled to practice after school, so I went. I kept feeling like I needed to leave and check on you, but I didn't." I shook my head in disappointment and sighed. "Anyway I left Blade's house and passed Mason standing outside his car. He was loading a few things from his house into the back of his car. I pulled over and got out to say hi and all. I asked what he was doing. He told me he was getting a few things to take back to Starkville with him. He mentioned he had just left your house, and then he told me why he had gone to see you. I told him he was an idiot and took off." I let out a slight chuckle and added, "Well, I kind of punched him too."

I left out some of the details of what had gone down. I didn't want her to know I knew of them. I figured it would embarrass her. I beat myself up for not listening to my instinct to go straight there from school. In shame I peered out the window. "If I would've left practice like I felt I should, I would have gotten there

261

before you did that." I shook my head vigorously in frustration.

With her free hand she touched my shoulder and gained my attention. "Ray, you saved my life. Don't act like you didn't do enough. Nothing is your fault; its mine," she assured me, and then rolling her eyes, she mumbled, "I'm the stupidest person on the face of the earth."

I sat down on the edge of the bed and looked her in the eyes. Gripping her hand tightly, I commanded her, "Yeah, you are stupid for attempting that. Don't you *ever* do anything like that again. Do you understand me? I thought you were gonna die, Aralyn." My heart rate increased as I remembered the look of death that consumed her pale body. My hands began to tremble as the thoughts flooded my mind. I tightened my grasp on her hand to steady my own.

She gazed back into my eyes with a look of sorrow and regret. "I'm sorry, Ray," she apologized. "I promise I won't."

I closed my eyes and sighed in relief. Then I heard her sweet voice say, "Ray, I can't really remember what happened. I mean, I remember what happened with Mason and all, but I can't remember your getting there. I just remember everything going black and being scared. I wanted the pain to go away, but it was still there. I dreamed I was trapped in a black abyss, but then there was a light. It was a small ray of light," she said, sharing her story with me. "The light was an angel, and he spoke to me. He said he loved me. He asked me not to leave him. It was his strength that forced my heart to continue beating, and it was his life that breathed fresh life into my lungs," she recounted her experience the way she had seen it take place. I silently listened as she described my rescue as that of an angel sent to save her. Being an angel was even better than being Superman.

Revelation washed over her face. She peered into my eyes and said, "It wasn't just a dream, and it wasn't an angel. It was you. You were the light that pulled me back, and you cried." She lifted her hand and lightly caressed the side of my face.

I gazed back into her blue eyes and responded, "Yeah, it was me."

"Thank you," she whispered. She smiled. "When I was coming to a little while ago, you were humming a song. I've heard you hum that song before. Is it a new one of yours?"

I smiled back, but I couldn't look her in the eyes any longer without completely revealing my heart to her, and I wasn't sure it was the time. "Yeah, it's new," I answered.

"Will you sing it to me?" she asked.

"Someday, I promise." A huge grin broke out across my face. It made me feel good that she appreciated my music despite the silly little song I had written for her two months prior.

"Why not today?" she pouted.

"Because, Aralyn, it's a special song. It has to be the perfect moment," I explained.

She poked her bottom lip out in an attempt to wear me down, but I stood my ground. If she only knew how close I was to giving in to her, she would've continued a little longer before giving up. She stretched her hand forward and tugged on my shirt. "Why are you still wearing what you had on yesterday morning? Have you been here all night?"

"I wasn't going to leave you here alone," I insisted.

"Hey, isn't tonight the gig with an agent listening to y'all?"

"Yeah." I hung my head.

"You are going, aren't you?"

"Nah. I've already called Blade. Your mom's still gone; I'm not leaving you alone," I explained with insistence.

She sighed. "Ray, music is your future; it's your life. I'll never forgive myself if you don't go. This is important to you," she urged.

"Aralyn, you're important to me. Yeah, music is important to me, but it's not my life; it's not what I value the most."

She sat silently for a moment. I could tell she was conjuring a plan in that brilliant mind of hers. "How about, if I get out of here today, and I promise not to drink or do anything else, and I go with you. Will you go then?"

I narrowed my eyes in suspicion and asked sternly, "And you *promise* not to touch a thing?"

She planted her arms across her chest with a huff and spouted, "Cross my heart."

I craned my head and stared out the window, deliberating her bargain. Releasing a deep breath, I gave in to her idea. "Okay, if the doctor releases you, we'll go."

Aralyn grabbed the remote attached to the hospital bed and flipped on the television hanging from the ceiling on the other side of the small room. I shifted my chair to face it. We occupied the time with a few shows while we waited on the doctor. Then it hit me I needed to inform her of who I was. "Oh, Aralyn, just so you know, they think I'm your brother. I knew they wouldn't give me any information otherwise, so I lied and told them I was your brother."

"Oh, okay." She smiled.

When the doctor finally showed up, I went to the cafeteria to grab a bite to eat. I returned after she was evaluated by a psychiatrist. I waited patiently while they typed her release orders, and I drove her home. She assured me she'd be fine long enough for me to go home and shower before returning. When I made it back, she was dressed and ready go. She sat sipping on a

Coca-Cola while we played that night.

Her mother took her down to the school and arranged for her to be able to graduate. That in itself lifted her spirit greatly. She began to smile again. I was certain she had found her own rose-colored glasses, put them back together, and slipped them back on. From that moment forward we spent every waking hour together. I walked close to her side in the hallways at school, never out of her presence except during class. I longed to reach out and touch her and hold her hand as I strolled next to her. Despite everything we had been through, I feared rejection.

The year was rapidly coming to an end. Our senior prom was upon us. I wanted to ask her to go with me, but I didn't have the guts to go through with it, so I opted to have Daniel be sure to tell Sheena to convince her she had to be there. Eventually I brought it up to her and assured her I could give her a ride if she needed one. At first she hesitated and told me she didn't want to encroach on my evening in case I had a date or something. I assured her I did not have a girlfriend much less a date; I planned to go stag, and she agreed to riding there with me. The day tickets went on sale, I bought one for me and one for her. I gave her hers when we pulled up at her house after school.

"Ray, you didn't have to get my ticket for me. I've been putting my allowance away," she proclaimed.

"It's okay. I make pretty good money playing at those parties. Well, you know how everybody pays five dollars to get in?"

She shook her head in acknowledgement.

"That goes mostly to the band. We split it evenly. I play at least two weekends out of the month, sometimes all of 'em." I worked on convincing her she could accept the ticket.

"I'll pay you back."

"No. I've got it. Don't worry about it. Spend your money on your dress, okay."

She gave in with a sigh, "Okay. You're really too sweet." She climbed out of the car. "See you tomorrow morning."

Along with the next weekend came the anticipated event. The class officers chose *Can You Feel the Love Tonight* as the theme. The Prom committee decorated the civic center to look like a starry night. They situated a fountain in the center of the room and scattered pink and red rose petals around it. Imitating stars, white lights hung from the ceiling, casting their romantic spell. I held my hand out for Aralyn's to escort her into the building. As we walked through searching for Daniel and Sheena, we were approached by several different people wondering when we had started dating. I didn't know what to say, so I just looked at Aralyn with puzzlement. She smiled back at me—astonished, just as I was, at their assumption. Neither of us ever responded to the questions.

We found Daniel and Sheena standing close to the fountain. Joining them, we all sat on the edge and watched everyone else dance. I knew Aralyn loved to dance, so I finally turned to her in the middle of a "safe" song and asked, "Would you like to dance? Maybe this time we won't feel so awkward," I asked, laughing my question off in case she declined.

She glanced around the room. "Okay, sure."

Not realizing we were heading out to the dance floor together, Sheena stopped Aralyn for advice. Aralyn solicited me to wait just a moment. She listened intently to Sheena's plight and advised her best she could. She joined me again and wrapped her arm in mine. Just as we made it to the dance floor, the song changed; the DJ began playing an old tune from REO Speedwagon, "I Can't Fight This Feeling."

I was slightly apprehensive, but I pressed through it and took her in my arms. As we danced across the room, I thought back to a lesson given to me about dance by my mother, *I believe when two people dance together, everyone who sees them is able to tell if their souls are made for one another because their movements will be as one. They lose themselves in the moment, and no longer are they two separate individuals twirling across the floor but one soul swaying to the beat of their heart, one heart. And when they find that song, the song that defines their relationship, their hearts synchronize to the beat of the song, and it's not just the two of them anymore; it's fate and destiny and all the stars in heaven joining in and surrounding them, telling them both the person they are with is the person who was carved just for them, that every fiber of their being was molded with them in mind, and when they come together, they are like two pieces of an incomplete puzzle. When those two pieces combine during that special rendezvous on the dance floor, the puzzle joins in creating a beautiful masterpiece of a picture, and life will never be the same again. No matter what happens, no matter how hard either of them try, that person will be forever branded into their soul.*

I had lost myself in the moment as we moved across the floor together in liquid motions. Just like my mother had said, we were moving as one to the song that defined our relationship. We had truly started off as friends, but I simply could not fight my feelings for her any longer. I was her Clark Kent, and she was my Lois Lane. I felt it in every fiber of my being. She and I both glanced up simultaneously at the twinkling lights representing the stars. That moment was our rendezvous, and we were joined by fate, destiny, and all the stars. They assured me she was the other half of my puzzle, and in that infinitesimal second, I was confident she felt it too. I wanted nothing more than to lean in and gently kiss her, so I gazed into her eyes prepared to complete our masterpiece.

CHAPTER 24

BED OF ROSES

In a small spin I pulled her body closer to mine. Our feet shuffled through the bed of rose petals. I was about to close my eyes and lean in when I caught them coming toward us from the corner of my eye. Apparently Darrell had broken things off with Tammy and showed up to prom with Emily, and Tammy planned to show her a thing or two. She marched right up to Emily and shoved her to the floor, and then with a shout, she slapped Darrell across the face. Emily stood to her feet, and a fight ensued as she lunged at Tammy. I spun around just in time to see them heading straight for us.

Holding her firmly against me, I jumped into defensive mode at the commotion. Disrupting our moment, I yanked her out of harm's way as the two girls smashed into the edge of the fountain. Aralyn's eyes widened as they tipped over the edge and splashed into the water, soaking those nearby. She decided quickly the senior prom dance floor was much too dangerous, so our night ended with us both reeling in our emotions while pretending we were merely friends.

It wasn't until graduation night, just a few weeks later, that another opportunity to take our relationship to the next level arose; this time she was the one willing to seize the moment. We had spent countless times together over those few weeks, but it seemed someone

269

else was always around, or our minds were consumed with finals. I was exempt from everything, but because of earlier in the year, Aralyn was not, so I offered my services in preparation. Unfortunately Daniel and Sheena had approached us as we were discussing it and invited themselves along for the "group" study. The Fates who had often spun turmoil into Aralyn's life seemed to be weaving obstacles in the path of our epoch.

Finals were taken, and then we spent endless time preparing for graduation. We had to mail invitations, buy new outfits to wear under our robes, and rehearse on the field. When the night decided to join us, we all stood in front of the bleachers waiting for the band to play the famous "Pomp and Circumstance." I stood next to Aralyn until I was told I must get in my place, which happened to be far away from her. Tenth in line, I graduated with highest honors. All of my hard work had brought me to that place. I would have never surpassed Aralyn had her life not fallen apart the way it did, and I understood that all too well. She would've been first in line. I knew she still struggled with beating herself up over that, so I never gloated or bragged about my place in line. In fact, I never mentioned it at all, but when they said for us to get in our places, she knew I had to leave her side.

The band began playing the famous song, and we marched onto the field and sat in our designated places. The valedictorian, salutatorian, and historian gave their speeches, encouraging us to all press on to higher education and commemorating our years together at Moss Point High. We all received our diplomas and threw our caps high into the air. I bent down to retrieve mine, and as I stood up, I eyed Aralyn running across the field through the crowd with a bright gleam on her face. Her hands were empty. She had not even attempted to pick up her cap. I saw in her eyes the Fates had lost their battle; running straight for me, she shoved the obstacles to the side. I smiled.

Before I knew it, she was before me. She threw herself in my arms and kissed me. It was perfect. She released her grip and slid to the ground. Throwing her hand over her mouth, she realized what she had impulsively done. "Oh, gosh, I'm sorry," she apologized. "You're not mad at me, are you? I didn't just cross a line that you didn't want to cross, did I?" She questioned her actions and my feelings.

I couldn't help but laugh because I had wanted to kiss her so many times before that moment, and I knew both of our feelings had already crossed that line long before any action was put to it. I kissed her forehead and answered, "No." Draping my arm over her shoulder, I smiled and uttered, "Come on. Let's go celebrate."

As we walked across the field, we passed Kristin and Carrie. Kristin snickered and whispered to Carrie in an obvious "I want you to hear me" way, "Can you believe she's smiling. She shouldn't even be on this field."

Letting Aralyn know I would be there for her, I tightened my grip around her. She responded to my gesture and lifted her head high and asked, "Okay, what are we gonna do?"

"We're gonna go get a couple of pints of triple chocolate ice cream, go back to your house, and watch a movie!" I exclaimed.

"Sounds good." She smiled.

Aralyn's life had fallen apart, yet it was being built back stronger than ever before. This time I was there to help her erect the supporting walls. Like a roof I covered her and protected her from the harmful elements of the world. She even allowed me to help her decorate her life with love and laughter.

All of my spare time was spent at her home. When I showed up to her door on June 12, I sensed immediately the change in her demeanor. She seemed depressed. Fright that she may regress washed over me, causing my heart to sink within my chest. All at once it hit me. The date. It was the anniversary of the day she had lost her baby. I had never brought the issue up to her, so she did not know I knew; originally, she suspected my presence on that day had given me insider knowledge, yet she clung to the hope Mason had told me she had food poisoning, but deep inside I figured she realized I knew the truth of that day. She tried to hide her emotions from me to no avail.

Desiring to make her feel better, I asked, "You wanna go somewhere?" I nimbly scanned through my options to myself: *Okay, a beach would only be a worse reminder, the movies would be too impersonal, the lake? Nah, that's for the day I sing her my song. I got it! Bellingrath Gardens. Flowers always make a girl feel better. Instead of bringing her flowers, I'll take her to them.*

"Oh, I—" she started.

"How about Bellingrath Gardens?" I interrupted before she could refuse my offer.

She caught herself in the middle of her rejection and stated, "Um...yeah...that'd be nice."

She dressed and we drove over to Theodore, Alabama, to see the beautiful summer gardens. We strolled through admiring all the colorful foliage as well as the huge orange and yellow ball-looking marigolds. She gazed at the begonias in amazement and awe. Her spirit seemed to be lifted out of the sad trench it had fallen into, and I recognized for the first time that my own happiness hinged upon hers. My heart overflowed with joy just watching her smile as she admired the beauty of the flowers.

We entered the rose garden laid out like a maze or

rather an English garden. Every time she leaned in to smell their fragrance, the beauty of her soul captivated me. Everything about her drew me toward her. As she breathed in the perfume wafting from a yellow rose, my emotions overtook me. In front of the bed of roses, for the second time (only this time I knew she would hear and understand me) I confessed, "I love you, Aralyn."

She spun around to face me, took two steps back, and stared at me with widened eyes. I saw straight through to her heart and knew I had frightened her with my confession. My heart sank at not having my love returned, yet I understood as I peered at her soul that while she cared for me deeply, she was merely terrified of letting the guard around her heart completely down for fear of it being shattered once again.

"I'm sorry." I reached for her hand. "I scared you; I didn't mean to."

"Yeah, you did. I'm sorry, Ray. I just don't know if I'm ready..." she trailed off.

Grasping her hand in mine, I assured her, "It's okay. I understand."

She stepped toward me and wrapped her arms securely around my back. I returned her embrace and accepted it for what it was—an assurance she did care.

On the Fourth of July weekend, her mom went to visit her friend Lydia. I had a gig that Saturday night, but Friday night was free. I stopped at the video store and rented a couple of movies to watch at her house that night. When I got to her house, I knocked on the door lightly, yet no one came. I knew she was home; I had just spoken to her before I left my house, so I entered and made my way back to her room. She sat at her desk writing poetry. I approached her from behind and leaned over to kiss her cheek. She smiled, laid her pencil down, and turned into my kiss. "Wanna watch a movie?" I asked, shaking the videos in front of her.

"Sounds good to me," she smiled.

I grabbed her hand and escorted her to the living room. She sat on the couch while I put *Sleepless in Seattle* in the VCR. We both lay snuggly on the couch watching Tom Hanks and Meg Ryan. Ten minutes into the movie, she twisted her body around and kissed me. "Ray," she whispered.

"Yeah," I pulled her hair out of her face.

"I know we've been seeing each other for a while and all, but I need to say something."

"What is it?" I asked as I intertwined my fingers with her hair.

"It's not that I don't love you or care about you, but I need you to know that things can't go any farther than this." She waved her hand between our proximity.

I shifted my hand and lightly traced my fingers over her cheek. "I know. It's okay, Aralyn." It was a big step for her. She admitted she loved me without actually saying "I love you." That in itself made my heart smile. "You just need somebody to love you, and somebody who loves you will want to give you what you need, not take what they want. I'm not gonna lie and say I haven't thought about it; I am a guy." I chuckled. "But I don't expect you to sleep with me to show me that you love me. I want to show you that I love you." I lifted my finger and placed it on the bridge of her nose. Running it all the way to the tip, I gently poked her. She nestled into my chest; I held her tightly.

We both enrolled at Mississippi Gulf Coast Community College in Gautier with plans to attend for at least a year before moving on to a four-year college. Aralyn started working with her mom and grandpa at Daisy's. Our time together naturally diminished, but we both arranged to take the same basic courses so we could study together. Sleep, band practice, and her work were the only things that separated us. Without her knowledge I began looking into courses I could take at the University of South Alabama. It was her heart's desire to attend that particular college, and I was bent on not allowing her to slip through my fingers by putting distance between us.

College began, and we spent every moment we could together. During our lunch break on October 10, I excused myself from her presence and drove down the road to a small flower shop. It had been nearly four months since I had told her I loved her in front of the bed of roses at Bellingrath Gardens. I wanted to surprise her by having flowers delivered to her on the anniversary of that date. I walked through the tiny shop full of several mingled aromas to pick out a dozen red roses to have delivered to her home on that Wednesday, the twelfth. The woman showed me a beautiful bunch of roses they had just received. I picked up one of them to examine it and found with a jab that the thorns were still there. I felt the stab but was unaware of the deepness until I signed the words *I love you* to the card. When I inspected the card to see if it said too little or too much, I saw a tiny drop of blood on the card. Roses signified beauty and undying love, but I became sorely aware painful thorns plagued the beauty of every one of them.

The lady in the shop gave me a small bandage, and I met Aralyn back at class. That afternoon when we pulled in her yard, I felt the prick in my finger once again as it stung. I spotted Mason's car parked in the shade. Aralyn saw it as well; we both glanced at one another and sighed.

"I wonder what he wants," she mumbled.

"Who knows?" I responded, but deep in my gut I knew exactly what he wanted. He wanted her. An immense thorn pricked the beauty and sweetness of our

275

relationship. I had been through this before. I knew Mason knew nothing of Aralyn's and my relationship; he still assumed we were merely friends.

I parked the car, and Aralyn hesitantly stepped out. The passenger door shut with a light thud. Mason sat waiting on the front steps, twisting pine straw between his thumbs and forefingers. He jerked his head at the sound of the car door and pounced to his feet. "Hey," he said, raising his brow. "You two riding to school together?"

Aralyn had a choice to make, and I knew it. He would confess his continued love for her despite how he had treated her and thrown her to the curb. For the first time since we had been together, she would face the reality of her feelings. She had yet to actually tell me she loved me. I wanted to believe with all my heart she was in love with me and no longer loved him, yet I knew how deep their relationship had been, and fear washed through me. I didn't want her to fess up to him immediately that we were dating because then she may never know what her true feelings were. I didn't want her to walk away from me several months down the road, and I *never* wanted to show up at her home to hear her giggling with him behind a closed door. I was sure of my love for her, but her lack of admittance left me with a seed of doubt as to whether she cared for me as much as she had him. He was her first love, and I knew that all too well.

I spoke up before she had a chance to hide from the decision the Fates had cast her way. "Yeah, something like that," I answered him with nonchalance.

He stepped forward to shake my hand. I extended my hand in return. "Do you mind if I speak to Aralyn alone?" he asked.

She glared at me with huge, fearful eyes, yet I couldn't protect her from this thorn. I swallowed hard over the lump forming in my throat. "Yeah, sure thing."

I turned and faced her. "Aralyn, call me when you're ready to study," I mumbled. I wanted her to know I still planned to be there. I didn't want her to think I was merely giving up on our relationship and handing her over to him, but I knew it had to be her decision.

She nodded her head. Trying to hide the torment my heart was already enduring, I smiled back. I climbed back into my car and drove away. I didn't make it too far down the road before I crumbled. I began having flashbacks of Loraine and that horrible day when I walked in on her and Willie. Loraine believed she was in love with me; she told me so many times that she did; nevertheless, she betrayed me and went back to the guy who was her first love. First loves were obviously powerful. From a distance I had watched Aralyn and Mason's relationship develop and crumble, yet I knew the power it held over her. It nearly destroyed her.

My foot shoved the gas petal to the floor. I raced through Escatawpa and crossed the bridge into Moss Point. When Loraine dumped me, every emotion I felt was intense, and the pain was raw; however, it didn't compare to the torment my mind braved knowing my world could easily be ripped to shreds with one small word—yes. If he asked her back, which I felt certain he was doing at that precise moment, and she said yes, they both would have robbed me of my oxygen, my life source.

I pulled in my drive and turned off the ignition. Shaking, I climbed out of my small car and headed for the door. Fear of the unknown twisted around my chest and squeezed it tight, crushing it. Gasping for breath, I flung open my bedroom door, slammed it shut, and collapsed to the floor. I hit my knees and begged, "God, if you're out there, please don't let him take her from me. I know he has it all, looks, money, charm, and he had her heart at one time, but I love her. I don't know what I would do without her. I watched him rip her heart out more than once. I don't think I'd be able to survive seeing it happen again. I've never been a religious person, and I know I have no right to ask anything of you, but I'm begging you please let him be by to apologize for the last time and nothing more. Please."

I grasped for hope in the midst of my torture. My thoughts and fears taunted me with every second the phone didn't ring. *It's been so long now. Surely she's said yes to his plea, and they're kissing right now. He's confessing how his heart has always belonged to her and how stupid he's been. He's asking her to marry him and spend the rest of her life with him. She's thrown herself into his kiss, and he's carrying her off to the bedroom now. She's giving herself to him once again,* my fears snarled.

With every thought implanted in my mind by fear, the pressure on my chest became heavier, and my breathing became more difficult. "Leave me alone," I screamed to them just as my phone rang. "Hello," I answered.

"Can you come over here, please?" Aralyn requested. Her voice sounded odd.

"Be right there," I answered.

As I drove to Escatawpa, my thoughts attacked again, *See, we told you. Didn't you hear that sniffle? She crying because she's going to break up with you, and she doesn't want to hurt you. She has no choice. She cares about you, sure, but you're not Mason. You don't make her feel the way he does. He was her first. You've never even been with her. She doesn't feel that kind of bond and connection to you.*

"Stop it!" I cried as I slammed my hand on the steering wheel with tears breaking through and rushing over my cheeks. "Get a hold of yourself, Ray," I told myself.

Driving down her road, I saw clearly that Mason's

car no longer sat in the shade. I pulled in and parked. I gathered myself together and took several deep breaths, slowly releasing them before exiting my car. I sauntered slowly and cautiously to the door. Inhaling a sharp breath, I steadied my trembling hand and knocked. The door swung open. She stood speechless before me with blood-red eyes and tear-streaked cheeks. I didn't know how to interpret that. I froze in apprehension. She threw her hand on her hip and snapped, "Are you gonna just stand there, or are you coming in?"

Why is she so snappy? "Are you okay?" I asked, hesitantly crossing the threshold.

"No thanks to you, I am. Why did you do that? Why didn't you tell him 'No way!'?" she fussed.

Whew, she's angry at me for leaving her. She's not cold and snappy because she wants to cut off her feelings for me.

In relief I grabbed her hand, sat in the chair, and pulled her into my lap. She laid her head on my shoulder and sighed. I wrapped my arms firmly around her and squeezed. "So, was he here for the reason I think he was?"

"Yes," she answered. "If you figured that's why he was here, why did you leave me here alone with him? Weren't you scared?" She sat up and looked in my eyes, searching for the truth.

Oh, if she only knew how frightened I'd been. "Scared to death, but, Aralyn, I didn't want you to be with me out of any kind of obligation or because you couldn't be with him. I didn't want to stop you from being with him if that's what your heart truly wanted. I wanted you to choose me," I explained my reasoning.

Sensing my struggle, she leaned over and rubbed her nose to mine. "Well, you won by a long shot." She smiled, cradling my face in her hands.

Joy flooded my heart, and peace reigned in my mind once again. I smiled. "Good," I whispered.

CHAPTER 25

PROMISES

The intense warfare my mind had just suffered combined with her profession that I had won told me it was time; I knew it. I couldn't wait until the flowers were delivered. I gently grazed her lips with mine and tasted their sweetness. She shifted her body; I cradled her in my arms. Her scent lingered and wrapped around me. I parted my lips to drink in her aroma. Without pulling her lips away, she whispered, "Ray."

"Hmmm?"

"I love you," she declared.

My heart leapt inside my chest. She had proclaimed her love for me only seconds before I was about to once again take a chance and share my heart with her. I tightened my grip around her body and pulled her closer to me. Our kiss became so passionate I couldn't respond to her instantly. I became acutely aware of my desire to take things farther, so I gently pulled away from her and smiled. "I love you more," I proclaimed.

She gazed into my eyes. Joy flitted across her face. "Promise?" she questioned, raising her brows in several quick motions.

Although I knew she asked in a playful manner, she had a serious need to know of the surety of my devotion. "I cross my heart, and I give it to you. I gave it to you a long time ago, but it belonged to you even before then. At the time I knew you weren't able to love me back, but I was willing to be there for you and wait until you could love again. You have no idea how difficult it was for me to rein in my feelings for you for so long."

My heart exploded with all of the emotions I had kept bottled inside it. They finally felt the freedom to release themselves. All the feelings I had ever experienced for her found words by which to express themselves and began painting the picture of my heart. "Aralyn, I noticed you the first time I laid eyes on you. That night at the graduation celebration, I caught a glimpse of you when you walked into the room. I hated Johnny Weatherton that night, and I wanted to yank you out of his arms when I saw him place his hand around your waist while you two danced. I had no idea you were the girl Mason was supposed to meet. Once I realized that, I knew I could never reveal the attraction I felt for you. He was my friend; we were blood brothers," I sighed at the obvious end to that relationship in my life. My countenance changed as my mouth turned down in a frown. A degree of sadness over the loss of childhood innocence and friendship lingered in my thoughts.

"I always thought you deserved better than him, but I never felt that was me; he was the one with all the looks and charm. When you almost died, I can't even begin to describe what I felt. I was so angry at him; I hated him for what he had done to you. I just wanted to love you and make every ounce of pain you felt go away, and when we started dating, I thought maybe I could, but today when I saw his car, I was so frightened you loved him more than you loved me. I would've let you go if that's what you wanted, but I begged God not to let him take you from me. It was really kinda selfish because I don't think I could live without you. With every fiber of my being, I love you."

Tears welled in her eyes and spilled over onto her cheeks as she gazed into my eyes while I professed my love and revealed my heart. I placed my hands on her face and wiped away her tears. She sniffled, "Thank you for loving me so much. I've been so afraid of getting hurt again that I've hidden my feelings from myself. When you told me you loved me that day in the rose garden, I wanted to believe it was real, but I was scared. You see, the first time Mason told me he loved me, he was trying to talk me into sleeping with him, and then when I finally gave in to his plea, he used those exact words to convince me. It wasn't long after that when everything started falling apart. I couldn't help thinking he never loved me at all. It messed with my head. I wanted to trust you wouldn't do the same thing, but I knew I wouldn't survive it if you did, so I denied my feelings."

She intertwined her hands with mine and continued, "It wasn't until today when I faced all that. When he came in earlier, he knelt down next to me and looked me in the eyes. I knew I could never deny what I had felt for him, yet as he began speaking and telling me how sorry he was and how he wished we could go back and start all over, I knew I would *never* choose to go back in time and start over with him. I realized finding true love is rare—you know, the kind of love that completes you. I felt something happen that day lying on the couch when I told you I didn't want us to sleep together. It was the strangest sensation I've ever felt; it felt as if I could literally feel my heart melt into yours. I felt it then, and I knew it then, but I just couldn't admit it until today when I looked Mason in the eyes and told him my heart belonged completely to you. The part that belonged to him only exists now as a distant memory. That's all it can ever be."

She glanced down at our hands. "I don't hate him, Ray, and I don't want you too either. I feel horrible that he was your blood brother, and I destroyed that—"

I released her hand and lifted her chin. "No, don't you ever think that. You didn't destroy anything. Aralyn, Mason chose popularity and being a part of the *team* over our friendship years before you came along. We patched things up and all, but it wasn't the same. I don't hate him at all. In a weird way I understand why he made the choices he made although I think they were wrong. He shoulda never slept with Samantha that weekend, but he was trying to do the right thing by agreeing to marry her. I'm assuming he didn't go through with it since he was here, and I'm sure you're part of the reason he didn't go through with it. That's what scared me so bad because I know how much you loved him. I also know he did love you. I beat myself up for a long time because I talked him into asking you back the first time—despite what I felt for you myself. I knew you loved him, and I wanted you to be happy. I also knew you were the best thing that ever happened to him."

"Oh, you're part of the reason he asked me back the first time?" Her voice rang with shock.

"Yeah and no, I guess. He told me he had broken up with you and gave his reasoning. He thought you'd start pressuring him into marriage, and he wasn't ready for that. I told him I didn't think you'd do that. I felt like you were more concerned with getting your education because I knew it was a priority for you. He was just struggling is all. He started feeling the responsibility of his choices, and it freaked him out. Regardless, I told him how stupid he was. In that way I guess yes is the answer, but honestly he probably would've still asked you back. He was already miserable, and I'm the big dummy sitting here telling you all this praying you don't change your mind."

Aralyn cupped her hand and caressed the side of my face. "Ray, you're not a big dummy. I appreciate your honesty with me. You're definitely not selfish for praying the way you did. A selfish person wouldn't have put my happiness first. You already cared about me then, and yet you knew I was heartbroken and wanted to make it better. That was the only way you knew how, and today you were willing to walk away if my heart desired him more. You're a strong, brave man. To me you prayed the way you did because you didn't want to lose the other half of yourself; that's all. It's definitely not selfish." She laid her head on my shoulder and whispered in my ear, "I promise you never have to worry about losing me. You're my true love, my soul mate."

"And I promise I'll never break your heart." I kissed the top of her head.

She turned into me, and we sealed our promises to one another with a lingering kiss. We had opened the door completely into each other's hearts and bore our souls to one another. We fit together perfectly, and I knew I wanted to wake up every morning looking into her crystal-blue eyes. I wanted to kiss her lips every night before I fell asleep and every morning before I left for work. I could picture our children perfectly—a dark-haired little girl with freckles scattered across her nose and cheeks and bright-blue eyes sparkling in the sun and a black-haired boy with deep-brown eyes like mine but with her nose and ears, of course.

Nestled into the pillows at the head of my bed, I tugged on the drawer of my nightstand and pulled out my notebook. I added a few additional lines at the end of the lyrics of my lullaby. Seeking the perfect spot to share my song and heart with her, I searched over the immediate area for the ideal lake and landscaping. I ended up deciding on a small, manmade lake in George County. Andy had a friend who had a large piece of property on which he dug the lake. As I stood on the hill amidst the huge oaks scattered throughout the property gazing at the bright blue waters, I knew I had found the perfect spot. Near the water on the opposite side of the lake, three weeping willows grew, their limbs drooping down seeking to submerge themselves in the frigid waters.

I explained my Christmas plans to her mother, and she gave me permission to steal her daughter away bright and early that morning. I bought a small, white metal bench and hid it in our garage. Early Christmas morning I woke up, dressed, and took the bench up to the property and set it facing the lake. Not wanting to obscure Aralyn's view of the lake, I set a folding chair off to the side facing the bench; then I drove to her house.

Still dressed in her snowman pajamas, her eyes widened when she opened her door to see me standing with a single rose in my hand. "Ray, oh, my gosh, I haven't even brushed my hair or teeth yet. What are you doing here?" she squealed.

I couldn't help but chuckle at the sight of her. Despite having hair in disarray, she was still so beautiful to me. "Go get dressed. I wanna give you my gift." I laughed.

"You're gonna have to give me a few minutes. Sit down and watch the television or look at the Christmas lights, whatever." She started toward the bathroom and stopped. "Hey, wait a minute. Why do I have to get dressed in order to get my present?"

"Because it's not here; that's why."

She squinted. "Where is it?" she pried, folding her arms across her chest.

"Somewhere special. Now go get dressed," I instructed.

Fifteen minutes later she came out sporting a Rudolph the red-nosed reindeer sweatshirt with a glowing red nose. "Cute," I smiled. I pulled a bandana from my back pocket and walked around behind her.

"What are you doing?"

285

"I'm blind folding you, dear."

"Why?"

"So you can't see your gift until I'm ready for you to." I tied the knot and grabbed her hand. "Just trust me. I won't let you stumble or fall."

"Okay, I trust you," she whispered through smiling lips.

I couldn't resist. I cupped my hand and lifted her chin. Pressing my lips against, I drew her close to me. "Sorry, I had to do that," I whispered.

"Hmmm..." she breathed.

I dropped her chin, stood to the side of her with my hands firmly supporting her arms, and guided her every step. I pulled up at the lake and helped her to the bench. Before untying the blind fold, I retrieved my acoustic guitar and leaned it against the folding chair. When I removed the bandana, she gasped at the starburst of sunlight glimmering over the waters in front of her. "Oh, Wow!"

I sat in the folding chair, picked up my guitar, and began to play the lullaby she had been longing to hear; then I sang:

"I Promise"

I see you from a distance
Standing with another guy.
He wraps his arm around you,
And I'm wishing you were mine.
I see you from a distance;
In his hands you place your heart.
If you'd only give it to me,
I'd never tear it apart.
If I promised to love you
And to stand by your side,
If I promised to love you,
Would you be mine tonight?

If I promised to love you,
And we would never be apart,
If I promised to love you,
Would you give me your heart?
If I promised to love you
And I sealed it with this ring,
Would you answer with a yes?
Would you make my heart sing?
'Cause I promise I love.

"I love you, Aralyn," I whispered. I laid my guitar to the side, pulled out the princess-cut ring I searched for relentlessly through several jewelry stores, knelt down, and asked, "Will you marry me?" I held up the token of my eternal love.

"Yes, yes, yes!" she squealed as she jumped into my arms.

We both ended up on the ground, and while we lay there, I slipped the ring on her shaking finger and caressed her lips with mine.

Aralyn desired a summer wedding, so we set the date for July 1. Silver Blade decided to go to Memphis, but I knew my place was with Aralyn. I declined going with them and resigned my position as lead guitar player. Kevin understood and found another guy to replace me within a few months. Of course, he assured me the dude couldn't touch my skills, and he was all too happy to say yes to being one of my groomsmen.

Aralyn struggled with my decision to give up the band. She felt I was giving up my dream for her, but I promised her my life and my dream was to be with her. Dreams often change, and sometimes they are placed on a back burner until time for the stars to align and bring them to pass.

I had remained in contact with Tramane since he

had moved away. I called and asked him if he would be my best man. He jumped at the chance to stand next to me. Daniel was all too happy to be a groomsman and escort Sheena down the aisle. I think he had it in his head it would appease her for a while.

I cut my hair for a job interview. I hired in at the shipyard and continued to go to school at night. Aralyn worked at her grandpa's store and enrolled in USA like she planned.

Our wedding day was wonderful. Aralyn's dad gave her away. Both of her parents got along beautifully. Despite Tramane being my best man, my stepdad proudly referred to me as his son to everyone who shook his hand. My mother looked beautiful; she beamed with pride as the usher seated her in the white chair set right in front of Aralyn's lake-side dream. My little sister walked ahead of Aralyn pouring out a bed of rose petals, guiding her to me.

We stood under a white archway with the lake glistening in the background. The minister spoke, "Dearly beloved, we come together today to join Ray and Aralyn as they give themselves to one another in holy matrimony. Rayford Sean Winstrom, do you take this woman to be your lawfully wedded wife, to have and to hold from this day forward, forsaking all others 'til death do you part?"

I peered deeply into Aralyn's eyes and proclaimed, "I do."

The minister turned to Aralyn. "Aralyn Paige Liddell, do you take this man to be your lawfully wedded husband, to have and to hold from this day forward, forsaking all others 'til death do you part?"

"I do." A smile stretched across her face, and her eyes shimmered.

"The couple has opted to say their own vows." The minister stepped back.

I felt butterflies in my stomach for the first time. It

288

wasn't cold feet; it was the knowledge I had to speak from my heart in front of all of the people there. The idea it was a small group didn't change the fact of my bashfulness. I cleared my throat and began, "Aralyn, you're everything I could ever want from life. I never imagined believing a person could be your destiny, but I was drawn to you the first time I saw you. It just took me a while to realize what I felt in that moment was my heart reaching out for its missing piece, its destiny. I give myself to you wholly. Every gift I have and every piece of my heart belongs to you."

Tears welled up in Aralyn's eyes. "Ray, you're everything I could ever want in life. You saw straight through to the depths of my heart and gave me what I needed—true love. You're the glittering golden thread woven into the tapestry of my life. You're what makes the picture of my life beautiful. I love you, and I'm giving you every part of me today—body, soul, and spirit," she whispered through broken sobs.

The minister interjected, "The ring is a symbol of eternity. It never ends. By placing these rings on one another's hands, these two young people are proclaiming their love for one another will be eternal. Ray, if you will get your ring from the best man." He nodded toward Tramane.

I turned to Tramane; he handed me the gold band. I gazed into Aralyn's eyes as I slipped the ring over her dainty finger. She slid my band on my swollen finger, glancing up at me with a raised brow as she wiggled it over my knuckle, forcing it into its permanent residence. The minister gave me permission to kiss my bride. I slipped my hand around her waist and pulled her body close to mine. I gazed longingly into her eyes before I pressed my lips against hers, drinking in the flavor of her soft mouth. Releasing her from my grasp, we turned to face the small crowd. The minister presented us to our family and friends as Mr. and Mrs.

Ray Winstrom.

We rented the community center in Escatawpa for our reception. The preacher instructed the crowd to go on ahead of us while the photographer took pictures. We took the usual ones with family and several of just her and me before joining everyone else at the reception.

We partook of the wedding cake and wine, completing the ceremony. Then we stepped out onto the dance floor. Aralyn picked out an older song by Anne Murray, "Could I Have This Dance." Fate, destiny, and all the stars in heaven joined us as we waltzed across the room.

It came time for Aralyn to throw the bouquet. All the single ladies scampered outside the building, eager to participate in the tradition. She slung the bouquet over her head. It soared through the evening sky. Sheena pounced from the ground and grasped the small cluster of flowers so many believed to hold a magical formula for future happiness. Daniel stumbled back and lost his footing as he peered across the parking lot watching Sheena jumping up and down with excitement. Her face glowed. I stretched my arms and caught him before he smashed into the guests behind him.

I removed the garter from Aralyn's leg and threw it to a crowd of zealous men, anxious for the dance promised with the woman who caught the bouquet. Sheena was an attractive young woman, and there were several available men interested in being the one to dance with her.

When Kevin caught the thing and led her out to the dance floor, Daniel grew so jealous that he cut in on them and proposed. Sheena just looked at him and laughed. "Daniel, I'm not gonna marry you 'cause you're jealous. It was just a dance, you crazy man." She laughed.

"You don't wanna marry me?" he pouted.

"Just ask me later when you're asking for the right reason, you big goofball." She smiled and wrapped her arms around him and finished out the dance.

I glanced at Aralyn and smiled. It was truly a wonderful day. She giggled at the sight we beheld, peered into my eyes, and whispered. "I love you."

Looking back down at her, I boldly proclaimed, "I love you more.

A delicate smile flitted across her face. "Promise?"

Leaning in for a kiss, I whispered, "I promise."

CHAPTER 26

HERE AND NOW

Aralyn and I enjoyed our reception and the company of our friends and family who came to celebrate our special day with us, but we craved the aloneness of the romantic night that lay ahead of us. Being so young, we didn't have a lot of money, but we put enough away for a three-day stay in a small cabin near Gatlinburg, Tennessee. That, combined with money given to us as a gift, made for a nice, romantic getaway. I had planned out a day at Dollywood, an adventure hiking through trails as well as rafting down a nearby river, and, of course, a day of shopping.

When the clocked chimed four, we slipped away from our guests, donned our going-away outfits, and climbed into my little car headed for Tennessee. Non-stop chatter, infused with excitement about our future together, filled the small vehicle as we drove to our destination. We explored all of our possibilities. "So, you should start your own band, Ray. I could come with you when you play in clubs and at parties and what not. I could sit there gleaming in pride that I'm the wife of the lead guitar player." Aralyn twisted in the passenger seat to face me and grinned.

"Umm...yeah, and you can write a story full of poetry, take it to New York to get published, and we can move to the Big Apple."

Hurt shot through her eyes and pierced my heart.

"Are you making fun of me?" She slumped back in her seat and folded her arms over her chest.

"No, I'm serious. I think you should write your story. I always have." I grasped her hand and squeezed it tight. "I'd never make fun of you, baby. Never."

A smile inched across her face. She curled in her seat and nestled her head on my shoulder. "Well, I'd love to visit New York, but I don't think I'd want to live there. I like small-town life."

"Huh, so glad you said that. Me, too, but I thought living in New York might be one of your dreams."

"Nope, not at all, but I do wanna see the Statue of Liberty. Ever since I watched *Planet of the Apes* and saw them ride around that mountain to find her stickin' out of the water, I've been fascinated with her."

"Well, one day I'll take you to New York to see her, baby," I promised.

"Ray?"

"Yeah, baby?"

"There's something we've never talked about before that I'd like to ask you about."

Apprehension wound itself around my chest. We had never crossed such a situation. We had been able to be open and honest with one another. I inhaled a sharp breath. "What's that?" I opened the door for her to share.

"Do you want to have children?" she blurted out as if she'd been fearful of asking.

"Yeah, I do." I had been wrong in my thinking of our ability to be open and honest with one another. The subject of children was an area of gray for me. I had refrained from asking about children on several occasions because of her loss. I feared the subject may be too touchy; therefore, I made a decision to allow her to bring it up in her own timing.

"How many?" she pried.

"Never thought about it. At least two, maybe more.

293

Do you want children?" Suddenly faced with the possibility she may not want any as a result of her prior experience, I hesitated.

"Yep, sure do. I'd like to have a house full of 'em, but not yet," she declared with boldness. "I was a little afraid you might not want any; I figured maybe that's why you hadn't brought it up," she explained.

"Honestly, Aralyn, I thought the subject might be too painful for you. That's why I haven't brought it up. It had nothing to do with my not wanting children."

"So you do know then? Did he tell you, or did you just figure it out?"

"He told me."

"So, when you told Sheena the doc said I had food poisoning?"

"I just didn't figure you wanted everyone to know. I thought maybe Daniel knowing would bother you."

"Thank you for protecting me even then. I had a feeling you knew. Look, I don't want you to be afraid of talking to me about things I've been through. I just gave myself to you completely. Every part of me belongs to you, even those painful places." She lifted her head from my shoulder. I craned my head and glanced for a split second into her lovely eyes. "I'm not gonna promise all things will be easy for me to talk about, but I definitely don't want you to fear bringing up something you're wondering about," she insisted. "Huh, I guess I should take my own advice. I obviously feared bringing up this subject of children before we got married." She laughed slightly. "I think I was a little afraid if we felt differently on the subject you may want to back out, and I was willing to go through with the marriage regardless. Silly, huh?"

I stretched my hand and grasped hers. "No, not silly at all," I assured her.

The evening wore on. We were still an hour outside of Gatlinburg when I looked over to see Aralyn sleeping peacefully. Despite her head lolling to the side and bobbing at every bump, she was so beautiful. It had been an extremely long day and evening, and I knew she was exhausted. We pulled up in front of the small cabin at 3:00 a.m. I stepped out of the car, unlocked the cabin door, and left it wide open. I walked back to the car, opened her door, and lifted her into my arms, cradling her next to me.

She was a heavy sleeper; nevertheless, the jostle from my lift aroused her from her slumber. She opened her heavy lids and whispered groggily, "We're here?"

"Sssshhh," I whispered. I carried her over the threshold and found the bedroom. Taking her swiftly back to dream world, the lateness of the hour consumed her again as I laid her on the bed and crawled in next to her. Propping on my side, I gazed at the beautiful sight sleeping next to me. It was our honeymoon night. I had been anticipating that night for a long time, yet I found myself content to simply watch her.

I grazed the side of her face with the backside of my fingers. With a moan Aralyn slowly peeled open her eyes and gazed back into mine. "What time is it?"

"Around 3:30 in the morning."

She glanced around to see where she was at. "You carried me in?"

"Yeah," I whispered.

"Why didn't you wake me?" she asked

"You've had a long day. You were tired. I figured I'd let you sleep."

Moving her body close to mine, her eyes took mine captive. "Ray, that was sweet of you," she lightly traced my lips with her fingers. Arching her neck, she placed her lips against my cheek. "But right here, right now, I want nothing more than you. Sleep can wait," she whispered in my ear as she grazed her lips softly over my neck. Her lips quickly found their way back to mine, and for the first time, we made love.

As we lay in the bed next to one another, I knew I was complete. I thought back to that day on the couch when she needed me to refrain from the physical expression of love in order for her to first feel loved intellectually and emotionally; I knew she had been worth the wait. The connection I felt with her as we made love far surpassed my expectations. Our hearts bonded into one heart. Our bodies may have been separate. Nevertheless, they were one. We fit together perfectly. Lying with her head on my chest and my arms securely wrapped around her, I closed my eyes. As my heartbeat drummed away, we both drifted into a sound sleep.

Not waking up until 11:00 a.m., we both slept in the following morning. Rolling over, Aralyn whispered, "I guess we need to find a grocery store. We're gonna want to eat while we're here."

I kissed her forehead. "Nope, you're not cooking a thing. It's our honeymoon. We're eating out every meal."

We both got dressed and found a small restaurant that served breakfast throughout the day. I took a bite of my pancakes just before asking, "So, where do you wanna go today? We can spend the rest of the day at Dollywood, or we can go grab our bathing suits and head to the river. I hear inner tubing through the rapids is a lot of fun. We can go shopping if you'd like."

"Hmmm...how about if today we don't go anywhere. We can just go back to the cabin and spend the day there." She glanced at me with anxious yet bashful eyes.

"Is that what you wanna do? You're not just saying that because you think that's all I wanna do, are you?"

A smile flitted across her face, and her eyes burned with desire. "No, Ray, I'm not just saying that. I wanna spend today with you and you alone."

"Hmmm...," I choked. "Sounds perfect."

She stretched across the table and pressed her lips against mine. "Perfect," she whispered.

"You ready for the check now?" I smiled.

"Yep."

We drove back to the cabin and spent the day in each other's arms until hunger pangs called so loudly we had to give into them. Once again she drifted off to sleep with her head snuggled into my chest while my heartbeat lulled her into dreamland. Admiring her while she slept, I ran my fingers through her hair and caressed the side of her face until the heaviness of my lids gave way to sleep.

I woke up bright and early the following morning to a cup of coffee being brought to me. Aralyn was dressed and ready to go to the river. A see thru lavender cover-up draped over her body slightly obscuring the view of her in her bathing suit. She sat on the edge of the bed and exclaimed, "I wanna go inner tubing today!"

"Okay, sure thing. Whatever you wanna do, we'll do."

A bright smile stretched across her face. She leaned in and whispered in my ear, "I enjoyed yesterday," just before planting an energetic kiss on the side of my face. Full of energy, she bounced to her feet.

"I did too." I laughed at her exhilaration.

We spent the day riding the rapids and swimming in the calmer waters of the river before drying off to go hiking through a nearby trail. The following day we decided to go into downtown Gatlinburg and do some shopping, and, of course, Aralyn insisted we go to the ice arena in the Ober Gatlinburg Mall. After that our little getaway was over, and it was time to head home and begin our life together.

Aralyn started at USA maintaining a 4.0 while I worked

days at the shipyard and went to school at night. We were both busy with homework and work, so our time spent together diminished; nevertheless, our bond remained strong. There were days in which we saw each other in passing, yet any spare moment either of us had was spent with the other. Our hectic schedules caused Christmas to creep up on us, and along with its jack-in-the-box appearance, a surprise sprang up.

On Christmas Eve morning Aralyn rolled over and draped her arm over my chest. "Ray, can you go to the store? I just remembered that I forgot to get the dinner rolls for tonight at your mom's," she mumbled.

"Yeah, all right. I will."

"If you don't get up and go now, you'll be standing in line for hours, honey," she said, reminding me of the craziness at the grocery store on Christmas Eve.

I rolled out of bed and plopped my feet on the floor and stretched. Yawning, I stumbled to the bathroom. When I strolled back into the room, Aralyn sat straight up in the bed with her hand secured over her mouth. "Aralyn, what's wrong?"

"Ummm...nothing...I'm not sure...I feel funny." A light bulb went off and flickered through her eyes. "Ray, when you head out, can you stop at the drug store and buy a pregnancy test?"

"A what?" I screeched.

"It may be nothing, baby, but I just wanna make sure; that's all," she assured me.

I came home from the store toting the rolls and the test. "Here's your test." I hesitantly handed it to her.

She came out of the bathroom with a look of relief and shook her head *no*. The next morning we exchanged the gifts we had gotten one another. We didn't have a lot of money, so we both wanted to be logical about our gift choices. She requested a comfortable housecoat and slippers, and I had requested warm gloves for my days at work in the weather. While trying on my new gloves, I saw Aralyn walk over to the tree and pull out a tiny wrapped package. Sitting next to me, she handed it to me and uttered, "I know we were supposed to stick to the logical gifts, but I have another one for you. Well, it's kind of for both of us." She placed it in my hands and sat impatiently waiting for me to open it.

Leery of what she had done to surprise me and concerned I had only gotten her the requested gift, I unraveled the paper. I opened it to find a small square with a plus sign in a small display window. My brow furrowed in confusion. "What is it?" I mumbled.

"I'm pregnant," she squealed.

"Pregnant? I thought you said you weren't."

"I wanted to surprise you. We're gonna have a baby. Can you believe it?" She threw herself in my arms.

Suddenly fear washed over me. *How am I going to support a baby? What if she has another miscarriage? What would that do to her? What is she going to do about her education?* I had always envisioned Aralyn and I having a family, yet the reality of it was a bit overwhelming. I had expected she would finish her college education first. Now we had to reevaluate our plans and goals.

"Are you okay with this?" I asked.

"Yeah, I am," she breathed. "I know I'll have to withdraw from school when the baby gets here, but I can finish out next semester and maybe even the summer semester. I'm taking 18 hours a semester, so I'll only lack an additional year and a half to have my bachelors in English. I know it's a little scary and all. Are you okay with it?" She suddenly seemed concerned.

"Yeah, baby. I'm okay with it. I think I'm just in shock is all. Look, this much I know: I love you with all my heart and regardless of whether we were planning this or not, that's our baby inside of you. How can I not love that? I just hope I'm a good dad." I chuckled.

Pressing the tip of her nose against mine, she

299

climbed in my lap and whispered, "You're gonna be the best daddy in the world."

Two weeks before our first anniversary, I took a trip to a small printing press and put in a request for a personalized journal. I specifically asked that the journal be leather bound and dyed crimson-red. I had a local artist paint the design I was looking for and took it with me for them to see. The collaboration was great, and between us all, I had the perfect anniversary present for Aralyn. I had always believed she needed to tell her story, and a journal was one way she could do that.

On our one-year anniversary, I took off work early and headed home to see my beautiful wife. I walked in with the gift-wrapped journal and went to our room where she sat writing her poetry. I slipped the gift in front of her and smiled at her look of astonishment. She jumped. "Oh, my gosh, Ray, what are you doing home?"

"It's our anniversary, so I took off early," I shrugged my shoulders in nonchalance.

"A gift? Now? You don't want to wait until after dinner?" she asked. Her eyes widened.

"Nope," I insisted, giving the gift a firm shake.

She tore through the paper and found the crimson-red journal. Around the perimeter of the 6 X 9 book was a scrolled vine. Hanging in the top left corner and stretching forth from the bottom right-hand corner were two wilting, white flowers. It had been embossed with the inscription *Plain Jane*, and wrapped around it was a yellow ribbon.

"What's this?" she asked.

"Well, the one-year anniversary gift is supposed to be paper, so I thought I'd get you a journal. It's paper, and it's red for your heart; also, you were wearing crimson-red the first night I met you." I smiled. Using my finger to point to the edging, I explained the significance of the image, "The scrolled vine and the white flowers are those parts of you that you used to keep hidden behind the wall, and," I tugged on the yellow ribbon and untied it, "the yellow ribbon symbolizes your intelligence that has always held you together. Now you can write your story and poetry. I've always thought you should." I kissed her on the cheek and stretched my hand to caress her bulging belly. "Concerning the title and your pen name, I've never thought you were a Plain Jane. Sometimes the way a person sees oneself is formed through false words spoken into their lives, and it is not who they truly are. To me you are the most beautiful woman in the world, inside and outside, and I happen to think you're even more beautiful pregnant."

"Thank you," she whispered. With a smile she placed her hands on top of mine and stared at the large bump that contained our baby. We both laughed when we felt a firm kick. Looking at her while she smiled, all the fears I had felt vanished.

Aralyn began writing her story that day. She decided not to attend school for summer, so she had spare time to write. Two months later to the day, the foreman over me hollered, "Winstrom, phone."

I sprinted to the phone, knowing the time drew near. "Hello."

"Ray, something's wrong. I don't know what it is. I'm bleeding," Aralyn cried.

"I'm on my way. Have you called anybody else?"

"No, I'm scared."

"Okay, call your mom. I'll be there in a minute," I assured her.

On the way to our little apartment, I passed an ambulance. I pulled in the parking lot and eyed her mom's car parked out front. I burst into the apartment. "Aralyn," I screamed as I sprinted into the living room. Silence filled the small apartment. A puddle of bloody water on the living room floor caught my eye. I raced into the bedroom screaming for them both, but no one answered. "The ambulance," I sighed.

I dashed out to the car and sped to the hospital, weaving in and out of traffic. I charged into the emergency room out of breath and desperate. The nurse calmed me down and assured me Aralyn was all right, and she would take me back to her immediately. As I rounded the corner into the hospital room, my eyes fell upon Aralyn propped up in the bed. She ran her hand through her matted hair, taming its disarray. The light thud of the door closing caught her attention. She craned her head and peered at me. "Ray," she said, stretching out her hand.

I darted to her side. "Are you okay? I got to the apartment and no one was there. I saw blood. I've been freaking out." My eyes shifted to her belly, which seemed to be missing. "What happened?" I grew frantic.

"You're a daddy; that's what happened." She smiled.

"I'm a daddy? The baby's okay?" I searched for an explanation.

"Yeah, by the time Mom got to the apartment, I was on the floor, and he was already coming. She didn't know what else to do besides call an ambulance and deliver him. The paramedics said she did a good job of helping me through. I'm so sorry you missed seeing him be born," she whispered.

"Him? It's a boy?" I leaned in and kissed her on the forehead.

"Yep, we have a boy. He's so handsome, Ray. He's got your black hair." She smiled.

"Where is he?"

"They took him to the nursery to check on a few

things. They said it was standard and that nothing's wrong," she assured me. "Come here." She patted the bed. "Lie next to me," she whispered.

I crawled in the bed next to her and held her in my arms. Within thirty minutes a nurse knocked on the door and strolled in with our baby boy. He was bundled in a blanket, sucking his thumb. The nurse handed him to Aralyn, and she fed him. After he finished nursing, she handed him to me. I gazed at the wonder in front of my eyes.

Aralyn craned her neck over my shoulder and whispered, "Are you happy?"

Without taking my eyes off him for a second, I sighed, "Right here and now, I'm the happiest man in the world."

CHAPTER 27

SWEET DREAMS

My dreams were coming true; albeit, a little faster than I had anticipated. There was a natural side of me that felt worry and concern, but when I gazed into the eyes of my handsome baby boy, whom we named Vick, and my lovely wife, peace dripped from my head and trickled its way down to my feet dissipating every anxious emotion along the way; unfortunately, I soon learned dreams are not always sweet; some of them are bad, and they can be invaded by nightmares!

It wasn't too long after Vick's birth that Kevin came into town; he stopped by to see the baby boy named after his childhood friend. He asked me if I felt I had been robbed of my dreams because of settling down and having a family. I didn't give his question a second thought before answering absolutely not. Dreams are funny that way. While one night you may have a wonderful dream and aspire to grab a hold of it and never let go, there's going to come a night when another dream comes along and sparks your interest. It may even be a better dream. The second dream doesn't rob you of your first dream; the two can simultaneously exist within your heart. Your focus may be centered on only one of them for a time, but when the stars line up and everything in the universe is prepared to manifest your heart's desire, you'll see all your dreams can come true.

I never gave up on my dream of music or Aralyn's dream of writing poetry, but at that point in my life, I knew the dream being fulfilled was my family life. I enjoyed watching Vick stretch and yawn and grow. When he first propped up on all fours and began rocking back and forth, you would have thought I was the proud daddy of a son who had just earned a medical degree. I boasted to everyone about how smart my boy was simply because of his posture. To me he was preparing to charge the world.

When our second anniversary rolled around, I took Aralyn out to dinner while my mom watched the baby. I had been thinking a lot about the satisfaction in having that dream fulfilled in my life, and I knew Aralyn felt the same. After the waiter seated us, I stretched my hand across the table and grasped Aralyn's. "Happy anniversary, sweetheart," I whispered.

"Happy anniversary." She smiled, slid off the bench, and scooted in next to me on my side of the booth.

"There's something I've been thinking about a lot lately."

"What's that?" She gave me a suspicious glance.

"Well, Vick will be a year old just a couple of weeks after the fall semester starts at USA. I think you need to go ahead and go back to college two or three days a week. Between my mom and yours, Vick won't have to go to daycare. What do you think?"

"Hmm...you wouldn't feel I was neglecting him?"

"Of course not. If you went three days a week, you'll still have two days a week home plus the weekend, and besides that it's good for his grandparents to spend time with him. My mom would probably enjoy watching him by herself, but she'd be willing to share him with your mom if she wanted one or two of those days," I insisted with an encouraging nudge.

"Okay, I'd like that. I'll call my mom about it tomorrow. What brought this up?"

I thought about my wording before I spoke, "Having a family is the most amazing dream in the world, but I don't want you to forget your other dreams," I gave her a serious stare. "I just think part of what we're meant to do for each other is to help each other's dreams be fulfilled." I smiled.

A bright gleam crossed her face. "So what about your dream, dear? Are you gonna start that band like I suggested?"

"I'm thinking about it. I still know a couple of people who play. I'll ask around to see if I can find anyone interested and good." I chuckled.

"Good. You deserve to be able to chase after that dream. I'll be your biggest fan."

I encouraged her, and she encouraged me to chase after our dreams that night; coincidentally, as we were leaving the restaurant, which had been filled with conversation of shared and individual dreams, a bad dream sought to invade our happiness.

As we prepared to leave the restaurant, Aralyn slipped out of the booth and excused herself, "I've gotta go to the restroom."

"All right, the check's already paid. I'll get the a/c kicking in the car and pick you up at the front door."

A large crowd of people flooded through the front door of the restaurant and obscured my view of her as she skirted around the corner, heading to the restroom. I squeezed through the crowd and headed to the car. Unbeknownst to me (at the time) as she rounded the corner, she walked right into Mason. "Oh, gosh, I'm sorry," she exclaimed as she bumped into him.

He reached out his hands and grabbed her shoulders. With a quick glance in her eyes, he roared,

"Whoa," just as he realized whose eyes he beheld. He cocked the half smile he was famous for and chuckled, "Ha, I'd recognize those beautiful eyes anywhere, Aralyn. It's quite all right. You can bump into me any day."

Shocked, Aralyn stuttered, "Oh...M...Mason, I didn't mean to run into you. W...when did you get back down in this direction?"

"Just graduated in May. I spent the month of June weighing my options and spending time with my daughter. I got here last night. Thought I'd spend a few days with my parents before heading to Virginia for my job," he updated her.

"Oh...that's right, you have a daughter. Umm...I have a son now. He's ten months old." She smiled at the thought of her black-haired boy at her mother-in-law's house.

"That's right. I remember Mom saying you married Ray."

"Yes, I did."

Aralyn shifted to go around him; he moved to prevent her. "Mason, I need to go to the restroom. Do you mind?" she said, her voice mingled with frustration. He seemed to be coming off a little flirty, and it made her uncomfortable.

"Why are you brushing me off. I'm simply trying to be nice to you and make conversation. We can be friends, can't we?"

"Sure, we can be friends, but I do have to go to the restroom, so if you'll let me pass, please," she begged with a sigh.

He moved to the side and allowed her to pass. As she wandered back out of the restroom, Mason strode back to her side. She jerked her head around. "Mason, what are you doing? You waited on me?" she spouted, aggravation and confusion filled her tone.

"I wanted to talk to you for a minute," he

mumbled as he followed her to the door. Seeing my car pulled up to the front door, he grabbed Aralyn's hand and pulled her to a halt.

She turned and glanced down at his hand as it held hers. "Mason, what are you doing?"

"Tell me. Are you happy?"

"Very," was her simple reply.

"I can't let you walk away from me. I should've fought for you back then. I still love you. I just wanted you to know that; that's all."

From the car I could see her talking with a guy. He had her hand in his, but I couldn't tell for sure who he was. I squinted to take away the slight blur around him. It looked like Mason! *What is he doing here? He's holding my wife's hand! They're talking. What is he saying to her? What is she saying to him?* My torment began.

I watched as Aralyn slipped her hand from his and pushed the glass door open. She climbed in the car and sat quietly. Awkwardness floated in the air between us. I tried to wait patiently for her to bring the situation up, but she sat glaring through the glass to her side. *Is she questioning her decision? Does she regret choosing me? Is she just upset about seeing him? Did seeing him spark an old flame?* My nightmare continued. My question finally burst forth, "Was that Mason?"

"Hmmm?" she asked in a daze. "Oh...yeah, it was."

I kept silent for a brief moment, but it drove me mad, so my interrogation began. "What did he want?"

"I don't want to talk about it right now, Ray." She cut me off.

Why does she not want to talk about it? Doesn't she understand that it's driving me insane not knowing what was said? Surely she must know I saw them holding hands. Anger brewed inside me; it was the first time I had felt that emotion toward her, and it scared me. What scared me worse than that was her vacancy. Her mind seemed to be somewhere else. I wanted to slam on the breaks and demand she tell me what was going on in her mind and exactly what had taken place, but we drove home in total silence.

Vick stayed at my mom's house, so as soon as I shut the door of our apartment, I spewed, "Why were you holding his hand?"

"What?" She jerked her head around. "He grabbed *my* hand, Ray, to stop me." Hurt shot through her eyes.

"If that's the case, why wouldn't you tell me what he wanted?" I demanded an answer. My blood boiled at the vision of them hand-in-hand.

"Because...I was upset, Ray. It's our anniversary, and he stopped me to see if I was happy...and...*to tell me he still loves me*," she blurted.

I took a step back. I had known Mason since early childhood. He was used to getting what he wanted. His ego had to have taken a big blow when Aralyn chose me over him. At the same time I also knew he did love Aralyn, and for that I felt sorry for him. I understood why he loved her; she was the most amazing woman in the world. Her heart was full of kindness and generosity. There wasn't a selfish bone in her body, and I knew, despite his own selfishness, he loved that about her more than anything.

Tears streamed down Aralyn's cheeks. They confused me. Pulling further away from her, I sat on the couch and hung my head. Seeing the distress on my face, she followed me and sat next to me. "Ray," she turned my face toward hers. "I'm not crying because of him; I'm crying because of your being mad at me. You just accused me of holding his hand. I wasn't. He grabbed mine."

The heat dissipated from my blood, and the raging madness stirring inside me settled. "I'm sorry. You just have no idea what went through my mind on that forty-five minute drive home not knowing what all was being said and seeing your hand in his. I guess I started to question if you regretted your decision."

"Not for a second. I was mad at him for saying what he did. I get quiet when I get mad. I just needed to calm down is all. I didn't want to ruin the rest of our anniversary. I'm sorry. I should've told you immediately what happened. Will you forgive me?" she asked, grabbing my hands and laying her head on my chest.

I wrapped my arms around her. "Only if you'll forgive me for being insanely jealous."

"I forgive you." She craned her neck to kiss my lips. The sweetness of her breath forced the nightmare away as her scent lingered. I scooped her up in my arms, carried her to our room, and laid her on the bed. As we made love, she assured me she was mine—body, soul, and spirit.

The following morning we drove to my mom's to pick up Vick. With my arm draped over Aralyn's shoulder, we strolled toward the front door laughing. From the corner of my eye, I saw Mason step into his yard. I could tell he watched us together. I knew it had to be difficult for him to see her happy without him. I kissed her on the cheek. "Why don't you go on in, baby. I think Mason wants to talk to me."

She glanced over her shoulder and whispered, "Are you okay?"

"I'm fine. I promise," I assured her.

Aralyn looked over her shoulder briefly as she entered the house, and I sauntered toward Mason. The time had come to put things to rest; it was necessary.

I stretched my hand forth as a sign of peace as I approached. "Mason," I acknowledged.

Mason sighed and reluctantly grasped my hand. "Ray." He rolled his eyes. "I'm not sure what to say to you. I mean, you're kind of married to the girl I loved, man." He inhaled a deep breath, "Isn't there supposed to be a code amongst blood brothers?"

310

I shook my head. "Man, I've been a good friend to you. I didn't just swoop in and steal her from you, Mason. I admit it; I cared about her for a long time. I stood by and watched you hurt her over and over. I never tried to undermine you during all that. I'm not the one who screwed things up with her; you are. I watched her fall apart, man. You shattered her life, and I picked up the pieces, but you had been out of her life for a long time when we got together. How can you be mad at me about that?" I said my peace.

Mason glanced at his feet and sighed, "Huh, I broke off my engagement with Samantha for her. I realized I couldn't go through with it. I loved Aralyn; I still do."

"I know you do, and I'm truly sorry your life hasn't turned out the way you expected it to, but I'm not gonna apologize for loving her. I would like things to remain peaceable between us, but I think we can both acknowledge that our friendship will never be the same. We just can't be blood brothers."

Mason looked away from me. I could see disappointment and hurt surfacing in his eyes as they watered. "You're right. At least I know you'll take care of her," he murmured as he grasped my hand with a final shake before climbing in his car and revving the engine. In a flash he was gone. My nightmare had been put to rest through Aralyn's reassurance, and now the bad dream of a severed friendship drove out of sight.

We spoke to both our moms that day, and they were more than happy to help out with babysitting for Aralyn to go back to college. They talked on the phone to one another and worked out a schedule amongst them to go around their jobs and responsibilities. Aralyn started back to school, and I found several guys who were interested in putting a band together. Don Fisher signed on as our lead singer. Lee Hand was our drummer, and Brad Harrison played bass. Every one of us lived in apartments apart from Don, but he lived in a small studio rental house off Ingalls Avenue in Pascagoula. There was barely standing room; thus, we had no place in which to practice.

My relationship with Andy flourished after Vick's birth. He felt such pride I named my son after his. We had even been camping together on occasion. When I told my mom I was getting a band together, Andy overheard and spoke up and offered for us to use their garage for rehearsals. As soon as the offer slipped past his lips, he yanked his head around to glance at my mom for approval. She simply smiled.

The guys all credited me for bringing the band together. Because my personality was such that I would not have taken the position on my own, they appointed me the lead man and gave me the job of choosing a name. I put a lot of thought into it. I wanted it to be different, yet I also wanted the name to have a hidden meaning. I searched through my past and found two words used against me to try to pull me down. I thought to myself, *I can take the negative forces of this world and the negative words they spew and turn their own words on them. When Pretty Boy makes it big, I'll have the last laugh.* Words are powerful, but even more so are hearts full of belief. In my heart I believed those words no longer held the power of feeling inferior over me. I may not have been what society expected me to be as a boy or a man, but I had something to offer the world—my music.

A year and a half later Aralyn graduated top of her class with a degree in English. During the meantime, she had completed her story, found an agent in New York to represent her, and had a publisher show interest. As a graduation gift I flew us both to New York. She longed to see the Statue of Liberty, so we took a cruise out at twilight to behold her beauty and awe. We strolled through the Metropolitan Museum of Art admiring the work of talented artists throughout history. We rode the elevator to the top of the Empire State Building and gazed at the city below us. It was thrilling.

As we strolled hand-in-hand through Central Park, Aralyn stopped in front of a fountain. Swinging our hands back and forth, she turned to me with a bright smile, stood on her tip toes, and pressed her soft lips against mine. "I love you so much," she whispered.

"I love you *more*." I grinned.

"Thank you for bringing me here. This is the most amazing graduation gift I could've ever imagined. We'll have to come back when Vick is older and bring him with us."

"I'm sure he'd love that."

She hung her head, staring at the pavement, and shuffled her feet. "But we'll need to purchase four tickets, not three," she mumbled.

Awareness of her declaration hit me. "You're pregnant?"

She looked up and grinned. "Yeah, I was calculating everything. I think I'm about three months. I guess I should tell Meagan. The publishers will need to know that."

"Yeah, probably so. When did you take the test?"

"This morning while you were still sleeping. I bought it the other day when I went to get a bottle of water. I didn't want to worry you unnecessarily. Are you okay with it?"

"Well, yeah! I just had no idea. At least you've gotten school out of the way. Do you wanna stay home for a while? Go to work?"

"I think I wanna stay home and write. Meagan secured me a good deal on my memoir, so it'll help financially, and I can continue to write while I'm taking care of our family," she explained her plans.

"Okay then. Are you sure it was okay for you to go to the top of that building?" I became worried.

"Ray, don't be silly. Pregnant women live in New York, you know." She laughed.

I couldn't help but laugh at myself.

That night we purchased front-row tickets to the *Phantom of the Opera* on Broadway and were totally captivated by the music as well as the talent. While in New York, Aralyn met with her agent and signed the appropriate contracts in order to seal a deal with the publisher. Her memoir was set to be released the following year. Her dreams had come true, and I was allowed to be a small part of it. That feeling was truly amazing.

After a week in the Big Apple, we flew back home to reality. Pretty Boy got back to regularly scheduled rehearsals and weekend gigs at local clubs and casinos. In May of '99 an agent named Matthew Silven sat in the crowd and listened as we played several of our own songs. He approached us afterwards and expressed an interest in taking us on as a client. He came back the following night and listened again. That night he offered to represent us. The following weekend we were in a recording studio making a demo for him to send out to record companies.

Within a month I received a phone call that Atlantic Records was interested in signing a deal. They wanted us in the studio in July, but I had to decline and have it set back to August. Aralyn was due in July, and I wasn't about to miss the birth of my second child. On July 18 our little girl was born. I was right there by her side the entire time. I watched Evelyn Paige enter the world weighing six pounds and seven ounces. She was the most beautiful baby in the world. I had a few weeks home with Aralyn and our precious bundle before leaving to record our first album.

When I made it back home, Matthew called me and informed me of an interview he had set up with a popular local magazine. They wanted to publicize us locally first. He told me to expect a call from a woman named Helen to schedule the interview. A few days later I received the anticipated phone call. Helen suggested we meet at the Tiki in Gautier for dinner.

The hostess of the restaurant led me to the table. "Good afternoon, Ray. My name is Helen. I'm with Mississippi Magazine. We spoke on the phone earlier." She grasped my hand with a firm shake.

"Hi, Helen."

"Please have a seat." She pointed to the small table situated against a massive window overlooking the water.

Journalistic materials covered large portion of the table for four. "Thank you," I uttered before seating myself in the chair across from where she had obviously already placed herself.

"It's nice to meet you, Ray. In preparing for this interview I listened to the demo of your first CD the recording studio gave me. You're talented," she began.

"Thank you."

"So, tell me, how long have you been playing the guitar and what got you started?" she asked.

"I was seven when I got my first guitar. My grandparents gave me the acoustic guitar they had given my dad on his seventh birthday. That's what got me started—a desire to connect with the man I never had a chance to know."

"And why is it you never had a chance to know him?" she warily questioned.

"He died before he knew my mom was pregnant."

"Oh, I'm very sorry about that." She took a sip of

her sweet tea, grabbed her pencil, and continued, "What's the one piece of advice you've been given about playing the guitar that has meant the most to you?"

"I met another guitarist at a young age. He taught me how to play the first rock song I learned. I ran into him again as a teenager. We were jamming together when he stopped dead in his tracks and said, "It's not about the speed, Ray. There are lots of speed demons out there who blaze all over the place. Every one of us has been guilty of doing it. The most important thing you need to know how to do with that baby in your hands is how to make it cry. If you can make it cry, the rest is gravy." A slight smile crossed my face. "That was the piece of advice I value the most."

"Sounds like it came from a man who truly loves music."

"Yes, I believe he does."

Changing the line of questioning, she switched gears. "It must be exciting to be picked up by a major recording label like Atlantic Records. A dream come true, huh?"

"Yes, it is a dream come true." I smiled. "It's exciting. I don't think there is a way to describe the exhilaration of it all."

"You're the lead guitar player. Now most people think of the lead singer as the front man of the band, but you started the band, right?"

"Yes, ma'am."

"Tell me about the band's name. How did you come up with Pretty Boy, and where did you get the idea for the band's logo, a Marine sword stabbed through an electric guitar surrounded by flames?"

"I wanted to take the two words used to taunt me as I was growing up and make something good out of them."

"So the words *pretty boy* were used to taunt you, huh? What's the story behind that? How did those words fit into your life? I want to know everything. Tell me about your life and your dad. How exactly did he die? Let's tell the readers of Mississippi Magazine exactly who you are."

"I would have to say the story goes back to the words *too pretty*. Hearing the words *too pretty to be a boy* can be a terrible thing for a little man, and I heard it all the time..."

WORKS CITED

Bon Jovi. "You Give Love a Bad Name." *Slippery When Wet*. Mercury Records, 1986.

Cutting Crew. "I Just Died in Your Arms Tonight." *Broadcast*. Virgin Records, 1986.

Van Halen. "Jump." *1984*. Warner Bros. Records, 1984.

Van Halen. "Hot for Teacher." *1984*. Warner Bros. Records, 1984.

Chicago. "Look Away." *Chicago 19*. Full Moon/Reprise, 1988.

Chicago. "Once In a Lifetime." *Chicago 17*. Full Moon/Reprise, 1984.

Scorpions. "Rock You Like a Hurricane." *Love at First Sting*. Mercury. 1984.

Surfing With the Alien. Joe Satriani. Relativity. 1987.

Joan Jett and the Blackhearts. "I Love Rock and Roll." *I Love Rock and Roll*. Boardwalk Records. 1981.
Guns N Roses. "Sweet Child 'O Mine." *Appetite for Destruction*. 1988.

Whitney Houston. "I'm Every Woman." *The Bodyguard: Original Soundtrack*. Arista. 1993.

Elton John. "Can You Feel The Love Tonight." *The Lion King*. Walt Disney. 1993.

REO Speedwagon. "Can't Fight This Feeling." *Wheels Are Turnin'*. Epic. 1985.

Anne Murray. "Could I Have This Dance." *Anne Murray's Greatest Hits*. Capitol. 1980.

Carcassi. (1792-1853) "25 Estudios."

Carcassi. (1792-1853) "Andantino."

Sir. Edward Elgar. "Pomp and Circumstance Military Marches."

Thriller. George Folsey Jr. Dir. John Landis. Michael Jackson, Ola Ray, Vincent Price. Columbia Pictures, Paramount Pictures, Epic Records Productions, 1983.

Leave It to Beaver. Creators: Joe Connelly, Dick Conway, Bob Mosher. Jerry Mathers, Hugh Beaumont, Barbara Billingsley. 1957-1963.

Father Knows Best. Creator: Ed James. Robert Young, Jane Wyatt, Billy Gray. 1954-1960.

My Three Sons. Fred MacMurray, Stanley Livingston, Don Grady. 1960-1972.

Planet of the Apes. Dir. Franklin J. Schaffner. Writer: Michael Wilson. Charlton Heston, Roddy Mcdowall, Kim Hunter. 1968.

Sleepless in Seattle. Dir. Nora Ephron. Tom Hanks, Meg Ryan. 1993.

LeFoux, Gaston. *Phantom of the Opera*. Pierre Lafitte and Cie., 1911.

Superman. Dir. Richard Donner. Writer: Jerry Siegel. Creator: Joe Shuster. Christopher Reeve, Margot

Kidder. 1978.

Kane, Bob. *Batman.* DC Comics, 1939.

Schledia Benefield lives on the Mississippi Gulf Coast. She is the author of YA companion novels *Pretty Boy* and *Plain Jane* and the NA romance novel *Wildflowers*. She dedicated eight years of her life to working with teenagers as a youth minister and has been invited to speak to high school students and women. Her goal as an author is to write stories that touch the hearts of readers and to tackle issues such as bullying, abuse, depression, domestic violence, and suicide. She formerly taught creative writing at a small private school and wrote skits and human videos for a drama team. She attended MGCCC, where she was majoring in math, secondary education, before giving in to her passion for words. She was the Keynote Speaker for The Key Club International's Division 14's Divisional Rally. In her spare time, the mother of five enjoys reading, spending time with her family, and visiting over a cup of coffee.

www.ingramcontent.com/pod-product-compliance
Lightning Source LLC
Chambersburg PA
CBHW020403260626
47156CB00007B/2213